GRAVE

MADNESS

GRAVE MADNESS

A Mining City Mystery

Marian Jensen

www.miningcitymysteries.com

This is a work of fiction based, to a greater or lesser extent depending on the story, on some actual events. Certain details have been changed and even more invented. All of the characters in this novel are either products of the author's imagination or are used fictitiously. Any resemblance to actual persons, living or dead, or organizations is entirely coincidental.

Cover Design by Terri Porter

Cover Photos by Michael Kello

Book Format by Luanne Thibault

ISBN-13: 978-1503000759

Dedication

To my brother Michael who, as a conscientious objector during the war in Viet Nam, completed his alternative service in a mental hospital, and inspired me in more ways than one.

I have myself been gravely mad,
and I can value with greater cause
than most the advantages of being sane.

To one who is mad, the world is still real,
but it has a new meaning; people are real too,
close and powerful and perhaps dangerous,
but among them all the individual is alone.

Morag Coate, *Beyond All Reason*

Chapter 1

Chance Dawson smelled the smoke long before he heard the sirens. Just like Butte's latest arsonist, the bastard (whoever he was), to torch a building on St. Patrick's Day. Angling through the massive crowd along Main Street, Chance knew he wouldn't be able to free himself for the next half hour, even if half the mountainside was on fire.

Shamrock-adorned revelers, clapping to the bagpipe music, had him hemmed in at the corner of Park and Main. It was barely noon and two thirds of the crowd was "a bit boiled." Their enthusiasm erupted as the Edmonton Police Drum and Piper Corps came into view, pouring forth with "Ireland Forever," their standard crowd pleaser. It was all Chance could do to avoid being sucked down the street by the horde.

The Pipers, who made their annual trek from Alberta south to Butte for the St. Patrick's Day Parade, were a too-good-to-be-missed highlight. Justifiably, *the Mining City Messenger* always included a front-page photo of the kilted cops as part of its St. Patrick's Day coverage, and Chance was perched to deliver.

Since his sister, Mesa, had taken over as editor of the weekly, Chance had curtailed his involvement as a sports reporter. His role as photographer was mostly a way to keep an eye on the paper in case Mesa needed him. Not that she ever did. In fact, she pretty much ran the paper without much trouble after only six months in the saddle. After all, she was a trained journalist with plenty of experience, even though she was only thirty. And she was smart enough not to part with tradition. A photo of the fire would have to wait.

Partiers jammed the streets at each corner along the parade route, oblivious to the possibility of fire. The skeleton crew of firefighters, streaming out of their uptown engine house at Mercury and Montana Street, would be stymied. A sea of people blocked the direct route up Main Street toward the ominous smoke that now billowed high above the hill.

And, thanks to the harsh winter, a frozen water main had burst at Woolman and Montana Streets two days before. The county had delivered gallons of drinking water to the affected families rather than force employees to work overtime on St. Paddy's Day. So, that route up the hill would be blocked as well. If Chance could find his way through the crowd and up Main Street on foot, eventually he might even beat the fire department.

The Pipers finally marched by, their Stuart tartans, white spats, and black ostrich-plumed bonnets shimmering in the sunshine. Chance pulled and pushed his way through the masses, craning to look up the hill to calculate how many blocks away the fire was, and whether he could find a ride. The two Irish coffees foisted upon him when Muldoon's started serving at nine a.m. weighed heavily on his decision.

It looked like the fire was just below Centerville, one of Butte's oldest neighborhoods and, with so many wood structures, one most vulnerable to fire. If the blaze was not extinguished quickly, another house would soon go up.

The pulsating sirens from Butte's fire engines were not going to be enough to clear the streets of the weekend crowd. Patrol officers on foot were doing their best to try to separate the throng, who were attired in every conceivable type of green clothing to enjoy Butte's oldest and largest free-for-all. Herding cats, drunken green cats, came to mind.

Chance fought his way back into Muldoon's, which now held three times the occupants dictated by the fire marshal, who was not likely to be issuing any citations as he was doubtless amongst the day's revelers. Don't cha know?

Fighting through the patrons, eight deep toward the bar, Chance saw Casey Van Zant, one of the three extra bartenders hired for the day. He was a mountain biker who Chance suspected might have ridden to work that morning, knowing the streets would be blocked off to car traffic until well after the bars closed at two a.m. A sudden change in the weather, this particular March 17th morning, made for one of the mildest St. Paddy's Days in recent memory, assuring large crowds who would stay late.

Before he could get Casey's attention, Chance felt the vibration of his cell phone. "Where are you?" he heard his sister, Mesa, yelling through the phone. A rush of people entering the bar obliterated whatever else she said. Chance squeezed through the doorway to stand outside, hoping he could get better reception.

"Chance?" he heard his sister blaring into the phone. "Where are you?"

"I'm outside Muldoon's," he screamed back.

"Look down the street," she said.

Across the street and a block away, Chance saw his sister with her former college roommate, Alexis Vandemere. She stood above the crowd on the concrete planter in front of the M & M, the one-hundred-year-old bar that served as the unofficial, holiday headquarters.

This was the first St. Patrick's Day that Mesa had celebrated since she departed Butte for college in Ohio a decade before. Even when she worked at the *River City Current*, an award-winning weekly in Cincinnati, she claimed the big city St. Patrick's Day celebration there lacked the spirit, or maybe the spirits, that made Butte's festivities legendary.

Alexis had come to town to make sure the celebration of Mesa's return reached the proper pitch. The pair had started early at Muldoon's as well. Alexis held onto the lamp pole next to the planter, her blonde ponytail, tinted green, swishing as she swung back and forth with a can of Guinness in her hand. Chance wondered what the two of them wanted.

Then Mesa pocketed her phone and leapt down into the chaos of the street. Running interference for her with a green, white, and orange sash across his chest was Shane Northey, a state legislator and her latest squeeze. He must have abandoned the contingent of politicians, including the governor, who had marched in the parade.

"Are you in any shape to chase after that siren?" Mesa asked when she reached Chance.

"I thought you were all about taking the day off?" he countered. "It being Sunday and you with company," he added, nodding knowingly toward Alexis. Now that Mesa had taken the job as editor of the *Messenger* permanently, he took more than a little enjoyment giving her a hard time. He had planned to end his St. Paddy's Day revelry early, in Adrienne's hot tub, staring at the side of Thunder Mountain. Taking photographs of the fire might get him warmed up, but probably not as enjoyably.

"I know I did, but that's because I figured with Alexis in town all the excitement would be here in the street. I didn't consider the arsonist would strike on St. Paddy's of all days."

"If everybody else thinks that way," Shane chimed in, "let's hope any house on fire is empty at least."

"Or littered with passed-out drunks," Mesa said with a roll of her eyes. "Especially if they started celebrating last night."

Above and beyond St. Patrick, Butte's citizens embraced the patron saint of the Finns, St. Urhu. Like the Irish, the Finns needed no excuse to drink heavily. Those Buttians with Finnish miners in their ancestry kept the celebration alive.

The specious holiday was the perfect way to get one up on all the Irish by starting a day early. Mesa and Shane had taken Alexis, a New Yorker who had traveled the world and never heard of St. Urhu, up to the Helsinki Bar and Yacht Club the previous night to witness the brawl first hand.

"You do have your camera," Mesa said sheepishly, "and I've got Alexis." His sister was on tiptoe, hoping to keep her friend in sight amidst the crowd.

"All right, all right, I'll see if I can get up there." He knew that Mesa would be reluctant to leave Alexis to fend for herself, not that she couldn't. But Mesa would feel responsible for the poor fools who ran up against her cocky wing woman.

As if the gods had pre-ordained it, Casey appeared outside the front door of Muldoon's. Bartending on St. Patrick's Day was a sacrifice made on behalf of one's community, and an act of endurance. He clearly needed a breather. Moments later, Chance had borrowed the mountain bike and begun the long slog up the hill. He had maybe a mile to go and it was straight uphill, about an eight per cent grade at an altitude of more than 5500 feet, but who was measuring?

Chance had already begun to gasp for air by the time he had ridden the five blocks to Woolman Street. He could see the Public Works barriers a block away to the west, obstructing the closest alternative route to get the oversized hook and ladder trucks up the hill to the fire.

The smoke filtered past the Mountain Con mine frame, its towering head frame a convenient landmark. It might make more sense to shuttle the Butte-Silver Bow's firefighters up to the Walkerville fire department, north of the Con mine yard, and bring their equipment, what was left of it, down the hill. Most of their volunteer fire department were on their hose truck in the parade, escorting the junior girls' world-series softball team, this year's parade marshals. Whatever the case, Chance wondered if much would be left of whatever was on fire.

Up the hill, the dark plumes of smoke, along with the growing smell of burnt plastic, guaranteed some kind of flammable material was well on its way to a first class blaze. If every able-bodied soul on the hill was down at the parade, which always used to be the case, then Chance hesitated to think how a fire had been started by accident. Surely, no one was smoking in bed or frying up a mess of trout on a day like today.

The bigger question was what an arsonist would find in Centerville that was worth setting on fire. Sadly, many houses in that neighborhood, once a proud community of Irish and Cornish miners, were little more than historic relics, with the emphasis on relics.

The previous summer, the community had recommitted itself to address its ragtag dwellings and had gotten a Habitat for Humanity grant. Concerned citizens were particularly pleased when the county had agreed to remove a mobile home, which was a vacant eyesore, and covered in obscene graffiti. The "butt-ugly blue trailer," as they called it, had attracted a steady stream of transients, and become a hangout for other n'er-do-wells. Its owner, a Bozeman developer, had made a last-ditch appearance at the Council of Commissioners meeting the previous Wednesday to protest the action. Too little too late, the removal was scheduled for the coming week. Maybe the developer had decided to recoup his losses through insurance.

Chance's thighs had begun to burn as he was spinning in first gear, pedaling like a circus clown on a tricycle while the bike's wheels inched forward. Meanwhile he was sucking air. At this rate, no one was going to get to the fire.

Finally, hopping off the bike to walk alongside, he managed the last two blocks, the fire department's sirens growing closer. He was only mildly deflated when he saw that the infamous "butt-ugly blue trailer" was almost engulfed, the remnants of "crack whore" graffiti being teased by flames, and not a soul anywhere to be seen.

This was the fourth fire in as many weeks. Maybe this was an accident but, if so, there were no current residents to question. And if it wasn't another of the latest arsonist's stunts, a hastily filed insurance claim might suggest another suspect. He pulled out his Nikon, and began circling the structure to document what was for sure going to be called a "suspicious fire."

❧

Chance pulled into the muddy driveway next to Adrienne DeBrooke's Sherpa hut, as she liked to call it. They had met the previous spring when she hired him to oversee the construction of the hut's cement daylight basement. To that, he had maneuvered and connected the prefabbed cabin that had arrived early one morning on a flatbed.

It had taken him awhile to understand why a successful, not to mention good-looking, San Francisco physician would want to live alone in a four-hundred-square-foot cabin on the side of a mountain. She had appreciated his work so much that she had called him again, a few weeks later, to help renovate the upper two floors of the Imperial Building on Park Street that she had just bought. Eventually, he discovered her true passion, when she opened an art gallery.

Adrienne's loft apartment above the gallery was smack dab in the middle of the day's festivities, which was exactly why she had retreated to her cabin for the weekend. Her mountain hideaway off the Moulton Reservoir Road was less than four miles from uptown, but it was worlds away from the evening's mayhem unfolding on the streets below.

He had planned to meet her well before sundown but covering the arson, if that was what it was, had gotten complicated. Not that Adrienne minded or likely even noticed. The cover of the hot tub on the deck above him was tightly in place, which meant she had probably spent a good part of the afternoon inside, lost in the canvas she had begun.

He grabbed her supplies from the back of his pickup and trotted up the stairs to the upper deck. Removing his shoes, he opened the sliding door to the piney smell of the cabin. As he suspected, she was standing at her easel, paintbrush in hand. She arched her back and said, "Thank goodness you're here. Did you hear my lumbar vertebrae calling to you for relief?"

He kissed her and said, "I love it when you talk medical to me." Then he handed her the groceries, kissed her again, but longer this time, and then went out to the hot tub, stripped down and got in. A nanosecond later, she appeared, wearing nothing but a bottle of champagne and two flutes. She joined him in the tub and said, "And how were the Celtic Bacchanals progressing?"

"Don't ask," he said with a sigh and wrapped her in his arms. "I lost sight of Mesa and company when I had to go up to Centerville to check out the arsonist's latest handiwork."

"I thought I caught a whiff of something odd this afternoon."

"Tell me about it," Chance said. "It was that eyesore of a trailer. Damn thing smelled to high heaven."

≈∾

Recovery from a weekend St. Patrick's Day was an art that, on Monday, the staff at the *Messenger* was delicately trying to practice. A group recovery session had convened in the newsroom.

The newspaper's college intern, Micah, appeared with a carton load of espressos from the Park and Main Café. Mesa had gone the triple espresso route.

Micah seemed showered and only slightly bleary-eyed, but Mesa could smell beer coming from his pores. Instead of his usual pressed, preppy look, he wore a green t-shirt emblazoned with "I drank a WEE toast to the Irish in these Butte bars," followed by a list of twelve local establishments.

"You know, Micah," Mesa said between sips, "don't feel like you have to take to heart that stereotype of the hard-drinking journalist."

Arnold Cinch appeared from his closet-sized ad office, a green plastic visor perched below the white tufts of what was left of his hair, just in time to counter Mesa's advice. "Don't believe it, kid. If you want to run with the big dogs, St. Paddy's is ideal practice." And then Cinch turned his sights on Mesa. "Besides, I hear you and some delectable damsel from back East were making the rounds."

Mesa hoped she wasn't turning too deep a shade of pink, as she was prone to do when she got embarrassed. Since her return to Butte the previous fall, she was still making adjustments to small-town life—like how everybody knew what everybody else was up to. She couldn't move from one bar to the next without meeting someone she "hadn't seen in forever."

"I was just trying to show an out-of-towner a good time," she countered. Alexis had been to St. Patrick's

Day once before, but she still qualified as an out-of-towner in Mesa's book.

"If you call the Irish Crimes a good time," Cinch continued. "I heard the two of you were huddled in a corner while half a dozen guys were busy pinning each other to the floor to defend her honor."

While the details remained hazy, Mesa did seem to recall that some time after midnight, Alexis had devised a chugging contest to win her attention, if not her affections. It had not ended well. Mesa made another mental note to stop by the Irish Times and make amends to the owner.

Irita, the *Mess's* office manager, had stepped in to give counsel. "I tell you numbskulls every year, drink a glass of water between beers." She tossed her large leather tote bag onto her desk outside Mesa's office. "Or better yet, give up alcohol altogether." Irita had been on the wagon for the better part of her adulthood, self-enforced abstinence brought on by her early years on the reservation.

"You ever use one of those porta-potties?" said Phade, the resident geek dressed all in black and sporting two nose rings through the septum. He stepped outside his cubicle to snag a cup from Micah. "I try to be a good Butte boy and not piss in the alley, but by noon those blue boxes are disgusting. I'm sure as hell not going to voluntarily drink water. I'd sooner suffer the day after."

"Speaking of the day after," Irita said, "some rancher gal's in the lobby, name's Jobe. She wants to know if she got any responses to her personal in last week's edition. Box 17. Cinchy, that's your gig, isn't it?"

This last directive Irita delivered with feigned delicacy. Cinch could be a bear even when he didn't have a hangover.

"I told you this was a bad idea," Cinch said to Mesa as he retreated to the wall of wooden cubbyholes that he and Chance had rehabbed from the basement of a corner grocery that had once doubled for a post office in Walkerville. The personals section of the paper represented Mesa's New Year promotion of the *Messenger's* reader-friendly, personal services.

The rest of the world might be posting its ads on Craigslist or Facebook, but in Butte, the search tended to remain on the ground. The hunt for some long-lost relative whose family had lived here when the mines were open seemed like a weekly occurrence. The *Messenger* and its reportedly knowledgeable local staff could offer more fruitful assistance.

"I just file the replies," said Cinch and pulled the three by five ad from the appropriate pigeonhole. "And you definitely don't want me to break the news to Ms. Jobe," he said to Mesa with an exaggerated air. "I knew her in a previous life."

Mesa took a long sip from her latte and grabbed the card from Cinch. A dull ache in the back of her head made her wish she'd never met Alexis Vandemere, who did not deign to work for a living. "Why bother?" she would say. "I like my trust fund and, besides, I'm too busy."

The three by five personal ads were the top of the line and cost twenty dollars per issue. If Mesa wanted this lady to be a satisfied customer, she knew she had better do the talking herself. She read the ad under her breath.

Do you know Dowling Jessup?

I am trying to reconnect with Mr. Jessup who lived at the Montana Children's Home in the '70s, and later in Deer Lodge. Help me find an old friend. Respond to Box 17 at the Messenger.

Seemed straightforward enough. St. Paddy's week was always an ideal time to look somebody up. With the highest per capita percentage of Irish ancestry of any town in America, Butte attracted a gigantic contingent of out-of-towners for the holiday. Former residents who now lived elsewhere returned in droves. The mine closures had created a migration of workers, but natives always came back to visit their extended families who had remained behind. And the town's population doubled when St. Patrick's Day fell on a weekend.

What tugged at Mesa's heart was the mention of the Children's Home. The orphanage, south of Butte in Twin Bridges, had seen several different owners since the state had closed the Home in the mid seventies. Each time the collection of buildings went on the selling block, a photo of the institution's turreted Queen Anne administration building made the papers, looking for all the world like the ideal setting for a Stephen King novel.

Mesa left the newsroom and its mewling occupants and walked out into the reception area to meet the woman looking for a long-lost orphan. She did her best to hide her surprise.

Fifty-ish and tall, the woman's stylishly frosted, blonde ponytail shifted nonchalantly as she turned from the window. Rosy cheeks and bright eyes accompanied her crisp, outdoorsy aura. The yellow lab, panting at her feet, confirmed her as an early morning dog walker, and nothing like Mesa had expected.

The dog rose with Mesa's approach. For a moment, the woman hesitated and then said in almost a whisper, "You're Mesa Dawson."

"That's right. Miss Jobe?" Mesa said, reading the name from the back of the ad mockup. This woman seemed so well-to-do.

"Please, call me Vivian," she said with a smile and offered her hand. She held Mesa's in both of hers, and nodded. "I knew your mother."

"Oh?" Mesa said, "You did?" not quite sure what else to say. Her mother had died of breast cancer fifteen years before, and Mesa rarely met strangers anymore who had known Sarah Ducharme. But the longer she looked at this statuesque woman, the more Mesa thought perhaps they might have met before.

"You look so much like her," the woman said. "It's uncanny."

Feeling her cheeks redden again, Mesa said, "Why don't we go back into my office," and motioned in that direction, "where we can talk." All thoughts about good customer service went out the window, even if, as Irita was constantly reminding her, every patron in sparsely populated southwest Montana had the potential to make or break a business.

Vivian Jobe angled onto the edge of the couch, knees together, her long legs crossed at the ankle. The dog, whom she introduced as Buddha, nestled in close. Vivian sighed, her hands clasped together, a gold signet ring on one finger and an emerald and diamond one on another.

"I knew you ran the paper, but I didn't expect to meet you," she said, continuing to smile. "Your mother and I were in school together, good friends actually," Vivian said, smoothing an imaginary wrinkle from her long skirt. "I was even in her wedding."

Now Mesa was smiling. "That's where I've seen you. My grandmother has a photo of my mom surrounded by her bridesmaids. I've walked by it a thousand times. You're the tall one," Mesa said with a laugh.

"God, I hated those pink dresses," Vivian said. "But don't tell your grandmother I said that. Sarah claimed her mother ordered the material especially from Seattle."

"It's so nice to meet you," Mesa said, despite vaguely recalling her grandmother's distress about the tall bridesmaid who had hoped to be a doctor one day but something had happened. Mesa couldn't remember what.

"I was so sorry to hear about Sarah's death," Vivian said, this time toying with the emerald ring. "I'm sorry I wasn't here for her. She was a good friend."

The pause came, the one Mesa always dreaded. Stuttering over her words, that is, if she didn't draw a complete blank, she became paralyzed in the face of people who were so kind—never knowing what to say, even all these years later. She fought back a lump in her throat. Thankfully, the rescue came quickly.

"Part of the reason I wasn't in Butte then," Vivian said, "has to do with my little ad." She pointed with one of her manicured fingers to the card Mesa still held. "Any luck, by the way?"

Mesa shook her head and said, "Afraid not."

Vivian let out a sigh. "I thought I might get some bites, maybe someone who knew of Dowl, if not in the present, then maybe the recent past."

"We could run the ad for another week," Mesa said, eager to help this friend of her mother's. It could take several days to recover from St. Paddy's Day. The old acquaintance Vivian sought might just be waking up to the *Messenger*.

"I suppose it's still possible someone could come around today," Vivian said, checking the time on her expensive wristwatch.

Mesa looked at the card again and thought about what Vivian Jobe might have looked like three decades ago—a bit thinner, a softer expression, blonde hair a little lighter. She also wondered what this Jessup guy had meant to her, and if he knew her mother as well. She wasn't sure if she wanted this to be the case, or not. The desire to know her mother as an adult had always warred with the fear of resurrecting her old grief.

"You said your search had something to do with why you weren't here in '99? Were you with him then? Not that it's anybody's business, certainly not the newspaper's. I mean, what makes you think you'd find Mr. Jessup in Butte now?"

"Well, as a matter of fact, I got the idea from a friend of yours—Sam Chavez."

Mesa had to smile. She had talked with Sam the previous Friday when he had been replacing a downspout at her grandmother's house. "You know Sam, too? He's the best."

Vivian nodded with a smile. "I work with dogs, agility training. Sam built a dog carrier for us. We got to talking the last time he was up at my place. I live between here and Whitehall. We talked about your mom. He told me all about how you had come back to Butte to run the paper and that you might be able to help me out. He thinks the world of you, especially how you've helped your grandmother."

"Likewise. Sam's like family." Mesa felt her cheeks reddening again, and reminded herself that she had a business to run. "Sometimes an ad in the paper can reach a lot of people," she said. "We started carrying these personals because we had so many people stopping in to ask for information. I think the paper feels a bit more user-friendly than, say, the courthouse or the police station, or even the archives. They can all seem more official," she said with another smile. "Some people just want to shoot the breeze, more or less. We've got time to do that."

"This search may prove to be more of a challenge, but now that I've met you, I get the feeling that you might be just the person to help me out."

"I like to think we take a more personal approach," Mesa said, "not that we always have any luck. Sometimes we can give people some pointers about contacts or places to check out. A retired teacher from California came through here a couple of weeks ago looking for a classmate from high school. We passed the name around the newsroom, made a call, and found out that she was living at the Waterford. You know the retirement home off Continental Drive?"

Vivian nodded and said, "Six degrees of separation. That's what I'm counting on."

"Exactly," Mesa said, feeling upbeat. She knew that strategy worked nowhere better than in Butte. "Thank goodness, or we'd be out of business. Can you give me some more background on your friend? We might be able to point you in the right direction ASAP."

She was glad Irita wasn't hearing this conversation. She'd be saying that acting as Miss Lonely Hearts wouldn't get any copy written for this week's edition. But that was one of the big pluses about being the boss. She could ignore Irita.

"I'm assuming you weren't at the Children's Home together," Mesa said, broaching the question she was most curious about. The idea of being so alone in the world that you had to go to an orphanage felt pit-of-your-stomach scary—right out of Dickens. Yet stories like David Copperfield and Oliver Twist that trumpeted overcoming those kinds of circumstances had always appealed to Mesa as a kid.

Vivian shook her head. "I grew up on a ranch this side of Deer Lodge, then moved into Butte when I reached high school. But Dowl told me about being at the Home. I know there are plenty of people who were there as kids who still live around here. I thought maybe he might have kept up with some of them."

Mesa was both disappointed and relieved. Some of the richest cattle ranches in Montana had once peppered the Deer Lodge Valley, thirty-some miles west of Butte. With her manicured nails and fashionable style, Vivian Jobe seemed more likely to have been the product of ranch owners than tenants. The Montana State Children's Home, on the other hand, fifty miles in the opposite direction, represented completely different circumstances. Mesa wondered how the two had met.

"Old boyfriend, then?" Mesa asked with a smile, feeling comfortable enough to tease.

"Not exactly," Vivian said. "This is where the story gets a little—," she paused and then finished, "—unconventional." She twirled the pinky ring again. "We knew each other the summer before my senior year in high school," she said, and then straightened her back and looked directly at Mesa.

Mesa had closed the office door, and then quietly moved over to sit on the other end of the sofa. She sensed that Vivian Jobe might not want the entire newsroom to hear her story, but Mesa did not want to miss a word. "What finally made you decide to get in touch? You waited a long time."

"It's a bit hard to explain." She paused and then smiled. "More than anything, I remember how sensitive he was. We spent a lot of time together that summer. Inseparable, I guess you could say." She arched her eyebrows as if there was a not-so-funny inside joke involved. "I was going through a tough time. He would bring me little bouquets of wildflowers, or be there with a squeeze of the hand or a reassuring word. Little things made a big difference where we were. It was all quite innocent, I assure you, but he helped me through what felt like an unlivable situation."

Mesa listened intently, curious about what Vivian meant by "where we were."

"Events that happen when you're young leave their mark. Then the memories return years later to haunt you. Images come back suddenly in a big stream, something you hadn't thought about for ages." She bent down to give her dog a quick hug. "Not a week goes by these days that I don't wonder about where he is and what he's doing. Sounds crazy, doesn't it?" she said with a half grin. "Well, we were. Or at least, I was."

"Crazy, how?" Mesa said in a voice that she hoped wasn't too suggestive. She liked this friend of her mother's and didn't want to risk offending her.

Vivian sighed deeply. "I feel like I can confide in you. After all, if you're as kind-hearted as your mother was, I think I can trust you. Sam certainly does."

Mesa made a note to thank Sam for the plug. He was her guardian angel. He knew if she made a promise to keep something confidential, she'd be true to her word.

"Dowl and I did a stint in Warm Springs together," Vivian said and paused. "The State Mental Hospital," she continued when Mesa didn't say anything. "Most people are a bit leery when they find out." She paused again, perhaps waiting to see Mesa's reaction.

A friend of her mother's had been in a mental hospital? Mesa had to admit that gave her an odd feeling. So that was what had distressed Nana.

Vivian's candor stunned Mesa. In a hardscrabble town like Butte, people didn't talk about such things, like Nana hadn't, or, if they did, too often it was with a sense of shame. Not that there weren't locals with issues. A recent string of teenage suicides had brought the town to its knees.

"Okay," Mesa said, scrambling to know what to say. "I admit I'm a little surprised. I mean it's not that I haven't had some friends who needed a little ... R and R. It's just that you don't look the type. I mean, I know that's not the most politically correct thing to say."

Vivian laughed, "Not to worry. We're in Butte. Truth is," she continued, "thanks to the wide-open spaces, and a maverick therapist, I finally got off my meds, and my life is stable. I've been taking stock of my past recently, and I came across some of my *prized* possessions from that time." She laughed and pulled out a carved wooden box from her purse. She poked around some old jewelry, a few handwritten notes, and pulled out a small object—

fine red and black yarn woven around a couple of wooden sticks crossed in the middle. Vivian handed it to Mesa.

"It's called a God's eye. Dowl made it for me. I carried it around with me for years."

Mesa held the talisman in her palm. She had seen similar objects that the Mexicans called *ojo de dios*. They were considered symbolic of the power to understand the unknown. Seemed like a thoughtful gift for one mental patient from another. "How long were you in the hospital?" Mesa asked, not wanting to pry, but curious.

"That first time, almost the entire summer. Back then you could do ninety days and be back on your feet, or so they thought." She shook her head. "I came back to school and finished my senior year. Your mom was one of the few friends who knew where I'd gone. Everybody else thought I'd been back East to visit relatives for the summer. That was the story my mother spread around."

Mesa thought about her mother, her gentle eyes, and her ready smile. She had a wry sense of humor, too. She and Vivian could well have been good friends. "I can see how the two of you would have hit it off," Mesa said and handed the God's eye back to Vivian.

"I was so lucky to have someone like Sarah who cared about me and treated me like normal." Vivian paused and twirled the God's eye by one of its sticks. "I found my way back to sanity, but Dowl had nobody—no friends, no family. That's part of the reason I want to find him. I've had advantages he didn't. I want to help him if I can."

"Do you have any idea how Dowl's doing?" Mesa had already begun to think about whom they might call.

Irita, for sure, would be able to do an impromptu check with her network of courthouse pals.

Vivian cocked her head to one side. "Not so sure. That's one of the things I'm hoping to find out. Last I saw him, he was accused of killing another patient."

Chapter 2

Mesa and Vivian Jobe talked for nearly an hour about how the trauma of her father's death had led to a breakdown that landed her in Warm Springs where she had met Dowling Jessup. Her grief had overwhelmed her but not so much that she didn't remember what had happened to Dowl.

His involvement in the death of another patient was the point of contention for Vivian because she was sure Dowl was innocent. "He was with me when they said it happened." But Vivian had had her own delirium to worry about, one that would eventually spin out of control and be diagnosed as schizophrenia. "I can tell you more about that eventually, but it's Dowl I'd like to focus on now."

Mesa had agreed to dig around to see what she could find, and contact Vivian in the next day or two. Hopefully, they could also get together for a little reunion with Nana Rose whom Mesa suspected would relish the chance to reconnect.

"Who was THAT who just left?" Chance said when he entered Mesa's office moments after Vivian had departed. He had a spring in his step that belied everyone else's Monday recovery. He carried a bag of jelly rolls and offered one to his sister, who turned away in disgust. "She from Bozeman?"

"What makes you ask that?" Mesa said. She liked the idea of stringing her brother along about a woman with Vivian Jobe's exotic history. And that's how her past sounded—this smart, attractive friend of her mother's suddenly appearing and saying she'd been in a mental hospital.

He shrugged. "She gave me kind of a long look, and she wears expensive boots and has an inside dog."

But it was his turn to grimace when Mesa, who was peeking out the narrow Venetian blinds at her office window, provided the TV Guide version of Vivian's story about Warm Springs, and the revelation that she had been a friend of their mom's. Chance joined her and watched Vivian cross the street to her pickup with the dog carriers. Sam Chavez was leaning on one elbow on the front hood.

"I never met a schizophrenic," Chance said, "at least not one with such nice clothes. Cool truck. Hey, isn't that Sam?"

"Careful," Mesa said and leaned back away from the window frame, pushing her brother back. "Don't let her see you. Didn't you hear me say I promised to keep her story confidential for the time being?"

Mesa felt suddenly protective. After all, who were they to hold it against Vivian that she had spent time in a mental hospital, especially since she was so candid about her past. She seemed no more deluded than you'd expect of any woman looking for a man she hadn't seen in thirty years. The woman had rights like everybody else.

"Weren't you telling me about some magazine article about a guy who'd recovered from schizophrenia,"

Chance said, "even wrote a book about it, then went bonkers again and killed his fiancée?"

"Well, if I heard Vivian correctly, she's never killed anybody and, even if this guy she's looking for served time for killing someone, she says he didn't do it. If he's out now, I'd like to help her find him."

"Well, you got your white hat on today, don't cha. Why are you so hot to help her out? She could be crazy as a bedbug."

Mesa knew Chance could be right. Butte seemed to have more than a few local characters who were short a full deck. "Sam Chavez sent her, and don't you think Mom would want us to do what we can? Plus, Jan Kaiser is her therapist and she thinks it's a good idea." Kaiser was one of a handful of therapists in town. She had treated Mesa after her mother's death.

"And she gave us another twenty for a personal ad and, on top of that, she's got the courage to talk about her illness, something this town could use more of."

"Say no more," Chance interrupted. "If she and mom were friends, AND Sam think she could use some help, that's good enough for me."

Mesa could see how Sam and Vivian might connect. He had known every kind of chaos, learning to drink at age seven with his alcoholic father, and then running away from abusive foster care. By the time he was nineteen and a ranch hand, he'd been thrown in prison for defending himself against locals who hated "Injuns." He was illiterate until Nana had taught him to read and write when he worked on the Ducharme ranch. Now known around town as a guy who could fix anything, he did odd jobs and functioned as Nana's 24/7 handyman. He was a survivor.

Suddenly weary, Mesa slumped into her chair, trying to ignore her queasy stomach, and making a mental note never to invite Alexis to town on St. Paddy's day ever again. "What are you doing here anyway? Make it good, please. My head and my stomach are in a race to see who can make me barf first."

"Well, then this might make your day. The fire in that trailer yesterday," he said as he shook powdered sugar from a jelly-roll donut off his hands and onto Mesa's coffee table, "they found a body inside. Some transient." Careful with the powdered sugar, he handed her the crumbled police report, holding it by a corner. "Our little St. Paddy's Day bonfire is now officially a suspicious fire and possible homicide."

Mesa looked up, only half listening. She scanned the report for the details. She knew the *Standard* would cover the arson angle as part of an ongoing story. Four fires in as many weeks was front page. But as any insurance adjuster in town would say, arsonists sprang up in Butte like weeds. Get rid of one and another took its place.

Arson was a time-tested crime story, if not an honorable one. The history of arsons in Butte could fill its own book. In the 1980's, after the Anaconda Company closed, half of the struggling, uptown businesses had gone up in flames. Arson was one of those tales of woe that needed coverage even if everyone hated reading about it.

"Why I busted my hump to get up there for a picture, I don't know. The *Standard* always beats us into print anyway," Chance said and held up the morning paper, which Mesa had yet to read.

She looked at the color photo—bright orange flames shooting into the air—and tossed the paper on top of half a dozen files on her desk.

"The police don't exactly know what happened," Chance said, taking back the form. "The trailer had been vacant for most of the winter and had no water or heat. They'd had complaints about squatters, I guess. Not like you could blame transients for using the place to get out of the cold. The fire department doused the fire before the dump was completely destroyed. The homeless guy probably died of smoke inhalation," Chance said, licking raspberry jelly from two fingers. "Nick said the guy was found lying on an old mattress with an empty fifth of Old Crow beside him and a lot of soot in his mouth."

Nick Philippoussis, the coroner's assistant and Chance's friend since high school, usually had solid information. "So, he torched himself?" Mesa said.

"Sheriff thinks more likely the transient was an innocent bystander, and the arsonist started the fire without knowing someone was inside. Course that's a minor detail, according to the sheriff. If someone dies in a fire started by an arsonist, it's a homicide."

Irita entered with an armful of manila folders and plopped them on Mesa's desk. "More applications that came in this morning's mail. Guess we're getting pretty popular, if everybody wants to work here. I'm not looking forward to going through all of these."

"Me neither," Chance said. "See ya." And he bolted for the door, almost careening into Irita.

"He's hell bent for leather," Irita said, motioning to the folders. "Leaving you to run the circus on your own, is he?"

When Mesa had put an ad in the *Messenger* to replace their ace reporter, the potential to generate a decent pool of applicants never crossed her mind. That said, she certainly hadn't expected more than half a dozen applicants.

She took a handful of the folders and left the rest to Irita who moved to the couch and began a quick review. Since the *Standard* had lured away Erin O' Rourke, the second raid they'd made on the *Messenger's* staff in nine months, her byline had graced the front page of the daily paper on a regular basis. She had certainly done her part, as promised, to help recruit.

Not that Mesa begrudged her former employee. The only position she dreaded having to fill was Phade's. She constantly had to come up with incentives to keep him happy. Geeks were hard to come by, and expensive. That said, Erin had been a good kid, worked hard, and rarely whined. She would be missed. Now if only Mesa could find another one just like her.

The first ten applicants had included everyone from a retired English teacher who knew Nana, to real estate agents who knew their way around town, to bartenders who knew "where the bodies were buried." Everybody knew something. But could they write about it in 750 words or less, on deadline, or help Phade with the blog and Facebook, maybe even fill his shoes some day?

"I don't know, Irita," Mesa said with a sigh. "Finding a replacement for Erin is turning out to be more complicated than I thought."

"That's because you insist on looking at the applicants' qualifications instead of hiring somebody you know, or are related to, like everybody else in town does."

"Now, now," Mesa teased, "don't forget this paper *is* a family business. Look at Chance and me."

"Yeah, but Chance doesn't draw a salary anymore. He just comes around to bug you and throw the occasional photo our way."

"Most of the applicants do have some decent skills, just not directly related."

"Don't make too big a fuss about it. You're hiring a reporter, not a prophet," Irita advised. "Get somebody who's straightforward, with some spine. Somebody who'll get angry rather than be indifferent or cynical. Somebody who'll write about who's not making it, about the America that's gotten left behind. Somebody who won't be bought out. Somebody who cares!"

With these last few words, Irita was shaking her fist in the air at Mesa. "Jesus, Irita, who got you so worked up?"

"I was watching Bill Moyers on PBS last night. God, that guy's great. If only he'd get a decent haircut. But don't pay any attention to me. I'll settle for a warm body with reasonable hygiene that can be on time in the morning."

"No, no. I liked what you said," Mesa said, thinking about her conversation with Vivian. She was a person who would buy that argument, that there was an America that's gotten left behind. And a Montana that got left behind, like Dowling Jessup.

She gathered up the rest of the files, and dropped them in Irita's lap. "Listen, take these files, pick three, ideally with Facebook and blog savvy who can get along with Phade, and set up some interviews for me. And remember, the budget is tight, so I'll settle for scrappy." Then she headed out the door.

❧

Chance had made a quick retreat from his sister's office. He knew too well how she could obsess about helping somebody, and he could see that look in her eye now, especially since this woman was a friend of their mom's, a connection that he could see meant a lot to Mesa.

She had taken their mother's death as hard as any teenage girl close to her mother would. Chance had been broken-hearted too. He wasn't ashamed to admit it. But at sixteen, he had his foot in adulthood and plenty to keep him busy. It was Mesa who had trouble bouncing back.

Sometimes he wondered if she didn't still harbor some deep-seated grief like their father did. Nate Dawson had been back to Butte exactly twice since his wife had died. He regularly splurged to get Chance and Mesa to visit him back East, but there had been no happy family reunions back in Montana. Colonel Dawson couldn't take the memories.

The biting March wind had returned. Not ideal weather to start the challenging renovation job on Granite Street he had recently been hired to do. A professor at the college had purchased a property adjacent to her home. She wanted him to gut the inside of the miner's cottage whose last tenant had died of a heart attack while filling the bathtub and whose death had gone undetected for two months owing to Butte's sub-zero winter temperatures.

Chance picked up his pace. He was heading toward the corner of Park and Main when he heard someone call his name. He turned to see Henry Gillis lumbering along the sidewalk, pushing his dayglo orange mountain bike. His cheeks and ears were pink from the wind. At least he wore his Spiderman gloves and matching headband.

"How's she going, Henry?" Chance said and crossed the street, keeping up his pace. Henry lived in the Leggett Hotel on Broadway along with numerous other developmentally challenged adults, thanks to subsidized housing. He liked to ride his bike around uptown, which was how he and Chance had met.

Chance had helped with a flat tire once, and since then knew that to talk to Henry was to have an extended chat. If you weren't moving, it was too hard to get out of the conversation, and Chance had no time to waste.

"I really need to talk to you, Chance. My friend might be in trouble."

"Which friend and what kind of trouble?" Chance asked, knowing that in Henry's mind trouble could mean a disagreement with another Leggett hotel resident, or the loss of a prized ball cap.

"See this picture in the paper," Henry said, and pointed to the photo of the burning trailer in the *Standard* he pulled from his back pocket. "I saw my friend go in there Saturday night."

❧

Chance cajoled Henry into the B&S diner on Main Street and ordered them an early lunch. If Henry had seen two men go into the trailer, then one of them might be the unidentified dead man. But that was a big "if." Henry had a vivid imagination, played a lot of video games, and was excitable. He was prone to misinterpret what he saw.

Henry regularly expressed his fear of the police, so Chance wanted to be certain that he was hearing from a witness to a crime. Convincing Henry to talk to the sheriff would be a battle. Maybe Chance would just pass along whatever he learned.

The morning coffee crowd had cleared out, and they had the café to themselves until the lunch bunch showed up. But, after fifteen minutes, Chance had begun to think his interest in Henry's concern for his friend was not helpful.

"I think I'll go home," Henry said, his eyes cast downward as if he were giving close inspection to the fiesta nachos Chance had bought him.

"You sure?" Chance asked in a quiet voice. He did not like the idea of shelving their discussion without making sure if Henry had really seen someone, and if that someone was actually his friend or a possible arsonist.

Henry had a way of embellishing events and relationships. If the driver said "hello" on the bus three days in a row, Henry would say he had a new friend.

"I was trying my best to explain it to you. You just don't understand," Henry said, refusing to look at Chance.

"I'm sorry," Chance said. In his haste to get details to turn over to the sheriff, maybe he had pressed Henry too quickly. He could see that Henry felt stupid, like it was his fault that he couldn't answer all Chance's questions, and that Chance didn't understand. Like most people, one thing Henry didn't like was to look stupid.

"Tell you what," Chance said, "if you'll stay and explain it to me one more time, I'll try harder to understand. And then afterward we can have some Wilkinson's. Chocolate's your favorite, right?"

Chance hated to resort to ice cream as a bribe, especially since Henry's Pillsbury doughboy appearance was a source of derision by some Leggett residents. But if Chance was going to go to the authorities with Henry's story, the details had better be as accurate as possible.

"Tell me again about what Stick said to you." Stick was the name of the friend that Henry was worried about.

"Nothing," Henry said in an agitated voice. "He always talked to me before. He always asked me how I was doing, and what I been watching on TV. But this time, he didn't say anything. He just stared right through me."

"Do you think he was high?"

Henry shrugged. "I know some people in my building do drugs, but I don't, and I don't like people who do. You believe me, don't cha?"

Chance nodded definitively. Henry had the elevated sense of right and wrong you'd find in a sixth-grader. The last thing he wanted was to get in trouble.

"Maybe he was," Henry said, his voice carrying the disappointment of one who'd been let down by someone important to him.

"You said he was with someone you never saw before. What did the other person look like?"

"He was taller than me. I'm six feet tall. You know that, don't cha? And he had strong arms."

"You mean he was muscular?"

Henry nodded once more. "He had one of those lumberjack shirts on with the sleeves rolled up to his elbow, and I could see his arms. He had one around Stick's shoulders."

"Did Stick need help standing?" Chance asked, wondering if the man was drunk.

"I think it was more like he was showing Stick which way to go."

"And you saw them walking up Main Street?"

Henry nodded several times. "Up past the Coffee Pot. I followed them a little ways. Sometimes people get mad at me if they think I'm following them. But I did it anyway."

Chance sensed Henry's defiance. "You weren't worried they'd get mad?"

Henry shook his head. "It was almost dark, so I didn't think they'd see me. I didn't like that guy. He looked mean. I wanted to be sure Stick was okay."

Chanced nodded. "How far did you get?"

"Not very far," Henry said, his voice dejected. "I stopped when I saw them go into the trailer. I was meeting my friend Thomas at AWARE House so I had to come back down to Copper Street. I wish I hadn't. Do you think Stick will get in trouble for what happened? He'd never start a fire or anything like that. He's real careful about stuff like that."

Chance hesitated before answering. So far, Henry had said nothing to indicate that he realized a dead man had been found in the trailer. Henry could read, but Chance had never actually seen him read much beyond a menu or the back of a video game cover. "Henry, did you read the article in the paper?"

❧❧

Mesa could never enter a library without thinking about when her father had taken Chance and her there for the first time. She could still see the smile on her father's face when he sat down in a tiny chair in the children's section to look at a book with her.

She was allowed to check out five books, a cruel limit, she thought. Her mother would put the books on top of the refrigerator and apportion them out so that Mesa would have something to read all week long. Now she did most of her research on the Internet and rarely found time to read at all, a situation she was always telling herself she had to remedy.

The Butte-Silver Bow Library, five blocks from the *Mess's* office, still gave her the same cozy feeling she had when she first came to story time twenty plus years before, but things were looking up. The building had received a welcomed face lift, with bright blue awnings above the large front windows, and a mural painted on the side. Inside, airport style security gates had been added.

Like most libraries back East, the usual allotment of homeless congregated there. She found herself looking at them differently since hearing Vivian's admission of her days on the street.

On her way to the section where the *Montana Standard* microfilm had been filed the last time she was in the library, she walked by an unkempt man with a battered backpack and several overstuffed paper shopping bags at his feet. He sat at a carrel, staring blankly into space, an opened book, upside down, in front of him. Evidently, he'd been made aware of the rule that the library was "reserved for active users of its resources."

Seeing no files of the *Standard*, Mesa turned to a nearby terminal and checked the library's website in hopes of finding an index for the newspaper. She discovered that the *Montana Standard's* online archives still only went back to 2000. The cyber highway could only take her so far on her exploration.

A helpful librarian redirected her to the files that had been moved to the second floor. She headed up the stairs for some good-old-fashioned, go-touch-the-hard-copy, or at least the microfilm, research. She actually enjoyed this part of newspaper work.

She exited the stairwell onto the second floor with its reference desk at the far end, the microfilm room beyond that. She figured a skip through the *Standard's* 1979 volume and she'd have the information she needed. Vivian had been clear about the time period when she had met Dowling Jessup. Her first stay at the adolescent unit of the hospital had begun the last of May. She had returned home in mid-August after Dowl had been accused of killing another patient. Mesa wondered if Vivian had confided in her mother about Dowling, and, if so, what she would have said.

On her way toward the back of the room, Mesa was surprised to see that a woman had fallen asleep under one of the oblong tables. She wore a rumpled camel coat with a dirty sheepskin collar. Her knees pulled up toward her chest, she clung to a large, half-eaten bag of Fritos while she slept.

One of the librarians, a tall blonde in a maroon sweater, chin up and shoulders back, approached and leaned under the table to rouse the sleeping woman, who had now begun to snore. She tapped the woman gently on the shoulder and said in a calm voice, "Excuse me, ma'am, you can't sleep or eat up here."

No response. The librarian offered another gentle tap on the arm, gingerly moving a chair to provide an easy exit for the prone patron.

Suddenly chairs went flying along with the books and magazines that had been on top of the table as the woman leapt from underneath, bucking the table and yelling, "This is my room and you can't come in. And these are my Fritos and you can't take them away from me!"

A man dressed in a voluminous overcoat and a leather and fur cap with earflaps stood up from a nearby carrel. Clutching a large, red plastic shopping bag that might well hold all his worldly possessions, Earflaps walked past Mesa, muttering, "not listening, not listening," and headed for the stairwell.

Mesa took refuge between two bookshelves. Not wanting to get in the way, she was still curious to see how the incident would play out.

The librarian held her ground and quietly repeated, "I'm sorry but you can't eat up here. If you'd like, you can go downstairs and sit in one of the armchairs by the front door. Food is allowed there."

Stocky and obviously used to having to defend herself, the street-savvy patron had adopted a wide protective stance. Looking around as though she had forgotten where she was, she eyed Mesa and then the librarian, who had continued her attempt at calm dialogue.

After a moment, the disheveled woman's shoulders relaxed as she paid more attention to what the librarian was saying. Taking a neon orange knit cap from her pocket, the woman pulled it down over her ears, yawned, and then started for the stairwell, the Fritos held in a vise-like grip.

The librarian began rearranging the chairs. Mesa picked up the one that had landed at her feet and brought it to the table, giving a supportive nod to the librarian who smiled back and said, "They call me The Enforcer."

Mesa introduced herself and complimented the librarian's good humor and the way she had defused the situation, wondering about the level of sympathy the staff could be expected to have. After all, they weren't social workers, although clearly the librarian had had some training to deal with ersatz library users.

"It's a shame," the librarian said. "These people don't really want to be here, but a lot of them have no place decent to go."

Mesa nodded in somber agreement, considering the possibility that Dowling Jessup might be one of "these people." The Butte Rescue Mission provided shelter at night but, during the day, transients were on their own. The library was the one place a person could go for free where no one would kick you out, at least if your behavior didn't attract attention.

Mesa returned to retrieving the correct roll of microfilm. Once she found it, she sat down at a microfilm reader and, for a moment, stared at her reflection in the screen. She thought about the expression on the homeless woman's face. Would she have done battle with the librarian if the situation had escalated? The unruly patron had clearly been ready for yet another person who would give her a hard time, but had become compliant when faced with someone who was calm.

The angle of the microfilm reader's screen was vicious, but there was no alternative. Mesa threaded the microfilm reel and started winding toward May of 1979 and details about Jessup.

She'd been staring at the screen for half an hour and had gotten as far as mid August. She rubbed the back of her neck and gave the room a quick scan, vaguely curious to see if Frito Lady or Earflaps had returned.

In the editions of the paper she'd scanned so far, she'd found no reference to the death of a teenager at the mental hospital, let alone at the hands of another patient, and that included checking the Police Blotter and Obituary sections. Could Vivian Jobe have been wrong about the date? By her own admission, she'd been taking some heavy meds.

But Mesa wanted to be sure she was thorough. She slowed the reel and renewed her search. Her doggedness paid off several feet of film later when she found an article entitled "Warm Springs State Hospital Subject of Review," complete with grainy photographs dated August 11, 1979.

The piece was filled with descriptions of wards and treatments, the problems of understaffing, and outdated facilities. As she read, Mesa found herself looking around again, wondering if Frito Lady had ever been a resident of Warm Springs or a place like it.

Not that she was unsympathetic to someone who had been institutionalized, particularly when she thought of Vivian. What she felt was discomfort. She was ashamed to admit that while she accepted that the Frito Ladies of the world needed to be cared for, she preferred someone else do it, in some place where she didn't have to notice.

The photograph in the article was unsettling. The subject of the picture was a nurse, blonde, with a natural attractiveness—if she hadn't seemed so haggard. She was standing in a hospital corridor in front of a door with a column window above the handle.

More revealing, the photographer had also captured several adolescent girls peering through the window like death camp survivors. She looked closely to see if any of the girls might look like a young Vivian.

The girls' heads seemed disembodied. They wore expressions, not of curiosity, but worry, as if they were wondering what would happen next, and how bad it might be. So much for the privacy rights of the mentally ill, Mesa thought, a sign of the times that the picture had made it into the newspaper. HIPAA laws would have protected those patients now.

The photo legend identified the employee as Jeanne Ann Lenin, psychiatric nurse and head of the adolescent unit. Jesus, Mesa thought, a nurse named Lenin. She could have been right out of *One Flew Over the Cuckoo's Nest*.

Mesa continued to scroll through the microfilm and found two more articles about the hospital that summer. The last, dated August 1979, detailed how a patient had wandered off the hospital grounds into someone's home, where he was found eating a homemade pie. After a frantic call to the Deer Lodge County sheriff by the homeowner, the patient had been apprehended and returned to the hospital. Mesa imagined a scrawny man with crumbs on his shirt trying to protect a huckleberry pie, much like Frito Lady.

The second story, two weeks later, buried in the back pages, was hardly fifty words long. But it was pay dirt. The article reported the investigation into the death of a male patient, Ethan Grainger, who had fallen off the Mound at the hospital.

The name Warm Springs was not a metaphor for a caring environment. A stock photograph showed the thermal outcropping, easily forty feet high, and steam rising out of its uneven crust. Sam had once explained to her about the hot springs' existence—long before white men arrived—and how deer, antelope, and other wildlife congregated there for warmth during the long Montana winters. Significant enough was its presence that the native name, Lodge of the Whitetail Deer, gave rise to the name of the valley, and eventually the county.

The article stated that a second patient, held in connection with the death, would undergo a court-ordered evaluation at the hospital. No name had been released, but if Vivian's account was accurate, this had to be Dowling Jessup. Some story—it was so generic the reporter might as well not have covered it, and probably had done nothing more than make a phone call.

That was it. At least, a death had occurred. There was no hallucination on Vivian's part. But Mesa was surprised the fatality had attracted so little attention. Were the victim and perpetrator so unremarkable that this was all the coverage they warranted?

She spent another half hour, scanning the rest of the newspapers from 1979, as well as those from 1980, looking for a follow-up story about any charges that were filed or any sentencing. But she found no further reference to the incident. Tired and beginning to see double after looking at the scrolling microfilm for so long, she copied the articles and the photo of the nurse, and headed back to the office.

A cold rain had begun to fall and was turning to snow. With the chill of the library and now the weather, Mesa pulled up her microfiber vest collar. She passed a man sitting on a sidewalk bench on the corner of Montana and Broadway, a block from the library. Cloaked in a well-worn parka and knitted gloves with no fingertips, he sat next to two garbage bags that appeared to contain his possessions. Rocking back and forth, he patted his lips with the fingers of both hands while he made a low but melodic sound, lost in his own one-man rhythm section. Mesa fought the urge to stare.

She thought of the photos of the mental hospital and how little the plight of the mentally ill had changed. She wondered how many of "these people," whom she often saw around town, had spent time in an institution, and if they preferred it. Somehow, she wouldn't blame them if they had chosen the street.

As she quickened her pace, she tried to imagine Vivian, unkempt and wild-eyed, taking refuge in a covered bus stop, but she couldn't do it. Then she tried to visualize Earflaps made over in a three-piece suit with a designer haircut and Ralph Lauren eyeglasses. But there'd be no hope of an extreme makeover for him, not unless some television producer could market it as a reality show.

Of course, now, everybody had issues and medication to address them. Several of her classmates at Damascus, probably like many of the fancy liberal arts colleges back East, had been admitted to a behavioral hospital ward on occasion. But Mesa had thought of that as a phase, a ploy to miss class and avoid term paper deadlines. Her college friends had been nothing like the Frito Lady.

When Alexis was fourteen, she had been shipped off to a school for troubled adolescents west of Flathead Lake. Not that Alexis was embarrassed by it. She had walked around campus her freshman year wearing a ball cap with the logo "Mission Valley." When Mesa realized Alexis had actually lived there, the two had bonded. No one else at Damascus had ever even been to Montana.

Alexis had complained about how she had endured a smorgasbord of prescription drugs to ensure her compliance. She entertained their dorm mates with endless stories of the "crazies" she'd met at Mission Valley: anorexics, obsessive compulsives, paranoids, the works. Of course, Mesa knew she had to take into account Alexis' tendency to exaggerate.

Mission Valley had cost four grand a month and there were three professionals for every student. Mental and emotional distress could be easily silver-coated in the right economic circumstances. The poor were crazy; the rich were eccentric and indulgent.

The snow had turned back into drizzle and a sudden chill, both mental and physical, enveloped Mesa. She sought solace in the Jailhouse Coffee shop on Park Street. Latte in hand, she sat at a corner table where she spread out the copies she had made at the library. She snapped photos of them with her iPhone while contemplating the effects of socioeconomic status on coping with one's mental health. Then she got down to brass tacks and looked more closely at the photo of this Nurse Lenin, wondering if it might jog Vivian 's memories further, and somehow lead to Dowling Jessup.

Chapter 3

Chance had never been beyond the foyer of Silver House, the community mental health center on Broadway. Its name had nothing to do with its vibe. The institutional, mint green paint, worn linoleum floor, and bare walls were a stark contrast.

At Christmas, Nana had asked him to drop off a shopping bag full of mittens and scarves there. Her War Brides Club had knitted them for the Gifts with a Lift program that insured the patients at Warm Springs received presents. The errand had left Chance slightly depressed, a rare state.

The Christmas decorations were gone now but the overall ambience remained the same. He stepped up to a glass-enclosed receptionist's office where a portly woman slid open a plexiglass window and growled at him. Chance announced his appointment with Henry's case manager.

J. D. Firestone appeared moments later dressed in jeans, combat boots, and a freshly pressed blue shirt with stiff creases in the sleeves. A turned-up cuff revealed a tattoo of a Celtic cross on the underside of his forearm. Except for a precisely trimmed mustache and goatee, he had shaved his face so closely that Chance could practically see his reflection in the sheen. Add to that a military crew cut and a left ear pierced with a small gold loop, the effect was somewhere between an Army recruiter and a punk rocker.

With a vise-like handshake and a deep glare, J.D. said, "So you're Chance. Henry talks about you all the time. Come on back."

Chance followed J.D. through the receptionist's office and out into a muddle of tables, chairs, and their listless occupants. He felt a tad uncomfortable, wondering what he might have said that he would have preferred not be repeated. Henry had a keen memory when he wanted to—something to keep in mind in the future.

Chance lengthened his stride to keep up though he could have closed his eyes and followed the scent of J.D.'s aftershave. Henry had mentioned on more than one occasion, "He stinks." Chance was glad Adrienne didn't go in for that stuff. She was the earthy type, natural smells only.

They entered a small office and J.D. pointed Chance toward a highly polished wood chair next to the desk, the top of which was empty except for a single folder. "So what's the deal with Henry and this trailer fire?" the caseworker said.

"Like I told you on the phone, Henry says he knows a guy called 'Stick,' and he saw the guy going into the trailer Saturday evening. I thought I'd talk to the sheriff about it, but I was kind of hoping to see if you might know this guy too. See if I could get some more details together."

"You're not sure you can believe Henry," Firestone said.

Chance squirmed in his chair, wishing he'd been more direct. "That about sums it up. But if Henry did see someone, the authorities need to know about it."

Firestone fingered the folder before him. "We guard our clients' privacy to the full extent of the law. Since I don't have any release of information—"

Chance interrupted, "Look, before you go down that road, let me say that, knowing Henry, I understand the struggles your clients face. We both know Henry has had run-ins with the police and he doesn't like them. I don't want to make it any harder on him."

"Why are you suddenly so interested?" Firestone quizzed. "The way I heard it the death was accidental. Is this about a story? Henry's told me you work at that weekly paper. You media people are usually interested in the more spectacular stories, and not necessarily sticking to the facts."

Chance sighed. "You wanna blame me for every story that perpetuates stereotypes about your clients?" Chance cocked his head in disbelief. "I can see how it happens, when everybody's so touchy about giving out information."

He paused for effect and to allow his frustration to settle. Then he said, "If you can't tell me if you know this guy Stick, could you at least tell me if he exists? Guys like Henry sometimes get confused."

J.D. let out a little chuckle. "Guys like Henry. You mean the mentally challenged? It's such a comfort when I meet people who act like our clients are another species."

Jesus, Chance thought, leaning back in his chair, instead of making headway, he was falling behind. "That's not what I meant. If Henry is hanging out with a possible arsonist, I think we might want to do something about it. If Henry's friend is this dead guy, and he actually was a friend of Henry's, we both know he'll be upset that his friend is dead. Aren't you worried about one or both of those situations?"

"Maybe. I'm more concerned that Henry saw fit to confide in you instead of coming here."

Chance did not want to mention that Henry didn't like his caseworker any more than he did the police. Now that he'd met Firestone, Chance could see how Henry had developed his attitude.

J.D. stared at Chance with an expression that he found uncomfortable. The thought crossed his mind that maybe the caseworker didn't want anybody looking further into this fire, especially if one of his clients was dead, but why not? No reason popped into his head, and he knew a question in that direction would likely alienate not only Firestone but also probably the rest of the Silver House staff, which would do him no good.

"Look, I don't mean to sound so harsh about this," Chance said. "I'm sure I do have a lot of stereotypes, and you're right, I don't know much about mental illness. I also don't work for the newspaper anymore except as the occasional photographer, but my sister definitely runs it. She could do Silver House a favor by informing the public about this story. It just might generate a more positive attitude about your other clients, which could be a good idea all around. But everybody gets touchy when we try to ask any questions."

"You know where I was first thing this morning?"

Chance sighed, sensing his little plea for better communication had gone nowhere. "No idea."

"One of the detectives thought he recognized the vic as one of ours. I was the lucky bastard whose turn it was to go down and ID the guy. Turns out, he was one of ours. Hopefully, he wasn't the arsonist."

Chance shook his head. "I'm sorry, I had no—"

"To do this job right, you have to be half saint and half robot," J.D. continued. "I'm neither."

"You seem to be doing okay with Henry," Chance said. "He's made—"

J. D. nodded and said, "Yeah, yeah. I told the police I'd send over a copy of the guy's file." He held up the folder, and then dropped it in front of Chance. "I'm gonna go get a cup of coffee. Should take me about ten minutes."

Then he left the room.

Chance was stunned by the sudden cooperation. Maybe Firestone did have a heart under that veneer. Was the precise appearance and highly controlled manner a defense against all the chaos around him? How else could he do his job? Whatever the cause for this opportunity, Chance intended to take advantage of it. He quickly grabbed the file and began to leaf through it. He found maybe twenty sheets of paper and a couple of photographs. Henry's friend was called Dowling Jessup.

Mesa had barely taken a sip of her latte when she heard someone call her name.

"Mesa, is that you?"

She looked up to see a woman in a navy knit pantsuit with a sequin-studded hummingbird design on the jacket. "Dr. Kaiser, you been on my mind," Mesa said with a chuckle at the inevitable aspects of small-town life. You couldn't predict when or where you were going to run into someone you knew, just that it was always happening.

"I don't normally speak to former patients in public but, for you, I'll make an exception," Dr. Kaiser said with a wink. "It has been more than ten years, give or take a phone call or two. That's my unofficial rule. The real surprise is that after all that time, we're both still in Butte."

Nana Rose had made arrangements for Dr. Kaiser to take Mesa on as a client three months after the death of her mother. Not quite fifteen and uninterested in school or friends, burying herself in Jane Austen and Charlotte Bronte, Mesa had languished.

At first, she had been reluctant. "I talk to you, Nana," she had argued. "Isn't that enough?" But her grandmother knew the difference between comfort and counseling and she suspected Mesa needed the latter.

But Mesa reassured herself that though she needed help, her depression and anxiety were a response to an inevitable occurrence, nothing wonky, and she had never needed any medication. The therapeutic relationship had tapered off the last year of high school. Mesa's grief at the loss of her mother had been profound and Dr. Kaiser had been skilled at helping Mesa process her loss and begin to take control of her future. The therapist had shepherded Mesa and her family through the decision-making that had led to her going to school back East. No small feat as her distant—emotionally and geographically—father had initially been totally against the idea.

Back then, Dr. Kaiser had been employed part time at St. James Hospital when they still had a behavioral medicine unit. The last time they had met, Mesa had gone to see her at the hospital. She still remembered being admitted to the locked ward by a brawny orderly who had eyed her through a small meshed-glass window as if she were a possible terrorist.

"Have time to catch up?" Mesa said. She genuinely liked the therapist, whom she now considered more a friend, not to mention an expert in her field. She really wanted to pick Dr. Kaiser's brain about what might have happened at Warm Springs.

"I do but, you know, I've come up in the world. I have a fancy office just up the street. Shall we?"

Chance scanned the recent notes in the file. As late as 2011, Jessup had been part of a special program for mentally ill offenders. A black and white mug shot of a man, who looked to be in his late thirties or forties, hard to tell which without the context of wardrobe and surroundings, stared out at him. In a prison uniform with cropped dark hair, he had well-proportioned features, his nose, brow, and chin angular.

He bore the unremarkable expression necessary to survive in prison, no overt signs of emotion. His eyes, the salient feature of his face, hid all but a hint of defiance. Chance turned the photo over and saw that it had been taken in 1985, when Jessup was probably in his late twenties. He most definitely looked older than his years.

A summary of institutionalizations formed the bulk of the files. Chance rifled through to the earliest records. Sure enough, after being initially charged with manslaughter in the death of Ethan Grainger, Jessup had been placed in the forensic ward at Warm Springs where the charges were dropped a year later.

After Warm Springs was re-organized in the early eighties, and the forensics ward downsized, Jessup was transferred to a special prison population at Deer Lodge, after an altercation with a guard. In '85, he had time added to his sentence after starting a fire in a vent as part of an attempted escape. And, in 1991, he'd been involved in the prison riots.

Jessup had spent a lifetime being in the wrong place at the wrong time. Nearly twenty years, Chance thought to himself. Hardened criminals spent less time behind bars. Chance wondered if that was the standard procedure back in the day. Of course, some people would say the state had done Jessup a favor. At least he hadn't been hanged.

He had finally been paroled in 2005 to a pre-release program for mentally ill offenders from which he had "wandered off." By 2006, he was back inside. Chance didn't want to think about how Jessup might have been treated at the penitentiary, or what he had learned from other criminals.

The last three years of confinement, he was back at the forensics unit at Warm Springs, diagnosed with bipolar disorder with obsessive compulsive episodes. He had gotten out three years later and was assigned to Silver House. He lived in a halfway house for six months and then he moved out to Twin Bridges.

The second photo, taken in '95 after Jessup had been transferred to the mental health unit, hardly looked like the same man. He looked "disturbed" now.

Jessup had spent his adult life locked up in one place or another. Was that what the system boiled down to—no family, no money, no lawyer, no early release?

The last entry was from J.D. Firestone. "Transitional housing program for mentally ill offenders seems successful. Client has been taking his medication and seeking employment."

Then, written in red, across the bottom of the page: "Program terminated."

Chance's reading was interrupted by the smell of coffee and Firestone's return. He quickly closed the file.

"Sorry I seemed impatient earlier," Firestone said. "I got three hundred plus clients on my caseload. I wish I could say I was on a first name basis with all of them. Some, like Dowling Jessup, I barely knew." He paused and sat down. "Get what you need?"

Chance nodded. "Just tell me one thing. Is it really possible for someone who had been admitted to a mental hospital to end up in prison without a trial?"

J.D. nodded slowly. "It's definitely possible to get shuttled back and forth between prison and the forensic ward in Warm Springs. Overcrowding creates problems. States have been warehousing people for years. Even now, the largest mental hospital in America is the Cook County Jail."

"Doesn't seem like he ever got outside an institution. What kind of life is that?"

J.D. picked up Jessup's folder and flipped to the pages in the back. "According to this summary, he was voluntarily admitted to avoid a misdemeanor charge of disorderly conduct. Then, while he was at Warm Springs, he was involved in a patient's death. He wasn't charged because he was suffering from mental illness, and was found unable to stand trial. Eventually the charges were dropped altogether."

"Who decided that?" Chance asked.

"The Forensic Review Board."

Chance was curious. He leaned over J.D.'s shoulder and saw X. Larraz typed under a scrawling signature.

J.D. continued reading from the several pages of Jessup's record. "He somehow became involved in a prison disturbance, which led to a felony charge of assault against a guard, which ended him up across the highway for a couple of more years."

"How would that have happened if he was supposed to be in the locked ward of the hospital?"

"Sometimes the programs shared facilities. If you run afoul of a state prison guard, no matter where it happens, you suffer for it. I'm not saying it's right, but that's the way they roll in the penitentiary. Mentally ill prisoners tend to serve longer sentences and experience more disciplinary problems, especially if they don't take their meds."

The longer J.D. talked, the more Chance realized that what Jessup lacked was someone to advocate for him. He languished in a system where everybody says they're innocent, and no one listened to much else.

"He might not have had an actual trial for the first beef," J.D. said, "but he added onto his time with those attempted escapes. Then, when he got sent to pre-release, he couldn't handle it. Says here he was only on the outside for four months before he got sent back for wandering away."

"Is there any record of who his attorney was?"

J.D. shook his head. "Montana didn't even have a state-wide Public Defender Office until 2006. Before that, the bigger counties took care of their own, or the court would appoint someone. In the hospital, the administrators met with county officials on the grounds. Maybe the patient was involved, maybe he wasn't."

"So what you're saying is if Jessup didn't have an attorney, his situation got sorted out in some office without him being any the wiser."

"Or he got ignored altogether. Some of these guys become so institutionalized, they're glad to be safe where they are. They don't cause any trouble. They learn not to attract any attention. In Jessup's case, I only recognized him because he would walk through this hallway when he came to get his meds."

Chance nodded. "Man, you got a tough job."

"Tell me about it," Firestone said. "It took me an hour to find his file and figure out his full name."

Chapter 4

Dr. Kaiser moved with her characteristic long stride. She was a big-boned woman but elegant, and liked to tease that she had only gone to med school because she never got to audition to be a Rockette at Radio City Music Hall in New York.

They reached the Silver Bow Building and up the stone steps they went. Dr. Kaiser led her to a large office down a hallway. Her office was furnished with a mahogany desk and chair and matching bookcases and woodwork. Expensively framed landscapes and photographs covered the walls. "This is considerably more chic than where we met the last time I saw you," she said with another chuckle.

Mesa sat in the deep leather chair in the office and thought about how circumstances had changed since they'd first met. She remembered the sharp clack of the hospital door's lock and the rush of escaping air that caused heat to radiate from Mesa's temples. Her hands had become clammy as she willed herself to take several deep breaths. Her unforgiving muscle memory had taken hold and, for an instant, she relived the fear of being locked in a small place.

She always wished Chance was with her at times like those. Forever guilty that as kids he'd tricked her into hiding in their father's footlocker and then closed the lid, he always found a way to divert her attention when a wave of claustrophobia overcame her. Thankfully, an orderly had directed her down the hallway to the nurse's station, and the walk had distracted her so that the stifling feeling had abated.

The grief over the loss of her mother became easier to bear, and the bouts of claustrophobia and the nightmares had eventually faded. Did Vivian have nightmares? Mesa wondered. Maybe that was one way to look at schizophrenia, a lifetime of nightmares.

Mesa remembered the behavioral unit with its offices and rooms with recessed handles and knobs on all the doors and cupboards to prevent injury. Thankfully, the ward didn't reek of antiseptic like the cancer ward where her mother had recovered from her mastectomy. Although her mother had ultimately died at home in her own bed, Mesa still thought of the hospital as a place where people got worse, not better. She could appreciate how Vivian would never want to go back to one.

"Do you remember that first meeting?" Dr. Kaiser asked. "I wouldn't have met you at the hospital, but I had an emergency and couldn't get to my consulting office. I told myself a walk through the loony bin might cheer you up," she laughed.

"Actually, I was just thinking about how hard I tried to act nonchalant about being in a psychiatric ward. Your sense of humor helped."

"You did well, although I think the Ninja Warrior and his posturing had you a little rattled."

Mesa smiled, remembering the teenager who had stationed himself in the middle of the ward's TV room, standing on one leg with arms outstretched in a pose reminiscent of the Karate Kid. "Good thing I didn't see *One Flew Over the Cuckoo's Nest* till I was in college. That wire-reinforced glass nurse's station looked like the lock-up in the county jail. I remember you joking about a patient in his fifties with Kleenex stuck in each nostril and both ears. Remember what you said about him?"

"Oh yeah," Dr. Kaiser said, "That old geezer said he was trying to keep the evil spirits from invading," she said in a deadpan voice. "And I wanted to convince him to run for Congress. My gallows humor got me through that job."

"What happened to the psychiatric ward at St. James anyway?" Mesa asked.

"Strategic planning, psychotropic drugs, the promise of community-based treatment. It's a much steadier and more lucrative stream of profit to offer emergency mental health evaluations off site, and then manage patients with pharmaceuticals. I still do my share of talk therapy, but much of the time I'm providing prescriptions for patients of counselors from here to the south Idaho border."

"Sounds like that keeps you busy. I'm surprised I haven't seen you since I got back into town." She found herself fiddling with the horsehair bracelet Sam had given her for Christmas, a "homecoming" present he had called it.

"That's because I'm just back from a six-month hitch with Doctors without Borders in Mozambique. Seems I'm an expert in rural mental health these days. But I heard about that plane crash you were in back in

September. I always did think you had a guardian angel."
She smiled. "Paper seems to have perked up too. This all
squaring with your ambitions to win a Pulitzer?"

Mesa smiled back. "You were always good at cutting
right to the heart of the matter. Coming back to Butte
wasn't in the original plan but that doesn't mean the
Pulitzer is out of the picture. Right now, I want to spend
as much time as I can with Nan. Her health isn't what it
used to be."

Dr. Kaiser nodded. "You certainly look like the
move agrees with you. I, for one, am glad to see you
back."

Mesa filled the therapist in on the other broad
strokes of her life, and then she explained about meeting
Vivian earlier in the day. "She told me that she was one
of your patients and that I should talk to you."

Kaiser nodded. "She left me a message earlier in the
day. Obviously, you left a good impression. I had no idea
that Vivian and your mother had been friends. Guess
that's one detail I missed." Then she looked at her watch
and said, "I've seen my last patient of the day, so fire
away. Now that I'm an expert," she said in jest, "what
exactly would you like me to pontificate upon?"

"I'm thinking I'll write a feature on mental illness
and focus on patients like Vivian. You know how this
town, and the state for that matter, deals—or, more
often, doesn't deal—with mental health issues. I get the
feeling that we haven't made that much progress in the
last decade or so. How about starting with a Mental
Health 101 lecture."

Dr. Kaiser laughed and Mesa pulled out her
notebook. "I'm mostly interested in background, the

stage that someone's life plays out on when they struggle with mental illness."

"Life in the psychotic lane?" Dr. Kaiser joked.

More visions of disheveled people flailing their arms filled Mesa's thoughts. "Psychotic?" she said, surprised. Somehow, she hadn't imagined that term could apply to Vivian.

"Nuts, loony tunes," Kaiser said, "you know, losing it. Fantasy and reality become one. What we're all afraid of. Erratic brain chemistry plays a hand, often triggered by stress, sometimes a traumatic event. In Vivian's case, the sudden death of her father, an alcoholic mother, and a chaotic home life took a toll."

"No violence, then?" Mesa said, remembering she'd promised Chance she'd ask.

"Not toward other people. Less than two percent of schizophrenics have a history of violence. Unfortunately, it's the minority's behavior that gets media attention. It only takes one nut blasting his way into our nation's Capitol to give the rest of them a bad name."

Mesa couldn't really imagine Vivian doing much damage, but she found herself relieved nonetheless. "She's waited so long to try to find Jessup. Why do you think she did that?"

"Takes time to come off heavier meds to lift the fog so a person can begin to differentiate between what actually happened, what were insidious side effects of the medication, and what's been hallucinated. That's when her memories would resurface. Then it takes time to stabilize your own life before you can begin to think about relating to the rest of the world."

"You think she'd reach back thirty-five years to find someone to relate to?"

Kaiser smiled. "You're still young but you ask your grandmother if she remembers her courtship with your grandfather. I'm betting she can recall the tiniest of details."

Mesa knew this was true. She'd heard those details.

"Significant events in anyone's life are etched in our brains."

Mesa nodded and wondered what life events had screwed up Frito Lady or the guy she'd seen making music on the street.

Working in Cincinnati, Mesa had learned early on that mental health problems and addictions were rampant in the urban areas of Ohio. She thought she'd left that all behind. "Montana is so rural. It never occurred to me that mental health issues were so widespread."

"Like a lot of problems out West, it's about economy of scale. We have so few medical facilities in state patients have to drive two hundred miles to get their meds, let alone treatment. Then there's the shortage of therapists, plus the cowboy mentality about sucking it up. It's easier to stay in bed with the cover over your head, or to hit the bottle. It might be cool back East to have a therapist, but here there's a definite stigma. It's no wonder Montana has one of the highest suicide rates in the country."

Nodding again, Mesa realized that everything Dr. Kaiser was saying about Montana probably went double for Butte, except it was the mining culture that left the legacy of stoicism.

Then she turned her attention to Vivian's quest. "You're not concerned that Vivian has an interest in a man with such a history of violence?"

"Some, but then she says he never hurt anybody. Besides, I'm a psychotherapist, not a judge. Former patients often look each other up. The shared experience gives them a bond. They can relate without having to explain every little thing like they often have to with outsiders."

Mesa found herself breathing more easily as Dr. Kaiser talked. She provided a reasonable explanation for Vivian's motivations, something that would reassure Chance. Mesa could also identify with the bond patients felt. Hell, military brats were the same way.

"This connection is also worthwhile because Vivian is in charge of her own life now. Finding Jessup is one of those things she wants to do. Hopefully, she'll succeed if he hasn't been swallowed up by the system."

"Swallowed up? How?"

"Ten per cent of the population in corrections facilities suffer some kind of severe emotional distress. Most are there for repeated non-violent offenses like drunk and disorderly, or crimes like dust-ups that arose because of their acting out when they've had no help. Without effective intervention, which they're not going to get in prison, they move between jails, homeless shelters, alleys, abandoned buildings, and ER's. 'Frequent fliers' is their buzzword. Long-term outcome for recovery is bleak."

"Well, that's cheery," Mesa said, thinking of a recent Police Blotter entry about a man who disrobed at the bus station and started swinging a large stick at police officers who tried to get him to put his clothes back on. "Do you think she could run into problems again if the search turns up nothing?" Mesa asked, realizing she was expressing a fear that had grown after she'd visited the library. The last thing she wanted to do at this stage was disappoint Vivian.

Kaiser shrugged. "Vivian has some expectations for this reunion and if it doesn't happen, she could experience some disappointment, even depression. If you have funky brain chemistry to start with, you don't always bounce back like most people, but her responses will be in the normal range. Otherwise, I wouldn't have supported her efforts to find the guy."

"But Vivian isn't manic depressive; she has schizophrenia."

"Well, schizophrenia as a diagnosis is problematic. It's a group of symptoms. Depression can be one part of it. You could do a lot to help your readers understand that the diagnosis of these conditions is not as clear cut as something like cancer or heart disease, maybe tear down some of the myths around the terms."

Mesa thought about the comments she frequently heard from her friends and people at the office who probably knew less than she did about treatment of the mentally ill. "I think readers would be interested to hear how the treatment has changed. What do you know about the period when Vivian and Dowling would have met?"

"Before my time, but I know it wasn't a pretty picture—overcrowded, cold sheets, heavy-duty shock treatments, restraints, straitjackets, the whole nine yards. Warm Springs received a lot of bad publicity when several patients escaped from their criminally insane unit. The place was re-organized in the late eighties during the downsizing of mental health programs across the country."

"Cold sheets?" Mesa muttered aloud.

"In the old days, if Thorazine or Haldol didn't make a zombie out of you, they'd wrap you in cold, wet sheets. I have a couple of clients who'd like to try the treatment on their teenagers."

Mesa smiled again at Dr. Kaiser's dark humor. She had always admired her relaxed, sometimes irreverent manner, though Mesa couldn't fathom how the doctor maintained it.

Then she thought of the independent, forthright woman who had visited the office that morning, and felt guilty. She imagined the humiliation Vivian Jobe might have felt if she had been wrapped in cold sheets.

Dr. Kaiser pulled out a pack of Misty cigarettes from a desk drawer and stood up. "Vivian also gave me permission to share her medical records, in case you'd like a fuller picture of her actual experiences. She obviously feels quite comfortable with your knowing, which is not usually the case."

Mesa suddenly felt the weight of Vivian's trust after only one meeting, imagining how embarrassing the history might be for her to share.

As they left the office and came outside where Dr. Kaiser could light up, she said in a quiet voice, "A lot of mental patients spend their lives believing they did something horrible to deserve their illness. Once they get effective treatment, they can understand that events have triggered their illness, rather than any weakness of character. And more important, they can stop letting mental illness define who they are. Vivian finally came to that recognition. She's learned how to take care of herself like anyone with a chronic medical condition, nothing more."

"Like an allergy that can flare up when you're exposed to sensitive situations?" Mesa said with a smile. That was the analogy that Dr. Kaiser had used when Mesa wondered if she would ever get over her grief that seemed to come and go.

"That's right. You always were a quick study," Kaiser said. "Your understanding of that makes you the perfect ally for Vivian. Finding Jessup represents a milestone for her. It's taken her thirty odd years to remember, but she is his alibi, and she wants whoever's still around to know the truth. You can help her accomplish that."

Mesa walked into the office forty-five minutes later feeling ready to tackle the interviews for the reporter job she hoped to fill by week's end. In the mean time, she felt confident about her ability to track down Jessup. The talk with Dr. Kaiser had given her a boost.

Nothing could have surprised her more than to find Chance lying on the couch, staring out the window. Strange as it might seem, he appeared to be in some form of deep contemplation.

She tossed her notes from the library and Dr. Kaiser on the desk. When Chance made no reaction to the thud, she had a moment of anxiety. Her brother rarely sat still. "Chance," she said, "are you all right?'

Her brother looked at her with an air of mystery and said, "I've just had a couple of curious conversations."

"Welcome to the club. It's called the newspaper business. We're all about conversation, the more curious the better. I had a few today myself." She tossed his feet onto the floor and sat in the corner of the couch just vacated. "So who did you talk to and what did they say?"

"You know that kid, Henry, the one who rides around town on the neon orange mountain bike?"

Mesa nodded. Henry had dogged Chance around town for much of the past fall. One afternoon she had found Henry actually shining Chance's bike, propped outside the *Messenger's* office. "What about him?"

"He's the first conversation. He says he saw the guy going into the trailer who got torched on Sunday, and there was another guy with him."

Mesa was skeptical. "Isn't Henry ..." she paused trying to choose the right words, "developmentally delayed? You know, Special Ed kind of thing. What I mean is, isn't he a bit slow?"

Chance sat up. "Well, he can't do calculus if that's what you mean, but he has an amazing capacity for certain kinds of detail, at least when it's about something or somebody he really likes."

Mesa gave Chance one of those sidelong glances like Nana used that essentially meant *are you sure you know what you're talking about?*

"For example," Chance countered, "he can give you the minutest details of scenes in *Home Alone*. It's one of his favorite movies, or the different levels of *Grand Theft Auto*, his favorite video game."

"So, you think he saw the transient, who was killed, with another person?" Mesa said trying not to sound too impatient.

"He saw someone he calls Stick. Apparently, Henry met him at Silver House about six months ago. They were both there to pick up their meds, and got to be friends, which says a lot about this Stick, I'll tell you that."

"How do you mean?" Mesa asked.

"Not a lot of your Silver House patients have much tolerance for a guy like Henry, who's thirty but has the demeanor of a thirteen-year-old."

"So what does his thirteen-year-old mind know about what happened to Stick?"

"He definitely thinks something bad happened to him, that's for sure."

"Yeah, I'd call dead pretty bad, unless of course he's the arsonist."

"No, he's not the arsonist and, well, Henry doesn't know he's dead ... yet."

Mesa shook her head. Sometimes Chance had a way of shielding people from bad news, and it wasn't always helpful. After all, that was how she had ended back in Butte. "And you don't think his suspicion is the result of too much *Grand Theft Auto*?"

"No, I don't. He saw his friend up close, and he looked high or drunk."

"Big shock," Mesa said. "Half of the people on the street in uptown probably fell into that category on St. Urhu's Day. A few beers combined with his meds probably lit him up like the proverbial Roman candle."

"Except that, according to Henry, Stick never drank. That's one of the reasons Henry liked him," Chance said. "And, even more curious, Henry said Stick had slowly been taking himself off his meds."

"Taking himself off? How?" Mesa said. How was this possible, she wondered, without some sort of side effects?

"He had used the computers at the library to look up the effects of his meds and how to wean himself off them."

"These guys were using computers?" Mesa once again thought about her afternoon at the library, trying to recall the computer patrons.

Chance nodded. "Henry bought an old Mac off EBay. He mostly uses it to get solutions to video games he plays. But Henry said Stick was wicked smart about plenty."

"So, what are you saying?" Mesa said. "Henry thinks he saw somebody who may have had something to do with the guy's death? If, in fact, Henry's friend is actually the dead guy, whether or not his death is something besides accidental?"

"Oh, it's him alright. I talked with the caseworker at Silver House who had to identify the victim. That's the second conversation. But I'm also saying that the cops' theory that the cause of death is an accidental overdose that led to a comatose state that resulted in his inhaling enough smoke to kill him might be oversimplified."

"An easy conclusion—" Mesa said, wondering what, if any, of this could be put into print.

"—to pin a homicide on a fricking arsonist the community is itching to see caught," Chance finished.

"You think there's some conspiracy here?" Mesa said, surprised at the suggestion from Chance who considered Sheriff Solheim a Dutch uncle.

"No way, but I doubt any overtime is gonna get spent on a homicide investigation when nobody will give two hoots about a homeless guy, and a mental patient to boot, who gets smoked in an abandoned trailer."

"Is that what the police actually told you?" Mesa said, willing to bet they would never actually express that opinion out loud.

"I haven't quite got Henry to the point of going to the police yet. First, I have to find a gentle way to break it to him that his buddy, Stick, is dead."

Not that Henry was likely to receive much of a hearing from the police anyway. "There might be something in this," she said finally, wondering if Silver House might be a place she and Vivian should investigate in search of Dowling Jessup.

"Do we have a full name for Stick?" Mesa asked. "Maybe we can dig something up on him."

"I looked at his file at Silver House, but you can't mention that in print. They're so paranoid there; the whole staff should be on medication."

"So who was it?" Mesa pressed.

"It's an unusual name, which is why he's got the nickname," Chance said. "Dowling Jessup. Get it? Dowl, like dowel rod, like stick?"

Chapter 5

"Unbelievable," Mesa said in whispered shock and then in a more matter-of-fact voice, "There IS no God in heaven."

"You better not let Nana hear you say that," Chance said.

Mesa jumped up from the couch and walked over to the window, leaning her hands on the sill as if to steady herself. "Damn it," she said even louder.

"What?" Chance said. "What's wrong? What am I missing?"

Mesa turned back toward her desk and picked up the classified card Cinch had given her that morning. She took it over to Chance. "Dowling Jessup," she said and then read from the card, pronouncing each word with a pause and a poke with her finger, "Do … you … know … Dowling … Jessup?"

"Okay, okay, take it easy, tiger. I'm on your side," Chance said.

Mesa took a deep breath. "Sorry," she said and collapsed on the sofa. "I don't mean to wig out on you. But I was just starting to think helping Vivian find Jessup might actually be possible. We could have turned it into a story with teeth too, a feature about mental illness with a happy ending." She shook her head. "What a shit coincidence."

"Well, she hadn't seen him in thirty years," Chance said, almost under his breath. "I mean it's not like she could miss the guy any more than she already does."

Mesa appreciated his attempt to relieve her distress, and its usual failure to do so. "Oh, Chance, that's not it. Vivian wanted to help Dowling clear his name. Maybe help give him a sense of worth again, if that's what he needed. She felt she owed him a debt that she could finally repay. It was an opportunity to pay it forward, you know?" Her heart sank as she recalled Vivian's enthusiasm at getting Mesa's help. "Now it's too late."

"I understand that she was a friend of Mom's and all, but you just met the woman this morning," he said. "I don't understand why you're so upset."

"It seems so damned unfair," Mesa said and threw the classified card across the room. "I just spent the last hour talking to Dr. Kaiser about how Vivian survived the shambles that our mental health system is in. I was getting a handle on what it all means, how it affects the whole community."

Mesa got up and walked across the room to pick up the card. She stared at it for a moment, rereading the text. "Plus, what if it isn't a coincidence? What if the ad in the *Mess* drew some unwanted attention to Jessup? I'd hate for Vivian to think that."

"Don't go there," Chance said quickly. "It was never your intention to do anything but help. Besides, it's probably for the best. The guy had a lot of baggage."

"What's that supposed to mean?" Mesa asked and sat down at her desk. Chance didn't usually deal in "baggage."

"Well, for starters, he ended up spending a lot of time locked up which, for a guy who didn't do the crime, if that's what you choose to believe, is a long time. If I was him, I'd have some serious grudges. I'd want to get even. Maybe that got him killed."

Chance explained what he had learned at Silver House about Jessup, the years back and forth between the mental hospital and prison, the halfway house, and then being dumped into the streets. "I talked to Henry's caseworker, a guy named J.D. Firestone. He was wound tighter than a golf ball by the way. Everybody in that place is hypersensitive."

Mesa listened as Chance detailed Jessup's institutional history from Warm Springs to Deer Lodge and back again. Dowl sounded like one of those "frequent fliers" Dr. Kaiser had described. The longer he talked, the more depressing the story became. She wondered how Vivian might react to Jessup's extended prison record.

By the time Chance had finished his narrative, Mesa was dumbfounded. The system had swallowed Dowling Jessup, just like Dr. Kaiser had described could happen. Maybe it was best that Vivian's search had been short-circuited.

"I'm sorry to be the bearer of bad news," her brother said and ran his fingers through his hair, a gesture that usually signaled his impatience. "It must be the day for it. Now I gotta tell Henry." Chance stood up and stretched. "Maybe the news will motivate him to talk to the cops. I'm gonna take him to see Adrienne to make a sketch of the man he saw. Then I'll talk to Rollie."

"You have more faith in Henry than I do," Mesa said. She had to admire Chance's confidence in the developmentally disabled. He often complained about how it was a shame Henry spent most of his waking hours watching cartoon shows and playing endless video games, that he was smart enough to be doing something useful.

Still, she wasn't convinced that Henry understood the difference between observation and imagination. "Make sure we get a copy of the sketch. I'll show it to Vivian when I take her this old photo from the *Standard*."

Chance took a look at the photo and the articles Mesa had found. "This nurse looks pretty intense—*One Flew Over the Cuckoo's Nest* and all that."

Mesa sighed, wondering why that particular movie stuck in everybody's head when it came to mental hospitals. "I doubt seriously that Vivian will have known any of Jessup's recent acquaintances, friends or not, or this nurse. But it's worth asking. Maybe she can shed some light on Dowl's death."

Mesa chewed on her cuticle thinking about the twists and turns of Vivian's story—lost lovebirds, a patient who ends up dead, Dowl falsely accused. Now, thirty years later, he's killed too. She stared out the window at the sky, now clear and bright, the snow squall long gone, the cosmic void high above the Mining City. Could it all be chalked up to bad timing? Or was there a connection?

If Dowling's death wasn't accidental, who would want to kill him? Who might have a grudge against him? Like Chance said, Jessup might have made enemies in the penitentiary. Ex-cons gravitated to Butte, which had a substantial pre-release program. Maybe one of them had seen the *Messenger's* ad.

Vivian was ready to clear Dowl from involvement in Ethan Grainger's death. Could the person actually responsible for his death know that? But why kill Jessup? And why wait so long? What might have triggered the killer's reappearance?

Maybe someone connected to Grainger thought Dowl hadn't been punished enough. Or maybe Dowl found out who was responsible for Grainger's death, or had known all along. Once Dowl was free, he was a threat.

But Dowl had been free for at least six months, which lent credence to the notion that Vivian's ad in the *Messenger* had prompted the killer's return. He had come looking for Dowl, and maybe the person who was asking questions about Dowl. Could Vivian be in danger too?

Or was the answer much simpler, and more in the present tense—Occam's razor, once again, the simplest explanation. Two violent ex-cons get drunk and one ends up dead, or perhaps one transient kills another over something inconsequential. It certainly wouldn't be the first time that happened in Butte, or elsewhere, for that matter.

Whatever the case, more information about the original murder might provide answers. At least she could find out enough to clear Dowl's name for Vivian's sake. That much Mesa could do for her.

More than once, Chance had witnessed Henry's capacity for high anxiety. One afternoon they had been standing outside the Leggett Hotel, and one of Butte's infamous stray dogs hurtled across the street toward them. Henry had begun to shout in a high-pitched voice,

"No! No! Get that dog away from me!" and then rushed into the hotel's lobby.

The black and white mutt had trotted on its way, none the wiser, and Chance had gone to retrieve Henry who was pacing back and forth like a caged wolf. Holding his hand up toward Chance to halt his approach, Henry said, "Dogs really scare me." Shaking his head vigorously, he had declared, "I'm never going to wait in the street again."

Faced with telling him about the death of his friend, Chance couldn't be sure how Henry would take it. On regular occasions, Henry would tear up just talking about the death of his foster mother. She had died of cancer years ago, but Henry still thought about her often, probably because she was the only woman he'd ever been close to that actually cared about him.

Chance had taken Henry to the Mountain Gallery so that Adrienne could act as backup in case he freaked out. She had that calm, bedside manner that made patients feel like everything was under control.

After Chance introduced Adrienne, he and Henry went into the workroom filled with framing supplies for her gallery. Adrienne also had a small office in one corner. That's where Chance decided to break the news to Henry.

Though he was brought to tears, he'd actually taken the death better than Chance expected. He had been careful to say that it was breathing the fumes inside the trailer that had killed Stick.

"You mean his body wasn't all burnt up? You know, all black and twisted?" Henry asked quietly.

Chance shook his head. "The sheriff's office thinks maybe he was drunk and didn't realize when the trailer caught on fire. Breathing in the smoke and toxic fumes is probably what killed him."

"I told you he didn't drink," Henry said. "I don't like people who drink."

Chance patted Henry's arm. "Don't blame yourself, Henry. You did the right thing."

"But maybe Stick would still be alive if I had gone after him," he said, his voice trailing off. "That man he was with, I didn't like him."

"I think your instincts were right on about that one," Chance said with a nod.

If the coroner's guess was correct, Jessup's death was indeed more than smoke inhalation. The fire marshal was still investigating but it was beginning to look like Jessup was somehow impaired. If he had entered the trailer the night before to sleep one off, why hadn't he awakened when the smoldering fire had finally ignited twelve or so hours later—unless he was too comatose to save himself? "How long had Stick been tapering off his meds?"

Henry looked away, seeming unsure how to respond. "I promised Stick I wouldn't say anything," he finally answered.

"Look, Henry," Chance said gently, "now that Stick's gone, I think you've fulfilled your promise. Don't you think he'd want you to help the police find out what happened to him? Maybe someone slipped him drugs to make sure he didn't get out of that trailer when the fire started. It would help to know what drugs he already had or didn't have in his system that night."

"I don't know for sure what all he took. I know he took some of the same ones I do. I have seven prescriptions but he only had three." Henry said this as though the number of meds a person took was part of some grand competition. "He told me once he didn't like the way he felt when he took his meds. You know a lot of these drugs have side effects, don't cha? Like my tics and stuff and when I stutter or talk fast, those are side effects. I can't help it."

Chance nodded again, more than aware of Henry's many stops and starts.

"He promised me one time that once he got completely off his meds, everything would be better." This last statement was accompanied by Henry's rocking his body in unison with his nodding head.

"He said maybe he would buy this little house in Twin Bridges and live there and not have to worry about anything. He said I could come and visit."

"What else did he talk about?" Chance asked. Maybe Henry knew more than he realized. "Did he ever mention other friends he had?"

Henry shook his head violently. "I was his best friend. We talked about all kinds of stuff. Dowl said he was going to teach me about cars, maybe help me get my driver's license some day. He warned me about not believing everything people said."

"How's everything going in here?" Adrienne asked. She had finished the frame she was working on, and come into the office. "Henry, are you ready to start on the sketch you want me to draw?"

Her voice was soft and unhurried. Chance admired how she seemed to make Henry think they had all the time in the world. She pulled out a sketchbook and sat in the chair that Chance vacated. She gave him a subtle "thumbs out" and he moved out into the workroom.

"Okay, Henry, I want you to close your eyes and see if you can take your mind back to the other evening when you saw this man Chance needs a picture of." She looked through the doorway at Chance while she talked.

"I don't see anything," Henry said, his eyes scrunched together. "It's dark."

Adrienne smiled and then said, "That's okay. Just relax for a minute and see if you can imagine your friend, Stick, and the other man. They were walking up Main Street together, weren't they?"

Chance could see Henry nodding his head ferociously.

"Tell me what you see," Adrienne continued quietly. "Do you recognize any of the buildings?"

Adrienne's soft voice seemed hypnotic but soon Henry was talking and Adrienne had begun to draw.

Chance thought about what Henry had said about Dowl buying a house in Twin Bridges. Almost all the clients at Silver House were on some type of disability. Where would he get the money to buy a house? How might a windfall come Jessup's way?

Most people like Henry lived on vocational rehabilitation funding—pensions with government subsidized housing. It was unlikely Jessup had some distant relative, some inheritance in his future. According to what Vivian Jobe said, Dowl didn't have any family, and that's why he had been in the Children's Home to start with. Maybe Vivian didn't know as much as she thought.

༄༅

Mesa stood in the foyer of her grandmother's house while Nana took down the eight-by-ten photograph from the wall. Removing a thin layer of dust from its frame, Nana said, "I can't believe, after all this time, you finally get to meet Vivian Jobe."

"Me either," Mesa said. "It was awkward and comforting all at the same time. She's really kind, and smart and …," she laughed, "still tall."

Nana chuckled. "You can see in this picture how the photographer had Vivian stand on the lower stair so that she wouldn't tower over Sarah and the other girls." Nana ran her finger over the photograph as she spoke and Mesa felt a twinge of sadness.

Nana had learned stoicism at her mother's knee. The family had survived the bombings of World War II in England and the deprivation afterward, stiff upper lip and all that. But, more than once, Mesa had heard her grandmother say that no parent should outlive their child. You never got over the loss.

"And she told you her story?" Nana said. "I should like to hear that myself. We shall have to have her to tea. Nana put the photograph back on the wall and headed for the kitchen. "Of course, I still remember that summer she went off. Dreadful it was. Sarah talking on the phone at odd hours of the night. In the end, there was nothing for it. Vivian had to go into hospital."

She tried to eat dinner with her grandmother at least one evening during the week. Not that Nan lacked for company. Her social life was far busier than Mesa's, especially now that the legislature was in session.

Mesa and Shane Northey had started hanging out regularly around Thanksgiving, after he had gotten elected to one of the House seats from Butte. Since he was a rookie delegate, he tried to be conscientious. So, once the session began in January, he spent most nights in Helena, sixty miles away, because he didn't want to miss any eight a.m. caucus meetings.

"How exactly did her father die?" Mesa asked. "She didn't really go into the specifics, just to say that his death was traumatic and her grief triggered a lot of anxiety."

Nana handed Mesa cutlery and the two set the dinner table while they talked. "It was a massive shock. Mr. Jobe was a lovely man, handsome and kind, and Vivian was a proper 'daddy's girl.' It was her horse that trampled him with her standing right there, unable to prevent it."

"Jesus," Mesa said, not wanting to think of the horror of it.

"Apparently, the horse had stepped in some deep hole and badly broken its leg, a tragedy in itself. When they came upon him and tried to help, in its agony the horse reared up and did Martin Jobe in. The foreman shot the horse on the spot. Vivian saw that too. Martin died in hospital from a massive skull fracture the next day."

"That's horrible," Mesa said. No wonder Vivian avoided talking about the details. "But Vivian did finish high school and go on to college," Mesa said while she brought water glasses to the table and Nan served up the shepherd's pie.

Nana nodded. "She wanted to go to medical school and, once she returned for her senior year, we thought life was back on track. She was so clever. I guess we all wanted to think she was all right."

"It must have been difficult for Vivian. Didn't people talk?" Mesa said. Butte High was a hotbed of gossip in her day. She could remember the whispers behind her back after her mother died, and those comments were meant to be kind.

Nana motioned to the table and they both sat down. She said grace and they tucked into dinner. "Vivian's mother was keen to keep everything hush-hush. I'm not sure any of Vivian's other friends had any idea. Sarah was her main confidante. They stayed in touch and, when the wedding came along, Vivian was the first person Sarah picked to be in the wedding. She was to have been the maid of honor but, in the end, they agreed bridesmaid was the ticket. I think Vivian was on a downward slide even then, and they both decided not to add any more stress. It was just after Chance was born that rumors surfaced about Vivian leaving medical school."

"Did you see her in Butte at all after that?" Mesa asked between bites.

"Sadly, no. And Sarah lost touch as well. At one point, she'd heard from another classmate that Vivian had gone on some pilgrimage to India. But I think that was a load of old tosh, the kind of rumor Vivian would have started just to thwart the nosey parkers. She had that kind of sense of humor."

Mesa had stopped eating. She imagined her mother wishing she could find her old friend, worried that she might be in trouble. "She still has that sense of humor. I'm going to try to help her figure out what happened to this friend of hers she knew at Warm Springs. I found some information at the library this afternoon, but I could use somebody on the ground to talk to. Who do you know who works at the hospital?"

"The person who can tell you all about the state hospital is Charlotte Haggis," said Nana. "She worked there for donkey's years."

"Charlotte who?" Mesa said. Her grandmother's heart attack might have slowed her down physically, but she still had plenty of contacts in town.

"Charlotte Haggis from Nottingham. She married Milton Haggis and came over in 1950 about the same time I did. He worked for the Water Department for years. She went to nursing school at St. James once she got here, and that led to a job at Warm Springs. She's been retired for several years, but she has a memory like St. Peter. I'll call her after dinner and have her over for a cuppa in the morning."

Mesa thought about resisting this idea, but she knew her grandmother liked to keep her hand in a story now and again. After all, she was still the *Messenger's* publisher. She had immediately taken an interest in the idea for a feature about the challenges of mental illness, especially since Dr. Kaiser, whom she greatly admired, also supported the idea.

Besides, Rose Ducharme did not make idle suggestions. If she said someone had some information, they did. Never mind that all her contacts seemed to come from her war brides' club.

"Mrs. Haggis?" Chance said as he appeared at the dining room entryway. "Why does that name sound familiar? Wait, isn't she the Tipsy Laird lady? You know," he said giving a quick touch to Mesa's shoulder, "the fantastic pudding with the booze in it."

"Oh, my god; she made the Tipsy Laird?" Mesa smiled. "I hadn't thought about her in years."

Nana hosted a Boxing Day party each year the day after Christmas. The parties were memorable because the war bride ladies brought fantastic holiday treats—mince pies, Yule logs, and homemade toffee and plum pudding. Mrs. Haggis was famous for her Tipsy Laird, a Scottish trifle made with raspberries, oats, custard, cream, and whiskey.

"Half her dessert was leftover that one year and you ate practically all of it," Mesa said and punched her brother in the arm as he sat down.

"You ate your share," Chance said, "I think we were both more than a little tipsy when it was all over. Speaking of which, what's for dessert, Nan?"

Their grandmother waved toward the sideboard where a pineapple upside down cake sat. "Help yourself," she said. "I take it you've already had dinner."

Chance nodded and stood up to cut a piece of cake. "Adrienne and I took Henry to Trumbo's pizza after she finished the sketch."

"How'd that go?" Mesa asked, still wondering just how much detail Henry would be able to put into words. "Let me see it."

"Haven't got anything yet. Adrienne wanted to add some finishing touches and then make a copy so we could have one when we turn the original over to Rollie."

He paused to take a bite of cake and then said, "I came over because I thought of somebody else in town that might be able to help with your story." Then he looked at his grandmother and said, "And because pizza joints never have decent desserts."

"Like who?" Mesa said, while she cut herself a piece of the cake half the size of Chance's, and one even smaller for Nana.

"Remember Mr. Sandifer, the art teacher at Butte High?"

"Sure. Didn't he retire a while back?"

Chanced nodded and then said, "He worked out at Warm Springs when he was first starting out. He always joked about helping a guy with a Ph.D. in physics make a potholder until the guy tried to stab Sandifer in the hand with a pair of scissors. Something about not having enough green loops."

"Right," Mesa said, teachers and their legendary stories. "Maybe check and see if he remembers hearing anything about Jessup, or Grainger's death, or maybe even Nurse Lenin?" She rolled her eyes at this last name.

They might be able to collect enough information for Vivian to help put this puzzle together, if only for her own satisfaction.

"Do be kind, you two," Nana said. "Silver House struggles so to make ends meet, and the number of people they serve seems to be growing by leaps and bounds."

"I know, Nan, sorry," Chance said. "And what you say definitely applies to Jessup. They hardly knew him in the short time he was under their care."

Mesa took one last bite of cake. She hoped she could maintain a sense of good will, and still write the hard-hitting story that she had a growing suspicion really needed to be told.

Chapter 6

At nine a.m. sharp on Tuesday, Mesa was back at her grandmother's house. Charlotte Haggis had clearly taken a page out of Mary Poppins' book. She sat poker straight on Nana's settee, hands clasped in her lap with nary a hair in her bun out of place, ready for the day. Mesa was sure the woman had been up before the dawn.

"Do let me pour, Rose," Charlotte said once Nana brought the tea tray into the parlor. "I know you've recuperated nicely, but one must pace oneself," Charlotte chided and poured milk then tea into three of Nana's best china cups.

As soon as she saw Charlotte, Mesa did indeed recognize her as the Tipsy Laird lady of childhood. But there was nothing frivolous about Mrs. Haggis this morning.

"Now then," she began once she'd handed teacups around, "your grandmother says you have some questions about the hospital I might be able to help you with?"

Mesa immediately put down her teacup and picked up her notebook. "I'm working on a story that focuses on mental health issues, and I'm doing some historical background, particularly the period around 1979. A patient was killed at Warm Springs that year. You were working there then?"

Mrs. Haggis nodded slowly, her teacup held in mid-air, a pensive look on her face as if she was reviewing files in her head. "That would have been a chap named Ethan Grainger, commonly referred to as Snake," she said with a dismissive shake of the head. "That was a proper cock up, all right, a real error in judgment on the part of a number of staff. Mind you, I'm not one to talk out of school, but I felt particularly bad for the young man who was blamed for what happened, a lad named Dowling Jessup. No doubt, you read about his death over the weekend. Is that part of what prompts your story?"

"Exactly. I'd be glad of any details you could give me," Mesa said and began writing in earnest, amazed at the woman's unfailing memory after thirty-five years. "You said you felt bad for him. How do you mean?"

"I supervised the admitting ward for nearly twenty years and saw my fair share of oddities. But I remember that one so well because he seemed so ordinary. He was a runaway, pure and simple. He was into drugs like so many of them were then, but down deep he was just lost and needed help finding his way back. In those days, we did a lot of that. Helped these young people find their way, and then sent them back home."

Mesa sensed a feeling of regret in the retired nurse's voice, as though she might have some misgivings about what happened to Dowling, just as Vivian did.

Mrs. Haggis sighed and brushed a tiny biscuit crumb from her well-pressed wool skirt. "There was no shortage of chin wagging about what happened. If it hadn't been for Dr. Larraz, lovely man, Jessup might have ended up in a prison cell with the key thrown way. As it was, he spent some time in the forensic ward instead."

"The forensic ward, what was that like?" Mesa asked. She had visions of psychotic murderers and serial killers licking their lips like Hannibal Lecter.

"The locked ward for patients with violent or criminal tendencies. I know it might not sound preferable to prison, but we had staff that did more than hand out pills in those days. He would have been well-treated, not taken advantage of as they often were in prison, weren't they?"

"Do you happen to know the outcome of his trial? I couldn't find any coverage about it in the newspaper."

"As far as I know, there wasn't a need for one. I think it was ruled an accident. In Dowling's case, he was put in seclusion, as was standard procedure. Eventually, he went back to his own unit."

"What unit would that have been?" Mesa made a mental note to find out more about how the hospital was organized in those days.

"The chronics ward—schizophrenics, paranoids, obsessive compulsives. That's where most of the general population ended up," she said matter-of-factly. "Sometime in the eighties, I suspect he was released with everybody else."

Clearly, Mrs. Haggis had no idea about the downward spiral of Jessup's behavior. "And what was the doctor's name again?"

"Dr. Xavier-Larraz, one of those double-barreled monikers," she said with a grin toward Nana. "He was the attending psychiatrist. Tall, dark, and handsome was our Dr. Xavier-Larraz. I think he was from somewhere in South America, family originally from Spain, I would say. Very European. Lovely manners. He did his best for the patients."

"What about a patient named Vivian Jobe?" Mesa asked.

"Beautiful name, but it doesn't ring any bells."

"You wouldn't happen to know what happened to Dowling after he was released in the eighties?" Mesa wondered where Dowling had gone before he ended up in Butte. Maybe he had made some enemies on the outside as well.

Mrs. Haggis shook her head, and then smiled. "I do see ex-patients from time to time. So many of them are in group homes in the community now. Half the time they want me to help them get back into Warm Springs."

This was news to Mesa, though she could hardly say she had ever had any discussions with former inmates.

"We took good care of them, you see," Miss Tipsy went on. "A disorganized mind craves order. It makes them feel safe. These group homes, I don't know." She wiped away more invisible crumbs. "I'm sure everyone does the best they can, wouldn't you say?"

"People can be cruel," Nana added as she warmed the trio's tea. "I've seen the residents made fun of when they're out and about on the streets here."

"Did you ever see Dowling?" Mesa asked. "Do you know how he adjusted?'

"Funniest thing," Mrs. Haggis said, suddenly animated. "I was on the Greyhound bus on my way back from my daughter's in Spokane. Dowling boarded in Missoula. We had a lovely chat."

"When was this?" Mesa wondered. Maybe Dowling had been living in Missoula and maybe they should be asking questions there.

"Must have been ..." and Mrs. Haggis began to count on her fingers. "Yes, eight years ago around Easter. I always go to my daughter's at Easter. She comes to me for Christmas," she said with maternal pride and then continued. "He said he was on his way to Butte. Much easier to blend in there, he said. That's what former patients want to do, you see. If they stand out, which they are more likely to do in upscale surroundings like Missoula or Bozeman, they attract attention, and trouble ensues, doesn't it?"

Okay, so maybe Missoula wasn't the place to look. "How did he seem then?" Mesa asked, hoping for any details she could give to Vivian.

"He'd kept himself neat and clean. You know the medications can give them a haggard look, but he was making an effort. And I could still see a hint of boyish charm. He helped a woman lift her suitcase above her seat. Shame, really, what's happened to him."

"Any details about the other boy?" Mesa looked at her notes. "Ethan Grainger? Do you know any details about how he died?"

"The fall, I should think, and third degree burns," Mrs. Haggis said grimly. "Fell through the crust on the Mound."

"At the hospital?" Mesa said in disbelief.

"You've never actually been to Warm Springs?" Mrs. Haggis asked, clearly surprised. "That's where the name comes from, a thermal out-cropping like the ones in Yellowstone, oozing scalding water and belching the most unpleasant gases." She made a peculiar face as if she could still smell the odor of rotten eggs.

"Never really had an occasion to visit," Mesa said, hoping not to sound offensive.

"Originally, Warm Springs was a health spa that attracted people from all over who came for the waters, so to speak. They could come for a week, have a daily soak in the mineral waters, and take the cure. There are partial remains of the concrete baths that were used. The Mound is behind the main residential building several hundred yards. It's easily forty feet high. They fenced it off after that mishap but, back then, you could walk right up the steps to the top. They even had a gazebo built up there. Patients could walk up to the top, sit on a bench, and take in the view."

Mesa knew Yellowstone Park took all sorts of precautions to keep tourists from stepping on or falling through thermal areas, but someone was always getting hurt anyway. The hazards were real enough.

"That's what I meant about errors in judgment," Miss Tipsy said quietly. "They may call it Warm Springs but, at the spot where they found the poor boy's body, the water temperature was nearly two hundred degrees."

Mesa arrived at the office by ten a.m., still mulling over what "Tipsy Laird" had said. Proper and precise as she was, she had been retired from the hospital nearly five years. Could her phenomenal memory of names and dates be accurate? They would need corroboration.

She had begun to make a mental list of who could talk to whom when she entered her office to find

Chance, once again, strewn across the couch, sipping coffee and flipping through one of three, thick folders on the coffee table. He was sufficiently entranced that he hardly noticed her arrival.

When she saw that he was reading medical files for Vivian Jobe, she picked up one of the folders and slapped him hard on the shoulder. "Those records are confidential," she said.

"Easy, tiger," Chance said. "They were dropped off about an hour ago by Dr. Kaiser. She said to put them on your desk, which I did. Then when you didn't show up ...." He looked at his watch, "I got bored. Besides you know I would never say anything."

Mesa slumped into her chair. "I know. It's just that I feel protective of Vivian. How would you like your personal problems spread all over town?"

"Don't have any," he smiled and took another sip of coffee.

"Besides, after talking to Jessup's caseworker, I thought Viv might have been biting off more than she could chew. So I got curious. Now that I've seen these psychiatric evaluations and discharge summaries, I can see she and Jessup might have been a match made in heaven. While he did time at Deer Lodge, she was hospitalized five times between 1980 and 2003."

Mesa opened one of the files and began to scan the pages as Chance talked. The reports described how Vivian, at twenty-six, had roamed the streets in the middle of the night only to be returned home at the hands of neighbors, strangers, and, sometimes, the police. Twice she had attempted to move away from home, only to have to return after giving away her money and belongings, mostly to street people she had met.

Chance picked at a Pork Chop John's sandwich and fries on the coffee table while he talked. "It's hard to believe this is the same person we met yesterday," he said. "Maybe she has a split personality."

"Dr. Kaiser cautioned me about using that phrase," Mesa said. "It's the tag for every crazy character in TV shows and movies, and it's a damaging misconception."

"Since when did you become so sensitive?" Chance said, "Kaiser must have given you some kind of indoctrination."

Mesa told herself to be patient. Chance had never known anyone with a mental illness, at least till Henry, and she wasn't exactly sure if he qualified. They did have the one cousin who was an alcoholic who had bouts of depression, but nothing as bizarre as all this. "Her hallucinations, which I'm about to tell you about, are bad enough," Mesa said, "without you making up stuff too."

During Vivian's longest hospitalization, she had finally admitted to her doctors that she was hearing voices. They called themselves the Dryads and gave her orders through trees and plants that spoke to her.

"Which means she talked to her plants," Chance said quietly as he put down one file and picked up another.

Mesa knew his whimsical comments were designed to irritate her, but the accounts of Vivian's bizarre behavior, even in retrospect, were unnerving. "So? I talk to my plants. Maybe, they don't give me orders ...." Mesa said and continued to listen to Chance's summary.

In the late eighties, Vivian lived on the streets in Spokane off and on, sometimes for as long as three months at a time. One commitment, nearly four months, had been in 1994 when the police had transported her to the hospital. She had resisted being removed from the lap of the Pieta, a marble statue in front of *St. Peter in Chains*, a Catholic cathedral near one of Spokane's trendier neighborhoods. She told the police she had been placed there by Mother Nature to guard the cathedral's lilac garden.

"Oh, my god," Mesa said, "Vivian Jobe homeless? Hanging out around the bus depot? Remember that guy with all his layers of dirty clothes and smudged cheeks? He used to panhandle on Park Street. I can't imagine Vivian asking anybody for anything. Let me see that file."

Chance shook his head and gave Mesa the last file without a fight. She could see he was a bit wigged-out by what he'd read.

"That was in '94," Mesa said. "Five years ago Vivian came back to Montana. She began taking medication to get stabilized and then slowly began to taper off once she settled in at her sister's ranch. Dr. Kaiser says that now, as long as Vivian monitors her condition, she can cope like any other adult. Physically, her condition is comparable to a pre-diabetic who has to watch her sugar intake. Emotionally, she's done well, but it's still a balance act."

"Maybe Jessup was on the road to be cured too," Chance said. "He was released from prison to a transitional housing program three years ago and then even left that six months ago."

"Cured is the wrong word, Dr. Kaiser says. Vivian's condition has a situational element to it, depending on her level of stress and anxiety. Part of her behavior patterns in the past may have resulted from side effects of the meds she was on. One in four schizophrenics doesn't respond well to them. Fatigue or constant drooling are common. And some of the drugs are so expensive, lots of patients can't even afford them. Besides, do we even know if Jessup was schizophrenic?"

"Chronic depression was the diagnosis I saw in his file at Silver House," Chance said. "No wonder she took her time trying to find him. If I'd been through all that, the last thing I'd want to do is tell people about it. Imagine having to figure out how to find somebody who might still be that bad off." He shook his head. "I took her story so lightly yesterday. She's been through a hell of a lot, Jessup too, for that matter."

"To look at her, you wouldn't think she heard voices," Mesa said, thinking aloud. "Of course, plenty of people hear voices, just usually not so strong and creepy that we're scared shitless and want to kill ourselves."

Chance rolled his eyes and kept eating.

"Instead we drink ourselves into oblivion to stop the jabbering," Mesa said. She picked up her cell and called Dr. Kaiser to thank her for dropping off the files, and to tell her Vivian's reunion with Jessup wasn't going to happen. "I didn't realize the amount of trauma Vivian's been through. And now she's about to experience some more."

Dr. Kaiser must have sensed Mesa's reticence in the face of the details of Vivian's history. "Don't worry, Mesa. Vivian has learned to deal with her voices so that she doesn't freak out about them. She knows that they're triggered by her stress level, so she can exercise some control over them."

"It's not just that, "Mesa said. "Jessup's dead. He was the transient in that trailer fire on Sunday."

"The arson?" Dr. Kaiser said, and then paused. "Well, Vivian can handle the news. She's got family around her now, and they'll be supportive. Her younger sister is a psychiatric nurse you know."

"Is that who Vivian lives with at Table Mountain?"

"It is. When Vivian had her last episode eight years ago, she ended up in Warm Springs briefly. Abby was a nurse and had been working at the mental hospital for six months, mostly in the chemical dependency unit. She hadn't even seen Vivian in several years."

Dr. Kaiser explained that Vivian had been living rough in Spokane in a halfway house, then a shelter, then finally on the streets. That Christmas, she'd been working as a bell ringer for the Salvation Army and had a little money. So she bought herself a bus ticket to Montana. But what she didn't know was that their mother had finally died.

"When she got off the bus in Deer Lodge," Dr. Kaiser said, "the sheriff recognized her walking down the street. She looked a bit rough, and when he asked her where she was going and she said home to see her mama, he knew he had to tell her the bad news. She had a meltdown then and there, so they called Abby who took her home after she calmed down."

Mesa thought about the impact of her own mother's death. Sarah Dawson had always been a vibrant, practical woman, and a straightforward Montana girl who had grown up horseback riding, and skiing, anything that could be done outdoors. She'd organized family vacation trips from the Swiss Alps to Lapland. She was the one who oversaw their moves from one base to the next, making sure her kids got integrated into the next community. She was the backbone of the family and her loss was devastating.

Thankfully, her last days had been at Nana's, and they had all been together. Mesa would have been distraught too to learn about the death of her mother the way Vivian had.

"Abby's married to a fellow who builds those eco-friendly houses, low impact, that sort of thing," Dr. Kaiser said. "You should go up to their place. Cordwood and straw-bale cabins. Once Vivian got on her feet again, she moved into one of them. She helps with construction, runs part of the business, plenty of open space and several dogs she's training to keep her busy."

"Does she take medication now?" Mesa asked, remembering what Henry had said about Dowl wanting to get off his.

"Only for her thyroid. I've never been sure the original diagnosis of schizophrenia was accurate anyway. I think Vivian was young, scared, sad, and alone, and now she's not."

The more Dr. Kaiser talked, the more fascinated Mesa became. "You can hear voices but only be afraid and depressed, not psychotic?" she asked.

"Unaddressed traumas trigger feelings of emptiness, isolation, and confusion. Agitation, like family chaos, or misdiagnosis and being shipped off to a mental institution where sleeplessness and anxiety are rampant, can create a toxic chemical imbalance in the brain that can generate all kinds of visual and auditory hallucinations. The newer medications may minimize the psychosis but restlessness and racing, obsessive thoughts are all side effects. Some experts, like R.D. Laing, would say hearing voices is a reasonable response to an unreasonable situation."

Mesa wondered how many people in Butte were overmedicated, misdiagnosed, or whose medical condition deteriorated because of the method of treatment or the side effects of their meds.

With all this information about Vivian's progress, Mesa had to wonder what had happened to Dowling Jessup. Had he recovered like Vivian? According to Chance's conversation with the caseworker at Silver House, Jessup had stopped by once a week to pick up medication for his depression. Whether he took the medication was unclear.

"One more thing, Dr. Kaiser," Mesa said. "You ever have any dealings with a psychiatrist who worked at Warm Springs, named Xavier-Larraz?"

"Not of late, but I did," Dr. Kaiser said after a moment. "He's a well-respected mental health advocate. He's been retired now for some time but he occasionally attends the state mental health meetings. He stays up on the research. Why do you ask?"

Mesa told Kaiser about how Miss Tipsy thought Larraz had tried to help Jessup after he was accused of killing Grainger.

"I'm not surprised," Kaiser said. "Larraz has always come across as a compassionate man. He may look old world in appearance, but his attitude about mental health treatment is cutting edge."

❧

"Henry, you always say that you shouldn't break a promise, right?" Chance said, making sure his voice was as neutral as possible. Any sign of criticism on his part could turn Henry into tears. "Yesterday you promised you would come to the police department with me, didn't you?"

Henry stood at the spotless kitchen counter at one end of the living room of his little one bedroom apartment at the Leggett Hotel. With the precision that only a person with OCD could muster, he was re-arranging four empty boxes of cereal, all with cartoon characters on the front. "You aren't mad at me, are ya?" he asked.

"I'm not mad," Chance said and looked out the window, trying to act as if he had all the time in the world. The view was mostly of the brick wall of the building next door, but there was a partial view of the East Ridge and the Lady of the Rockies statue, something else Henry was obsessed with. "But I thought you wanted to give the drawings to the sheriff."

"Not the one of Stick. I want to keep that one. But he can have the other one. I don't like that other guy."

Chance felt like this was progress. He'd been at the apartment for twenty minutes trying to cajole Henry into walking the four blocks to the police station. "Okay, so we'll just give him the one of the stranger."

"I don't like the police. They make me nervous," Henry said. "Want to see my DVDs I got for Christmas?"

Henry always bought his own Christmas presents since he had no family and few friends. Chance had made sure to get him a gift certificate for the movies at the mall. "You showed those to me the last time I was here, Henry. Why don't you put on your jacket, and we can take a quick walk over to the police station. You can give Sheriff Solheim the sketch, and we'll be back here in no time flat."

"I don't like the police," Henry repeated. "They never do anything when I tell them someone's mean to me, and sometimes they aren't very nice either."

Chance knew that Henry, like a number of the developmentally delayed adults in town, had a habit of calling the police at the least provocation. They tended to see the world in black and white, with a precise view of right and wrong, and everything in the latter category required punishment. "Well, I'll be with you this time, and I'll make sure the sheriff listens to you. He's my friend, you know."

For the first time that morning, Henry looked up at Chance. "He is? Do you think he'll let me see his badge?"

❧

Mesa walked into the outer office, tossed the new hire applicants' files onto Irita's desk, and wondered why everything was so quiet. The newsroom usually whirred with a steady hum punctuated by Irita orchestrating the work.

Irita and Cinch stood outside Phade's cubicle whispering heatedly to one another. When Mesa approached, Cinch trudged off in the direction of his office, and Irita turned Mesa back the way she'd come.

"Wait a minute," Mesa said. "I wanna hear what's going on."

"I'll tell you in a minute," she said conspiratorially. "I don't want Cinch thinking I've ratted him out."

Mesa stopped in her tracks. Irita's favorite pastime was tormenting Cinch. Irita pushed forward into Mesa's office. "What are you talking about?" Mesa asked, looking straight into Irita's animated stare.

"When Cinch came into work early this morning, he found Phade asleep at his computer terminal."

"That's hardly the end of the world. I've given Phade his own office key so he can come and go when he's working on the blog."

"Except the blog he was working on belongs to Cascade Utility, not the *Mess*. Apparently, he's been moonlighting and now he has plans to go out on his own. So Cinch ran roughshod over him, and said that he was the worst thing that ever happened to the paper. Then Phade told Cinch to eff off, and that he quit."

Chapter 7

After repeated attempts to reach Phade on his cell, Mesa, with clenched teeth, dragged Cinch into the office to discuss the particulars of his conversation with Phade. "What's wrong with this generation?" he had said. "No loyalty, that's what."

Cinch had worked at the *Mess* since Sol Ramey had bought the paper in the eighties. Every one of the paper's advertisers knew they could count on Cinch to keep them happy. He knew where the ads needed to be placed to minimize competition between retailers, long ago having mastered the give and take that kept Butte's finite number of businesses and their customers satisfied. And everything he knew he kept in his head.

But the *Mess's* print readership was aging. Mesa had no illusions about that. Cinch's view of the world mirrored the forty percent of locals who still wanted to hold the newsprint. But Phade was the person who would put their advertisers in cyberspace. He was the future. That said, for the moment Mesa knew she needed both of them.

If Phade was serious about quitting, she felt sure he would have come directly to her first. After all, she was one of the few people in town with whom he had anything in common. But she had promised to get him some help. She needed to get that "sorted," as Nan would say, before she talked to him. But she didn't have time for that now. She needed to talk to Vivian about Jessup's death as soon as possible.

She put Phade out of her mind and drove the seventeen miles up to Lime Kiln Hill, thinking about her mother and wishing she were there to talk about her friendship with Vivian. Life as a military family meant that Mesa had never really gotten to know any of her mother's Butte friends. Plenty of them had shown up for the funeral, but the names and faces were soon forgotten. No one had made a solid connection with Sarah's surviving children.

Mesa imagined her mother and Vivian brushing their horses after an afternoon ride, trading barbs, and laughing the whole time. Sarah Dawson had loved to ride and those times riding with her were among Mesa's best memories. When they had moved to Italy, they had all missed the horses.

The turnoff to Table Mountain ranch was easy to spot and, once over a short rise, she stopped on the gravel drive in front of a long house with four dormers. She'd seen the *Standard's* news article that described Table Mountain with its cordwood and straw-bale construction that gave the buildings their distinctive adobe look.

Vivian's brother-in-law, Wally Germane, a self-described throwback, taught classes in voluntary simplicity at the Adult Education program in town, which included the methods he'd used to build the house. Maybe she'd offer to send Phade to some of the classes. It wouldn't cost her that much and he would feel like she understood him. Despite his tech savvy, he had a "back to the earth" side.

Mesa parked the SUV next to a peeled log fence and gate, clearly hand-carved and neatly finished—like the house. A sense of calm precision and quiet permeated the grounds. No cell phone could interrupt this silence.

"Be right down," Mesa heard a woman's voice calling. A face at the window above the front door came and went, then reappeared at the door. "I'm Abby, Vivian's sister."

Four inches shorter and probably ten years younger, Abby reached out her hand to Mesa. Her handshake was confident and reassuring—the hand of a nurse. "Hope you don't mind my visiting on short notice," Mesa said.

"I told Vivian you were coming. How was the drive up Lime Kiln? That spell of warm weather turned the ice on the road to slush pretty quick."

"Nothing the car wash can't handle."

Behind the house, the mountainside of Douglas fir sheltered the ranch. With no hustle and bustle anywhere, Mesa thought, the place epitomized the term "mountain retreat." If a mind in turmoil sought order as Tipsy had said, nature provided some here.

"Vivian is so pleased you wanted to come up and see us."

Mesa released a long sigh, her breath calm and peaceful. Her earlier anxiety aside, she could not help but relax. "You sure have a beautiful place."

Irita had said so when Mesa told her where she was going. What she'd said was, "Those two been working on that place for a decade. It should look good."

Cinch had chimed in, when he overheard their conversation, that he thought Table Mountain was a commune for religious nuts and homosexuals. Not exactly two groups likely to join forces, Mesa had tried to argue.

"Would you like the nickel tour?" Abby asked. She opened the bareback log gate and Mesa followed. They strolled leisurely past the long house toward a smaller house just behind.

Mesa was devoid of any desire for home ownership and was usually immune to anyone's house beautiful. But the Germanes had managed to build three distinctly different examples of energy-efficient homes without benefit of a single brick, nothing but straw bales, logs, and adobe. The occasional local granite was spread around for good measure. The complex was plain clever.

"When Vivian first came here, she lived in Leaning Tree cottage." Abby pointed off to the left at a small building fifty yards away. "One large room with one side all glass, and a wood stove that makes it as warm as the womb. It was the only place where we could get her to be calm in those first months."

Mesa could see the little cabin wedged next to a gigantic fir tree. It almost seemed like a human nest.

"She became a first class birder," Abby said. She explained how Vivian would sit on the floor staring out the window, watching the birds at the feeder and taking a ton of notes. "Sometimes sitting for days at a time, at one point she said they were talking to her.

"It was hard at first," Abby said and shook her head. "But we just left her alone and, over time, her energy changed. She would come out of whatever world had taken her away."

"Did you develop an approach specific to her? How did you do it? Your training must have helped you to deal with her illness."

"You mean being a psych nurse and her sister would be to my advantage?" Abby chuckled. "Not really. Once you no longer have to monitor a patient's compliance, there's not that much to do. Except, of course, be kind. In the end, I think that having a lot of space to wander in and no one monitoring her every move was what did it. That and an understanding therapist who didn't believe in the diagnosis or the drugs. You know Jan Kaiser?"

Mesa nodded. "I talked to her before I came up here. She gave me a lot of background and, of course, Vivian allowed me to see her medical records."

"Jan has the courage of three armies, if you ask me," Abby said. "She's been questioning the prevailing wisdom about mental health care for as long as I've been in nursing."

They left Leaning Tree and walked to another house, this one called simply the Guesthouse. "This is where Vivian hangs her hat these days. She has the second floor. When folks stay over, they use these downstairs rooms."

Each of the rooms, once again, had floor to ceiling windows with breathtaking views of the forest and the mountains beyond. The care that had gone into the construction of this private retreat was obvious. They went upstairs but Vivian wasn't there.

"Vivian has a couple of Labs who follow her everywhere. She must have taken them for a walk," Abby said. "Buddha and Gandhi." She explained that her husband had given Vivian a pup early on. "It was the first thing we did that managed to shift her focus to something she didn't have to be afraid of."

Mesa smiled. Animal therapy, why not?

"Come over to the Long House. We'll make tea. Vivian should be back soon."

They went out the side door through a small green house made of recycled plastic siding and salvaged windows. Rock planters were filled with herbs and seedling tomatoes. A two-track led down into a glen away from the houses. "Where's that go?" Mesa asked.

"We have sixty acres total," Abby said. "That two-track leads down to a creek and 40,000 acres of the Beaverhead National Forest. It's a nice buffer," she said with a smile.

They entered the house through a side door where Abby took off her shoes. Mesa followed suit. "This is where we host groups who come here for workshops."

The long dining table was handmade from larch and had been buffed to a golden sheen. Beyond the dining room, a small living room, and a circular stairway with a hand-hewn, curved aspen for the banister completed the first floor. Order and warmth permeated everything the Germanes had built.

Mesa chuckled to herself. "Amazing," was all she could say as she let her fingers trail along the banister.

"This is our control center," Vivian said. She pointed to a series of dials, knobs, switches, and thermometer on the wall. "We monitor the solar panels and wind mill that generate the ranch's electricity, so we can operate off the grid. No power bills for us."

The Germanes' careful attention to every aspect of their environment was obvious. They'd taken the same attitude toward Vivian's care. They had taken her out of the system and off the mental health system's grid. Would that others had the opportunity, or the courage, to do the same.

The ranch was more than fifteen miles from the nearest town, Butte in one direction and tiny Whitehall in the other. Mesa shuddered to think of the emergencies that could come up, but that was Montana for you. Take care of your own, because nobody's coming to the rescue.

Abby had just set some mugs of tea on the table when the consistent bark of dogs interrupted the quiet, followed by Vivian's appearance at the door. "See how I got my sanity back?" she said after a nod of greeting. "They kept me busy chopping wood and carrying bales."

The three women sipped tea companionably while Vivian and her sister traded stories about the challenge of living outside the boundaries of traditional communities, both the mental health one and the environmental one. "I guess when it comes right down to it," Abby said, "we didn't have a choice. Once we'd sunk all our savings into the land, we had to find a cheaper way to build a home. And, once Vivian reappeared, I was the only family left. So this was where we brought her."

"I'm glad you decided to come see the place so soon," Vivian said after Abby had excused herself to make a run to the grocery in Whitehall.

"I hope I'm not imposing," Mesa said, while her hostess sipped her tea. She started to add that Vivian's description of Table Mountain had been so intriguing, but her host intervened.

"I realize we've only just met, Mesa," she said quietly and put her tea down. "But I know that vibe when someone has bad news." She sat back in her chair and folded her hands in her lap. "I've seen it over and over in my life. If you have an emotional illness, people are inclined to treat you like a child. They speaker slower and quieter, and they have trouble looking you in the eye. 'The court has decided to commit you.' 'Your mother has died.' 'You have to take these drugs or go back into an institution.' People worry that I might not be able to handle bad news, that they'll trigger an episode."

Mesa, at a loss for words, had stopped looking at Vivian.

Vivian smiled and said, "But I can handle it, Mesa. It's Dowl, isn't it? What's happened? You want to tell me something about him that's going to be hard to hear. Is he back in prison?"

Mesa felt even worse. "If only he were," she answered.

In the three-minute walk from the Leggett to the police station, Henry had turned around to go back home twice. Chance considered it a major victory that they were finally sitting in the Sheriff's office. When Rollie Solheim was sitting down and smiling, he looked vaguely like an old time Santa Claus, except with a buzz cut, which was a comfort. He had also shown his badge to Henry as soon as they'd arrived. He even let Henry hold it.

After hearing Henry explain what he had seen, Sheriff Solheim said, "So, Henry, you're sure this sketch is a man you saw this past Saturday evening with your friend, Stick?" He held up each sketch as he mentioned each man.

Henry nodded and nodded. Chance had to touch his friend on the arm so he'd stop.

"And you know how important it is not to get people into trouble by saying they did something when they didn't?"

Henry started nodding again. Chance had been over this earlier, knowing that Henry was supersensitive to the idea that anyone thought he was lying about anything. More than once Henry had gone into meltdown when somebody accused him of lying. "I always tell the truth, Chance," he would say. "Lots of people don't believe that, but it's true. You believe me, don't cha, Chance?"

"Okay, Henry, would you wait out in the hall please while I talk to Chance," the sheriff said.

Henry retreated quickly. Chance watched him, glad that the sheriff's office door had a window in the upper half so that he could keep an eye on Henry pacing in the hall. "So, what do you think?" he said to Rollie.

"Well, I see what you mean about the kid. He does have a mind for detail. You gotta remember, though, just because Henry saw somebody with this arson victim doesn't mean this mystery man killed anyone. He might not even be our arsonist."

"I get it," Chance said. "But I wouldn't bring this to your attention if I didn't think there was something to it. And neither would Henry. He hates the police station. No offense, Rollie."

"You know, guys like Henry don't have the best reputation as accurate witnesses," Rollie answered. "I can't guarantee how our detectives will take this information. They don't like spending a lot of time working a case that gets blown out of the water when their witness falls apart in court."

Now Chance was nodding. He didn't even want to think about having to get Henry into a courtroom.

"First thing, let's see if anybody else saw this guy around," Rollie said. "He doesn't resemble any or our usual suspects, at least not as far as I know, so it might take awhile."

Chance accompanied Henry back to the Leggett, wondering what, if any, good their trip had done. The sheriff was hardly convinced that the stranger, if he existed at all, had anything to do with Jessup's death. Maybe the lawman was right. What didn't square for Chance was why Jessup had crawled into that trailer to avoid a cold March night, when he could easily have gone to Henry's apartment and slept on the sofa.

It was time to find out more about what shape Jessup had been in the night of St. Urhu's. What had he been up to before Henry had seen him? More than what Henry knew.

≈≈≈

"There's no easy way to say it," Mesa said, looking directly at Vivian. "Jessup died some time Saturday night, early Sunday morning, most likely from inhaling smoke and toxic fumes in a trailer fire."

Vivian chewed her lip. The yellow Lab at her feet cozied up close and whined. She reached for the dog, hugging her neck and whispering, "It's okay."

"I'm so sorry, Vivian. Just when I thought—"

Vivian reached out and touched Mesa's hand. "Thank you for coming in person to tell me. It's a shock, but one I can take." She took a deep breath, patted the dog, and continued. "After all these years," she said and her voice faded.

"I know. Some coincidence, huh?"

"What actually happened? Was it an accident? I would be broken-hearted if it was suicide. Do the police even know?"

Mesa explained the arson theory, and then Chance and Henry's speculation about the second man.

"Your brother thinks he could have been lured there?" Vivian's voice had become stronger. "You think it's possible someone killed him? But why?" And then Vivian sat back in her chair. "Oh, my god. The ad might have brought attention to Dowl. Could someone have come after him after all these years?"

Mesa shrugged. "We have no way of knowing, but Chance and I think it's worth looking into. We could use your help."

Mesa described the man Henry had seen, showed the sketch of the stranger to Vivian who slowly shook her head. "No one I know."

Mesa explained that originally the police were pursuing the case as arson but that Dowl's death made the case a homicide, which gave it more priority. Or at least she hoped it would become a priority.

She assured Vivian that the question of what had happened to Dowling was important, and that she intended to make the sheriff's office aware that his death might be related to what had happened at Warm Springs.

"I feel like it's the least we can do," Mesa said, looking as much as anything for a simple response, some hint of how Vivian was taking it all.

She pulled out the other sketch in the folder in her lap. It was the one of Stick. Mesa handed the sketch over and Vivian smoothed the fold in the paper.

At that moment, Mesa realized that this might be the only picture Vivian had ever seen of Dowl. "Would you like to keep that?" Mesa said.

A long moment passed, and then she nodded and said, "He looks better than I thought he might." She continued to smooth the fold with both her hands as if she were touching the outline of his face. "He had such a sweet smile when I knew him."

"I feel like we got derailed before we even got started," Mesa said, wondering for a moment if her zeal for this story was misplaced.

"I never really thought about what I would do if I found him. I wanted him to know that he made things easier for me then. I never got to thank him for what he did for me, and I might have been able to give him a helping hand if he needed it." She paused and reached down to pat the dog. Then she said, "Clearing his name was something I would have helped to do if he thought it was important."

She paused again, and finally said with a sigh, "I guess now it's left to me. Maybe we should try, even if no one else cares."

Mesa explained about Henry going to the police, and about Mr. Sandifer. At least they had some leads. Mesa took out the photo of the nurse she had copied from the microfilm at the library the afternoon before. "Let's start with this article about Warm Springs that ran in the *Standard* in August 1979. This photo was part of the piece." She handed the news clipping to Vivian.

After a long look, she shook her head. "The girls in the background look the part but I don't really remember them, or the nurse."

"Do you remember a doctor named Larraz?" Mesa said. "A psychiatrist?"

Vivian looked up from the news clipping. "Maybe. I do remember a therapist that Dowl would talk to. He seemed to admire him. I think he was Spanish. He had a daughter who we were allowed to visit sometimes."

"At the mental hospital?"

"There were staff cottages on the grounds. A couple of times, we went to a picnic at one of them, you know, adolescents trying to act normal. It might have been his house. I don't know. As usual the details are faint."

"We might be able to track him down," Mesa said. "I talked to a retired nurse, Charlotte Haggis. Is that name familiar?"

Again, Vivian shook her head.

"She remembers Larraz helping Dowl. Maybe he remembers something that would help clear Dowl's name."

Vivian shrugged and sighed, the dog sitting up and leaning in to her. "I'll admit my memories come in waves. But maybe if I talked to some of the staff from that time; that might help."

"Can you think of any other reason anyone else might want to kill Dowl?

Vivian shook her head. "I know it's been a long time, but I don't think a person's core personality changes. He was a gentle man."

"He was friends with a young man at Silver House who said that Dowl made comments that suggested he might come into some cash, maybe an inheritance," Mesa said. "What do you make of that?"

Again, Vivian could only shake her head. She added, "As far as I know, Dowling had no family. After he left the Children's Home, he had lived briefly with an older sister, but she had died in childbirth. He was alone."

Mesa had begun to sit on the edge of her chair. The thought of vindicating Jessup and telling the story of Vivian's triumph over a crushing mental health system begged to be told. But Vivian wouldn't be the first person to feel swamped by Mesa's enthusiasm, and she wanted to avoid that. "Maybe we need a day or two to let this sink in."

Vivian smiled and, once again, Mesa felt like she was the one being comforted. The older woman clapped her hands to her knees and stood up. She walked over to the wide window with its view of the Leaning Tree Cottage and the mountains beyond. She put her hands on her hips, and turned back to Mesa. "That's the last thing we need to do. I've spent years fighting inertia. I don't intend to let it get a hold on my life again. I think maybe a road trip to Warm Springs might be in order."

Chapter 8

Whenever Chance thought of his high school art teacher, his father's words came ringing through. "*There's a guy who marches to the beat of a different drum.*" Chance was never quite sure if his father was being sarcastic or complimentary. After all, Colonel Nathaniel Dawson had served all his adult life in the Air Force. He and Ken Sandifer were polar opposites. Chance never mentioned how much he admired his teacher.

Chance parked his pickup on Copper Street in front of Ken Sandifer's house. He and his wife, Mitsy, had bought a dilapidated miner's cottage for back taxes for less than $3000, and completely transformed it into a livable home with a loft and a walk-in basement. They had also bought two lots to the east of the cottage, torn down a second collapsing cabin, and proceeded to create a miniature farm right behind the Butte-Silver Bow jail.

They raised their own chickens along with a small goat and several rescued hounds. A couple of metal sculptures graced the garden along with a fire pit around which everyone could graze. All of this was surrounded by a wood and hog-wire fence and a gate with a trellis over it.

Over the years, Mr. Sandifer had thrown a couple of graduation parties that included bonfires that had attracted the attention of the police department, which was only a stone's throw away. In the end, he was deemed harmless enough and had developed a reputation as one of Butte's eccentric artists.

Through the gate's arch, Chance could see Sandifer with his speckled gray hair that now grew mostly on his face. What little hair he had on his head was cropped but, on his chin, he sported what Nana would call a naval beard—trimmed only with scissors. He reminded Chance of a photo of Sigmund Freud he'd seen on the Internet.

Sandifer stood at the back of his house in the driveway, unloading firewood from his pickup. When Chance called his name, the teacher turned, looked over his wire-rimmed spectacles, and then nodded his approval. "Chance, it's been a while," he said.

Chance crossed the yard, navigating his way around a sculpture—made from various chains, metal piping, nuts, and bolts—quietly rusting. Another sculpture, decidedly abstract, seemed to be some sort of molded plastic, shiny black and red loops.

Sandifer's handshake was firm, and they half embraced in a way that made Chance feel like the older man was genuinely glad to see him. "Want some help?"

They began stacking the firewood in a lean-to next to the garage, chatting as they walked to and from the back of the pickup. "What you working on these days?" Chance asked, and nodded toward the long wooden worktable beyond the wood shed where every conceivable color of paint had been spilled or splashed. His gaze was fixed on a dinner plate.

"I started glazing old china with these enamels that you can bake in the oven," and he waved his hand toward a collection of brightly colored little jars and tubes. "Beats going down to the high school to use their kiln, and I can work any time I want. Enamel stinks so Mitsy drove me out here."

Chance nodded, silently making a note that he thought Adrienne might like to meet Sandifer.

"So, what you been up to lately? Haven't seen you since you came round to help tear down the Mad Hatter's place."

Chance smiled. The Mad Hatter had been the Sandifers' neighbor, known for the exotic headgear she would wear whenever she worked in her garden or put the garbage out. "Who could resist an afternoon of swinging a sledgehammer through a bunch of plaster and asbestos?"

"You were swinging that roughneck like you had something to prove."

Chance had left Butte after high school, gone to college, got married, and got divorced back East. His return to Butte afterward had been on the down low. That day had been the beginning of his reintegration.

After his divorce, Chance had made the conscious decision to abandon the urban and corporate hubbub in favor of a competition solely with himself and the wilderness. That what had really split him and Stephanie up, her perception that he lacked ambition.

As far as he was concerned, the Western tradition of self-determination had saved him. "Enjoyed that day. Got me going too. Made some good contacts."

"I like what you did with that art gallery in the Imperial Building," Sandifer said laying his armful of logs on the stack. "You still helping your sister with the paper or are you just doing the restoration work?"

"Matter of fact, that's why I stopped by, for the newspaper, that is. Mesa's working on this story about Warm Springs. We both remembered you talking about working there when you were in college."

"That's a tale worth telling, all right. Let's take a break." He motioned to the steps that led up to the back porch. They both sat down on the top step. Sandifer reached into a cooler on the porch and pulled out a couple of Moose Drools. "Sun's over the yardarm somewhere. Have one."

The March wind had died down and the sun was high overhead, "Why not?" said Chance.

After a long pull on the beer, Sandifer said, "Funny how when you're young you don't realize which of your life experiences is going to shape your character into the person you'll become. I'll tell you what though, that was one helluva time." He shook his head, and then chuckled. "So, what part of life in the loony bin piqued your interest?"

"I know it might be asking a lot, but I'm hoping you might remember a couple of patients who were there about the time you were. That was the late seventies, right? I realize it was quite a while ago."

Sandifer smiled. "Sometimes it feels like it was just yesterday." He shook his head again. "Never thought I'd be working in a mental institution with a bunch of schizophrenics." He paused, scratched his beard, and then said, "We were all castaways."

"What were you doing there in the first place?" Chance asked.

"Nam," Sandifer said, and explained that the hospital had been staffing the place with conscientious objectors, using them as orderlies, food service workers, and occupational therapist's aides. Then, when the war was over, no more draft. No more COs. "The hospital had a hard time attracting help."

Chance could see that. He'd be the first to admit working at an asylum, even a place like Silver House, would make him crazy as well.

"Trying to make ends meet on a new teacher's salary, it was all I could get. My mother made me promise I wouldn't go down in the mine. So, I started working part-time in the summer, taking the place of staff on vacation in the OT department, and then covering weekends, and holidays."

All but one of Butte's mines had long since closed by the time Chance might have considered working in one but, in the seventies, work in the mines was still common. Nevertheless, a generation of parents had sacrificed to get their sons into college so that they could enter safer occupations. Guys like Sandifer were lucky, and thankful.

"Working in a mental hospital couldn't have been a walk in the park," Chance said.

"It was intense at times. Then again, I was pharmaceutically altered about half of it, like most of the people there—patients *and* staff." He gave another quick shake of his head. "Who you trying to track down anyway?"

"Anybody who might have been involved in an incident where an adolescent male patient died."

"The Grainger kid?"

Chance nodded, only slightly surprised. Sandifer had a great memory for names. It was part of the reason he was such a good teacher. "You remember him?"

Sandifer jigged on the step and then said, "Remember him? Hell, I found his body."

❧

Driving away from Vivian and Table Mountain ranch, Mesa could hardly contain her excitement. Vivian had phoned Warm Springs and been referred to the Patient Advocate's office, a position that had been established some ten years before when the hospital had undergone review.

She had made arrangements to meet there the next day. Although the receptionist doubted there would be any staff Vivian would know, the grounds were open to the public. "Maybe a look around might jog my memory," Vivian said. "And you can take some photographs for your story."

And to think Mesa had contemplated dumping the project because Vivian might not be up to it. The stereotype that those who struggled with mental illness could flip out so easily was one of several she promised herself she would write about. Vivian was no Frito Lady.

She had left Vivian to put together a statement she could give to the Butte-Silver Bow police about what she knew about Dowling Jessup. Meanwhile, Mesa had explained she was making a trip to Twin Bridges to learn more about Dowl's life there and would let Vivian know what turned up.

Thirty some miles down Highway 41, Mesa was taking in the Tobacco Root Mountains bordering the

Ruby Valley when she drove past the sign that said, "Welcome to Twin Bridges – The Little Town that Cares."

Long before meeting Vivian and learning about Jessup's time at the Montana Children's Home, Mesa had begun to consider expanding the *Mess's* coverage to smaller markets in the surrounding counties. Madison County and Twin Bridges being one of them, she had asked Irita about her friends in that direction. Irita's contacts almost always included food.

Twin Bridges, unlike many Montana towns its size, had one upscale restaurant to which folks would drive thirty plus miles to dine. But that fine establishment was only open on the weekend, usually for the benefit of the celebrity ranchers or retired government officials like Ted Turner or Donald Rumsfeld, who often brought out-of-town visitors and left large tips.

Conversely, the mainstay establishment, the Green Anchor Bar and Restaurant, with its saloon on one side and the restaurant on the other, served three meals a day, seven days a week. Admittedly, the name was an odd choice for such a landlocked part of the country, but the blue neon-lit anchor was just odd enough to be memorable. At the three-way intersection of Main Street and Highway 41 to Dillon, all the traffic passed by the restaurant one way or the other, and much of it stopped in.

Researching a feature story about the status of the Children's Home had the potential to demonstrate the *Messenger's* commitment to outlying areas in Southwest Montana. In the process, Mesa would find out what Dowl had been doing at the orphanage. According to Irita, the person to talk to on both accounts was Gladys

Pylypew, Irita's sister-in-law from her first marriage, and the manager of the Green Anchor.

"Gladdie can tell you all there is to know about the Children's Home, Twin Bridges, and anything else that goes on in Madison County," Irita had said. Given that Madison County had about two people per square mile, and Twin Bridges was a town of four hundred, it wouldn't surprise Mesa if Gladdie knew every resident on a first name basis.

Mesa wandered into the restaurant around one p.m., following the smell of fried onions and cheeseburgers from the sidewalk. The lunch crowd had begun to thin. With the increased daylight of March afternoons, plenty of ranch work could still be done before dark.

Gladdie wasn't hard to spot, a middle-aged woman with clear blue eyes and gold rings on every other finger. She was bussing tables, taking orders without a note pad, and acting as cashier.

Mesa sat on a stool at the counter and tried not to take offense at some patrons' slightly longer stares at her unfamiliar face. She ordered a bowl of chili and a grilled cheese and hoped the comfort food would have a warming effect. Once the food arrived, she told Gladdie she worked for the *Messenger* and the beginning of a vital confidence had begun.

According to Gladdie, "If Irita sent you, all doors are opened."

Of course she knew Dowl and had only heard the evening before about his death. "Damn shame. What do you want to know?"

Mesa was impressed with Irita's sphere of influence. Between the ebb and flow of customers, Gladdie began to draw a picture of Dowl's life in Twin Bridges. He had come back around Labor Day, months ago, and taken up residence in the Home without anyone really noticing. Since its last owner, some Japanese real estate developer with businesses in California, had defaulted on his taxes, the town had adjusted to the place being abandoned again.

The Beaverhead River flowed gently through Twin Bridges, and the Children's Home had once flourished with its ranch bordered by the river. Since the Home's closure, the river attracted fly fishermen from all over the country and the world. But the Home and its history remained a proud part of the culture of the town.

"He became a fixture here till recently when the Home was sold again and he got tossed."

Gladdie's tone suggested that the locals didn't think Dowl had received a square deal either. "He saved that woman who bought the place a good deal of money. His work might have been makeshift, but he patched the holes in the castle roof."

The castle was the turreted building Mesa thought belonged in a Stephen King novel.

Gladdie explained that Dowl became a familiar figure along Main Street. At least a couple of times a week, he'd walk across the bridge and visit the post office, and then buy some Copenhagen at the Trading Post. He received a monthly check of some sort though no one knew what for as he looked able-bodied. He told people he was working on the roof of the superintendent's house. He wore Carhartt overalls and looked the part so no one thought to ask who said he could. He drove a tore-up old truck that he bought from Dale, who owned the tire store. He said Dowl kept it in good running order.

"What kind of truck?" Mesa said, wondering where it might be and what might be in it.

"The usual Ford or Chevy. Ask Dale. He was the one said Dowl was living at the Home out of his truck," Gladdie continued as if reliving how she'd discovered that Dowl was sleeping rough. "He took a quick look inside the camper one afternoon. Neat as a pin, it was. A mattress with a quilt on it, some cooking utensils in a wooden crate and a lantern was all."

"You ever see him with anybody?" Mesa asked. She showed Gladdie Adrienne's sketch of Henry's mystery man. "Like this guy, or anyone come to visit?"

Gladdie looked at the sketch. "A lot of fishermen stop in here through the summer and fall. They all start to look alike. If he passed this way, it was probably only once. Dowl ate lunch in here a couple times a week. If he'd had a visitor, I'd have met him when they came in here for coffee."

༺ঌৡ༻

"How was it that you were the one to find Snake's body?" Chance asked, as excited as Sandifer about his revelation. They were back to stacking wood.

"I was taking a smoke. Some of the patients had a less than healthy attitude about open flames, so we had to smoke out on the grounds. That particular night I had a joint with me. Like I said, that job could be brutal. Anyway, I liked to walk out to the Mound because it was at the back of the property, away from most of the buildings. Some people didn't like to go back there because of the sulfur smell.

"Besides sulfur, that thermal water is filled with iron and magnesia salts. Makes these far-out colors on the rocks—metallic blues, and greens, and yellows. Anyway, it was nearly midnight, and that old Montana moon was bright. I thought I'd check it out. That's when I saw something odd on the side of the Mound."

"Nobody had missed him?" Chance said, wondering why no one had reported anything unusual.

"He had missed the first bed check," Sandifer continued, "but, by the time staff had figured that out, they were making excuses. Snake could be dark and brooding. We thought he was off pouting in some stairwell somewhere, that kind of thing. Course, they had him stoked up on so much Thorazine, I'm surprised he could lift his fork. We figured he couldn't be far, and he wasn't."

"What happened after you found the body?"

"After all hell broke loose, you mean? Anaconda cops showed up. Took him to the infirmary, but he was already dead. Next day they put this kid they thought did it in isolation. A nice kid, good with a paintbrush, but he'd all but fried his brains on LSD by the time he got to us. Grainger called him Stick. Couple days after that, he was moved to the locked ward."

"He wasn't taken into Anaconda to the jail?" Chance asked.

"Don't think so," Sandifer said. "But that wasn't so unusual. We'd have blow ups at the hospital on a regular basis, nothing as serious, mind you. But whenever the cops were called in, they didn't take anybody into custody. They didn't want to be responsible for some nut case in their jail. The Chief of Police back then was happy to defer to the experts, and they were at the hospital."

Sandifer was confirming what J.D. Firestone had said, but Chance made a mental note to check it out with Rollie Solheim. "Then no arraignment either?"

"Beats me. Sometimes we'd have hearings right there on the premises. But I never got asked to appear at one, if that's what you're wondering."

"No one wanted you to talk about finding the body? That seem odd to you?"

Sandifer shrugged, sat on the truck tailgate, and then said, "I gave the cops a statement that night. That's all. You gotta remember, this was thirty-plus years ago. Things were different then, no CSI and all. We had over a thousand patients, a lot of them with minimal diagnoses, but all of them with the stigma of the place. And often their families didn't want anything to do with them. Course, Dowl and Snake didn't have much family that I ever saw. Maybe if they had, things would have turned out different."

So what was up with this kid who ended up dead?"

"I had only worked there about three months," Sandifer continued without needing any more probing, "when Snake—Ethan Grainger was his given name—bought it. Had a cobra tattooed on his arm." Sandifer drew a squiggle with his little finger on the underside of his forearm. "He's the one that caused all the trouble."

Two guys get into a fight, hardly an unusual scenario Chance had to admit, but one ends up dead, now that was something different. Chance wondered how something like that could have happened within the confines of a hospital where kids were being medicated and closely supervised. "You ever hear what they fought about?"

"Hear about it? Seems like it was all we talked about for weeks afterward."

Sandifer's version of the story synced with what Charlotte Haggis had told Mesa. Snake was the mean one with the temper. He had been abused and neglected as a kid. It was all in his file; he nearly killed his own father once he was big enough to fight back.

"Even though he was a small, wiry kid," Sandifer continued, "everybody was scared of him except for the two girls and Stick. And for some reason, Snake took Stick under his wing so the other patients didn't pick on him. He was a gentle kid and laughed at Snake's jokes."

"Seems strange that Stick would have turned on Snake," Chance said.

"But that's what the official word was. Stick pummeled him and then pushed him off the gazebo. Snake fell down the side and cracked through the crust of the Mound with his head. Supposedly, his neck was practically broken, not to mention he was half scalded."

"Man, that is bleak."

Chance couldn't see the sense of it. But then they were in a mental institution where sense tended to be in limited supply. "You ever see anything about their diagnosis that might suggest that kind of violence?" Chance asked.

"Couldn't swear to it after all this time, but when we didn't have anything better to do, the head nurse would make us read the patients' case files. As I recall, both of them were diagnosed schizophrenics. But back then, that was the general diagnosis for most of the adolescents, no matter what kind of craziness they were into. Stick tried to pickle his demons in alcohol and acid. But, as far as I can remember, all his assaults were self-directed."

Chance wondered how those habits might have played out over the last thirty years. Jessup could have made a lot of enemies who might have wanted him dead once he was back on the streets. Accidental death in a trailer fire was looking more and more doubtful.

It was clear that Gladdie had taken good care of Dowl. One day when Dowl sat at the counter eating some stew, she got to thinking he looked cold, and asked him how long was this roofing job going to take him. He said not long and that he thought he would move on to the cafeteria next. She told him she was worried about how he was doing in that truck of his. He told her not to fret, that he'd bought a propane heater and had moved into the smoke house, which is small enough to stay warm.

"That's when we realized he hadn't been hired by anybody," she said. He had come back to the Home because it meant something to him. "I guess he felt safe there."

Mesa had begun to take notes as Gladdie filled in much about the part of Dowl's life that Vivian had never known. "Did he ever say anything about what happened to his family and why he ended up in the orphanage?"

"Well, apparently he wasn't an orphan," Gladdie said while pouring herself a cup of coffee. "A lot of those kids weren't. The parents just couldn't take care of their kids. Dowl said once that his father wasn't much count, and his mother ran him off. Don't know what happened to her."

"But he ended up in the home in the years right before it closed?"

"The state emptied the place out in '75. That was the year I moved here."

"Lots of kids hit the road in those years," Mesa said. Her mom used to tell her stories about wishing she had been able to go to Woodstock. Her father had laughed. "You? Hitch to Haight-Ashbury or live on some commune?"

"Maybe in the rest of the country, but I wouldn't think most Montana kids would leave the state," Gladdie said. "Usually kids would get taken in by family unless times were really tough, or there just wasn't anybody else, which sounded like was the case with Dowl."

"So Dowl is living at the Home, doing odd jobs, and another out-of-stater, this time a woman from Arizona, comes along and buys the place." Mesa had done her homework. She knew of the more recent sale of the home. "What happened then?"

"Don't get me wrong. She's nice enough," Gladdie said. "Her father bought a small ranch south of here and when she came to visit she took a liking to the place. I'm sure the state gave her a good deal on it. She has big plans to turn it into some kind of conference center or meditation retreat, some damn thing. The insurance company told her the place wasn't fit to live in the way it was, mold and pigeon shit everywhere, so Dowl couldn't stay. He had to go."

"How did he react to that? Was he upset with the new owner?"

"Not exactly. I mean by then we all knew him. It's true he was kind of a loner but Hazel Menafee and her husband cleared out an old shed they had. He moved in his propane heater, and he was doing okay for a while, but I think he had too much time on his hands. He seemed to have lost his purpose when he couldn't work at the Home. He started making more and more trips up to Butte." Her voice trailed off.

"Apparently he told a friend there that he was going to come into some money, maybe buy a house. He ever mention anything like that to you?

"News to me," she said and began wiping down the counter for the umpteenth time.

Mesa could tell Gladdie was more affected by Jessup's death than she wanted to let on. "Do you know why he was going over to Butte? Did he ever mention knowing anybody over there?"

Gladdie shrugged and let out a disapproving grunt. "Something about that town, people end up in more fixes."

Mesa walked across the street to Dale's Garage, and introduced herself to its owner, who had his head underneath the hood of a maroon and white sedan of indeterminate age that had been primped and polished to the nth degree. "Nice car," she said with a big grin. And she meant it. She couldn't imagine the patience it would take to put that much effort into an automobile.

"Yours?"

Dale nodded and wiped his hand on a rag. "1955 Buick Century, all original. One owner. 72,000 miles.

Stored on blocks in a barn for the last twenty years. Strapped rancher traded it to me for services rendered on a much-in-demand combine with a temperamental fuel system."

Mesa listened while Dale regaled her with the finer details of the classic car before she asked him about Dowl. That changed his mood completely.

"Hell of a note. Just when he was pickin' up a head of steam," Dale said with a shake of his head.

"When was the last time you saw him?" Mesa asked.

"Last Friday morning. Fishing season's comin' on. Showed me how to buy my fishing license online, if you can believe that. He liked to tie his own flies. Had a new one he wanted to try and thought maybe we could cast a few one afternoon next week." Dale shrugged. "I said good, and he left here about an hour later."

"Say where he was headed?"

Dale shook his head. "Got in his truck, waved so long, and headed down 41. That's the last I saw of him."

"You said he was getting up a head of steam?"

"He still owed me a hundred bucks on that truck I sold him. He'd been workin' it off, odd jobs around here. He's real good with motors. But last week he said he'd have the cash for me. That his patience had paid off."

"What did you make of that?" Mesa asked, hoping Dowl might have taken his fishing buddy into his confidence.

"Not a damn thing. I know Dowl had his share of hard knocks. When he first came here, he didn't look good. All thin and kinda scraggly. His thinking was a bit cloudy too but, after a bit, seemed like he sharpened up. Workin' over at the Home seemed to give him a real sense of purpose. Course, he was down after he had to leave. But he got goin' again. He started helpin' me out of a morning. Then in the afternoon, he'd go over to the library and use the Internet. Seemed content for a while."

"He ever talk about friends or his past, anything that might help to explain how he ended up like he did?"

"Nothin' like that. Every once in a while, we'd get to talkin' about something in the paper. He was always goin' on about how poorly the government was run. What people got away with. Course that's nothing new around here. I started seein' less of him as winter came on. I think he must have gotten something goin' in Butte, going back and forth."

"Any idea what or who with? Anybody he could have had a problem with?"

Dale shook his head and got out of the car. "He wasn't like that. Once you got to know him, Dowl was a likeable sort, not the kind to start trouble. I'll miss him."

Chapter 9

"We had a former patient come to the *Messenger* office yesterday hoping to find out more about what happened to Jessup," Chance said. He stacked the logs he had in his arms, and then took out his iPhone. He showed Sandifer a photo of Vivian that Mesa had taken the day before, along with one that had been in the medical records from Dr. Kaiser. "Here's a snap from 1979 and then one taken recently."

Sandifer looked long and hard at the first photo, shook his head, and then looked at the second. "She looks none the worse for wear," he said and handed Chance a couple of logs.

Chance had hoped that since Sandifer had direct knowledge of Grainger's death and Jessup's involvement, he might remember Vivian as well, and that might jog his memory about who else they could talk to. No such luck. But then as Chance was closing out of the photos, one from the newspaper article that Mesa had forwarded to him popped up.

Sandifer, looking over Chance's shoulder, said, "Now her, that's a face I'll never forget. We called her the Red Menace."

"Jeanne Lenin?" Chance said. "You're sure?"

"With a name like that in a mental institution? You make up nicknames just to lighten things up," Sandifer said. "She came to see me, God, it's been about fifteen years ago probably, to make amends, as they say in twelve-step lingo." He chuckled. "She's a perfect example."

"Of what?" Chance said.

"She was the biggest addict in the place, stealing the patients' meds, eventually got canned. Can't say as it broke anybody's heart. She liked to give all the draft-aged guys a hard time. Looking back on it, I can understand. Her brother had been a Marine in Nam. Poor bastard came home in a body bag, and she resented the hell out of the ones of us who didn't serve."

"She still live around here?" Chance wondered aloud.

Sandifer shrugged. "I heard she got religion and started preaching, but you know how that goes, 'saved today, lost tomorrow.'"

Chance made a mental note to check with Irita about the local Evangelical churches. Butte was mostly a Catholic town, but there were a couple of startup evangelicals that tried to serve the transient population, which was large. Irita's sister changed churches habitually, looking for the perfect one. "If she found it, they wouldn't let her belong," Irita had said. Anyway, the sister might be able to help.

"How about the patients in the background?"

Sandifer stared at the photo more closely. "Hard to tell. Somebody doped up on Thorazine starts to have that washed out, hangdog look. Besides, I mostly worked with the guys."

"Can you remember any other background on Stick, any details that might help to explain what happened between him and Snake? Could they have gotten into it over a girl? You know, your typical boy-girl thing? Okay, maybe not typical."

Sandifer laughed and then said, "Now that you mention it, Snake, he used to stroll the grounds with this gal with long dark hair. And another girl, a sweet blonde. Never said much. She and Stick always had their heads together."

"This is her, this is that other girl," Chance said shaking the phone. "Name's Vivian Jobe."

"Seriously?" Sandifer took the phone to look at the photos again. "She was pretty when she was young. Used to remind me of Joni Mitchell." He sighed and then said, "That's what psychotropic drugs will do for ya."

"You say they could walk the grounds freely?" Chance asked, wondering what the grounds of the hospital would have been like.

"Sure. The hospital was surrounded by enough acreage to support a farm with cattle, hay fields, plus they grew their own vegetables. Then there was housing for staff. From the highway, you might think it was a ranch with a cattle barn and a cluster of outbuildings, fair number of trees, and a lake."

Chance had driven past Warm Springs hundreds of times over the years. It was visible from the Interstate that headed west to Missoula, but he never gave any thought to who was there.

"You have to keep in mind that this was back in the day before the state dumped all the mental patients out into the streets," Sandifer said. "The real scary folks were locked up all right, but most of the patients could get ground privileges, if they hadn't had any problems of late. Besides, Snake's girl wasn't a patient."

"Who was she?" Chance asked.

"Her father was one of the staff psychiatrists. One of the Cubans."

"Cubans?" Chance said with a curious expression.

Sandifer smiled in return. "Yeah, that's what we all said. Once the revolution came, Castro scared off a lot of the professionals who escaped to Miami. They expected the shooting to be over quick so they could go back to their middle class lives. But that never happened.

"State-run health care being what it was, low salaries, and less than ideal working conditions, English as a second language wasn't a deficit. A lot of the medical people ended up with state jobs. Some even made it out West."

"Do you know this young woman's name?" Chance said. He had never run across anybody in Montana from Cuba, at least that he knew of. It was a long shot but hey, maybe she could help shed light on what had happened.

Sandifer shook his head. "The girl's father was Dr. Xavier-Larraz. He was a real taskmaster. Signed everything with his initials, XL. We called him Extra Large. You had to run to keep up with him, but he was a decent doc."

"How do you mean?" Chance asked.

"God, we gossiped about the Cubans all the time. You know, somebody to lean on. It got around that the other Cubans snubbed Xavier-Larraz because his family back in Havana was in the gambling business, the Mafia even. Kind of implied he was riffraff. Every once in a while, he'd come into the cafeteria and eat lunch with the orderlies. I had the feeling he was definitely an outsider, and kind of lonely."

"What about the girl's mother? Wasn't she around?"

"Not that I ever saw."

"Did he do a good job? I mean, could he still be around?" If he was, he might be an ideal source of information.

Sandifer shrugged. "You got to wonder what the administrators were thinking when they hired a bunch of Cuban shrinks. At least XL's English was reasonable. Every once in a while, he'd come looking for me to translate something one of his patients had said in a session. Seemed like he was trying to do more than just medicate everybody."

Mesa pulled up alongside an old timber garage converted into a cabin, square-shaped with an addition to the back. Gladdie had called Hazel who said Mesa could have a look-see at the place Dowl had rented. Hazel was shopping in Bozeman but said the front door was unlocked as they had lost the key years ago, and Dowl had felt no need to buy a new lock. There was no sign of the '73 Chevy pickup Dale had described. Mesa figured it must be in Butte. She texted Chance to be on the lookout for it and to pass the info onto the Sheriff's office.

She walked into the sparsely furnished house, careful not to disturb anything. Though it could hardly be called much beyond a cabin, the space allowed for three rooms—a living room/ kitchen with a small bedroom and bathroom. A narrow back porch was stacked with cordwood for the stove inside that smelled of ash long ago gone cold.

"Lookee here," Mesa said aloud once she closed the front door. On the wall to the left, someone had rigged up a slab of half-inch plywood on top of a couple of sawhorses for a makeshift table. She studied the collage of photos and notes on the tabletop.

In the middle was a newspaper photograph of an elegant woman dressed in an old world riding get-up, an A-line skirt with a single pleat, a bolero jacket and a flat gaucho hat, that reminded her of women on horseback she'd seen in Spain in the processions before a bull fight. The photo's caption had been cut away.

Next to that picture were several clippings from the *Standard*. The first was about an outbreak of swamp fever in southwest Montana. The second, a follow-up, described the owner of the horses on one ranch as devastated to learn she might have to have her horses put down. Instead, they had elected to quarantine them. Mesa thought about a conversation she'd had with Alexis on St. Paddy's Day about the delay in shipping her mustangs because of a recent breakout of some disease.

Next to the news clippings was a Xerox copy of a page from some sort of medical directory, with each entry of eight or ten lines about various doctors and their specialties.

Could Dowl have been looking for a new shrink on his own? How could that be? How would he even pay for a private doctor? As she skimmed through the profiles on the page, she could see these were distinguished medical people, Yale, Harvard, Georgetown, with specialties like addictions, eating disorders and social anxiety, schizophrenia and forensic psychiatry.

Finally, there was a copy of the Dillon *Tribune* folded to the classified section. Several jobs for ranch hands were circled. Mesa couldn't make sense of it. Was Dowl having fantasies of becoming a ranch hand?

God knows, ranch hands had plenty of work to choose from. Country songs aside, there was nothing romantic about ranching. The hours were long, in all kinds of weather conditions, working with stock whose needs did not correspond to a nine-to-five schedule. She'd met plenty of cowboys who weren't that big, but they were wiry and strong and weren't on mind-numbing pharmaceuticals. Was that why Dowl was tapering off his meds? So that he could get back in the saddle again?

As she photographed each of the items on the table with her cell phone, she wondered what Jessup had been planning. It had not occurred to her that he had an organized mind, or that he was living a life with plans, places to go, people to see. It hadn't occurred to her to ask Vivian. It had seemed too personal, but that was when she thought Dowl was alive and that he and Vivian might become friends again. What did it matter now?

She was familiar enough with the genius madman stereotype, like Hannibal Lecter, but she had assumed that Dowl was below average in intelligence. After all, he had been hanging out with the likes of Henry Gillis. But then again, Vivian was a bright woman. Why couldn't he have been just as clever?

In the closet-sized bathroom, she checked the medicine cabinet but found nothing but a blue and black plastic razor and two prescription containers, complete with cotton jammed in them. Both were dated from the past year and neither container looked liked it had any pills missing.

The medication was alprazolam, brand name Xanax. She knew from a feature they'd done in the River City *Current*, before she had left Cincinnati the previous year, that the blue pills were called footballs on the street, and sold for a couple of dollars a pop. Maybe more in Montana, distribution requiring considerably more effort. A bona fide party drug, hipsters used them to enhance their alcohol buzz, or when they were coming down hard from Ecstasy.

It looked as though Jessup had stopped taking the medication more than six months ago. Yet, he hadn't sold them on the street.

She moved to the bedroom, her steps echoing off the walls. The room was devoid of much of anything personal. A single bed, half-made with a threadbare quilt, sagged next to a nightstand. A white coffee mug sat on the table top, coffee stain at the bottom. An out-of-date copy of *Montana – the Magazine of Western History*, with a free coffee coupon from a café in Dillon that bookmarked an article about the Children's Home, lay nearby.

The article focused on the grown children of the Home, the ones who had returned for reunions, and their stories about how much the Home had meant to them. Photos of one-time residents showed smiling, seemingly well-adjusted adults with spouses, happy to be reunited with old friends. She wondered if Jessup recognized any of the faces, whether he'd tried to get in touch, or whether he felt left out. Clearly, his adjustment, once he left the Home, had not gone as well.

The bed wheezed as Mesa sat down to collect her thoughts. She took a minute to fill her senses with the surroundings so that she could write about it all later. On the windowsill was a well-worn hardback of *The Count of Monte Cristo*. Its spine cracked, the book fell open to that place when she picked it up. Inside, written on a half-folded sheet of paper were a dozen or so quotes, presumably from Dumas. The first one she recognized. "All human wisdom is contained in these two words— Wait and Hope."

"Dowling Jessup, what were you up to?" Mesa muttered and put the book back on the window ledge.

The cabin's walls creaked from a gust of wind. She could see the darkening sky out the window and knew that she should pay attention to the weather and head back to Butte. But she was finding it hard to move.

The meager remnants of Dowling Jessup's life depressed her. She thought about the tone in Dale's voice when he talked about Dowl and the look on Gladdie's face. The place he had been trying to make for himself in Twin Bridges had all come to nothing, or at least nothing good. She wondered what direction Dowl's life had gone in. Mesa didn't relish having to make sense of it with Vivian. Finally, she headed for the door, reminding herself she needed to be able to write about Jessup's life without getting sentimental.

Chance still couldn't understand why Vivian had said nothing to anyone at the hospital if Jessup had meant so much to her. "Do you remember how Vivian reacted after all this happened?"

"I recall Dr. Xavier-Larraz being real worried about her," Sandifer said. "He had a round-the-clock watch put on her after they locked Jessup away. I remember because I scored some overtime helping out; they were still short-staffed in that ward. Seems like she was discharged a couple weeks later. Never saw much of XL's daughter after that either. Guess her old man figured the patients weren't as safe as he thought."

If Jessup wasn't guilty, being falsely accused of his friend's death must have been traumatic. That is, if his reactions weren't medicated away. "You see much of Dowl during the rest of the time you worked at Warm Springs?"

Sandifer shook his head again. "They transferred him to the forensics unit. I'd go over there occasionally, but there wasn't much need for occupational therapy with that bunch. That's where the potholder story comes from—handicrafts with an edge. Stick was still there when I left. They reorganized the place a couple of years later."

"Any idea where he might have gone from there? Any other friends he might have connected with once he finally got out?" Chance wondered if he might be able to find a trail that J.D. Firestone didn't know anything about.

"Most of the patients ended up in group homes or on the street, half of 'em homeless. The hospital's forensics unit's still there."

Chance grimaced. If Dowl was as sensitive as Vivian had implied, how had he endured the harshness of his confinement with other violent offenders? And, if he was innocent, his resentment about what had happened must have festered.

"I read in the papers that Dr. Larraz put up a real fuss to limit the number of patients who were released on their own," Sandifer said. "I guess nobody would listen, him being Cuban and all. Funny what passes for progress in mental health care. Sure seemed like one step forward and two steps back to me."

Sandifer offered Chance another beer but he declined. Day drinking would have to wait until he was retired too.

Reaching for another Moose Drool, Sandifer said, "You mentioned that Stick's girl showed up at the *Mess* office. How's she doing? Maybe she knows what happened to him."

For the third time in fewer days, Chance realized someone else, who wouldn't want to hear it, was learning that Dowling Jessup was dead. "Maybe I'll have that beer after all."

❧

The Sweetgrass Café reminded Mesa of the lobby of an old hotel. She had decided to take a break at the café whose card she had found in Dowl's cabin. Driving out of Twin Bridges on the way to Dillon, she had stopped at the Children's Home. A chain link fence closed off the road that led into the grounds, but Mesa could see the slowly deteriorating buildings of the once-bustling facility that had meant so much to Dowl. She tried to imagine what it had been like when he had lived there, when he'd apparently enjoyed a stable life for a time. Maybe the last place he ever felt safe.

Flipping through the photos on her phone, she looked at the one of the Montana Children's Center sign—substantial, made of wood and stone, but starting to look dilapidated, like the system of social services to which it had belonged. Yep, she had definitely needed a pick-me-up.

Mesa sat on a shabby chic sofa next to the storefront window, waiting for her latte and wondering what had brought Dowling Jessup here. Well-used, upholstered chairs in reds and oranges, low coffee tables covered with dog-eared magazines and free wifi encouraged customers to stick around. Jessup seemed more like a guy who would have hung out at Gamers'. He'd want a fat mug of the Butte café's hot drip coffee, legendary because you could walk behind the counter and refill your own cup if you wanted.

She imagined this place was popular in the morning and at lunch with the college crowd, but it was already four o'clock and on a Tuesday. Dillon's streets were mostly empty. She was able to snag the last blueberry muffin under a glass dome and sat enjoying the tart but sweet berries. Flipping through the photos on her iPhone to find the picture of Dowling Jessup, she looked up to see the brightly colored sign across the street—the Galleria Arroyo.

Dillon had a modest arts community, fostered by the art museum at the local College of Western Montana. It was the Spanish sounding name that made her wonder.

She took her latte up to the cashier and asked to have it transferred to a 'to go' cup. "I work for *the Mining City Messenger* and I'm following a story about a man who was killed in Butte over the weekend. I'm trying to trace his movements, and I hear he was in Dillon. I was wondering if he came in here." She showed the young woman a photo of Adrienne's sketch of Stick.

"It does kinda look like a guy who was in here last week. I remember because he didn't know what a latte was. He just wanted a 'regular cup of coffee.'" She made quotation marks in the air. "Yeah, I think that was him."

"Was he with anybody? Maybe meet somebody here?"

The clerk shrugged and handed Mesa her coffee. "Couldn't say."

"How about that gallery across the street, do you know who owns it?" she asked while the young woman looked for a lid for the cup.

"It's a Mexican woman, I think. I don't know her name. I only started working here this semester. She comes in here occasionally. She's wears beautiful jewelry."

Mesa left the café and walked over to the storefront, pulling the collar of her quilted vest close to her neck as she went. She had to shield her eyes from the intermittent sun to see inside the gallery's window.

Paintings, sketches, and photographs were arranged in small groups along two walls and depicted what Mesa suspected was some South American revolution. Black and white portraits of street urchins, grandmothers sitting on porches of dilapidated buildings, and brunette women with high cheekbones and frayed dresses were mounted in high-quality frames. Watercolors of marinas and rural landscapes were dramatically rendered with a bright palette. But she could have been looking at the walls of someone's den. That's how personal the collection seemed, someone's individual taste displayed as if the gallery were that person's home.

In one corner of the storefront, an assortment of red and blue candles, and small bones and seashells were arranged along with several crosses and a collection of religious statues. An interpretative sign read Santeria artifacts. Mesa googled the term on her cell phone where she found "Santeria—a blend of Afro-Caribbean and Catholic rituals used in divination and healing practices." This part of the gallery seemed out of place, more of an exhibit, even an altar, than anything for sale.

Still, no cheap imitations or trendy, overpriced items like chia plants were on exhibit here. The gallery was aimed at customers who could afford to pay for what appeared to be the original work of gifted artists.

Once inside the gallery, Mesa saw a woman at the glass counter wrapping a framed photograph. She was turned toward a side wall so Mesa could not see her face. But she had the same dark hair and square shoulders of the woman in the news photo that she had seen in Dowl's cabin.

Mesa slowly wandered from one table to another, pausing to admire the paintings on the wall, reading the descriptions of various sculptures. She was contemplating what she would say to the woman when the old-fashioned bell that hung on the door jingled and a sixty-something rancher clomped toward the counter.

"Let me have a half dozen of those Havanas," he said in a gruff voice to the woman who had come to meet him by the register.

Mesa stopped in her tracks. It was definitely the woman in the photograph that Dowling had pinned to the table in his cabin.

The prominent forehead and nose, the jet-black hair pulled tightly back and held in place with a purple and gold scarf called up an image of a proud Latina. She nodded quietly and went about the business of opening a sliding door of a humidor next to the counter. She removed the cigars and wrapped them carefully in thin tissue paper. She placed them in front of the crusty cowboy who plopped a fifty-dollar bill on the counter.

The woman opened the register and silently returned the change to the counter, avoiding the customer's outstretched palm. The customer picked up his change and left. The woman immediately began polishing the counter with a dust rag as if the previous transaction had left handprints.

Could this woman be Xavier-Larraz's daughter? Mesa saw an easel of business cards on the counter and picked one up. It read "Galleria Arroyo – Afro-Cuban Artifacts, Mariposa Arroyo – Purveyor of Fine Art and Gifts." The name, Spanish for butterfly, certainly fit. The woman was folding the dust rag with the precision of a flag bearer. She had yet to utter a word. Mesa introduced herself and then said, "You're the owner?"

Mariposa nodded.

"Your gallery is filled with some unique art for this part of the country," Mesa said, hoping to establish a little rapport.

Mariposa nodded acceptance but said nothing.

"Actually, I stopped by because I'm working on a story about the death of a man called Dowling Jessup. I'm hoping you can help me." Mesa produced her phone with the sketch. "We know he was in Dillon last week. Perhaps you saw him?"

Mariposa leaned over the counter tentatively to look at the photo and then stepped back as if she'd seen a rabid dog.

"The barista in the café across the street told me she saw him come into this gallery." Okay, that was a bit of an exaggeration, but that probably was what happened. "Did you talk to him?"

Mesa sensed that the woman recognized Dowling, maybe not by name, but she had seen the face. "You do recognize him. When was he here?"

Mariposa seemed paralyzed, clutching the dust rag to her chest, her gaze focused on the photo. Maybe the direct approach was a mistake, Mesa thought.

Lowering the tone in her voice, Mesa said, "Forgive me, I don't mean to suggest for a second that you had anything to do with his death. I'm just hoping to get some background information. The woman in the Sweetgrass Café says she saw him there last week."

"He's dead?" Mariposa said in a whisper.

"Killed in a fire in Butte this past weekend." Mesa paused, trying to decide whether to go for the jugular. Then she said, "He did visit your gallery, didn't he. What did he say?"

She nodded, and spoke haltingly. "He said didn't I remember him. That I had known him a long time ago. He said we had some catching up to do, but I had no idea what he was talking about. Then some customers came into the gallery. He said he'd be back and he left."

"And did he come back?"

Mariposa shook her head and looked at the counter again. Mesa suddenly felt like she was in junior high again in the principal's office, only she was the principal. There was something about Mariposa's demeanor that seemed stunted. She looked like a competent adult but she acted like a stuttering adolescent.

"Please, if you don't mind, I am closing the gallery early. A storm warning has been issued."

Mesa left her card and encouraged Mariposa to call if she thought of anything that might help, and then she returned to her car. She sat thinking about their conversation when a white SUV pulled into a parking spot in front of the gallery. A tall, older man, dressed in tailored slacks and a tweed jacket, got out of the car. He ran his hand over his thinning gray-black hair, smoothing it into place as the wind had picked up, and went into the gallery.

Moments later, Mariposa stepped out with the man. Together, the pair hurried back to the SUV and drove away.

Mesa started her car, wondering if she had just seen Señor Larraz picking up his daughter. Were they the reason that Dowling Jessup had come to the Sweetgrass Café? Had he hoped to reconnect with the people he had known at Warm Springs three decades before?

Maybe she had found several pieces of the puzzle of Dowling Jessup after all. But she only had a vague idea what the whole picture should look like. Why, after all this time, had he decided to look Larraz and Mariposa up, and what did he mean by "catching up"? That was a question she needed to ask them. Beyond that, she wasn't sure what to do next. She was left with only the faint smell of cigar smoke, and the coming storm.

Driving out of Dillon, she was still stuck on the big question of whether there was any connection between two deaths so many years apart. Maybe Jessup was simply the victim of random violence, or maybe he had died at the hands of someone he had pissed off much more recently.

If Snake and Jessup's deaths were connected, Mesa hoped to recreate as accurate a picture as possible to support that theory. Jessup's murder could be a window to the past, a wormhole through which they could climb to find out what had happened to Snake.

Pulling onto the Interstate with the snow falling steadily, her thoughts drifted back to the loneliness and isolation of Jessup's cabin in Twin Bridges. What irony that Jessup's death might be the key to establishing his innocence. After all these years, someone was finally coming to his rescue.

Corny as it might sound, she felt a sense of duty to clear Jessup's name, to set the record straight. Her obligation was to Jessup, Vivian, and even Snake, not to mention Henry, to sort out the truth of their stories in a way they couldn't for themselves.

Chapter 10

By the time Chance left the Sandifers' place, a persistent growl from his stomach could not be ignored. He decided to head to the gallery where he and Adrienne were meeting Mesa after work. He prayed there would be something in the fridge besides celery stalks and hummus.

He got into his pickup and dialed Nick Philippoussis' number. The assistant coroner had promised to track down any paperwork he could find about Ethan Grainger's death. "Jesus, Chance," he had said, "You're asking about a dead guy from thirty plus years ago."

When Nick answered the phone, Chance could hear the ambulance siren in the background. "You want me to call you back?" Chance shouted.

"Sorry. I forgot I had that thing on," Nick said and the siren fell silent. "I can talk. I'm just on my way back to the garage from an emergency room run."

"Did you find anything about the Grainger death?"

"Like I figured, the records are all screwed up. Anaconda and Deer Lodge County consolidated back in '76 just like Butte-Silver Bow did. Back then, the county coroner was elected but the city job was a regular hire. So they combined the two offices when the term ran out."

"And, so?" Chance said, patience never his strong suit, and Nick loved to talk.

"The city coroner was appointed, so the Anaconda Chief of Police had the coroner's duties added to his office, like county sheriffs have done. In my humble opinion, it is a complete conflict of interest. But, whatever. He took the title, maybe even did a little work, but the paperwork apparently slipped his mind and sat in a big pile."

"What do you mean about conflict of interest?" Petty squabbles, jealousies, and jurisdictional issues might limit cooperation in large urban bureaucracies, but that was rare in a sparsely populated state like Montana. Law enforcement types, no matter which agency they worked for, were more often than not hunting and fishing buddies. Everybody knew everybody and wanted to get along.

"Like here, we work right alongside law enforcement but, as coroners, we focus on the body and cause of death. We decide if a homicide has been committed, and then law enforcement investigates. If the same person is doing both jobs, you're putting a lot of power into one set of hands. Enough pressure mixed with a little uncertainty and a homicide or a suicide could become an accident, and no investigation ever happens. Or vice versa, and all kinda people get rounded up."

Chance thought about this possibility. Could this have been the case with Grainger's death? Maybe the situation wasn't so cut and dried, and Dowl being put in the forensics ward kept him from causing more harm without having to go to trial. "You think that could have happened in this case?"

"No idea. I did talk to one of the county maintenance guys who said they have boxes of county records stored in the old police station if I wanna have a look-see. I said no thanks."

Chance sighed. Nick already had three jobs. Besides being the assistant coroner in Butte-Silver Bow, he drove ambulance and worked at Duggan Dolan Funeral Home. It wasn't like he had any extra time to drive seventeen miles to Anaconda to dig around in some old files but it couldn't hurt to ask. "C'mon, Nick, you know you'll have a lot more luck with them than I will."

"You're such a whiner. Turns out, I've got a call into Jackie Mondale's dad. He's the day sergeant at the police department over there. We might have better luck finding a police report. And I mean might. They moved to a new police building eight years ago, and left their old records in boxes too."

Chance smiled and made a mental note to buy Nick a bottle of Neversweat bourbon from Headframes, the new distillery in town. "What about the fire marshall on the trailer fire? They really calling it arson? Could have been accidental, right?" Chance had been curious from the get-go about the fire's timing. Henry saw the mystery man walking toward the trailer with Stick Saturday evening, but the actual fire had not broken out until almost twelve hours later on Sunday morning.

"He hasn't filed a report yet. What I heard was lots of talk about alcohol, cigarettes, and smoldering underneath the trailer, which eventually broke into flames when the wind picked up. Either way the smoke and the gases were gonna kill the guy sooner or later.

❧

"Anybody home?" Mesa called. She shook the snow off her vest and took off her hiking boots. A log fire crackled in the giant stone fireplace across the living room so she knew that somebody was close by, even if Alexis wasn't around.

After the Sweetgrass Café and seeing Larraz and his daughter, Mesa had been anxious to return to Butte and talk to Chance to see what, if anything, he might have learned from Mr. Sandifer. She had put the hammer down and headed for home, sensing the storm would build quickly.

She had done her civic duty and called Sheriff Solheim's office to report what she had found in Dowl's cabin and the particulars of the 1973 Chevy 383 pick-up Dale had sold him, white with a red stripe. But the sheriff, along with most of the police department, was already dealing with weather-related fender benders. She left him a detailed phone message.

The heavy spring snow was relentless and soon semis were roaring past her, each one creating a mini white-out. The SUV provided plenty of traction but she had slowed to a crawl, the visibility was so bad. At this rate, she wouldn't be in Butte before midnight.

She had tried to call Chance to say she would be late joining him and Adrienne for a drink. But the cell service had become spotty.

Then she saw the aging iron bridge over the Big Hole River near Glen, and the decision was made. "Screw this," she had said out loud, and inched off the exit onto the Frontage Road toward Alexis' new digs.

Though she had not actually visited Alexis' ranch since her father had purchased it six months before, the Hollister place was well known. The hundred-year-old cattle operation had been in the family for four generations before it was finally sold off. When no one in the family wanted to stay on and work the ranch, the last generation had sold it in parcels over a five-year period. Alexis' family had bought ten sections, including prime bottom irrigated land in three locations. Mesa'd been thankful to finally see a light in a window through the blinding snow.

"Alexis, are you here?" Mesa called again. The home place sat next to the Big Hole with the bridge a familiar landmark. The central part of the house was probably a hundred years old too, with numerous additions—a wing here, a wing there. Open wood beams, gray river stone halfway up the walls, mounted antlers, Red Indian blankets thrown over furniture. Yep, Alexis had herself a bona fide hobby ranch.

The glow of the fire drew Mesa toward it like a magnet. She was happy to warm herself, wondering with a twinge of guilt if maybe everyone was out in the storm, rounding up cattle. Newborn calves would be particularly vulnerable if they were separated from their mommas in this weather.

She was thawed enough to consider going in search of something warm to drink when she heard a rustling toward the back of the house. Alexis appeared in a doorway, barefoot, with half-done-up blue jeans and a tee shirt, topped off with a towel wrapped around her head. She would look good in rags, Mesa thought.

"Hey, it's you—an orphan in a storm," Alexis said. "Dang, I thought it might be somebody fun."

"Thanks a lot," Mesa said, taking no offense. This was Alexis' modus operandi. If she said anything polite, it was usually because she wanted something.

Alexis came over and offered a substantial hug. "Seriously, glad you've finally showed up to see the place. Like it?"

Mesa looked around the room while Alexis cleared away newspapers, clothes, boots, and dirty dishes that littered the fireside furniture. "Sorry about that," she said. "Housekeeper only comes twice a week."

Mesa smiled and shook her head. Alexis was a legendary slob. One year in college, she had actually paid one of their classmates to double up with another student so she could use the additional dorm room for a walk-in closet. "What's up?" Alexis asked.

"Duh," Mesa said with her hands thrown in the air. "I'm stranded by the storm and need a place to crash. Seriously, I'm too tired to fight the semis any more. I'll head home in the a.m."

"Stay as long as you like, doll," Alexis said. "Now, belly up to the bar." And she walked over to a walnut hutch that covered half the wall. "What may we offer you?"

"I could use a cup of coffee," Mesa said rubbing her hands together.

Alexis laughed. "Seriously? We're snowbound. Where's the brandy?" she said and dived into a mélange of liquor bottles on the hutch. "I've been out seeing to the horses for the last couple of hours. I had to take a hot shower to defrost."

Alexis might be filthy rich but she didn't mind a bit of hard work if it had to do with animals. She hunted around for a couple of snifters, filled them half full, and gave one to Mesa.

They stood warming their backsides in front of the fire and watched the steady fall of snow out the wide front window. "I haven't seen a storm like this since the last time I was skiing in Garmisch." She winked at Mesa and then said, "Managed to find safe haven with a Swiss skier that time, Olympic hopeful."

Mesa sipped the brandy, rich and smooth, spreading warmth through her whole body—Hennessy's probably. Alexis never skimped on the booze.

"That blizzard went on for three days," Alexis mused. "Luckily, the Swiss Miss was quite fit and extremely imaginative," she added with a wide grin.

Mesa was used to these stories. She was never quite sure how much was true, or meant simply to shock. The skier could just as easily been male.

"Hope you're not sharing those tasty little anecdotes with the locals," Mesa said. "This is Beaverhead County, not the Upper West Side. A gathering of socially-conscious, progressively-minded liberals around here could meet in a broom closet."

Alexis walked over to her friend, slipped her arm into Mesa's, and steered her toward the kitchen. "From what I hear, every ranch family worth its salt has a few eccentric members with bad habits. I could fit right in."

"Speaking of ranch families," Mesa said. "Remember you said that you had neighbors around here that had horses with swamp fever?"

Alexis paused in front of the opened refrigerator and handed a triangle of Brie to Mesa along with a jar of artichokes. "See, that's just what I was talking about. The Xavier-Larraz's remind me of *The Addams Family*." She opened a plastic container of black olives, smelled them, and put them back in the fridge. "They hole up south of here on a big old place near the Beaverhead across from Morton Ditch."

"What's the family's name?" Mesa said, wanting to be sure she had it right, and wondering where Arroyo (the name Mariposa used) fit in.

"It's one of those old world, double-barrelled names. You know, Spanish, where they include the father's and the mother's surnames. Xavier-Larraz."

"Is he the one with the horses?"

"I suspect he owns them, but it's his wife who is so torn up about it all. I can see why. I'd be devastated too. They're Andalusians."

"Xavier-Larraz is from Spain?" Mesa said, mildly surprised that a Spaniard would end up working in Warm Springs, assuming she had the right name, which surely she did. The number of psychiatrists in Montana was a short enough list that could be checked.

"I think they're from Cuba. At least the mother is. The Andalusians, now they're from Spain. They're really rare in this part of the country. You couldn't even import them legally until the sixties. You see them more often back East in dressage competition. I guess wifey had her heart set on raising them out here, and now, if she gets to keep them at all, they'll have to live in quarantine, if that's even possible."

"Have you met the Xavier-Larrazes?"

"When I first moved in, I drove down to introduce myself. Actually, I wanted to see the horses and where they were set up. They're hard as hell to have a conversation with, if you want to know the truth. He's older and doesn't seem to do much beyond smoke expensive cigars and drive into Dillon on occasion. I guess he used to work at the college."

That was Alexis for you, far more interested in the horses than the people.

"Mariposa, that's the wife, splits her time between the horses and a little art gallery she's opened in Dillon. Doesn't even drive a car if you can believe that. Somebody chauffeurs her everywhere."

"Mariposa is his wife's name? I thought she was the daughter," Mesa said, recalling what Vivian had said about visiting the psychiatrist's home and meeting his daughter.

"Her mother lives at the ranch too. Her name's Domenica Arroyo. She's the most normal one, if you ask me. She has her own little house, and is a go-getter in an old-fashioned kind of way. She owns that roadhouse down by Apex, the Hacienda Supper Club. Been there a couple of times. Not bad. We should check it out some time."

Mesa had blown by the club on her way to Alexis. The place had been remodeled and looked far more upscale than most roadhouses in Montana.

A sign on a couple of tall black metal poles in the substantial parking lot had said, "Open this weekend. Special show." Consistent with her on again, off again attitude, Mesa had made a mental note to call Shane to see what he might know about the place, and if she could entice him to accompany her to the show.

She had driven by the location many times. A couple of businesses had failed to make a go of it there, including a restaurant with a bar and casino, and even a strip club, which had been done in by embezzlement. Strip clubs in rural Montana were few and far between. With such a small population, folks were too likely to meet someone they knew there, and wished they didn't.

"I don't think she and the señor see eye to eye on much," Alexis continued. "Mariposa seems to go back and forth between the two houses."

"Then there's the guy who manages her horses. I'm not sure what his name is. I call him Lurch."

Mesa grimaced.

"Well, not to his face. Knows his horses all right but he's weird. Follows Mariposa around like a puppy."

Mesa was snuggled deep under layers of blankets in one of the many spare bedrooms when her cell phone woke her. She patted around the blankets looking for it.

As usual, it had been impossible to convince Alexis of the hangovers they would succumb to if they continued doing Liquid Bourbon Balls. A shot of Maker's Mark chased by a tablespoon of chocolate syrup was a recipe for disaster passed on to them by a Damascus classmate from Kentucky. At least they'd passed out fairly early.

Throwing off all the covers, she got out of bed and found the phone in the back pocket of her jeans. She jumped back under the covers and answered just in time.

"I was about to hang up," Shane said. "What are you up to?"

It was past eleven, a time when Mesa tended to be at home on a weeknight, not that Shane always called. He was often out and about in Helena, being wined and dined by some lobbyist. She explained the storm and holing up at Alexis'. She didn't mention the Bourbon Balls as Shane already had a less than positive attitude about Alexis' drinking since the dust-up at the Irish Times. He thought she was trouble with a capital T.

Mesa began telling Shane about meeting Vivian, her friendship with her mother, her search for Jessup and his death; and decrying the state of mental health in Montana.

"There's a bill to bump the funding to put that transitional housing program back on its feet," he told her. "Probably never get out of the Human Services Committee though, at least not while the Tea Partiers have the majority."

Mesa continued her rant and Shane finally interrupted, "Mesa, I'm glad you're concerned, but you know you're preaching to the choir, right?"

Mesa stopped talking. He had that impatient voice that signaled he wanted to change the subject. She licked at a smidgen of chocolate syrup at the corner of her mouth and said, "That's me, getting carried away, I guess."

"I'll be home on Friday," Shane countered. "We can dissect the subject over dinner, if you want. You're not busy, are you?"

When she hung up the phone, she snuggled back under the covers, rerunning that last question in her mind. Yep, it definitely irritated her that he assumed she'd be waiting for him.

Adrienne sipped her wine and tried not to listen to Chance's phone conversation with Mesa. Sitting on the sofa in the loft above her gallery, she enjoyed looking through the tall windows at the falling snow. In fact, she had planned it that way.

She had designed the apartment from scratch like a cake, but with a far more lasting effect. She had visualized not only the room and its furnishings but also the floor plan for the entire apartment, right down to where the fireplace needed to be in order to enjoy the view before her.

She had accounted for everything about this apartment except for the recurring appearance of the attractive, charming man who stood several feet away talking animatedly on the phone. She had not planned for Chance Dawson in any way, shape, or form.

Her solo journey to Montana was meant to be about re-discovering art in her life. No more long hours at a career, that drained her of the energy for the painting that made her whole. She had enough money to live modestly, and time to make the last third of her life more fulfilling. It wasn't that Chance was unwelcome, just unplanned.

"Everything okay?" Adrienne asked as Chance tossed his cell phone on his pilot's jacket and plopped back down onto the sofa next to her.

He nodded. "She's holed up with Alexis Vandemere at her place in Glen. Storm's socked them in. She'll be back tomorrow."

He sounded vaguely uneasy about Mesa, as usual. As younger sisters went, Mesa was a breath of fresh air in Adrienne's opinion. Intelligent, ambitious and most of all, independent, Mesa had qualities not so common in a lot of her generation. She didn't fawn over men, or feel her life needed to revolve around one. She was far more self-assured than Adrienne had been at that age.

Yet Chance seemed overly protective. He often behaved as if he needed to be the net to Mesa's high-wire act.

Adrienne began to massage the muscle just below the nape of his neck that always seemed tight. "You don't like Alexis, do you?"

Chance turned to her and smiled. "She's a little prickly for my taste, but it's not that I dislike her. Alexis parties hard, and her family's got enough money that she doesn't have to think twice about what she does. She did St. Paddy's up in grand style, and Mesa did her best to keep up with her."

"That doesn't make her much different than a lot of people in Butte on St. Paddy's, does it?"

"Maybe not," Chance said and took a swig of his Moose Drool, "but Alexis doesn't have family here. On top of that, I'm betting she's not likely to stick around. I'll be surprised if her fascination with mustangs and that hobby ranch hold her attention for more than a year or two. Ranching is hard work."

"Now, now," Adrienne said, only half teasing. "Do you think I'm a fly-by-night? Open an art gallery, have some good times, and then pull up stakes?"

"Not if I can help it," Chance said, and pulled her wine glass away so he could engulf her in one of his bear hugs.

≪≫

Chance bounded up the stairs carrying an armful of firewood. He hadn't minded going out into the storm as much as he'd minded putting his clothes back on first.

Adrienne, now re-clothed as well, met him at the door and brushed the snow off his head.

She reclaimed her spot in the corner of the sofa, fiddling with her laptop as she settled in. "This is a video I found on YouTube about the latest efforts to help patients who hear voices. It's groundbreaking stuff."

Chance tended the fire, thinking about Mesa's interest in Vivian Jobe. Her connection to his mother might be all well and good, but he was still uneasy about the mental health issue. He sat down next to Adrienne, enjoying the closeness of her body as he listened to a psychologist talk about the challenge of living with voices. "So you think schizophrenics aren't scary crazy?" he asked when the video was over. He was relieved that Adrienne had such a matter of fact attitude about it all.

She shrugged and said, "I don't think that medication and institutionalization is always the answer. People can address their mental health using a multitude of alternatives."

Chance thought about his conversation with Ken Sandifer earlier in the day, wondering what he would think. Chance shook his head, "Sure sounds like this kid who got killed at Warm Springs was surrounded by people who were psycho."

Adrienne shrugged. "That was thirty-plus years ago. I'm not saying that there aren't people who need to be in mental institutions, such as they are. But people can get better, slowly, over time, and in the right circumstances."

"You think a guy like Dowling Jessup could have improved over time?"

Adrienne shrugged. "We've been underfunding mental health programs for years. Being poor, on your own, and living on the street is not what I call the right circumstances."

"Good to know. Mesa says this Vivian Jobe's family has got a sweet setup. Apparently she took the death of Jessup better than Mesa expected."

"You sound a bit surprised," Adrienne said.

Chance nodded again. "I guess so. From what Sandifer told me, it's hard not to think of Dowl Jessup as a violent guy and Vivian Jobe as a timid teenager not exactly grounded in reality."

"Henry seemed to like him," Adrienne said.

"True," Chance said, "and Henry's afraid of his own shadow. Maybe Dowl was able to get better, as you say."

"Tomorrow, Mesa and I are going to try to talk to a couple more of the hospital staff. This doctor that Ken mentioned has a ranch outside Dillon. And I'll try to track down this nurse through one of the evangelical churches."

"I thought you decided to back off working with the paper," Adrienne said. "You seem pretty involved."

Chance knew what Adrienne was getting at. Restoration of Butte's many run down but architecturally significant buildings was his real passion, though the projects tended to come and go with long gaps in between. He did enough regular remodeling to have a steady income, but he had handed the family paper off to Mesa when she had returned to town the previous fall.

Chance stood up to stoke the fire, thinking about the work he hadn't done on the miner's cottage that morning. "Just this one story," he said with a sigh. "I'm mostly doing it for Henry's sake. He did ask me for help, and he sounded so pathetic when I told him Jessup had died. I'd like to help figure out what happened. I mean,

I'm not so sure about the whole schizophrenia thing, but Henry, I understand. He just needs a helping hand now and then."

Adrienne pulled Chance down into her arms and kissed him. "For a strapping big fella, you can be a big sweetie sometimes, you know that?"

"Jeez, don't say that in public," he teased. "I gotta reputation to protect. Tomorrow I'm gonna track down this Jeanne Lenin who was a nurse at the loony bin."

"That name sounds familiar," Adrienne said.

Chance got up and brought her his cell phone photo of Lenin. In the slow months of winter, Adrienne had taken some ad locum work at the hospital and the community health center, when they were short-staffed. Maybe Lenin had somehow finagled herself into a healthcare job again.

"You know that new place up on Main Street," Adrienne sat up and said, "It's a soup kitchen where you can help out in exchange for food. I worked a clinic there one evening and met the woman who runs the place. I do believe that might be who you're looking for."

"Irita, I said I'm on my way," Mesa said.

She listened to Irita's rant over the cell phone while trying to negotiate the winding drive that formed the access to and from Alexis' ranch. It was nearly eight a.m. and the sun was high enough in the sky that the sparkling snow created a glare that made visibility hazardous.

"Why didn't you tell me you didn't get back into town?" Irita fussed. "You could have called me at home, you know."

Irita had arranged three interviews back to back, starting at ten a.m. She was going to be damn sure Mesa didn't miss them.

Irita sounded hurt. She was so conscientious that, at times, Mesa felt like she took advantage. She had been out of the office all day yesterday and had not even called in. She'd gotten so carried away hunting down details about Jessup and Vivian's story that she'd neglected her job as editor.

"I'm sorry," Mesa said with a sigh. "You're a trooper, Irita. The interstate's clear. I should be in the office well before ten. I'll just stop off at home, change clothes, and then I'll be there." And then, almost as an afterthought, she asked, "So, is Phade there?"

"Yep, he's in his cubicle as usual, smelling like Cannabis Connections."

"Let him know gently that I'd like a chat and keep him away from Cinch."

Predictably, the spring snow had ended well before morning. The steady flow of semis headed from Salt Lake to points north and west had cleared the highway, and meant the drive would be uneventful. She had hoped to talk Alexis into making a trip to the Larraz place, Rancho Esmeralda, as it was now known, but the weather meant Alexis had calves that needed attention.

Mesa sped home, her thoughts turning to what Chance had told her on the phone the night before, comparing notes in her head. Sandifer confirmed what Charlotte Haggis had said. Dowling Jessup had been a drugged-out runaway whose guilt in Ethan Grainger's death seemed less than straightforward. Vivian wasn't the only one who thought that Dowl hadn't gotten a fair shake.

Neither Sandifer nor Haggis recalled any trial, perhaps thanks to Dr. Larraz. Jessup had spent considerable time in the hospital's forensic unit—hopefully getting treatment—before eventually being warehoused in the prison at Deer Lodge.

Then there was new background on Mariposa, whom Alexis had identified as the woman in the article Mesa had photographed in Dowl's little house in Twin Bridges. According to Alexis, Mariposa was the younger, horse-loving wife of Xavier-Larraz.

But Sandifer had said that Mariposa was Xavier-Larraz's daughter, something that Vivian seemed to confirm. Could her memory be trusted? Mesa wondered and not for the first time. Mesa didn't like the implication of this confusion of roles. That ought to be cleared up sooner than later.

Once she finished the interviews Irita had lined up in the morning, and had a little heart to heart with Phade, she would regroup with Chance. His enthusiasm for helping her seemed to have grown after he found out that Sandifer had been directly involved.

Chapter 11

Irita stood in Mesa's office, clutching three file folders and tapping her foot. If Mesa didn't show up, she sure as hell didn't know what she was going to tell these three sitting in the lobby. She went to the edge of the lobby door and peeked in. Two women, one a soccer mom checking her smart phone, another with streaked purple and nearly white hair, and a guy who looked like the fourteen-year-old reincarnation of John Belushi, had all turned up promptly.

She retreated to the editor's office and looked at her watch. It was ten after ten when she heard the rush of wind as the outer office door opened. Mesa blew in, dressed in a metallic green parka with a fur trim hood and a big smile.

"See, I told you I'd be here," she said. "Okay, let's get the show on the road," Mesa said, taking off her coat. "You sure they all have some computer background?" she said, wondering how Phade might take to "soccer mom." He did claim to be developing an interest in older women although she wasn't sure if he'd meant it, or if he was making a veiled reference to Adrienne and Chance. Phade knew how to push Mesa's buttons.

Irita handed her three files with relief. "I think you should start with—"

Mesa's cell phone rang and she grabbed it while she looked at the file on top. "Oh no, how long?" she said. "Have they called search and rescue?"

Irita did not like the sound of what she was hearing. Someone was missing. It couldn't be Chance. He'd come in earlier looking for Mesa. Now both of them seemed to be obsessing about this Warm Springs woman and the arson victim. Thank God, the copy for Wednesday's edition was in the hopper.

When the phone call ended, Mesa had an expression on her face that Irita recognized. It was that rank-pulling look, the one the boss got when she was gonna stick Irita with something Mesa had promised to do.

"Vivian Jobe didn't come home last night. That was her therapist on the phone. They've been searching for her since first light."

Irita looked at her watch, mentally calculating how much daylight the searchers had to work with. She didn't know the territory up at Table Mountain, just that it was mostly national forest. The potential for a mishap was ever present, and who knew with this Jobe woman? Maybe once she heard her man was dead, she might have gone off the deep end.

"Irita, I want to go back up there." Mesa was slipping her parka back on.

Irita sighed though she was not surprised at her boss's response. Why the situation was taking precedent over the paper was a discussion for another time. "What am I going to do with these applicants?" she said. "We need to hire somebody *macht schnell*."

"Can't you just pick one?

"No, I can't pick one," Irita said, through clenched teeth, her voice going to that testy place even she didn't like. "If I could, I would have already. You're the journalist. You're the best judge of who to hire. Please don't leave me stranded with these people."

Now Mesa sighed. "Okay, here's what we'll do. If they want to work in the newspaper business, they have to be ready to roll with the punches. Tell them I have to cover a breaking story. Give them Nan's lecture about the holy Trinity of small town papers. You know, the police blotter, obits, and high school sports. While I'm gone, they can nose around and churn out five hundred words. Tell them to have the piece back here by the end of the day. I'll look at their stories and pick the best one."

"You promise you'll pick one by the end of the day?"

"I promise," she said and grabbed her shoulder bag and left the office in a whirlwind.

"What about Phade?" Irita called out and then shook her head. She really liked the kid, and most of the time Mesa was great to work for. But when she got a burr under her saddle about a story like this one about the nut hut, she just wouldn't let go.

The smell of corned beef and cabbage made Chance's stomach growl as he and Adrienne entered the Bread and Roses Café. Clanging pots and pans and the low chatter of three red-apron-clad workers filled the worn but comfortable café, a former bakery in uptown Butte.

The café started serving lunch at eleven so Jeanne had invited them around ten to talk. Adrienne waved to the woman behind the serving counter. Despite the years since the news photo had been taken, Chance had no trouble recognizing Jeanne Lenin. Except for about a pound a year, three decades had barely changed her.

She wore her hair in much the same style, a relaxed pageboy, vintage fifties. But now its color was more gray than blonde, and she wore a tortoise shell hair clip on top to keep the loose strands in place. Her face was still attractive, only rounder, made kind by the plumpness.

"Hey, Jeanne, thanks for taking time to talk," Adrienne said when the woman approached. "This is my friend I told you about, Chance Dawson."

Wiping sweat from her brow and then her palms with a white handkerchief, Jeanne gave Chance a strong handshake and said, "Grab yourselves some lemonade." She motioned to a large stainless steel urn and a stack of Dixie cups. "Just let me give these folks some marching orders, and I'll come join you."

Adrienne and Chance sat at a corner table, covered with a red and white checked cloth and an artificial flower in a small vase. All of the tables sat four and were covered with similar homey linens. Chance tasted the lemonade, cringed at its excessive sweetness, and then turned to watch Jeanne as she gathered the staff into a small cluster near the oven in the back. She called for quiet, and then gave out some instructions. Then he heard her say, "Let us pray."

The workers held hands and bowed their heads, while Chance contemplated the paper rose in a small glass urn, and his own religious underpinnings. Organized religion in general made him uncomfortable.

He called himself a secular humanist, if anyone asked, nothing New Age, no tree hugging, just a general notion that everything and everyone was connected. The label was convenient as it allowed him to avoid going to church without giving up on God.

Adrienne was studying the card holder on the table, which listed the phone numbers of the Food Bank, Community Health, and other resources for those in need. Chance watched Jeanne, who had apparently embarked on a lengthy petition.

"Had any religious experiences of late?" Adrienne asked in the tone he thought of as her "come hither" voice.

"I went to a revival once when I was eleven or so," he said. He told her about the makeshift tent church that had appeared one summer. It was on the other side of the woods that bordered the base housing where they lived when their father was stationed in Ohio. Talk among the local kids was that snake handling was part of the service.

"Who took you?" Adrienne said.

"I snuck out one Friday night to see for myself."

"You did not," Adrienne said.

Chance laughed. Adrienne had a "good boy" image of him that he loved to dispel. "Ask Mesa; she followed me." Of course, he had spotted her. He had let her come along and peek under the edge of the tent with him. Even then, when all the other boys claimed not to be able to stand their little sisters, he had never run her off.

Their discussion was interrupted by Jeanne Lenin, who put a small plate of ginger snaps on the table as she sat down. Chance dove into the cookies, hoping they were not half sugar like the lemonade, while Adrienne and Jeanne made nice. They seemed to have struck up an authentic connection.

They had met when Adrienne had been subbing for a physician at the Community Health Center. She had been sent to staff a clinic at the Butte Rescue Mission but on that evening, the Mission had plumbing problems so the clinic had met at the café after hours.

Since then, Adrienne had taken to dropping in to the café for a coffee. "I like the concept," she had told Chance. "Besides, no one proselytizes doctors. Everybody thinks we're gods already."

Chance had filled Adrienne in on Jeanne Lenin's background à la Ken Sandifer. He was happy to have her take the lead. After all, Jeanne could easily tell Chance her former life was none of his business.

"Now, how can I help?" Jeanne began.

Without hesitation, Adrienne jumped in. "Remember when I was in the other day and we were talking about reinventing ourselves?" The two women smiled at each other, with Jeanne giving a subtle nod in Chance's direction.

"There's a woman in town that could use your help." Adrienne gave a quick summary of Vivian's quest, ending with a simple, "Chance learned that you used to work at Warm Springs during that time. You could really help by telling us what you remember about the death of Ethan Grainger."

Chance tried not to look at Adrienne. He loved how she had cut to the chase so quickly without being even the least bit threatening. People just opened up to her. If she saw him smiling at her, he knew she'd blush.

Jeanne tugged at the cuffs of her long-sleeved sweater and straightened in her chair as if she had made the decision to face their questions into her past with decorum.

"Honest to John, that's so long ago and there were so many young ones. She remembered my name?"

Chance didn't bother correcting Jeanne's faulty conclusion. Instead, he pulled out the copy of the news photo and handed it to her. "Maybe this will jog your memory."

Jeanne perused the article, methodically straightened the folds of the paper. Her face took on a grim expression for a split second then relaxed when she looked up and answered, "Can't say any of these faces look familiar, not even my own."

"Mostly we're interested in the patient who was killed," Chance said. "You remember that?"

"Remember?" she said with a sigh. "I lost my job on account of it. People thought I was a scapegoat, Dr. Larraz covering his tail, but I know it was the Lord at work."

Thankfully, the previous night's storm had not crossed over the Divide and Highway 2 south of Butte and through the East Ridge was clear and dry. Mesa sped as fast as safety would allow on the winding old two-lane highway until she hit the turnoff to Table Mountain ranch.

She hadn't checked the weather the night before, but March was a roller coaster month with nighttime temperatures that could fall below zero but also stay well above it. On the other side of a storm front, the weather could be balmy, a regular Banana Belt.

Mesa looked up at the bright blue sky, thankful that yesterday's storm had moved north away from Table Mountain. In any case, hypothermia was still a real possibility for anyone who was lost or injured overnight in the mountains, no matter the temperature.

Chance's pal, Tank Sorich, had gotten turned around one afternoon in November when they were deer hunting in the Tobacco Root. He'd huddled between two boulders and managed to survive the night. He even found his way back to the road, meeting the Search and Rescue dogs coming to look for him.

But thinking about the weather could not distract her from wondering how Vivian had ended up in this predicament. Mesa was convinced there was no way Vivian had taken a downward spiral after they had parted the day before, quite the opposite. She was ready to press on.

Nevertheless, Mesa, in her eagerness, had pushed Vivian to think back through one of the most difficult times of her life. Yet she'd seemed determined to help figure out what had happened to Dowl.

True, this might be one of those situations in which she could have left well enough alone. If only she had a nickel for every time someone had suggested that. It always came down to a line she felt the need to cross. After all, that's what made a good journalist, knowing when a situation wasn't "well enough." She'd had a professor who liked to quote George Orwell: "Journalism is printing something someone else doesn't want printed. Everything else is public relations."

Mesa shifted into second gear, and muttered out loud, "What does a guy who writes about talking animals know anyway?" Then she laughed. People had thought Orwell was off his rocker half the time.

෪ঌ৯

"Dr. Larraz?" Chance said, remembering the name from his conversation the day before with Ken Sandifer.

Jeanne leaned back in her chair and a smile engulfed her. "Juan Xavier-Larraz. He was about the most handsome man I had ever seen. Like Ricky Ricardo but without the nonsense." She looked up, and then said, "Maybe you're too young to remember *I Love Lucy*."

"Not at all," Chance said. Between the ages of eight and thirteen while living on military bases all over Europe, Chance and Mesa had seen endless reruns of American sitcoms. Whenever Mesa got in trouble with their mother, which was often given her feisty nature, Chance used to mimic Ricky Ricardo's singsong directive to Lucy, "Mesa, joo got some splaining to do."

"This Dr. Larraz," Chance asked, "was he Cuban like Ricky Ricardo? What was he doing at the hospital?"

"Chief psychiatrist, a smart one too," Jeanne nodded. "That afternoon the boy was killed, I was in his office with him, trying to help the nursing staff deal with the other doctors. The Cuban doctors—we had two others—could barely understand half of what their patients were saying. The treatment orders on the charts were half in English and half in Spanish. Confusion was the order of the day."

"Vivian Jobe would have been on the adolescent girls' ward," Chance said and showed Lenin the photo of Vivian on his iPhone. "She was diagnosed schizophrenic. That ring any bells?"

The former nurse took the phone and shook her head. "Fraid not. That job was a nightmare," Jeanne said, leaning toward Chance as if to take him into her confidence. "Probably not much older than you are now, I was, and had charge of all the staff in the adolescent ward."

Chance watched Jeanne as she reached for a cookie from the plate on the table, readjusting her sleeve cuffs as she went. She was a woman with appetites, all right.

"They found that boy's body round midnight, dead since afternoon. There was a hullabaloo with the state board. The sign-out charts were incomplete. He'd been missed at the last bed count, but we were short-handed on that shift and nobody reported it up the line." She wiped cookie crumbs from the tabletop and then said, "The hospital needed a scapegoat, and I was let go."

"So you did know the boy who was killed?" Chance said, unsure suddenly if Jeanne Lenin was to be believed or if she was covering for herself.

"Snake," she said, "Just like in the Garden of Eden."

Chance wondered what temperament Ethan Grainger might have had to warrant the off-putting nickname. Did he lie in wait in the grass, or strike without warning?

"That's what they called him. I believe his last name was Grainger. I didn't have much to do with the boys' ward."

"And the boy held responsible for Snake's death, supposedly his name was Jessup," Chance said. "Do you remember him?"

Jeanne shook her head. "It's shameful, but I can't recall."

"What happened between the boys?" Chance asked. He'd heard Sandifer's version and wanted to see how Jeanne's matched up.

"Like I said, I was pretty wrapped up in my own misery, but I believe it was a fight over a girl. Like what we see here, you have kids with a lot of anger and nowhere to put it. I know Juan did everything he could to help those kids."

"Can you think of anybody else who might still be around who could tell us more?" Chance asked, trying to prompt the woman's memory and noting her reference to the chief psychiatrist by his first name. "What about this Dr. Larraz. Have you seen him since?"

Jeanne stared into her Dixie cup for a moment, and then shook her head with a faint smile of regret. Chance tried to read the woman's expression, wondering how accurate her memories were. She seemed good-hearted, but he knew she was leaving out part of the story about her own addiction. He could understand why she might choose to do that after so long, but it also made him wonder what else she wasn't telling.

The wind went right out of Mesa when she saw the Search and Rescue truck coming down the road from Table Mountain Ranch. If they had been called that morning and were already on their way elsewhere, that meant one thing. Vivian had already been found. The question was in what condition.

She rolled down her window and signaled for the truck to slow down. She wanted to find out what she was getting into. The Search and Rescue truck barely slowed, just long enough to say they were on their way to a "bigger situation farther down the line." This one, meaning Vivian's rescue, was "under control."

Mesa continued up the mountain still with a knot in her stomach. A Jefferson County sheriff's car was parked in front of the long house, but no one was in it. She tore out of her car and banged on the front door. No one answered, so she walked in. The warm smell of pine met her, though it did nothing to relieve her tension.

The Beaverhead National Forest stretched for miles in every direction. The effort to search for someone lost in it seemed like an overwhelming task. Vivian could have wandered off in any direction.

Mesa paced the floor, wondering what her next move should be. Her first thought was to call Dr. Kaiser, but she didn't see the Germanes' landline and, without cell service, her own phone was no help.

First Dowl and now Vivian. Was there something much more sinister about what had happened that summer at Warm Springs? Maybe someone was trying to create the illusion that Vivian was unstable. Any given summer in Montana, a set of human remains would be discovered, often the only thing that was left of someone for whom life had become too difficult.

Then, through the window, she saw Vivian's sister, Abby, running toward the house. Mesa went out the side door to meet her. "I saw Search and Rescue headed down the hill," Mesa paused, and then hoping for the best said, "How is she? Dr. Kaiser called me to say Vivian hadn't come home."

"Yes, yes, she's going to be all right," her sister said, her face taut but managing a quick smile when she spoke. "I have to get upstairs to get more blankets."

Mesa looked back down the hill, and saw a sheriff's deputy and Wally Germane carrying Vivian on a portable stretcher. Her two dogs were trotting alongside.

"The ambulance is coming up the mountain," Abby said and ran up the stairs calling to Mesa to get the door for the men.

Mesa, her sigh of relief audible, did her best to stay out of the way as the men entered. Vivian was conscious, wrapped in Mylar foil blankets, the dogs licking her hand as the stretcher was lowered to the floor.

Abby returned with more blankets. "Let's get something warm into Vivian too," Wally said.

Abby went into the kitchen. The deputy had gone to his cruiser to use his radio. "I need to wash my hands," Wally said and headed to the bathroom. "You'll sit with her in case she needs anything?"

"Sure," Mesa said, glad for the opportunity to talk to Vivian. She knelt down next to the injured woman who was shivering under the blankets. Vivian looked, if anything, cheerful. Mesa smiled tentatively. "You had me going on the drive up here," she said half laughing. "It's a relief to see you in one piece."

"Thank God for my dogs," Vivian said. The blonde Lab gave her a tender lick on the cheek and Vivian murmured, "Good girl, Buddha. They kept me toasty, so I didn't go into shock. Plus it helps to have a couple of years of med school under your belt so you don't panic."

"I'm so sorry," Mesa said, and then fumbled around for what to say next. "I …."

"Nothing you did. Got myself into a minor fix," she said in a quiet voice through chattering teeth. "Took Buddha and Gandhi down to the creek. It's a long walk, but we do it all the time. About an hour down the mountain, a couple of young bucks came out of nowhere and Gandhi started to go after them. I sprinted to call him back and, in the process, I tripped over a downed aspen and went ass over teacup about thirty yards. Heard my leg snap when I smacked a boulder halfway down."

Mesa could see Vivian's left leg had been placed in a temporary splint. Otherwise, she looked none the worse for wear for someone who had spent a cold night in the mountains. Vivian was tougher than she looked.

Abby returned now with some warmed milk and honey. "Dogs kept her warm all night," Abby said with a smile as Vivian propped herself up to drink. Buddha nuzzled closer, her chin on Vivian's good leg. "Gandhi," Abby nodded toward the black Lab who sat nearby keeping a watchful eye, "woke us up toward morning. He had Viv's scarf tied around his neck. Thank God. Last night, we'd searched and called until it was too dark to do much more. We couldn't do anything but wait for sunrise. It was a long night," she said with a sigh and walked back into the kitchen.

"I won't argue," Vivian said, waiting for her sister to reach the kitchen. "And it wasn't just because of the temperature. Gandhi was growling off and on for half the night. I'd sure like to know what spooked those deer. I had that odd feeling that we weren't the only ones out there."

Chapter 12

Chance sat at the drawing table in his townhouse, staring at the plans for the Dead Guy House on Granite Street. That was how his client, Professor MacMillan, referred to it. Nick had suggested Chance for the job after saying it was one of the worst deaths he'd ever attended. "The stench was unbelievable. I can't believe you'll ever get it out of that house, but I told the lady that if anybody could do it, you could. That guy was in that tub for weeks. It was the water meter guy came to check on the leak that called it in. Vomited all over the porch."

Chance had drawn up several designs to make over the hundred-year-old miner's cottage into a guesthouse. After a year and half in probate, at least the smell was said to have decreased. Chance's musings about who to hire to redo the chimney were interrupted by a call from Ken Sandifer.

"After you left yesterday, I got to talking to Mitsy about Warm Springs and all. She reminded me about Tommy Little Boy."

"Who's he?" Chance asked, hoping it might be someone like Vivian with new information about Jessup.

"He's an interpreter with Mitsy, and when he was a kid he was in the bin. That's how I first met him. Then he and Mitsy became friends later on when they started working together. Anyway, she thinks he might have more accurate memories since he wasn't crazy to start with."

"How do you mean?" Chance said, turning away from the drawing and giving Sandifer his full attention.

"Tommy was deaf and he'd grown up on the reservation without any real medical care. After his mother died, he ended up in Warm Springs until he was about fourteen when one of his teachers figured out he wasn't a mental case. He just couldn't hear."

"Jesus," Chance said, "what a nightmare."

"At least this one had a happy ending," Sandifer said. "He got released from the bin and adopted by a family where the father had deaf parents."

"And another thing, Mitsy's aunt is on the Foundation Board at the Paul Clark Home. She says they used to have a Cuban doctor who had been a big donor. Mitsy wonders if it's Larraz."

❦

By the time Mesa had come back from Table Mountain to the emergency room at St. James, it was nearly one p.m. Vivian was already in the process of being admitted. The storm had passed and the number of injuries from fender benders had subsided, so the ER was quiet.

Mesa wanted to be sure that Vivian was out of danger before heading back to the office—anything to avoid having to face Irita, not to mention Phade, and the decision about a new reporter. Mesa prayed that the kid who looked like John Belushi was a lousy writer.

Abby had accompanied Vivian in the ambulance and Mesa could see her hovering in one of the ER's treatment bays, but couldn't get her attention. Finally, she decided to go back to the office and call later to see how Vivian was doing. That road trip to Warm Springs would have to be delayed.

On the way up to the parking lot, she passed Adrienne, who turned out to be filling in for a doctor on leave. The two women smiled when they saw each other and Adrienne was quick to ask what brought Mesa to the hospital. "Anything I can help you with?" she said.

Mesa sighed inwardly. She continued to wrestle with the fact that while she genuinely liked Adrienne DeBrook, and thought she was perfect for Chance in many ways, she was nearly twenty years older. Mesa shook her head to rid herself of a vision of Chance as a first-grader when Adrienne would have been a med student. Stick to the present, she told herself, and then said, "Did Chance tell you about Vivian Jobe?"

Adrienne nodded. "The woman who was at Warm Springs."

"She took a bad fall and ended up out all night. I want to find out how she's doing. They brought her into the ER about twenty minutes ago. Any chance you could reconnoiter for me?" she asked sheepishly, knowing full well that not being family, any information Mesa received would be a breach of privacy. "I'd like to be able to visit her as soon as I can."

"I can probably look over a shoulder or two," Adrienne said with a conspiratorial air. "How about I give you a call as soon as I know anything?"

෧ඹ

Mesa had just sat down at her desk in the office, Irita hovering in the hallway, when Adrienne's call came in. Vivian had suffered the early stages of hypothermia but was responding to treatment. The break in her leg was a simple fracture and would not require surgery. She would likely be discharged in the next day or two depending on how her vitals looked.

"She's a lot tougher physically than I would have thought," Mesa confided.

"I didn't hear anybody raising concern about her emotional well-being either," Adrienne said. "She was sitting up in bed and talking to her sister when I walked by, more worried about her dogs than anything else."

Mesa had no sooner switched off her phone than Phade appeared at her door. Despite two days' growth of beard and serious bed head, his dark looks never failed to arouse. She cocked her head at him and then motioned him in, reminding herself that now that she was boss, flirting was no longer appropriate communication even if it had been known to get results. He cocked his head back at her, pushed the door closed with his foot, and all but fell into the corner of the sofa.

She came toward him and Phade drew in his long legs, allowing her to sit next to him. "How nice to see you," she said and stifled a smile as she realized he still wore a hint of eyeliner. Had he been out partying before returning to the *Mess* office and passing out the night before? "What happened this morning?"

"That geezer creeps me out. You gotta keep him away from me."

"He's not exactly ready to join your fan club either. He tells me you're moonlighting."

"Nosy prick. I'm not doing anything outta line. You said as long as I took care of Mess business first you didn't care what I was doing on my own time as long as it didn't have anything to do with porn."

"So what projects am I subsidizing?" Mesa said and reached over to touch a new silver bracelet he was wearing.

"Like it?" Phade asked. "It's a Viking bracelet. Friend of mine just got back from Denmark." Then he added in an apologetic tone. "It was just a quick fix for a buddy. Cascade's system sucks. I gota better setup here."

Mesa was glad the money she'd put into their computer system was paying off. "So I take it that means you quitting was play time."

Phade studied the bracelet and then looked up. "You know I like our arrangement," he said. "But I need more help with the everyday maintenance. How else can I think big thoughts? So keep the creep away from me, and hire somebody I can work with, or it's all over between us." He gave his eyebrows a quick up and down, and then left.

Irita scurried in moments later. "What's the verdict?"

Mesa sighed and said. "He's becoming a regular prima donna, that's what. But he's still here for the moment. Let Cinch know he's to keep his distance from now on."

Irita nodded. "Everything okay with the Jobe woman?"

"Good as can be expected when you've been hunkered down under the stars for the night with your two best Labrador buddies."

"I've had worse offers," Irita chuckled and handed Mesa a thin stack of paper. "And now, on to the ongoing humdrum of the newspaper business. I just printed out stories from two of the three applicants." She tossed the hard copies on Mesa's desk. "We're still waiting on 'soccer mom.'"

Nana had long ago insisted that when Chance and Mesa came for a meal, the occasion would be civil, not that she didn't enjoy a lively discussion—just no gory details while eating. Since their grandmother seldom made demands and because they would do anything for her, the pair avoided any unsavory topics at table.

They'd consumed the bulk of the mid-week pork roast without mentioning autopsies or arson. When Chance finished his second piece of Dutch apple pie and brought up Jessup, Mesa guessed his curiosity had gotten the best of him, or the sugar had gone to his head. Then again, maybe he thought Nana really could shed some light on the deaths of Grainger and Jessup.

"You can't help wondering," Chance said to Mesa, "that if Dowl Jessup wasn't guilty, as Vivian believes and Sandifer certainly questions, then who did kill Ethan Grainger thirty years ago?"

"More on the Warm Springs death?" Nana Rose said over her bifocals.

"Still some unanswered questions," Mesa said. It had been a long day, but she welcomed the chat. She'd worked out more than a few knotty problems sitting with her grandmother at this dining table.

"Didn't Charlotte say that Vivian's young man was held responsible?" Nana said. "Who wants more tea?"

"That's the curious part," Chance said as he shook his head at the offer of tea. "Vivian says he was with her when the other boy died. What do you think? Based on what you remember about Vivian during that time, would you take her word?"

Sipping the last of her tea, Nana gazed at the bottom of the cup for a moment and then said, "Your mother's antics on the ski slopes may have garnered some respect, but she idolized Vivian, who was smart and ambitious and had plans, as they used to say. Sarah was heartbroken by what Vivian went through. I'm sure if your mother was alive today she'd say that of course Vivian is to be trusted."

Mesa and Chance exchanged a glance, but said nothing. Their grandmother rarely mentioned their mother's name. She spoke of her daughter's faith in her friend with reverence, a deep respect for someone whose opinion could no longer be consulted.

Finally, to break what was becoming an awkward silence, Chance said, "I think we need to track down this Cuban doctor. His name seems to come up often enough."

Rose Ducharme folded her cloth napkin and placed it to the side of her teacup, signaling the end of the meal. Mesa loved the precision with which her grandmother attended to the smallest detail, never in a rush, and never allowing any task to be performed half-heartedly. "A Cuban." Nana said. "Probably a refugee."

"Don't you think that's odd, Nana," Mesa said, following Chance's entree, "hiring Cuban doctors back then to work in a mental hospital?"

"They were professionals in their own country, and refugees who needed work. It would have been a viable opportunity. You weren't likely to find many American doctors accepting the state's wages to work in a mental hospital back then."

No one had a better sense of history than their grandmother, or a greater appreciation of refugees, having been an immigrant herself. Mesa welcomed someone to fill in the blanks. "What do you remember about the Cuban crisis?" Mesa asked.

"Bay of Pigs was in 1962, the year before the assassination," Nana mused and then recalled Kennedy and Castro and the standoff about nuclear missiles. "Everyone was building bomb shelters."

One question was all it took for their grandmother to hold forth. She made her way to the barrister's bookcase and the journals that she kept at one end of the dining room. She referred to them as her "Out of Montana" series—with apologies to Isak Dinesen, she would add. Nana often said that the remoteness of Montana in the fifties had had more than a few similarities to the wilds of Kenya.

Nana had started a journal to record life on the ranch that became her new home after she had left Cambridge. When she first came to Montana as an English war bride, the journal grew out of the letters she wrote to her family in Sussex and her reflections on her married life.

As small children, Mesa and Chance had watched with curiosity when Nana had written with a fountain pen in what then seemed like a giant ledger. Over the years, their grandmother had kept a running narrative of social and political events and their effect on the Ducharme family. Mesa and Chance had huddled around her to hear about the weather and the ups and downs of the ranch and whatever else they'd missed while they'd been overseas.

Once their grandfather's heart had weakened and the Ducharmes moved to town, the journal's focus narrowed. In college, when Mesa had finally read *Out of Africa*, she realized how much her grandmother's journals had been fashioned after the Danish writer's work.

Mesa grinned at Chance as they watched their grandmother bring two volumes to the table—her version of the sixties. The black books, now looking like an ordinary size, covered five-year periods or so and were marked accordingly.

Nana flipped through the appropriate book as she sat down, and then said, "School children doing air raid drills, hiding under their desks, nervous about missiles in Cuba. Quite dreadful, really."

"So when did all the refugees show up?" Chance asked. Mesa could have listened to Nana's entire narrative but Chance wanted to get to the heart of the matter.

"Once the embargo began," Nana said, "the Cubans who could afford it began leaving in droves. Before Castro and the communists, Cuba, especially Havana, was rather like Las Vegas. I remember *Life* magazine doing an article on Hemingway in Havana, deep-sea fishing, flamenco, quite romantic. The nightlife attracted movie stars, gamblers, and lots of money, even the Mafia. Many Cubans had become accustomed to a standard of living the communists weren't going to provide." Her voice trailed off as she continued flipping the pages.

"I could see Xavier-Larraz fitting in," Mesa said. "He still smokes fancy cigars, and wears well-made clothes."

Mesa thought about the image of the doctor picking up Mariposa in his expensive tweed jacket. Xavier-Larraz might have the fashionable look, but she wondered if he had the heart for a glitzy lifestyle. Sandifer had made him sound more like Albert Schweitzer than Al Capone.

While Chance finished his pie, Nana talked about Monsignor Flanagan, the leader of the local Catholic churches, there being eight of them then, bringing a couple of Cuban boys to Butte. An article about them appeared in the church bulletin, appealing for suitable lodgings. In the end, the language barrier was the element that led to their placement at the Paul Clark home where one of the teachers spoke Spanish.

Nana's sympathies had gone out to the children whose plight reminded her of her cousin who had been sent to the English countryside when the Nazis were poised to invade the island of Guernsey. "She was only eight, and she was never really quite right afterwards. That kind of separation at such an impressionable age and under a dark cloud was simply too difficult."

"Were there lots of those refugees?" Mesa asked. She wondered about Mariposa—whether she and her father had been taken in as exiles. Perhaps that was what the job at the mental hospital had helped Xavier-Larraz avoid.

"Most went to Florida, I think," Nana said, "Miami. Though, eventually, they went all over the country. I do remember a Cuban family came to Helena. The father was hired at Carroll College. People were wary of him, saying he was a spy. He wore tinted glasses like Aristotle Onassis, which did make him look a bit mysterious. It was speculated that he was an unscrupulous lawyer who'd worked in Batista's government, but who couldn't practice law when he escaped to this country. So he became a professor and taught Spanish instead."

Mesa wondered what it must have been like for Xavier-Larraz, coming to start a new life, working in a mental hospital in Montana. She wondered what he'd been told to recruit him and what he must have thought when he saw what he had to work with. The first winter must have been grueling. Talk about culture shock.

"So, we didn't like Batista either?" Chance said. "I thought it was Castro we didn't like. Who were the bad guys?"

"That's the question all right," Nana said. "It was the beginning of the time when one could no longer tell. Half of Miami is still waiting to go back to Cuba once Castro's government is gone. It's ironic, really. It's been so long that many of the exiles are grandparents by now. Most of them probably don't even remember the country they left. My heart goes out to them, caught between the world of the immigrant and the exile."

Mesa understood how her grandmother felt. She'd left England an immigrant, voluntarily, and wasn't going back. Nana Rose had made it clear she planned to be buried in the Mount Moriah cemetery next to their grandfather and their mother. Montana was her home now. Only the exiled wanted to return.

"Wow," Chance said, "Fidel's still around and his Soviet buddies are long gone."

Mesa's curiosity about Xavier-Larraz had spiraled. What had he come to America to escape—revolution? family? maybe both? She wished she had talked to him when she had seen him in Dillon.

"We have never lifted the embargo," Nana said. "The war in Vietnam diverted everyone's attention. Cuba was left to its own devices."

Nana was sipping her tea and stared into the cup for a moment as if to consider her words before speaking, then said, "So much conflict among the young people then. It wasn't like my generation when we all saw the war as a noble effort."

"I guess guys did some drastic stuff to stay out of it," Chance said.

"If it hadn't been for those war clouds, you might not be here today," Nana said with a smile. Mesa and Chance grinned too. They had heard the story many times of how their parents had met at the Malstrom Air Force base movie theater.

Their father had joined up out of high school, rather than face Montana's ebbing job market, and was stationed at the base in Great Falls. Their parents had married young despite their grandmother's objections, but she could hardly complain since she had done the same thing. Was it any wonder where Sarah had gotten her strong will?

"Ken Sandifer called today," Chance said, "to say his wife has an aunt who is on the board at the Paul Clark Home. She says that one of their deep-pocket donors is a Cuban doctor."

"You think it could be Larraz?" Mesa said.

Chance shrugged. "How many Cuban doctors do you know in Montana?"

"Wonder what Dr. Xavier-Larraz considers himself—immigrant or exile?" Mesa said as she lifted a dessert plate with another slice of pie toward Chance.

Chapter 13

While Adrienne preferred to spend most nights at the cabin out at Moulton, when she worked in the evenings in town, the loft above the gallery was more convenient. Chance often joined her. This evening he poked mindlessly at the logs in the fireplace, the orange embers so bright they lit up the loft. She would be home from her shift at the ER soon.

He hoped she wouldn't be worn out. He ought to get up and turn on a light, but he liked the space his mind was in. All the questions about the arsonist and Henry and Stick, and now Larraz and his life as an exile had been crammed into his head. Sitting alone in the dark, the logjam had broken and ideas floated free.

The Cuban was a hero for sure. He had saved Mariposa from the clutches of communism, and Jessup from a murder charge, and he had motivated Jeanne Lenin to get sober and go into recovery. Too bad he hadn't been able to save Jessup a second time.

Vivian could call on Ken Sandifer to support the possibility of Jessup's innocence, and now this Tommy Little Boy might join the bandwagon. Maybe the thing to do was to bring Little Boy to the hospital to meet Vivian,

Sandifer too. Between the three of them, maybe they could fit together all the pieces of the puzzle.

Chance heard the door open. "Sitting in the dark again?" he heard Adrienne say. "Is this your idea of some kind of sexual fantasy?" she asked.

He could hear willingness in her words. She wasn't tired at all. "Yes, ma'am," he said and hung the poker on the stand.

"Father Difranco. You met him in the cafeteria one night when you came over to the hospital to have dinner—tortoise-shell glasses, salt and pepper beard, collar around his neck."

"Okay, smarty pants," Chance said and pinched her nipple. They lay half-clothed on the rug in front of the fire. "I know the guy. Glasses, graying beard. He always wears mismatched black pants and jackets. Probably shops at Goodwill."

"Exactly. So we were having coffee and I asked him about Warm Springs and if he knew any of the psych docs who'd worked out there."

"You know, I really appreciate you taking an interest in this whole thing," Chance said and continued to circle her nipple.

She turned over on her stomach. "I'm trying to tell you something that might be pertinent."

Chance smiled, turned over as well, and then said, "Okay, okay. The priest had a friend in seminary and …."

"I mentioned something about Cuban doctors and he started telling me about this friend who was Cuban and how he came to the States through a special visa program back in the sixties after Fidel took over."

"Seriously? That's some departure from the usual State Department red tape," Chance said.

"That's what I said. Remember the hullabaloo around Elian Gonzalez?"

"Let's see, I think I was a senior in high school when that happened," Chance said, and Adrienne gave him a quick, but gentle slap on the cheek. Then he recounted the conversation with Nana about the children who'd come to the Paul Clark Home. Maybe that was where they'd come from.

"The seminarian Difranco knew went to foster parents in Florida."

Mesa snuggled under the down cover after her phone conversation with Shane. She had wanted to pick his brain about Warm Springs and how they might get their hands on the records about what happened to Dowling Jessup, but he wanted to talk about the Tea Party jerks that continued to make his life on the Human Services Committee a nightmare. How could she not listen and offer her condolences?

Such phone calls after a long day always ended with his thanking her for allowing him to blow off steam but, lately, it felt like a competition to see who had the more important thing to say.

Initially, she had enjoyed the connection. Their relationship had become steadier after New Year's. For one, they actually had a good time New Year's Eve, which was a first. Most of her New Year's Eves, at least the ones she hadn't spent at home, had been disasters.

Maybe it was the realization that they wouldn't see much of each other once the Legislature was in session.

But he had come back on weekends and encouraged Mesa to move out of Nana's house, which she had finally done. Chance had recently bought and remodeled a duplex on Granite St. in walking distance of, and midway between, the office and Nan's house. The unit was on the second floor, and Mesa enjoyed the view from the upstairs rooms. Shane had helped her move what little furniture she owned, including a newly purchased queen-sized bed that he had helped a shorthanded delivery guy haul upstairs for her. Shane scored points for loyalty.

They had enjoyed some good times skiing at Discovery, the local ski resort near Georgetown Lake, and searching for out-of-the-way hot springs where they could skinny dip. But lately, when they spent time together, routine had begun to set in.

Earlier in the month, on a Sunday evening at the Silver Dollar Saloon, they had gone to listen to Big Sky Revival, a Bluegrass trio that included one of Shane's fellow legislators. The effects of numerous pints of Guinness being what they were, they had snuck out the side exit at intermission to continue the evening in bed. The only decision left was whether it would be her place or his. They chose Mesa's because she had to be up early, while he didn't have to be back in Helena until four in the afternoon for once.

As they sat up in bed leaning against the headboard, having the cigarette moment without the cigarette, she felt slightly impatient. Waking up next to him in the morning could have benefits. But on the other hand, she enjoyed her mornings alone with her own thoughts.

As if mindreading, he had solved her dilemma. "I think I'd better be going. I'd love to stay but you have an early start tomorrow," he said. "And if I stay I'll just want to repeat this in the morning, and you'd be late …."

They were becoming predictable already. Like the phone conversation they'd just had, the moments felt prescribed. He hadn't called because he wanted to, as much as that he thought he should. Wait a minute—was she grousing because a man was being thoughtful?

She didn't want to seem unappreciative, but she could see life with Shane developing into the traditional progression of events—date for two years, become engaged, married, then kids. A progression of events that Mesa knew was not her—at least not her with him.

She was constantly meeting guys she found attractive: a new prof at the college, her dentist, the manager at Bugs 'n Bullets, and that was just in Butte. Throw in Helena and Missoula and the potential for meeting a few unspoiled, refreshing, outdoorsy kinda guys was unlimited. No, she definitely was not ready to settle down. And these regular nightly phone calls were an ongoing reminder.

She opened the file folder to read the drafts submitted by the three reporter applicants, looked at a copy of the soccer mom's blog entry entitled "27 Ways to Use Leftover Wine," and then closed the folder. She would have to find the right time to tell Shane.

❧

Chance had gone downstairs in the Imperial Building to retrieve the newspaper on Thursday morning. He had developed a morning ritual around reading the paper with coffee while Adrienne exercised.

There was something both peaceful and erotic about watching her do yoga every morning in the studio apartment. She wore this lavender leotard that was set off by the dark wood floor and the morning sun streaming through the long windows. His day was starting off the way he liked. At least until he saw the paper. "Police Have Lead in Arsons" the headline read, and below the fold, a photo showed two uniforms leading Henry, thankfully unidentified, into the police station.

Chance grabbed his phone. Before he could punch in the sheriff's number, he saw the voice message from Henry. He cried, "Chance, you said the police would be nice to me. But they brought me to the station and they won't let me go home. Don't ever talk to me again!" The tirade tore at Chance's insides.

He called the sheriff's office, but his call was forwarded to the receptionist. She explained that the arson suspect had put up such a fuss at the station that he'd been taken to Gilder House for his own safety. That was where the sheriff was now.

Chance yelled, "Gotta go" to Adrienne and without further explanation, flew down the steps and jumped into his pickup. Gilder House was where the cops took anybody they picked up who was mental. It was only four blocks away, straight up Main Street.

સ્ટું

It was past eight when Mesa woke with a start. She'd been having a restless night, dreaming about snowstorms and immigrants adrift at sea, but then she'd sat straight up in bed as if someone had pulled her out of deep water. Maybe it was her frazzled psyche anticipating a visit to the Archives.

Adrienne's call the night before about special visas for Cuban kids, and Chance chiming in about Larraz possibly being a member of the Board of the Paul Clark Home had her thinking about how and when he and Mariposa had come to Montana. The Home had been established a hundred years ago by copper baron William Clark in honor of a son who had died in childhood.

But, much like the Montana Children's Home, the city's need for such an institution had faded in the seventies. The Paul Clark Home morphed into a McDonald's Family Place, serving a different population in the community. Mesa's hunch was that the Archives likely had records from the Home that could be informative about its earlier days.

Her attitude toward the Archives, and the renovated fire station in which they were housed, hardened as she entered the beautifully restored building. Memories of an experience there in the days before the renovation still unsettled her.

She had come on a school tour only a few months after her mother had died. Mostly sleep-walking through her classes, she found the tour of the dilapidated fire station that housed a bunch of dreary old records crushingly boring. That is, until the tour guide began talking about the building's paranormal reputation. Volunteers working in the evening had reported, more than once, that they heard what sounded like the voices of firemen murmuring in dark corners and that the disconnected alarm bells had been heard clanging on occasion, both at night and during the day, as though the fire department still inhabited the place.

For Mesa's money, thoughts about communication from the "other side" seemed morbid, if not stupid. So, when the class was led through the alarm room, Mesa was the unenthusiastic last in line. She was almost out the door when the bells began to clamor as if to call her back. When the tour guide, the kindly white-haired Mr. Shannon, said "Someone trying to reach ya, darling?" Mesa had sped out the building and back onto the bus. It would be months before she told Nana Rose what had happened.

Mesa flew up the two flights of stairs at the Quartz Street entrance, a mere two blocks from her duplex. Adelaide Faraday, the assistant director, greeted her fondly at the research desk. Addie, as she was known to all, had been there for as long as Mesa could remember, and she was a walking history book of Butte in her own right.

"Hey, Addie," Mesa said and explained her interest in data from the Paul Clark Home. Addie expressed some doubt about any Cubans settling in Butte but turned to her computer terminal and inputted Mesa's request for any data about the Paul Clark Home anyway. Moments later Mesa was sitting in front of a cardboard box with records dating from 1904 through 1971 that Addie had brought out from one of the now state-of-the-art, temperature-controlled storage bays.

After inspecting a copying book of correspondence from the 1900s, a set of index cards from the 1920s and 30s with typed information about each child, and several folders of old bank statements and board minutes, Mesa opened a large red ledger with accounts entered from

1938 until 1981. Handwritten, ink entries tallied the expenses and donations and other revenues of the Home that were deposited in the now-defunct Metals Bank.

Mesa let out the tiniest peep of delight when she found what she'd hoped. From 1968 onwards, an increasingly large donation appeared in the last month of each year from J. Xavier-Larraz, M.D.

"Find what you were looking for?" asked Addie, an encouraging smile on her face.

"I certainly did," Mesa said and scribbled dates and amounts in her notebook. She wasn't sure of its implications yet, but there was always something comforting about a paper trail.

"You might be interested in something else I found," Addie said. "It's not specific to Butte or even Montana but it is about Cubans from that period."

Addie waved Mesa around the wooden counter so that she could see the computer screen. "I googled special visas for Cuban kids." She looked sheepish and then said, "Brilliant, huh? Check this out."

"Operation Pedro Pan?" Mesa asked, and looked up at Addie, who shrugged.

"I've never heard of it."

❧

Gilder House therapists and staff worked with the police to keep people in crisis in Butte from having to go to Warm Springs. Cops didn't want to make that trip and probably most detainees didn't want to be there either.

Intentions were good but Chance knew that Henry didn't feel safe anywhere but home. He would be scared of the police who had brought him there, and angry at Chance whose idea it had been to talk to the authorities.

Chance tore through the front door, conscious of his own anger. "Is Henry Gillis here?" A woman with a plastic name badge that read "Evie Swanson, House Manager" greeted him with a firm hand.

"I'm sorry, sir. This is a private facility, and unless you're family—"

Chance didn't wait to hear the rest of her spiel. "I need to see the sheriff immediately," he said in a tone that he knew was too strident. "You can tell me if he's here, can't you?"

The caseworker was the voice of reason. "I'm sure the sheriff will speak with you, but you need to calm yourself first, sir. Okay? Now, what's your name?"

Chance took a breath, and identified himself in more measured tones.

The manager disappeared and then returned moments later to lead Chance down a hallway to a bedroom where Solheim stood in the doorway, hands on his hips. Just beyond the lawman, Chance could see Henry rocking back and forth on a bed with a uniformed officer nearby.

"Can we talk a sec?" Chance asked the sheriff, and the two of them went into the kitchen farther down the hall.

"What happened, Rollie?" Chance said. "I brought Henry in to help you guys out. Now you've put him under lock and key? I don't get it."

"Easy, Chance," the sheriff said. "He's not under arrest. I talked to the detectives working the case and we all agreed that Henry represents a solid enough lead in this string of arsons that we needed to have an in-depth discussion with him."

"Oh, come on, Rollie," Chance said, "You know Henry's not capable of any in-depth discussion. You'll just scare the life out of him. Besides he told you everything he knows in that sketch."

"Yeah, well, that's why we brought him here. When we picked him up at the Leggett last night, he got all hysterical on us when we said we wanted him at the station. The detectives questioned him last night and this morning. We got a lot of background on the deceased but not much on the other guy."

"Then why don't you let me take him home?" Chance said.

"We need to hold him until we can eliminate his prints from the ones we lifted from the trailer."

"You think Henry could have been involved in the arsons?" Chance said, trying not to sound incredulous.

"We're just trying to reduce the number of suspects, Chance. It's standard police protocol. Your pal Henry can place a suspect at the scene of an arson. That's a substantial connection and the first decent lead we've had. For all we know, his pal WAS the arsonist. It wouldn't be the first time one of them torched themselves."

Chance shook his head. "I get that you need to make headway in these arsons, but you can't really believe that Henry is involved."

Solheim shook his head, "Look, Chance, Henry may be your special little friend, but I've seen how guys like him can be taken advantage of. Jessup had been involved in his share of dust-ups. Maybe it wasn't the rosy picture Henry described. The arsonist turns out to be some shit bag that shows Henry a little attention, or threatens him and coerces him into helping out, maybe telling us some rum story. We only have Henry's word that he didn't go into that trailer himself. I'm not saying that's what's happening here. I'm just saying we're gonna be careful and check."

Addie and Mesa sat, transfixed, reading aloud in rapid whispers, first from Wikipedia and then from the websites the article referenced. "From December 1960 to October 1962, more than fourteen thousand Cuban youths arrived alone in the United States. What is now known as Operation Pedro Pan was the largest recorded exodus of unaccompanied minors in the Western Hemisphere."

The article explained that parents thought they were sending their kids to Miami until Castro could be overthrown. Fueled by rumors that the revolutionary government would close the Catholic schools and take the children into indoctrination camps, concerned Americans in Havana contacted the Archbishop in Miami. He contacted the State Department. The children's temporary visas were predicated on the Church's agreement to assume responsibility for them in the short term.

"Oh, my god," Mesa said aloud as she read about the fiasco that ensued. The children were unable to return. The Bay of Pigs and the Cuban missile crisis that Nana had mentioned resulted in the embargo that still exists. No flights were allowed in or out of Cuba. The church had to find permanent homes for all of the young exiles.

Children were placed in foster homes, Catholic boarding schools, even orphanages until arrangements could be made for relatives, even family friends, to take them in. Mesa shook her head. Was this what happened to Mariposa?

"Come to think of it," Addie said, "six or eight years ago, before the renovations, we did have a fellow come in here, his wife and a college-aged daughter with him. He was trying to locate a woman in the area whose ranch he used to visit on the weekends. Tall and dark, he'd been staying at the Paul Clark Home. Maybe he was part of this bunch too."

❧

Chance slammed the door of his pickup. After listening to Solheim's lecture, he had asked to see Henry who had repeated what he said on the phone message.

He stared out the windshield and looked at the horizon. After last night's storm, low hung clouds hid the top of the East Ridge but the valley below looked as clean and crisp as a newly washed car. Taking a deep breath, he felt himself relax.

He had made a mistake, taking Henry's fears so lightly. Now he was on the police's radar, and not just in this case. He'd be added to their list of usual suspects from now on. Chance had to find a way to make this up to Henry—but how? He needed to talk to Adrienne.

His phone vibrated. A text from Mesa said that Tommy Little Boy and the Sandifers were meeting with Vivian at the hospital at ten a.m.

❧

When Chance met Mesa in the lobby of St. James, she was excited to tell him what she'd learned but she sensed he was a little off kilter. Meanwhile, Ken and Mitsy Sandifer and Tommy Little Boy were already there and jabbering away. She promised herself she would check in with him after their meeting with Vivian.

Mesa watched with fascination as Tommy Little Boy's hands moved steadily as he communicated with Mitsy while they waited for the elevator. Montana's deaf population was among the smallest in the country, and seeing people use sign language was a rarity in Butte. On top of that, Little Boy wasn't anything like Mesa expected after hearing Chance's background on him. She had been ready to meet a diffident man who had been an abandoned child, deaf and dumb, wrongly placed in a mental asylum.

But Tommy stood tall in cowboy boots, broken in but well shined. With a bright smile, his gentle brown eyes moved quickly at the least gesture. He wore a plaid shirt, his sleeves rolled to the elbow, his black hair pulled back in a ponytail. She shook his hand when introduced, and she could tell by his constant gaze, he was reading her lips as she spoke to Sandifer. Once again, her negative stereotype had led her in the wrong direction.

"Vivian is looking forward to meeting you," Mesa said. She had called ahead to Dr. Kaiser to make sure that their visit wasn't a disruption. Kaiser was happy to report that her patient was being discharged around lunchtime, and then handed the phone over, saying that Vivian was perfectly capable of deciding who she wanted to see.

Mitsy talked as she signed to Tommy, who responded with a smile, and they made their way into the elevator. When they entered Vivian's room, she was dressed in street clothes and sitting on the edge of her made bed, a dark blue boot on her injured leg. Her face had regained its color, her eyes their twinkle. She reached her hand out to welcome Mesa who then sat on the bed next to her.

When Mesa introduced Ken, Mitsy, Tommy, and Chance, Vivian responded warmly, her eyes lingering for a moment on Chance. "A bon voyage party!" she said with a chuckle. A curious, half smile crept over Vivian's face when she looked at Little Boy. "I remember you," she said in a surprised voice. "You were the one who never talked. And you liked to draw animals."

"I remember you too," Mitsy translated aloud as Tommy signed. Mesa could see from Ken Sandifer's expression that he was touched by the reunion. He couldn't seem to stop smiling. Neither could Little Boy who also couldn't seem to take his eyes off Vivian.

Mesa wondered what thoughts must have been going through all their heads, given the trauma they'd experienced so long ago. She knew from her Air Force brat days the torrent of feelings that could accompany reunions, even with fewer years in between. And, while life on a military base could be bad, even on the worst days, it could hardly be compared to life in an asylum.

"We brought these two to see you," Mesa said, motioning to Ken and Tommy, "because we thought they might help us learn more about what happened to Snake. Like I told you on Tuesday, Chance has been working with Henry Gillis who saw Jessup Saturday night before he died, maybe his killer too. We think it's possible that there's a direct connection between their deaths. "

"I've been wracking my brain, trying to come up with anything that could help," Vivian said, her voice vital and strong. "That's how I got through half the night in the woods. I kept telling myself it's the least we can do, figuring out what really happened. It's frustrating that my memories are so scattered."

"Maybe Ken and Tommy can add some details that might jog your memory," Mesa said. It was worth seeing if they could generate any collective memories.

Vivian nodded. "Let's have at it."

Mesa gave her an encouraging smile. "Why don't you start with what you remember about the day Snake died?"

Vivian took a deep breath and began to speak slowly. "The gazebo is what always pops into my head. The darn thing seemed so out of place, like something out of a Disney movie. We used to walk up there and sit in the afternoons, when they would let us, as if we were anywhere but a mental institution," she said with a chuckle.

"You and Dowl, and Snake and Marie," Ken said, Mitsy signing all the while, so Tommy could be sure to understand.

"Mariposa," Mesa said. "We've learned her name is Mariposa."

"Do you remember her?" Chance asked Vivian.

"Coal black hair, pretty," Mesa added.

"I remember her, the psychiatrist's daughter," Vivian said. "She was with Snake a lot, but I don't remember seeing her that day. Dowl and I didn't go for a walk that afternoon though. I can't remember why."

Tommy's hands began to move quickly, punching the air with urgency. "Wait," Mitsy signed to Tommy, "you're going too fast." Then she translated: "Dowl had one of those pre-Bic, metal lighters, rectangular with stripes and stars like the American flag. He liked to flick its lid open and closed."

"That's right," Vivian said in an excited voice. "He'd traded with one of the orderlies for it."

"But Dr. Larraz took it away from him," Mitsy said, translating more slowly now. "Tommy says he and Dowl and Vivian were standing in the annex after lunch when Dr. Larraz came through the double doors all of a sudden. He saw Dowl flicking the lighter and went to take it. Dowl didn't want to comply, but eventually Larraz took it from him."

Mitsy translated Tommy's explanation, "Patients could smoke, but not in the wards. Even if they had smoke privileges, they couldn't keep matches or lighters with them."

"What happened after he took the lighter?" Chance asked. "Was Dowl angry?" Chance looked in Vivian's direction for an answer.

"Dowl never got mad, at least not that I remember. But I think the doctor could be strict, and it intimidated him," Vivian said. "I looked forward to being outside where you could sit on the bench and see the mountains, but Dowl wouldn't even do that. Instead we just sat in the stairwell until it was time to go back to the ward."

"What else do you remember about Larraz or Mariposa?" Chance asked Tommy.

"She was easily spooked," Mitsy translated, and then Ken added, "I never noticed that. Course, she wasn't a patient, so I never saw her in OT."

Tommy continued to sign saying that he had drawn a picture of a horse and wanted to give it to Mariposa one day when he saw her leaving XL's office. To get her to turn around and see him, he had touched her arm. She had turned around all right, her arms flailing at him. She tore his shirt and hit him hard enough to knock him into Larraz's door.

"Come to think of it, she and Snake didn't hold hands or anything, not like Dowl and Vivian," Ken said, almost embarrassed as he nodded to Vivian.

Mitsy continued to translate. XL came charging out, wondering what had happened. Tommy thought he would be in trouble. Instead, XL seemed to grasp the problem right away. He picked up the drawing and managed to calm Mariposa down enough for her to accept the gift. He made sure Tommy wasn't hurt, and the next day XL brought him a new shirt.

Tommy finished signing and Mitsy added, "Tommy couldn't understand then much of what XL said but obviously he was trying to apologize for Mariposa's behavior."

"What made you think Larraz and Mariposa were father and daughter?" Chance asked Ken. "We've been doing some checking and there's no record of Larraz having any children."

Sandifer jerked his head in surprise. "That's weird. I mean, he talked to her like you would talk to a child. He never corrected any of us when we made that assumption."

"I might have an explanation for that," Mesa said.

Chapter 14

Mitsy led Mesa to the hand-carved oak door of a well-preserved Craftsman bungalow on the west side, and walked in. "Cokie, we're here," she called.

After Mesa's revelation about the Pedro Pan program, Mitsy had suggested that they should make a quick stop at her Aunt Cokie's after they left the hospital. Mesa sensed that she wasn't the only one fascinated by Operation Pedro Pan. How had fourteen thousand Cuban children come to the US and no one in Butte besides Father DiFranco have even an inkling of such an exodus? Had Monsignor Flanagan known, she wondered, and been told not to go public?

"If anybody knows, it'll be Aunt Cokie," Mitsy had said.

"I'm in the kitchen, hon," Cokie called from the back of the house.

"She's always baking," Mitsy said as they walked toward the smell of what Mesa guessed were chocolate chip cookies. "If my Kenny had married her instead of me, he would weigh three hundred pounds."

A woman who could have been Mitsy's twin emerged from the kitchen. The women hugged and laughed. Sensing Mesa's confusion, Mitsy explained,

"This is my Aunt Cokie. We come from one of those large Irish families with kids who are practically the same age as some of their aunts and uncles. My dad is Cokie's oldest brother. She was born just three years before me."

Mitsy pulled Mesa forward by the arm to introduce her. "Mesa's the new editor of the *Messenger*," Mitsy said.

"I like what you're doing with that paper, hon," Cokie said. "I was just saying to Bridget, my youngest, that "Family Ties," the new section that lists events to do with reunions and visiting family, is just what Butte needs."

Mitsy helped Cokie serve up coffee and warm cookies while explaining their visit. "We don't wanna take up too much of your morning," Mitsy said. "I just wanna pick your brain for a sec."

Mitsy filled Cokie in about the story Mesa was working on, and about being particularly curious about Operation Pedro Pan since it was news to everybody else. "Remember that handsome Cuban you used to talk about at the Paul Clark Home? What was his name?"

"Juan Xavier-Larraz." Cokie pursed her lips and grinned. "He was easy on the eyes."

Bingo again, Mesa thought. They were on a roll. "Did he ever mention this Operation Pedro Pan?" she asked.

Cokie shook her head. "We got to know each other pretty well, though mostly on the porch," she laughed. "Him with his cigars and me with my Marlboros, we were the smokers. Cigar smoking was frowned on in the Home even then, but I didn't like to see him out there on his own."

Mitsy added, "Her son had leukemia, and they were living in Ennis at the time." She explained how the Paul

Clark Home had allowed Cokie to spend as much time as possible with her son before he died. "There was only so much they could do back then."

Cokie smiled and said, "We've had four others, and that's helped, though you never really get over the loss of a child."

Mitsy reached over and squeezed her aunt's arm.

Cokie continued. "He'd made some hefty donations to the Home, and we felt it made sense to have him involved in running the place. The truth was he mostly wanted to repay the Home for the care they'd given to several Cuban refugees including his sister, Mariposa. So maybe they were all from this Pedro Pan program."

"Then Mariposa Larraz was here at the Paul Clark Home and you say she was his sister?" Mesa said. The Operation Pedro Pan explanation did make sense then. If Mariposa was Larraz's sister, he must have come to Montana to find her.

"Was she not supposed to be here then?" Cokie asked.

"No, no," Mesa said more politely. "We've been trying to pull together the pieces about Mariposa so this is somewhat of a surprise. I spoke with someone recently who thought that Mariposa Larraz and Dr. Juan Xavier-Larraz were married."

Cokie shook her head. "No, that's not right, but I could see how people get confused. Juan took an entire afternoon explaining Spanish matronyms to me," Cokie said. She explained that Mariposa Arroyo-Larraz had come to the Home in 1966, some years before our Stevie passed. She and Juan shared the same patronym, the last name, but had different matronyms, the middle name.

"Mariposa's mother is Domenica Arroyo. She lives with them on the ranch now, at least she used to."

"Sounds like you knew him fairly well," Mesa said.

"It was a difficult time for me and he was very …," she paused and then said, "understanding. He had a way about him that made you feel like you could confide in him, not like a lot of Butte men who hide their emotions."

Mitsy was nodding along. "My Kenny's pretty good, not like a lot of them."

Mesa understood what they were getting at. Mining's legacy of stoicism left little room for tenderness. Add to that the generic cowboy mentality for which the state was well known, and sensitive New Age men were scarce on the ground.

"If anything, I'd say Mariposa looked upon Juan as a father figure," Cokie said while she refilled their coffee cups. "He rescued her from the hands of fate. He told me about her spending months in Miami, and then a place in Iowa before he found her here. He was grateful for all we had done for her after what she'd been through."

"How do you mean?" Mesa asked. "Had she been in some trouble?"

"Mind you, I heard about this from Celia Voinovich, the Director of the Home, who was a teacher then. She's retired now. She said that Mariposa was only six years old when she came to America alone. Imagine the trauma of that. She'd come to the Home from a girls' school in Iowa City. A nun from the Sisters of Leavenworth, who was coming to teach at St. Joseph's School, brought her here. The child was so pretty, but thin and just about afraid of her own shadow. She spent most of her time in the corner avoiding the other children. It must have been strange, all right."

"How exactly did it work? I mean, how did he claim her?" Mesa said. She still couldn't get her head around all these Cuban kids up for grabs.

"The way I heard it, he had forwarded a stack of paperwork and photographs, showing that he was her half-brother. Then one summer afternoon, he came to fetch her.

Cokie described Larraz being taken into the garden to meet Mariposa. He knelt down on one knee and called to her in Spanish. She came right away. She wouldn't let anyone else even touch her, but she took one look at him and then came right away.

"Must have been the sound of his voice or maybe the Spanish. Brings a tear to my eye just to tell the story," Cokie said and pulled a Kleenex from her pocket.

"It must have been quite the reunion," Mesa said, realizing she had goose bumps on her arms.

"He was relieved all right," Cokie said. "He had been in Iowa and tracked her here. He asked a lot of questions about the condition she was in when she first came to us, and if she had been examined by a doctor. Apparently, there were all sorts of innuendos about mistreatment of the girls at that Iowa orphanage, not that anything came of it."

"Mitsy said he joined the board of the Home?" Mesa said, wondering if he was still involved when the trouble came up at the hospital.

Cokie nodded and said, "He wanted to stay in the area and was hired on at Warm Springs where Mariposa could live on the grounds with him. We'd see him at our Festival of the Christmas tree each year and we'd catch up. Then we'd see him every couple of years. Eventually, Mariposa's mother came to the US. Not long after, he married one of the Lorimar sisters. He still lives on that big spread down in Dillon."

"That's an incredible story, Cokie," Mesa said. "I'd like to talk to the Larrazes. Would you mind if I used your name to get in touch with them?"

"Don't see why not. We don't see much of him now, but he still sends a check like clockwork every December."

୧ର

Mesa drove back to the *Mess* office after leaving Mitsy and her aunt. She wanted to talk to Cinch as he served as institutional memory at the paper. He might have a take on it all. And she was still curious about why Chance seemed so out of sorts. She wanted to check in with him.

Before she could find either of them, Irita greeted Mesa at the door. "Well, who's it gonna be?" she said expectantly. "I got features to be written, council meetings to be covered. You know, the regular stuff that our readers want to know while you're gallivanting around the countryside trying to save the world."

Mesa smiled. Irita's bluster made her day. "Weren't you the one who said write about the Montana that's been left behind? Well, that's what I'm doing." They both turned into Mesa's office where Irita stood her ground in front of the desk, arms akimbo. "At least Phade's back on the job," Mesa added.

"Whatever. I still need another pair of hands to work with, preferably a pair connected to half a brain."

Mesa pulled the folders from her satchel, along with the three stories the candidates had submitted. "Can't say as I was bowled over by any of them but in the interest of harmony, I'm afraid I have to go with the John Belushi lookalike. He has a ton of computer background, and he's just geeky enough that Phade will tolerate him."

His story entitled "Lady in Red" was actually a bit of a scoop—an interview with one of the pranksters who had scaled the East Ridge recently and covered the Lady of the Rockies floodlight with red cellophane. Half the community had been up in arms about the shenanigan, especially since the police had not released the names of those involved. It was exactly the kind of story Mesa hoped to post on the *Messenger's* new blog. And it sure as hell beat the soccer mom's "Spring Storms Present Fashion Challenges," and her recipes blog.

The purple-haired applicant had submitted a piece about Southwest Montana's growing music scene, a retreaded though well-written article, she had no doubt submitted elsewhere. She probably had the makings of a bona fide print journalist but the *Mess* was not the place for her yet, plus Mesa was not bowled over by the corner cutting.

Irita grabbed the folder, punching the kid's number into her cell as she left the office. As her own cell rang, Mesa made a mental note that Irita deserved a bonus.

It was Alexis on the phone in her usual spirited form. "You're so curious about the Larraz bunch, I'm headed over there this afternoon if you want to tag along," Alexis said. "I'm in a hay-buying mood."

❧

With a quick text, Mesa had located Chance who was down the block at Pork Chop John's. She found him sitting at the far end of the counter fortifying himself with his usual Deluxe. The addition of lettuce and tomato, along with the onion and pickle, constituted his daily allotment of vegetables.

Mesa ordered a Diet Coke and sat on the stool next to him, trying to gauge his mood. This was an odd sensation, as he was usually so upbeat. "Thought you'd be eating at the hospital with Adrienne. Everything cozy there?"

He nodded. "There was a three-car pile-up at Homestake Pass and they were slammed in the ER," he said, wiping mustard from the corner of his mouth. "Why do you ask?"

"Just that you seemed a bit off when you came to the powwow with Vivian."

"Rollie is holding Henry in custody as a 'person of interest.'"

"Seriously?" Mesa said and grimaced. "Poor kid." Chance had told Mesa how uneasy Henry had been about going to the police station. She knew Chance would not feel good about this newest predicament.

"The sheriff is really into solving these arsons. He's feeling a lot of pressure to make some headway. He doesn't seem to understand he has permanently traumatized a completely innocent person. Henry won't even speak to me."

"Did any of his detectives go over to Jessup's cabin in Twin Bridges? I didn't see anything there that would suggest Jessup was an arsonist. Or, what about the truck? Have they found it yet?"

Chance shrugged. "Rollie wasn't exactly in the mood to share details about any other evidence."

"Sorry, Chance," Mesa said. "I pushed you to convince Henry to talk to the cops."

"It's not your fault," he said finishing off his sandwich. "Henry came to me. I was just trying to help him feel better about his pal." He sighed. "You sure this story about Vivian and Jessup is worth the trouble? I mean, what if Jessup really did kill Grainger? How she going to take that? We don't need two people traumatized."

"She can handle it. Besides, Chance, the whole point is to get to the bottom of the story, to the truth. That's what Vivian has wanted from the get-go. And that's what drew me to this story from the beginning. Irita's got a list of things a mile long that she thinks I should be doing instead."

"I get that, but you're writing for the *Messenger*, not *The Washington Post*. You sure you're not trying to impress Vivian because she was Mom's friend?"

"Of course not, idiot. It's about writing the facts as they are, not as we might like them to be," Mesa said with a sigh. "You can't expect me to fill the paper with fluff. This is a story about real people's lives, people who don't always have a voice. It deserves to see the light of day."

The sun was high and most of the snow from the recent storm had melted. The pungent smell of manure and horses greeted Mesa as she got out of Alexis' pickup at Rancho Esmeralda as the Lorimar Ranch was now renamed.

Lurch, Alexis' nickname for the Esmeralda foreman, had called the day before to say they had some premium grade alfalfa they wanted to get rid of. "Just what my mustangs love, not that I coddle them," Alexis had told Mesa.

She couldn't decide if Alexis was putting her on, or really trying to help with background on the Larrazes. Either way, Mesa was game, and had left the office to rendezvous with her friend. Thirty minutes later, she had pulled into Alexis' place where they switched to her pickup and drove south on Highway 41 through Glen and past endless pastures to the turnoff to the Esmeralda.

Finally, they drove through the tall, timber gateway to the ranch. A spacious white clapboard house with red shutters, a rock chimney and a red roof, stood next to a smaller and newer house nearby. A massive barn of the same construction sat at the rear of the houses. Alexis pulled up next to the barn doors in the front by the corral.

"This setup looks like it belongs in Ohio, not Montana," Mesa said while Alexis parked.

"The history of this ranch is wacky," Alexis said. "Once upon a time it was one of the largest sheep ranches in the whole country. Seventy years ago, some railroad magnate developed it, and then left it to his daughters who never really lived here."

"Wonder how Larraz could afford it?" Mesa said aloud. Unless he'd taken money out of Cuba, he couldn't have been living large on a state salary and pension.

"Married one of the daughters after a whirlwind romance," Alexis said with a grin.

"Well, aren't you a wealth of information," Mesa said. Alexis never read a book or sat down at a computer unless she had to. "How'd you find out all about that?"

"Ranch hands. They gossip like old women at the bingo. Larraz married the surviving sister. She was way older than he was, like in her sixties. Then she died about five years after that, apparently a very satisfied woman, because she left everything to him."

A paddock door opened and a sturdy ranch hand, outfitted in Carhartts and a leather Stetson, sauntered toward the truck. Alexis got out and greeted him. "Hey, Frisco. Brought my friend along. I want to introduce her to the señor. He around?"

Mesa turned toward Alexis and mouthed "The señor?" She couldn't remember the last time she had heard Alexis be so deferential to a man.

Frisco looked Mesa up and down like she'd been out in the hall during class, and he'd found her wanting. There was nothing polite or folksy about him. He wasn't exactly like *The Addam's Family* Lurch, but he did have a hefty scar over his left brow that gave him a menacing look.

"Take her up to the house. I'll load the pickup. You want both rolls?"

Alexis nodded and turned Mesa back the way they'd come.

❧

Chance continued to have reservations about Mesa's determination to investigate the circumstances of Ethan

Grainger's death and Dowling Jessup's involvement in it. For one, he didn't think they'd have much luck convincing the police that there was any connection between two deaths more than thirty years apart. The sheriff had made it clear that his priority was solving the arsons. Once again, Jessup, with no family and no money, had no one who would advocate for the investigation of any injustice he might have suffered.

Chance had to admit the Operation Pedro Pan story was a curious blast from the past, thousands of kids from Cuba without visas or family. Presumably, those kids had grown up in the US since the situation in Cuba had not changed. He couldn't help but wonder what had happened to them.

He also knew Mesa would go ahead no matter what. And, as usual, Chance did not feel it was wise, or fair, to let his sister go it alone.

So, here he was, waiting for Nick who had agreed to meet across from the Courthouse at the Venus Rising Coffee House. Chance sat at a corner table after ordering. He knew Nick would rather be caught dead than order a tall, double shot espresso, but when put in a plain mug it would look like the motor oil he was used to drinking. As long as it was hot, was all he would say.

"You owe me big time," Nick said when he finally arrived. "You can't believe the hellhole where Anaconda stores their old records. And damned if I didn't have to listen to this old-timer, another maintenance guy, tell war stories."

"Come on, Nick, you know you love that stuff. Whaddaya got for me?"

"Half a coroner's report that is pretty straight up. A Warm Springs doc named Larraz is listed as attending.

The deceased had lacerations on his face and arms, bruises and contusions on his head and neck, and third degree burns all over on account of he ended up face first when a part of the crust on the thermal outcropping known as the Mound collapsed and he fell into it."

Chance cringed at the thought of what that must have felt like. "So it was called a homicide?" Chance asked.

"Well, that page of the report is missing," Nick said. "But don't act all conspiratorial on me. Like I told you on the phone, the county and city coroners' offices combined files, which got jammed into cardboard boxes and stored. I'll bet the rest of that report is probably stuck to the back of another one, only I don't got the rest of my life to look for it. Lucky for you I also copied the police report, which is complete." He tossed several pages in Chance's direction.

Chance shook his head. He liked cops so he rarely poor-mouthed them. They had a tough job. But he couldn't help wondering if this lost page was mere coincidence. All he said to Nick was, "Bureaucracy."

Nick explained that the records were tossed into one office, stacked near to the ceiling. Which was no surprise to him since when he was hired by Butte-Silver Bow in '99, he had to reorganize files that were ten years old. The previous coroner, who had decided not to run again, had let things slide as election day neared. Meanwhile, people were still dying and when somebody dies, as any coroner would say, there's a lot of paperwork.

Chance leafed through the police report, which was signed off by the Chief of Law Enforcement for Anaconda-Deer Lodge County. "So, if Warm Springs is a state hospital, who has jurisdiction over a death that occurs there? Would they have called in the state police, or the county, or what?"

"The county coroner, shithead. You know that. The bodies belong to us by state statute," Nick said. He explained that the Anaconda police would also investigate if there was a complaint and somebody needed to be arrested. In this case, it was a little fuzzy because the bulldozer who was police chief then was also the coroner. Clearly, Nick did not have a high opinion of all coroners. "He went down as a double-dipping weasel that did as little as possible and collected the equivalent of two salaries."

Chance flipped through the report that showed that the suspect, Dowling Jessup, was remanded to the custody of the hospital and placed in the forensics ward pending a review in the Anaconda-Deer Lodge District Court. A review that, as best as Chance could tell, never took place.

"So what do you think happened?" Chance said.

Nick shrugged. "Without a complete coroner's report, it's hard to tell. The way I read the police report, the deceased and the suspect Jessup had an altercation up on the Gazebo and the deceased fell to his death. Manslaughter would be my call, but Jessup is locked up in the forensics unit and the police chief slash coroner calls it good."

"So, no hearing, no lawyer, no nothing?" Chance said. "I still can't believe it could happen that way."

"The coroner and the police chief consult and decisions are made about how to proceed, who to charge with what. In this case, you had a police chief who was also the coroner. He probably called the county attorney and they decided the best way to handle the situation."

"The county attorney?" Chance said.

And before he could ask, Nick said, "Long time dead, and don't look so surprised. This is why we all want friends in local government."

"Yeah? Well, maybe if you could count on your friends to do the right thing."

"Which you can, and I do." He gulped his coffee and then said, "The tox report on the vic from the trailer came back. He had more than his fair share of alprazolam, a.k.a. zannies or footballs, in his system though not enough to off himself. Basically, he popped a couple of extra meds to chill out. Washed down with a dose of Jim Beam, he wasn't gonna wake up for a good twenty-four hours if you'd started a fire on his ass."

Chapter 15

"Hi, Rosita," Alexis said to a Mexican housekeeper who had opened the back door to Alexis's knock. "Can we see the señor?"

Dressed crisply in blouse, skirt, and pressed apron, Rosita led Mesa and Alexis through the large, modern kitchen that smelled of strong coffee and furniture polish. They walked to the front of the house and into a foyer with a gleaming, pine floor where the housekeeper asked them to wait a moment.

"This isn't like any ranch house I've been in before," Mesa whispered. "Feels more like a mansion back East."

"I heard the Lorimar sisters spent a lot of time on the West Coast, Seattle, or Portland, I forget which. At least until the señor convinced the younger one to stick around."

Mesa chuckled, "You make their lives sound like an episode of Dallas."

Rosita reappeared and said, "The señor will see you now." She motioned them into what turned out to be a spacious den with knotty pine walls inset with brimming bookshelves and a roaring fire in a stone hearth.

The señor, clad in clothes more suited to a librarian than a rancher, stood up when they entered. The earthy smell of his cigar permeated the room even with the fire burning. He reached out a hand to Alexis. "It's always good to see you, Alexis. Please sit down. Introduce me to your friend."

Mesa sat down on a deep red brocade-upholstered sofa across from the fire, happy to enjoy its warmth. Alexis' grandmother had been a stickler for manners and, when she most needed them, Alexis could deliver. Beginning with a "May I present," she described Mesa as her college roommate without whom Alexis would never have survived. It was only partly an exaggeration.

"She's the editor of *the Mining City Messenger*. It's the weekly newspaper in Butte."

The señor had resumed his seat and smoking his cigar. "I think I have seen the paper when I have had occasion to be in Butte, which is not often," he said, nodding to Mesa, "but I will certainly regard it more closely when next I visit."

Watching her friend edge toward the door, Mesa could see Alexis was in no mood to take part in a serious conversation with the señor. She excused herself to deal with Frisco and talk horses.

"What brings you to the Esmeralda?" the señor asked, his tone formal but inviting.

Mesa could see Larraz still had the charm that Cokie remembered. His good looks had probably gotten him a long way, but it was the gentleness in his eyes she warmed to, and his accent, which she couldn't resist in any man. His gaze did not leave her while they talked.

"I recently spoke with Mrs. Claire Winsot. She's on the Board at the Paul Clark Home in Butte. She told me you've been a longtime supporter of theirs."

"Mrs. Winsot?" he paused. "Of course, Cokie! Now I remember. Most kind. How is she?"

"Quite well. Actually, I saw her this morning. We happened to be discussing Operation Pedro Pan. It's quite a story and one not a lot of people around here know. She thought your sister was part of that group of children. I was wondering if you might be willing to talk about it."

Larraz put down his cigar, and nodded, "Mariposa was sent to Miami in 1963. She was only six. I had already left Cuba and was in the States studying medicine. Unfortunately, it had become difficult for families to communicate during the revolution, and so it was some time before I found out what had happened to her. Without the care she received at the Home, I'm not sure how well she would have survived. We will always be grateful."

He paused to puff on his cigar, as if he needed a moment to recover. Mesa could see how the memory of those days still touched him.

"How did this subject come to your attention?" he asked. "You have an interest in this story for your paper?"

As he spoke, Mesa could see that he was sincere in his gratitude. She hoped he would be as sensitive when she switched the conversation to Jessup, so she dodged his first question and went on to the second.

"Perhaps, if Mariposa were willing to talk about her experience, we might do a feature." She spoke confidently. After all, she'd had people refuse to talk before. It was part of the job. But if Larraz didn't choose to discuss Grainger's death, what then? She had no editor to run back to, to ask what to do. It was up to her.

"Right now, I have a more pressing story I'm covering that concerns Warm Springs. Mrs. Winsot thought you might be able to help me with that as well."

"If I can, I've been retired now for more than ten years," Larraz said.

"I recently spoke with a woman who came to our paper searching for an old friend she knew at Warm Springs. I believe you worked there at the same time in the late seventies."

He nodded. "You do realize that as a physician I'm not at liberty to talk about individual patients, even if I am retired."

"I understand," she said, sensing a reluctance forming on his part. "Let me tell you the story I'm hoping to write about, and then if there is any information you can give, I'd appreciate it."

"I am happy to help if I can," he said, and sat back in his armchair to listen. He seemed at ease.

Mesa explained the details of Vivian's search for Dowling, her desire to prove his innocence, and his subsequent death. Larraz listened quietly, his undivided attention on Mesa as she spoke.

"I remember the two young men—boys really," he said when Mesa finished. "The incident upset the staff terribly. We saw so many young people tormented by emotions they couldn't manage." He shook his head.

"I know this is meaningless for Jessup," Mesa said, "but for Vivian Jobe, it could be an emotional watershed. She'd be helping to set the record straight for someone she cared a great deal about, particularly if Dowling Jessup's recent death was not an accident."

"Ah, I see. So the Butte police think Jessup's death was a suicide? How sad."

"Quite the contrary, they're treating his death as part of the arson. And that may be the case. But Vivian says that Dowling didn't kill Ethan Grainger, and I'm exploring the possibility that his death and Jessup's could have been linked."

Larraz was leaning forward now, holding an ashtray, and toying with his cigar ash. "That would be the long shot, as you say? But it would make for a good story, no?"

Mesa smiled and nodded. She was not ashamed to want to write a story that captured the public's interest. "Particularly if the connection turned out to be true. You were the attending physician at Grainger's death, and Jessup was never officially charged as best we can tell. Do you know why that was?"

"Do you know of Chief Bonney?" Larraz said with a smile. "He was, as my ranch foreman will say, a piece of work. He had his own way of meting out justice. I certainly would not presume to guess his thinking. Sadly, he is no longer with us."

Sadly indeed, thought Mesa as she scribbled in her notebook. Another avenue to investigate was blocked.

The señor relit his cigar with a match, and looked for a moment into the fire. "Violence in mental health institutions has always been a problem. It was present then, as it is now. You may find that these boys involved were good friends, but disagreements between two friends are often more extreme than with those who are not as close. You would agree?"

Mesa nodded, and said, "But there were no witnesses to what actually happened, isn't that right?"

"The police investigated the incident, so I can't speak to that entirely. I know they found evidence on the body that linked Jessup to the dead boy."

"Do you know what that was?" Mesa asked.

The señor shook his head. "In the end, my job was to ensure the safety of the patients in the hospital, something at which I failed that day. That is on my conscience, I assure you."

"I spoke with a former nurse, Jeanne Lenin. She said she thought you'd done everything you could to help Jessup. Do you think he could have killed Grainger? You were his therapist, weren't you? Do you think he actually could have killed another human being?"

Larraz clasped his chin in his hand in a Freud-like pose and spoke deliberately. "I'll tell you what I told Chief Bonney. If it was anything, it was an accident, a mistake."

"Is that why you had Dowling Jessup put in the forensics ward?"

"Bonney said that as long as Jessup had no alibi and refused to cooperate, he made himself look guilty. The boy kept insisting he was nowhere near the gazebo that day. In the end, I felt, as my patient, he would receive better treatment with us than if he was placed in jail, which is what Chief Bonney wanted to do."

Mesa nodded. "Were there others who might have wanted to harm Grainger?"

"No doubt," Larraz admitted, "but none that had ground privileges that day. I'm sorry I can't be more helpful."

"Just one more question," Mesa said. "Jessup left Warm Springs about three years ago as part of a special residential program for offenders with a history of mental illness. Did he ever try to make contact with you or with Mariposa?"

The señor stood up and said, "Not at all."

Mesa stopped writing. Was it likely that Mariposa failed to mention to Larraz that Jessup had come calling? Or was the señor lying? She thought not. Mariposa would not want the attention.

In that split second, she decided to let the question slide. Their rapport was warm and she didn't want that to change, yet. If she needed to, she could call him out on it later.

"If you think of anything about the incident you could share, I'd appreciate hearing from you," she said and gave him one of her cards.

He nodded, and then said, as Mesa prepared to leave, "Operation Pedro Pan was a blessing in some ways but it also had long-term, emotionally devastating consequences for many. Some scars are so deep that sharing how one gets them is too painful. Any attention a story might bring to Mariposa would be difficult for her. I hope you'll consider this if you should decide to write one."

She shook the señor's hand and thanked him for his time. "I've heard good things about you, Dr. Larraz. It was a pleasure to meet you."

Mesa could see how concerned he still was for Mariposa, even after all these years but, as her former editor always said, "Once you let people think they can influence what goes into the newspaper, you might as well start working for the Chamber of Commerce."

The señor bowed to her and then accompanied her to the rear of the house where the housekeeper was looking out a picture window into the late afternoon light. Meticulously, she dried teacups and saucers and placed them on the dining table, intermittently watching the unfolding scene outside.

Mesa and the señor walked toward the corral where Alexis leaned against her pickup, arms crossed, watching Frisco examine the back hoof of an Andalusian. Dappled gray with a thick braided black mane, the horse was massive but calm, and so well groomed she could not remember seeing a more pampered animal.

Next to the horse was a wooden mounting block with three steps. Mariposa was dressed as she was in the photo Dowling had pinned to his table in Twin Bridges. Mesa held her head high, wondering if Mariposa would acknowledge her, but the other woman was completely engrossed in the horse.

Once Frisco had finished examining the stallion's hoof, Mariposa stepped up to the mounting block. Her boot must have slipped on the second step. As she fell back, Frisco reached to steady her. But Mariposa regained her balance and sternly rejected Frisco's helping hand with her riding crop, making it clear that she neither needed nor wanted help.

Mesa was distracted from the awkward moment by the señor, who asked, "Are you a horsewoman like Alexis? Perhaps you would like to visit us again and ride."

"I'm afraid I'd have trouble keeping up," she said off-handedly, her attention on the scene near the corral and the cautious attention everyone seemed to pay Mariposa. Clearly, something was not quite right with her, and those around her knew it.

৵৶

"What are those white markings on their necks?" Mesa asked, examining what looked like Morse code dots and dashes. The black, gray, and white gelding with a thick black and white mane walked from the barn past Mesa into the corral, following a smaller horse with similar markings. Alexis called them "grulla paint" mustangs.

"Haven't you ever seen a freeze brand? Tells what sanctuary the mustang came from," Alexis said. "I swear, Mesa. For somebody who has spent so much time in Montana, you don't know jack about horses. Hope you were more on the ball when you talked to the señor."

"He was charming enough, but he didn't really have that much to say. "

"Told you they were dull and boring," Alexis said. A whinny came from inside the barn, and she went into the corral again and opened the top half of one of the stall doors. A chestnut with a star on its forelock poked its head out and neighed. "Don't worry," she called to the horse, "you're not missing anything."

"I thought you just bought two mustangs," Mesa said, admiring the spirited animals.

"This one belongs to Jesse, the foreman. That's how I got him to work for me—by agreeing to let him board his horse and help to train mine. I'm getting eaten out of house and home."

"By me or the horse?"

Mesa turned to see a tall, lanky cowboy with broad shoulders and an easy gait come up behind her.

He tipped his hat to her, and then walked into the corral. "Sorry I wasn't out here to help you unload. Got caught up with a couple of calves down in the bottom.

I'll take over," he said to Alexis and she moved back out of the corral.

"You're forgiven, this once," Alexis said. "We just got back from the Esmeralda."

Jesse gave an eye roll and went over to the chestnut to let the mare out of the stall and into the corral.

"Jesse used to be in the señor's employ," Alexis said. She explained that much as Jesse did not want to be considered a quitter, he had left the Esmeralda when he couldn't get time off to go with his brother to the Mustang Makeover in Texas where he was competing. Jesse had returned from Ft. Worth just in time to get hired by Alexis. "He knows just about all there is to know about training mustangs."

Jesse sauntered over to stand next to the two women. He leaned against the corral next to Alexis.

"You got to know Mariposa?" Mesa asked him, doing her best not to dwell on the cowboy's dark brown eyes.

"Some," he said. "She's a pretty good horse woman. Spends a lot of time with those Andalusians, I'll tell you that."

"And Frisco," Alexis said. "You worked with him too."

The cowboy said nothing.

"Go ahead," Alexis said. "Tell her what you told me."

Jesse shrugged. "He's okay, I guess. Why they kept him and let me go, I'll never understand. I forgot more about horses than he'll ever know. He spent most of his time keeping an eye on her, riding with her everywhere almost like a bodyguard. Not that she gave two cents about him."

"That was odd the way she got snippy with him when he tried to help her when she slipped on the mounting box today. Don't you think?" Mesa asked Alexis, who shrugged.

"Wouldn't be the first time," Jesse said. "Only things she cares about is horses."

"That I can understand," Alexis said.

"Don't say much either," Jesse said, and then looked at Alexis with a grin. "Just as well."

Mesa wondered if Frisco knew about Mariposa's history with Operation Pedro Pan. Could he have been part of that too? "He ever talk about where he came from?"

"Haven't you heard? That's just the kind of thing cowboys don't ask each other," Alexis said. The taller of the two grulla mustangs had come over to Alexis who was scratching its neck and cooing, "Good boy, Baron."

Mesa looked toward Jesse who said, "That's true," then he leaned down and said in a low voice, "Housekeeper said he did a stint in that Recovery program in Warm Springs. The señor hired him from there because he don't drink. He fell off the wagon once and señor told him if it ever happened again he'd see to it that Frisco was sent back to face the music. Guess he's got something on him."

Sent back where, Mesa wondered.

It was well past midnight when Chance heard from Adrienne, who was working the third shift at the ER. The two of them had spent a leisurely evening at his place. It was only when he'd reached for the ringing phone that he realized her side of the bed was empty, and that he had fallen asleep.

"What? You forget your lunchbox?" he said with a yawn.

Chance had learned that when something was wrong, Adrienne's voice became calm. He sat up in bed the minute she began to talk. "Henry's been brought to the ER," she said in muted tones. "An auto accident of some sort. He's unconscious and he's pretty well banged up."

Chance had barely said, "I'll be right there," before he hung up, grabbed his jeans and shirt and tore out the back door, through the alley and into the street. He ran the remaining two blocks to the ER, telling himself to be thankful that Adrienne had been on duty.

Henry had taken a liking to her after she had drawn the sketches of Stick and the mystery man. Though he'd spent his share of time in hospitals, Henry did not like to spend the night anywhere but at his apartment. More than once Chance had offered to take Henry camping but he always said he liked his own bed. "Sleeping bags make me itch," he had said by way of explanation.

Chance slowed his pace as he entered the hospital, grateful that the ER was practically empty. He looked though the door to the treatment bays where he could see Adrienne entering information at a keyboard.

"What the hell is happening?" Chance said when Adrienne approached.

She sighed and maneuvered him to a quiet corner where she helped him re-button the shirt he'd thrown on. "I'm not entirely sure. The police found him lying on the sidewalk on Park Street just past Rocky Mountain

Archery. They think he might have been a victim of a hit and run."

"Did anybody see anything?" Chance said. He knew that end of Park St. had several empty lots and, at that time of the evening, the traffic could have been light.

"Apparently not, but there were skid marks on the road and a sapling that got sheared off at ground level.

Sparky's Garage on the corner of Park and Wyoming was having some March Madness special. Cinch had sold them an ad in the *Messenger*. The barbeque restaurant had a spacious bar and it could have gotten rowdy. Maybe a drunk driver had over-corrected, hit Henry and then, the driver knowing he couldn't pass a breathalyzer test, had taken off. "Did he say anything?" Chance asked.

"He was in and out of consciousness when they took him upstairs to x-ray," Adrienne said, "which isn't unusual for someone who has sustained a nasty bump on the head and is in shock. I heard him mumble something about his headlight being on."

Chance plopped down into one of the plastic waiting chairs. Adrienne sat next to him, and gently hugged his shoulder.

"I bought him the headlight for that bike. Made him promise to use it," he said. "This poor kid's had nothing but bad luck since St. Patrick's Day."

Chance looked up at Adrienne. "You don't suppose this could have something to do with Henry seeing that guy at the trailer?"

"The arsonist, you mean?" she said, and then shook her head. "The police were here earlier in the evening, delivering some guy who'd lost a fight outside Sparky's. Somebody who had one too many Moose Drools probably tore down the street in their pickup and smacked Henry along the way."

Despite Adrienne's similar logic, Chance couldn't shake the feeling that maybe Henry was on someone's radar. "Can I see him when he's awake?" Chance said.

She nodded. "Let's hope that's sooner than later."

Chapter 16

"A trucker on a night run to Sioux Falls saw the explosion. Cinch heard it on the scanner," Irita said. "I guess we can be thankful the arsonist torched an empty pick-up in the middle of nowhere and not somebody's house. Then there's the possible hit and run on East Park." It was Friday morning and Irita was in the middle of her morning round up of the news, talking to no one in particular, since Mesa had stopped by only long enough to meet Vivian for their drive to Warm Springs.

Irita walked into Mesa's office, talking to herself, "What about the new hire? I thought you could indoctrinate him today. He can stop by any time. When can you fit him in?" She began flipping the pages of Mesa's calendar.

Chance followed her in, interrupting Irita's monologue. "Where's Mesa? Who are you talking to?"

When she explained where Mesa had gone, Chance sat down on the sofa and said, "Damn it." Then he began to unwrap a breakfast burrito from the Park and Main Café. "I need to talk to her."

"Call her on her cell. She's gone to Warm Springs, not the North Pole."

"She better watch herself, is all. What with Henry and now this pickup, we may be in over our heads."

Not that Chance would expect any TLC from Irita, but she could see he was not his usual happy-go-lucky self. "Chance, hon, what are you talking about? What's happened to Henry and what about the truck?"

"The hit and run you were just calling into the wilderness about? That was Henry."

"What?" Irita barked and took her warlord stance with her fists on her hips. You couldn't take this kind of news lightly. "I like the kid, even though he can be a nuisance," she said. "Sure don't like to hear that he got hurt."

"I think it was a warning to keep his mouth shut," Chance said, telling Irita he was convinced that the man Henry had seen, in turn, had seen Henry's photo in the *Standard* and decided to shut him up.

"You think they meant to come after Henry?" Irita said, wondering just how much the kid could know.

"He figured out where Henry lived. Anybody uptown could have told him where the 'loopers' hang out. And to make it all the easier, Henry's habits are like clockwork. He rides up Park Street to look at the Lady almost every evening. He's obsessed with that damn statue. All mystery man had to do was wait for him, and then he could scare him to death, if not worse."

Irita conceded that Henry trudging along the street uptown with or without his neon orange bike was a common enough occurrence. The mostly open area on East Park had been flattened by the Anaconda Company years ago to make way for pit mining. The unobstructed view of the Lady of the Rockies statue on the East Ridge was an unintended byproduct. Henry would be hard to miss.

"I called Rollie first thing this morning to see if he would reconsider running the sketch in the *Standard*, but he won't." Chance took the folded sketch out of his pocket and tossed it on the table in clear frustration. "He still thinks Henry's delusional and that this is probably a sketch of his mailman."

"And the truck, the big ball of fire that exploded in the night over by the college, you want to tell me why we should be worried about that?" Irita said, patting her fingertips together and telling herself not to get too excited. Everything would be fine, just fine.

"According to the Sheriff, the truck is registered to a guy who owns a garage over in Twin Bridges, and the one last in the possession of Dowling Jessup."

"Why would the arsonist target that truck?" Irita said.

"Good question, Irita. The same one I asked the Sheriff, who ignored me. That's because I don't think it was the arsonist. I think it's another warning. We're asking too many questions about Jessup and someone doesn't like it."

"It's more of an inconvenience, really," Vivian was saying as she and Mesa sped along the Interstate past Rocker and Ramsay on the way to Warm Springs. "I feel like such a fool to be honest, all that worry. Search and Rescue, oh, my god, how embarrassing." These last words she said with a chuckle.

Mesa smiled at Vivian and wondered how many women her age would have handled a cold night in the woods so cavalierly, let alone a broken leg. "You do realize, you could have died of hypothermia."

"Now, now, I gave up awful-izing not long after I came into Dr. Kaiser's care," the older woman said in a gentle voice. "I still can't quite fathom how it happened, but compared to what's transpired since I started this whole mess, well ...." and her voice trailed off. "Although, I'll admit I'm certainly glad I had my dogs with me." She petted Gandhi who sat in the back seat with her head on the console between the two of them.

"So, what do you think we'll learn from this Patient Advocate?"

"I'm not entirely sure. She's who the switchboard referred me to when I said I had questions about access to patient records. The office has been around for about ten years and, as far as I can tell from the website, this same woman has been in the job since it was created. So she should be able to give us some perspective. Basically, her position was established when the hospital went through its last major review. A major criticism was that patients had no one to assist them in understanding their rights in the process of commitment."

"You can say that again," Mesa said. "Too bad this Advocate wasn't around when Dowl needed her."

"Exactly what I thought," Vivian said with a sigh.

"Have you been back here since you were last ...?" Mesa still wasn't comfortable thinking of Vivian as a mental patient.

"It's okay," she said with a smile. "I don't mind being called crazy." Then she said, "Now that I'm not. And no, I haven't been back for a decade and even then,

I never saw the Mound again. For some reason I feel the need to go back there for Dowl's sake. Call it a pilgrimage."

"I hear ya," Mesa said and they pulled off the exit ramp, past Uncle Buck's, the local bar complete with several racks of antlers above the door, across the railroad tracks, and onto the hospital grounds.

"It looks just as I remember it," Vivian said in a quiet voice. "The gazebo, the peculiar colors of the Mound. The more substantial railing around the gazebo is new. Probably wise."

Mesa was surprised by the peaceful atmosphere of the hospital grounds. The buildings were a mixture of old and new brick structures, but there were no fences, iron bars, or gates to ask permission to get through. She had no doubt there were doors inside, much like the ones she remembered at St. James—the ones that locked you in. But, as far as the outside, she was surrounded by empty pastures, old farm buildings in the distance, and the freedom of the open spaces.

The Mound stood at the back edge of the compound. The receptionist at the Advocate's office suggested that they head out there, and the Advocate, who was late back from a meeting, would catch up with them.

Surprisingly, they'd been able to drive right up to the outcropping. Taller than it seemed in the photo in the newspaper, it looked strangely out of place, except that the Mound had been there for centuries. It was the hospital that was the newcomer.

The March sunlight was warm but the wind off the fields created a chill. Vivian held her cardigan close, lost in thought. "I feel sort of like the recovering alcoholic who goes into a bar to see if she'll feel tempted. I was always so anxious and confused when I was here before, but not anymore. This place and my illness have no hold on me now. I get that my institutionalization caused as many problems as it cured."

Mesa didn't know what to say. She was impressed with the way Vivian had been able to put such a difficult situation in perspective. Clearly, she had let go of any shame or stigma. Maybe that's what made Mesa tongue-tied—realizing she needed to do the same thing.

They strolled around the Mound in silence, careful to step over the occasional streams of hot water escaping through the thermal crust. "Well, I was hoping to have some revelation about Dowl and the whole grisly mess, but nothing's coming up, at least nothing new."

"Did he ever talk about what he was going to do once he was released? You know, before Grainger's death short-circuited his future?"

"You'll get a kick out of this," Vivian said, "especially after what you told me about that Frito Lady and the Butte Library. That's what got me thinking about how Dowl used to read aloud to me. We'd sit in the stairwell. It was kind of a natural echo chamber and he would read Dickens to me." She smiled. "He talked about becoming a librarian."

Mesa smiled back, remembering *The Count of Monte Cristo* she'd found in Dowl's cabin. She hoped the vindication and sense of justice meted out in the novels he read had given him comfort. There certainly had been none as a result of that afternoon at the Mound.

Chance had relayed from Nick the details of the original crime scene and Mesa ran through them in her head. She could see how it had all happened—a sudden fall over the rail of the gazebo after a struggle, the blunt force trauma when Grainger's skull collided with limestone, and the body parboiling in the stream of bubbling water when it broke through the travertine crust.

It was easy to see how there had been no witnesses. The nearest buildings were a grove of cottages nearly three football fields away. "What are those houses over there?" Mesa asked, more out of curiosity than a belief that there might have been a witness the Anaconda police chief had failed to question.

"Those were staff cottages. Remember the picnic at Dr. Larraz's house? That's where he and his sister lived."

Once back on the Interstate and headed home, Mesa called into the office, mindful about keeping Irita happy. Her assistant had nothing but bad news to share—Henry in a coma, Dowl's truck being torched, and Chance suddenly feeling very uneasy about their investigation into Jessup's death. "Call Chance and have him order up some pizzas. We can have a summit meeting at the office when we get back."

Vivian couldn't help but overhear. "Thanks for coming with me. I know you're busy," she said. "The Patient Advocate wasn't much help, but I'm glad I made the trip."

Mesa reached over and squeezed the older woman's hand. "No worries. I think it was important to see the hospital, and the Mound, especially if I'm going to write about it. I can't believe I've lived in Butte for as long as I have and I've never been out here. Now I can visualize what actually happened, whoever was involved."

Vivian was right, though, about the Patient Advocate. A forty-something lawyer named Lydia Vartok, she had no access to previous patients' records, and knew only cursory information about what had happened in the '70s and '80s. But her primary responsibility was an important one, acting as an informal counsel to the patients. She couldn't actually represent them, but she did know the law and she was a reliable record-keeper for what did or didn't happen.

She did say that if Dowl had been moved to the penitentiary, he would have had to have committed a felony, something that would have involved an assault like hitting a guard hard enough to warrant medical attention. She also said that transferring mentally ill offenders from the state hospital to the state prison without giving them a chance to present evidence or witnesses to argue against the transfer was just what her position had been designed to prevent.

"Meaning it might well have happened in the past?" Mesa had clarified. Lydia gave a quiet but emphatic nod.

Chance was halfway through the double pepperoni when the women arrived. He explained about Henry's accident and the Sheriff's refusal to run the mystery man's sketch in the paper.

"When does unconscious turn into coma?" Mesa said, taking another look at the sketch on the coffee table.

Chance shrugged, "Adrienne says the first twenty-four hours it's hard to tell."

Mesa could see how down Chance was about Henry. But, in her mind, he seemed overly concerned that someone had torched Dowl's truck as a warning.

She was aggravated that the police hadn't found the truck first. More likely, it had been torched to destroy evidence. If it was a warning, she was even more irritated. "What we need to do is redouble our efforts. I think we're getting closer to figuring this thing out."

"Look, Mesa," Chance said and put down his slice of pizza. "What if the one person who knew where to find that truck saw Jessup get out of it, meaning our mystery man? And what if he knows who's asking questions about him? Don't be naive."

Mesa knew better than to openly scoff at Chance. "I won't do anything stupid, I promise, but we need to focus on mystery man. Now that the truck is gone, we still don't know anything more about him than what Henry told you on Monday, which was next to nothing. If he left any fingerprints in the trailer, the police haven't identified them. Nothing we've found out about Dowling even hints at a connection with another man, besides Dale at the garage. Vivian, you have any ideas?"

"What about the items you found at Jessup's cabin?" she asked. "Why don't we go through them again? Maybe something will occur to me."

Mesa turned to her computer and pulled up the file of photos she had taken in Twin Bridges. Vivian and Chance stood looking over her shoulder as she went through the pictures. The photo of Mariposa on horseback was first.

"We know this is Mariposa," Mesa said deliberately. "Yesterday, she was wearing an outfit just like this one, except a slightly different color and design. I think she's obsessed with the get-up, as well as the horses. We know Jessup knew where to find her, even made contact. What's suspicious about that though is that Larraz claimed not to know anything about the visit to the gallery. It's hard to believe Mariposa wouldn't tell him. He's definitely the kingpin at the ranch."

"Maybe that was all completely innocent?" Chance asked.

"Didn't sound innocent when Mariposa described the conversation. She seemed frightened, at the very least confused. Of course, we can't be entirely sure that what Mariposa said she heard was what Jessup actually said or meant."

"What did he say?" Vivian asked, clearly curious.

"That they'd known each other a long time ago and that they had some catching up to do."

"That does sound fairly innocent. After all, that's what I hoped to do with Dowl," Vivian said.

She chimed in again when she saw the magazine article about the Children's Home reunions. "Maybe the article put Dowl in mind to reconnect with friends he made there. He always talked fondly of that time. Maybe he'd seen some of his old classmates around town."

"I thought about that," Mesa said. "But we have no evidence he contacted anyone but friends from Warm Springs, and why Mariposa and not you?"

"Out of sight out of mind?" Vivian said. "Mariposa did get her picture in the paper."

Mesa gave Vivian a consoling glance, not wanting her to feel like she had been forgotten.

She smiled back, and said, "My own fault. I try to avoid the limelight."

"What's with the list of doctors?" Chance asked and squinted closer to the screen to see.

Mesa enlarged the page copied from the medical directory, and then almost simultaneously, they said, "It's Larraz. He's listed on the page."

Enlarging the page still further, Mesa could see the psychiatrist's name under X, listing his education and specialty, and that he remained a licensed therapist in Montana. The directory also gave an office address in Dillon.

"Jessup was trying to find Larraz," Chance said. "What if he did? What if Jessup met up with Larraz?"

"If he did, Larraz denied it when I spoke with him yesterday. I asked him specifically." Mesa kicked herself for not taking a closer look at the listing. She could have shown it to Larraz. Now she was really concerned about the possibility that he had lied about seeing Jessup. She had made the mistake of putting Larraz on a pedestal like everyone else did.

Chance had not succumbed. "Why would he lie— unless he was trying to cover something up or protect someone?" His phone rang and he turned away to answer it.

"What would Jessup want with Larraz after all this time?" Mesa said, looking at Vivian.

"I wish I knew," Vivian said, deflated.

"That was Adrienne," Chance said. "Henry still hasn't woken up, and the truck wasn't the only arson last night. Somebody tried to start a fire at the back of Bread and Roses around four a.m."

 славу

Mesa had no trouble convincing Shane to take a drive down to the Hacienda on Friday evening when he arrived in Butte. He knew all about the place, which was a surprise. She hadn't mentioned that it was Alexis' idea.

"I was there for a bachelor party about five years ago when it first opened," he said with a bigger than usual smile as they drove toward tiny Apex.

"Now, don't get the wrong idea," he had said in response to her frown. "It was mild by comparison to some blowouts I've seen in Butte."

"Nobody got beat up or arrested for firing their six-shooter?" Mesa taunted.

Shane shook his head. "The señora throws a decent party. She had a couple of long-legged gals dance for us. All decked out in feathers and flowers."

"And not much else, I'll bet," Mesa chuckled. She had no particular critique of women who liked to take their clothes off for a living. It would certainly beat waiting tables. If anything, she'd probably admit to feeling intimidated. She had the body of a teenage boy—nothing any guy would pay to see.

"They looked like exotic birds with yellow and red costumes and feathers that barely covered the tantalizing parts."

"Not your local strippers?" Mesa said. She knew the local dancers only by tidbits she heard from Cinch, who feigned a platonic interest in their careers. "There actually IS an art to it," he would argue. One had supposedly come from Reno recently, another from rehab, and natural talent and on-the-job training were heavily relied on.

They all performed at Sagebrush Sam's, the club in Rocker, west of Butte, and a favorite of truckers traveling I-15 from San Diego County to Canada, and I-90 from Boston to Seattle. Butte bachelor parties, not to mention the occasional bachelorette bash, provided the additional audience.

"God, don't call them strippers," Shane laughed. "The señora would go ballistic. She called them exotic dancers, professionally trained."

"And were they?"

"Beats me. The music was more than your average jukebox—Caribbean, lots of drums, really fast. The dancers did seem to have some choreography involved in what they did. It wasn't your standard bump and grind."

Shane became caught up telling the story of the Hacienda Club bachelor party while Mesa's thoughts drifted back to the Bread and Roses Café's brush with arson the night before. The wooden back door, which had been a temporary substitute for a metal one on order, had been the starting point for the fire.

Someone had lit a tea light candle in an open cardboard box of old newspaper soaked in cooking oil. Fortunately, a couple of late-night drinkers from Club 13, walking home through the alley, had seen the smoke and the fire department had been called.

The café would need that new back door sooner than later, but otherwise the damage was minimal. Still the phantom arsonist had struck again, twice if the sheriff insisted on counting Dowl's pickup. No witnesses. No fingerprints. No nothing.

Jeanne Lenin, living above the café, had not seen or heard anything. She had called Adrienne in despair early Friday morning. When they rendezvoused at the café after lunch to survey the damage, Mesa and Chance had joined them.

Together they examined the partially scorched wooden landing and the blackened door. "It looks like a pretty feeble attempt to burn down a brick building if you ask me," Adrienne had said.

Jeanne stood apart from the other three, her hands held in supplication against her lips. Mesa sensed her fear. Perhaps Lenin's past as an addict was finally catching up with her. Could it be that getting fired from Warm Springs when Ethan Grainger had died was more than a coincidence? Did the former nurse know more than she had told Adrienne and Chance? Was someone trying to keep her quiet too, now that interest in Grainger's death had resurfaced? Mesa was beginning to think that the personal ad asking for info on Dowling Jessup had received wider distribution than she'd imagined.

"I agree," Mesa said to Adrienne, "Maybe this was meant as a warning too."

Despite a conversation with the sheriff later that day, Chance could not convince the lawman that there was any connection between the burnt-out pickup, the fire at the café, and Jessup's death at the previous arson. The sheriff said Chance was beginning to sound like a broken record.

At least the detectives assigned to the arson case had shown both of Adrienne's sketches to the few businesses in the area of upper Main Street. One of the waitresses working at the Copper Pot thought maybe the mystery man looked familiar, but she was uncertain.

Just because Lenin and Jessup had once crossed paths at Warm Springs thirty years before hardly seemed relevant. Since the college was on spring break, Solheim held out little hope that anyone saw Dowl's pickup traveling along Park St. through the deserted campus and on past the gun range where it was eventually set on fire. His focus now was on finding a witness to the fire at the café. At least Henry, who remained unconscious in the hospital, was in the clear.

It was nearly ten p.m. when they pulled into a parking lot half full. The Hacienda Supper Club sat along the frontage road north of Dillon, at the Apex exit. The building's construction was common in Montana—cedar-planked siding with a dark green, tin roof. A couple of imitation wrought iron balconies created an ornate façade above the entryway. Matching post lamps on either side of the dark wooden double doors revealed decorative wrought iron handles.

Sagebrush Sam's in Rocker was a nondescript gray aluminum-sided rectangular building that could be mistaken for a dentist's office except for the exceedingly large parking lot made to accommodate semis. The Hacienda was way classier.

Mesa wasn't sure what she expected to learn at the club. She did think a strip bar seemed like an odd business for this upstanding, old-world family. Then she remembered what Sandifer had told Chance about the other Cuban docs looking down on XL because of the family business back in Havana. Old habits?

Alexis thought talking to the señora in her own element might make her willing to talk about the business. Mariposa might even show up. Somehow, Mesa didn't expect that to happen, but maybe talking to the mother could be revealing.

A couple of men in dress shirts and bolo ties stood outside smoking. Mesa wondered if there was some special event going on inside when Shane opened the door and the sound of dance music and people laughing spilled out into the darkness. A lobby with curved walls and hanging planters filled with red geraniums gave patrons a chance to shake off the weather and hang up their coats. Above one planter, Mesa saw a red and white Santeria statue with candles like the ones in the window of the Galleria Arroyo. Again, this seemed an odd mix— religion and exotic dancing.

Mesa followed the music into a large, darkened room where several long tables were filled by a party of thirty-something couples. Judging from the leftovers on their plates, the supper part of the club seemed to consist of steaks, locally produced no doubt, and side dishes of rice and beans. Mesa knew little about Cuban cuisine but the unmistakable aroma of garlic and lime made her wish they'd come earlier for dinner.

Mesa scanned the crowd for Alexis who predictably was nowhere to be found. Just like her to suggest a plan and then not show up.

Nevertheless, Mesa liked the feel of the place, which reminded her of old photographs she'd seen of Las Vegas in the fifties, not to mention that the Hacienda was spotless, a quality missing in many Butte bars. Toward the front of the room, a half moon stage fronted a shiny, wooden dance floor.

Shane motioned toward a table in the middle of the room. A cardholder on it read "Floor show at 11pm – Tropicana Nights." If the Hacienda Club wanted to prove it was magical, the transition from rural Montana to a tropical paradise would be proof positive.

All Mesa knew about Cuba she had learned from biographies of Hemingway and old black and white movies. The tall drinks with umbrella decorations that Shane brought from the bar fit right in. "This is the rum concoction we drank at the bachelor party. They were a favorite of Hemingway's. Thought you'd want to try one in memory of your fellow journalist."

She had to give Shane credit for trying. "It's a mojito," she told him. She had had more than her share of the cocktail once at a bar in Sun Valley, Idaho. The writer had often slummed there before he succumbed to depression and shot himself. Mesa clinked her glass with Shane's. "What else do you know about this place?"

Shane had an uncle who ran a fishing guide service out of Melrose, fifteen miles north, and was a decent source of local background a.k.a. gossip. "They do all right with Orvis fly-fishermen and during hunting season. Serve up a hunter's buffet on the weekend. Some of the guides will haul over four or five guys for the food and even dancing, although that makes for a late night unless you're flying home the next day."

"Ever hear of any trouble?" Mesa asked, not that she could imagine Dowling Jessup ever stopping by. She knew the strip club in Rocker had the occasional dust up, usually truckers arguing with college guys over a girl.

He shook his head. "Their regular bartender knows the locals. He's pretty burly, too. Imagine he'd toss anybody who was feisty. Plus, I had the impression the señora runs a tight ship. These dancers don't exactly fraternize, if you know what I mean."

"No lap dances?" Mesa asked with a pout. She was hardly an expert on the economics of the trade. But the law of supply and demand suggested that individual attention usually resulted in substantial cash flow.

Shane shook his head. "Once the girls finish dancing, they walk around with a tip basket and say 'howdy.' They do all right, best I can tell. Other than that, the señora keeps a close rein on the ride. It's kind of this fantasy thing, you know. Trading on the unattainable. Kinda like you."

Mesa slapped Shane on the shoulder, saying, "Stop it," though she knew he was only half-kidding. In the months of their on-again-off-again relationship, Mesa was the switch flipper.

"Time out," he said. "I'll buy us another Hemingway special before the action starts."

Mesa mulled over what Shane had said about the club. If the Hacienda only had one dance show a week and no side action, even if they did special events at holidays, which she knew they did at Labor Day to draw in the rodeo crowd from Dillon, could they be making enough money to break even? And what if they didn't? Could Jessup have known something about the Hacienda Club that would be an embarrassment to Larraz and his family?

A number of locals greeted the bartender by name as a steady flow of them began to arrive. Maybe the Hacienda was as much a local bar as anything else. Assuming the señora owned the property including the building, her only overhead was the bartender, a cook and a waitress, the alcohol, and utilities. At least the club was a decent enough place to bring someone on a bona fide night out where the guy would shell out a few bucks.

"Show's about to start," Shane said, when he returned with the drinks.

Mesa looked toward the stage and sure enough, a woman with salt and pepper hair pulled back in a bun high on the crown of her head was adjusting the sound system. A fanfare erupted, the crowd calmed, and the woman waited for the flourish to fade. Then in crisp but accented English, "Señoritas and señors, Ladies and Gentlemen," she said with a quick bow to the long table of patrons and then to the several tables of couples that included Mesa and Shane, and finally to the crowd at the bar, "The Hacienda is proud to present Tropicana Nights."

With a welcoming hand to her right, a curtain opened behind the stage, the music was cued, and out strode a stunning dancer of Vegas proportions and costume with dramatic, sparkling make up. The music was a rhythmic combination of drum, guitar, and brass. Dressed as Shane had described, the tall dancer moved her shoulders and hips fluidly across the small stage. She made eye contact with her audience, smiled, and genuinely seemed to enjoy herself for the next several minutes.

The music ended abruptly and the lights went down. Then another song was cued, the lights went up again, and another dancer replaced the first. The second dancer was a bit older, but even more regal and striking. Drawn into the intimacy of her performance, Mesa couldn't take her eyes off her.

The partiers at the table had stopped talking. Likewise, the bar patrons had turned away from their drinks as the dancer stepped down from the stage to the dance floor. Everyone was watching the movement of this tall, dark woman with her yellow and orange plumes who pushed the limits of even the most limber body to the increasingly hypnotic music. Again, the music stopped abruptly, and the dancer struck a dramatic final pose, like a tropical bird in mid flight.

Mesa found herself clapping almost involuntarily when the music ended. The dancer took a quick bow to the accompaniment of whistling and yells. Then the lights changed again, first into darkness, more cued music, a few moments of overture, spotlights slowly moving, a fanfare for what was to come.

Mesa was struck by how cleverly the audience was being manipulated into anticipation of the next segment of the program. Just at the moment she was wondering how long the music would last, the curtains opened. Both dancers appeared, striking a pose in yet another breathtaking costume revealing deep cleavage and rising high up the hips. Mesa was sure the outfits struck at the heart, if not other body parts, of every man at the bar.

The second dancer stood just behind and to the left of the first. The music began to thump and their bodies moved in unison. As they stepped out onto the dance floor, Mesa took a quick glance at Shane, whose mouth had dropped open when the women's hips began to gyrate together only inches apart.

Mesa could not have accurately estimated how long the next series of dances lasted. It was as if everyone in the bar had been sucked up into a vortex of sensuality that no one wanted to end, including the dancers.

When the music came to its crescendo, the dancers, who had separated to perform on both sides of the room, reunited in a pose that, in its final flourish, left them with arms held high, leaning back to back. The crowd erupted with appreciation. The exhausted dancers smiled and made deep curtsies, holding hands, congratulating each other, and acknowledging their admirers.

The señora returned to the microphone and introduced the performers, both of whom were from Miami, and extolled their training and careers. Soon, she said, they would be appearing in Boise, and then Seattle. Eventually the dancers meandered through the crowd with baskets into which both men and women were tossing paper bills. Shane tossed twenties into each.

Mesa was not surprised to see the señora step off the stage to be greeted by Alexis, who emerged from the crowd at the bar, holding a glass of champagne for the older woman. Despite her age, the señora glided across the floor elegantly. They hugged, and Mesa waved nonchalantly at her friend to join them.

Alexis turned the señora in the direction of Mesa's table. Shane had taken his eyes off the dancers long enough to say, "Here comes trouble."

Mesa sighed. Men, particularly Mesa's friends, often had a love/hate attitude about Alexis. They loved her looks, but they hated her attitude. She and Alexis had made a pact long ago never to let a man come between them, at least not seriously, and definitely not the same man. Although after Alexis' high jinks on St. Patrick's Day, where she had nearly incited a riot at the Irish Times, Mesa could understand Shane's reaction. But she ignored him anyway, and invited the two women to sit down at the table.

Shane said hello, asked the ladies if he could bring them drinks, and dutifully went off to fetch them. Mesa made a mental note to reward his cooperative manner later.

Alexis was, in fact, on her best behavior, properly introducing Señora Domenica Arroyo to "her best friend in all the world." Domenica must have been a great beauty when she was young. Mesa guessed her age about the same as Nana's, but the Cuban woman knew how to accentuate good bone structure with a touch of makeup and plum lipstick that showcased her high cheekbones.

Mesa gushed about the dancers, saying their performance exceeded what anyone would expect at a roadside entertainment spot in Montana. Señora Arroyo nodded slightly. "The dancing is as much for me as for our patrons. Juan knows how much I miss Cuba, and so he has indulged me. We have good rum and Cuban cigars," she waved toward the bar. "It's about remembering the past." She pointed to a bronze plaque hanging above the bar and read aloud, "Hoy como ayer!" and toasted with her champagne glass.

Today like yesterday, Mesa said to herself and raised her glass. She'd seen the slogan on the Internet when she was researching Operation Pedro Pan. It was a rallying cry for Cuban exiles who gathered each year in various parts of the United States to celebrate the traditions of a homeland to which they were not likely to return.

"I noticed the statue in the entryway, almost like an altar piece," Mesa said. "It's Santeria, isn't it?"

"Yes, yes. That's right, the señora said. "You know about this?"

"Just a little. Are you a practitioner?" According to what she'd read, Santeria was an Afro-Cuban tradition that relied heavily on amulets, charms, and the occasional animal sacrifice, mostly practiced in agricultural areas of the island. Sounded a little edgy.

"The statue is meant to bring health to all those who enter, and to keep away the evil. Some call it voodoo, superstition, but I believe in the healing power of Santeria."

"The señora danced once upon a time," Alexis said, turning the conversation to a more upbeat topic. "I've even seen a photograph. In the biggest club in Havana."

The señora patted Alexis's hand. "Until Juan's father swept me away." Her tone had changed. "I was only nineteen."

"Is that when you came to the United States?" Mesa knew that this was not the case but she wanted to keep the señora talking.

"No, no. I came much later. Juan helped get me out. Mariposa needed me. Despite his objections to my relationship with his father, he did not want Mariposa to be separated from her mama any longer. He has always been such a good brother to her, and she adored him. She used to follow him around the house when she was small." Domenica seemed genuinely touched when she spoke of Larraz.

At that moment, Shane appeared with the drinks and the señora excused herself, "I must greet my other guests." She took her champagne and made her way to the rest of the tables.

"Damn," Mesa said and shot a look at Shane. "She was just starting to talk." Then to Alexis, "Think you can wrangle her back to join us?" Alexis shrugged and followed the señora.

Twenty minutes later, the señora, attending to business, thanked the crowd for its generosity, mentioned a coming attraction for the Memorial Day weekend, and encouraged the crowd to stay as long as it liked. Mesa was surprised to see that it was almost two a.m. when the stage went dark and the sensuous Caribbean music gave way to Lady Gaga from the jukebox. Not long after, the tables of couples began to depart. Alexis and the señora were nowhere to be found.

Finally, Shane and Mesa headed for home. On the way back to Butte, she thought about the evening. Nothing she saw suggested any kind of unusual activity. No Mexican drug lords or Russian mobsters had appeared. No high-priced call girls lounged in dark corners. Quite the opposite. All she could be sure of was that many in the audience would go home thinking that the appropriate end to a night of exotic dancing would be a horizontal mambo of their own making.

Saturday morning, Mesa lay awake thinking about the señora, her daughter, and Xavier-Larraz and what an odd threesome they made. Her thoughts were interrupted by Shane who appeared at the door of the bathroom, showered and apologetic. Pulling on a navy sweater, he sat at the foot of the bed.

"You can't say no to a sitting United States senator," he said. "It's not like there are a lot of Democrats in Beaverhead County to welcome him."

Mesa answered with a noncommittal, "Hmmm." She knew he was trying to make up for leaving on a Saturday when he didn't need to be in Helena. He was accompanying Montana's senior Senator to a luncheon in Dillon where he was receiving an award.

"It's actually an honor," Shane muttered.

"I know," Mesa said. "You've done good work. It's a feather in your cap." She felt only slightly guilty because on some level she didn't necessarily care that he was leaving. It was just that Cuban music that had put her in the mood for an extended morning in bed.

Shane kissed her gently on the lips, and then said he'd call later when he was back in town, and then he was gone. Mesa pulled the pillow over her face and sighed. Shane's sense of duty was admirable, but also frustrating.

Her annoyance was interrupted by a phone call from Alexis. "Enjoy your evening out with Mr. Straight and Narrow?" she teased.

"Shut up, loser," Mesa teased back. "What's with you, up and at 'em before nine a.m.?"

"I could ask you the same thing," she said in that smarmy voice of someone who was sleeping alone.

"Shane had to go put on his string tie. He's meeting Senator Krueger for a whistle stop in Butte and then they're flying down to Dillon."

"Boring," Alexis said.

Mesa had heard this before. Alexis left politics to her high-roller father unless an issue affected her directly.

"Thank God I've got something juicy to talk about. Thought you'd be interested to know that I gave the señora a ride home last night."

Mesa sat up in bed. "Seriously?"

"Juan usually acts as her chauffeur, but apparently something came up, and she was going to have to wait for the bartender to close out before he could take her home. So I volunteered."

"Well, aren't you the Good Samaritan. What did you learn, or are you just calling to gloat?"

"No, well, maybe. I thought you'd be jealous as hell to know she talked my ear off. I think she had one too many glasses of champagne while she was waiting for her ride."

Damn, Mesa thought, Alexis always had the luck. "So how did this all happen?"

"I hike her up into the pickup and the first thing she says is she's going to spit on Fidel's grave some day." Alexis laughed. "She's a pistol. She blames Castro for having to send Mariposa away. They thought she would be back in a year. She says Juan is a saint. Apparently, he was already in the US as he and his father were not speaking since he had hooked up with Domenica."

"Ouch," Mesa said. "That couldn't have gone over well." Life on military bases had taught her plenty about the male ego and machismo. She imagined a pre-Revolutionary, ultra-patriarchal haven like Cuba where heat and corruption could go to the head – and loins – of fathers and sons. "Open infidelity had to breed resentment." Mesa said.

"Maybe so, but they all seem like one happy family now, even if Mariposa is a little weird," Alexis said. "The señora says Juan never took out his feelings on Mariposa. She says he's done everything to help her with her sickness of the heart."

"Strange," Mesa said, "What do you think she meant by that?"

"Who knows," Alexis said. "Seems more like sickness in the head, if you ask me. She also said that Juan gave up any kind of social life of his own to care for Mariposa. Then, finally, he got Domenica out of Cuba so she could be the nursemaid, her and her Santeria statues, which she apparently clutched to her bosom the whole way. She thinks they can fix everything."

"Did she say when she came to the States?" Mesa asked, still trying to grasp the timeline.

"No, but some ranch hands told Jesse that the old gal showed up just before Juan married the Lorimar sister. Apparently, they were oil and water, which is why Juan built a separate house for Domenica and, I guess, Mariposa to live in as well. The señora says The Hacienda Club is his way to keep her busy."

"Did you get any idea just what kind of sickness of the heart Mariposa has?" Mesa said. She had wondered this from the beginning when Vivian said that Mariposa lived on the grounds of the mental hospital with Dr. Larraz. It didn't seem like the ideal upbringing for someone who suffered from a lot of childhood trauma unless it had developed into much more.

"Domenica said that when they had to put down one of the Andalusians, Mariposa didn't move from bed for weeks afterward. What I heard is that she came into the barn when Frisco was about to euthanize one of the horses, and Mariposa wigged out. He tried to restrain her and she attacked him with a pitchfork. Nearly took his eye out. That's where that scar came from."

Mesa remembered what the *Standard* article had said about how horses infected with West Nile virus would likely have to be destroyed leaving their owner devastated. "Jesus," Mesa said, "she doesn't look that strong." Then she remembered Dr. Kaiser's comment about the strength of someone in the midst of a psychosis.

"Not that I blame her," Alexis added. "If those horses had been mine, I would have been sick in the heart too."

The larger question for Mesa was why this had mattered to Dowling Jessup enough for him to clip Mariposa's photo from the paper.

"Seems like the señora is glad Mariposa is more interested in horses," Alexis said. "The art of exotic dancing was definitely never the path for *her* daughter."

Chapter 17

Chance had spent the morning trying to catch up on the renovation of the Dead Guy House or the DGH as the pre-releasers he'd hired called it. He'd bought face masks for his workers plus a large jar of Vicks VapoRub to coat the upper lips. Nick had assured him that this was the best way to keep from gagging from the smell that still lingered. It was not working.

The result was lots of smoke breaks, which Chance could hardly say no to. Most of the crew was hard core AA'ers for whom smoking remained their only legal vice. Along about the fourth smoke break in two hours, since he didn't smoke, he was sitting in his pickup. Less than pleased with the unavoidable delay, he began sorting through the paperwork in the passenger seat, trying to get something done.

He realized he had forgotten to give Mesa a copy of the police report from Grainger's death, which was at the bottom of the paper pile. She was way better at keeping track of the bits and pieces of a story.

Later, he would tell Adrienne that he didn't know what had made him read over the report again. But when he came to the section about the items found on the deceased, he was so stunned he called out, "Oh, my god" so loudly that one of the workers came over to the pickup and asked if he was okay.

He gave his three workers an early lunch and tore away in his pickup to find Mesa. Driving toward the *Mess* office, where she often spent Saturday mornings, he almost missed her walking up Granite Street. He stomped on the brake with sufficient force that Mesa looked toward the street when she heard the skid. She walked out into the street, pulled open the door, and said, "What the hell is wrong with you?"

"Just be glad I caught up with you." He handed her the police report and pointed to the revealing section. "Read that," he said.

Mesa read aloud, "Contents of the deceased's pockets: sixty cents in change, Juicy Fruit gum package and a red, white and blue, metal cigarette lighter decorated like the flag."

Puzzled, she looked up at him and, for a moment, Chance experienced that rare moment of remembering something before his frustratingly clever sister did. "Day before yesterday, at the hospital, Tommy Little Boy said that Larraz took that lighter from Jessup. So how did it end up in Grainger's pocket unless Larraz put it there?"

"You think he was trying to implicate Jessup?" Mesa thought for a moment, then said, "Wouldn't you think that Chief Bonney would have realized that? It must not have been a critical piece of evidence. Maybe there were two lighters?"

"How would the Chief have known? Tommy Little Boy couldn't have told him. Vivian, by her own account, wasn't even able to provide Jessup with an alibi. It would have been Larraz's word against Jessup's, if it ever came up at all, which I'd guess it never did."

Mesa said, biting the corner of her lip, "But Dr. Larraz knows." She grabbed the police report saying she'd take it to the office with her for safekeeping.

"What are you going to do now?" he asked, wary about Mesa's cavalier attitude after the torching of Dowl's pickup. The police hadn't spotted that truck since Mesa had reported it on Tuesday. But two days later, the local arsonist chose that particular vehicle to set alight? All the copper in Butte couldn't convince Chance of such a coincidence.

"To talk to Jeanne Lenin, even with this lighter connection, we still don't have any kind of motive for Larraz killing Grainger. It could have been an accident even. But I think she knows, and someone doesn't want her telling, which is why that fire was set at her door."

"Well, don't do anything else until you tell me what she says, okay?" Nothing they knew now was really going to change what had happened to Jessup. But he didn't want Mesa to go off half-cocked in the excitement of what he'd discovered, like confront Larraz on her own. The specter of that burnt-out pickup truck haunted him even if Mesa was a disbeliever.

"Will do," Mesa said and she was halfway down the block.

≈⋙

Mesa hiked over to the Bread and Roses Café, remembering its previous incarnation, the Renaissance Bakery. When it went out of business, the storefront had done a brief stint as a Tea Party campaign office before the Bakery's industrial-sized oven had formed the core of the café's work. Resurrection for Jeanne Lenin, as for much of Butte, was the name of the game.

The aroma of freshly baked bread wafted through the door as Mesa walked into the café, which was doing a brisk Saturday morning coffee and donut business. When she asked about Jeanne, one of the workers said she was still in her apartment on the upper floor.

Mesa walked the long flight up and knocked at the door. After a few moments, the weary-eyed platinum blonde answered. "Me, again," Mesa said. "You remember, Chance's sister, Mesa?"

Jeanne nodded with a smile, then added, "Good looking fella, your brother."

Then, somewhat to Mesa's surprise, she was invited into the cramped apartment. Mesa couldn't see beyond the first room—a combination living room, dining room, and kitchen that overflowed with furniture, books, and magazines. Excess appeared to be how Jeanne found comfort in the world.

She moved around her kitchen corner in a short-sleeved, plaid housedress with the efficiency of a short-order cook. She invited Mesa to sit down, and then proceeded to make coffee. They made small talk about the neighborhood while she set out the coffee and donuts complete with Melmac plates and paper napkins.

Meanwhile, Mesa thought about what tack to take. "I've been giving more thought to the possibility that the fire last night might be some kind of warning. Have you given any thought to that idea?"

When Jeanne gave no response, Mesa pushed on. "Any thoughts about who could have set that fire?"

"Look, I know your brother thought I might know something about the death of that Grainger boy, but I can't see how that's connected. I haven't thought about anybody at Warm Springs in years."

"I tell you what I think is odd," Mesa said. "I visit Dr. Larraz Thursday afternoon and within twenty-four hours a possible witness to the trailer fire is involved in a hit and run, Dowling Jessup's missing truck is found torched, and your café receives a little wake up call."

"You think Dr. Larraz has something to do with this?" Jeanne said, wide-eyed.

"Chance says you spoke highly of Larraz, and that he helped you get sober and start this café. Dowling Jessup hoped to put his life back on track too. He was trying to contact Larraz and Mariposa. At least he had collected some information that would lead him to them. Did he ever come to the café?"

"Jessup?" Jeanne asked and shook her head. "If he did, I probably wouldn't have recognized him. He never talked to me, that's for sure."

"Dr. Larraz seems to have a knack for saving people, wouldn't you say? He saved Mariposa from the orphanage. He got her mother out of Cuba, and he helped you. Did that help require your silence about something that happened a long time ago? Maybe he was trying to remind you of your promise to keep quiet."

Jeanne focused on her donut and then said, "Why would you think such a thing about a man who has helped so many?"

Mesa pulled out the police report that Chance had given her a half hour before and showed it to Jeanne, explaining that the lighter was the one Larraz had confiscated.

"That might not mean much to you right now. After all, Jessup can't defend himself, but two other people saw

Larraz take that lighter and even though they couldn't speak up thirty years ago, they can now."

Jeanne stirred the mug of coffee in front of her, but said nothing.

"Look, Jeanne," Mesa said in a solemn voice, "I talked to Dr. Larraz yesterday. He knows we're looking into Jessup's death. I'd hate to think the past stands to haunt you like it did Dowling Jessup. For all we know, you may be next. Maybe you should think about cooperating, and tell me what you know about his death before it's too late. I'll go to the sheriff with you."

"I never knew Dowling Jessup, I swear," she said. Her voice sounded tinny and Mesa could hear the fear seeping into it like oil across water. "How could I know anything that might help the police figure out who killed him?"

"Maybe you know more than you realize," Mesa said. "To find out who killed Jessup I think we need to know more about the day Snake died, including where Dr. Xavier-Larraz and his sister were."

"You know about Mariposa?" Lenin said with a shake of her head.

"Surprised?" Mesa said. "What's so curious about her, and why didn't you mention her when you talked to Chance?"

"Juan tried so hard to give her a normal life," she said. "After what happened to her, he thought it best to try to treat her like a daughter, fewer questions that way."

"What do you mean by normal life?" Mesa asked, wondering how Jeanne's version of events might match up to Aunt Cokie's story.

"She ended up in a Catholic orphanage after she came to the States. Juan had heard about it somehow. He was back East and set out to find her. Eventually he traced her to the Paul Clark Home. She was traumatized—couldn't be alone, awful nightmares. Half the time, she wouldn't let anyone touch her.

"He had no idea what had happened to her. I think he got suspicious when the nuns seemed so willing to tell him where she'd been sent, even with him having no proof that they were even related. Like one Cuban was the same as the next and glad to be rid of both of them."

Mesa thought about Larraz and his concern for how the Pedro Pan fiasco had affected Mariposa. She couldn't help feeling sorry for his situation, but she reminded herself she needed to feel sorrier for Jessup.

"What about the day Snake was killed?" she said. "Chance says you were with Larraz that day. Is that true? What really happened?"

"It was like I told your brother, I swear. We were together that afternoon."

"Together how?" Mesa said with a hint of sarcasm.

"Just as I said, and no more."

Mesa could tell from the way that the other woman avoided eye contact she knew more, but was afraid to say. "But you saw something, didn't you?" Mesa said. "Did you see who killed Snake?"

"I never saw anything—except the girl," Jeanne said putting her hand up as if to draw a limit to what she could be accused of. "Late in the afternoon, Juan called me to come over to their cottage and to bring a sedative. Mariposa was hysterical, crouched in a corner, her dress torn, and blood on the front of it. He couldn't handle her."

She looked up at Mesa, her eyes pleading. "I helped her get cleaned up and sat with her until the sedative took effect. I didn't know for sure what she'd done, or what had been done to her, and I didn't ask any questions. I know that was wrong, but nobody even knew Snake was dead at that point. Juan told me I had to keep quiet about Mariposa's hysteria. If I ever said anything, he'd be forced to tell the authorities about suspecting me of stealing drugs from the infirmary. I had no choice."

Mesa thought about Jessup, confined to the forensic ward, probably not ever knowing how or why he'd ended up there. "You let an innocent young man take the blame," Mesa said.

"I have never known what really happened," Lenin said, "As far as I could tell, only Juan knows. I had no idea there were no witnesses, or that Jessup would be suspected. And for all I know, he was guilty."

"If you were fired anyway, then why have you been protecting Larraz all these years?" Mesa asked. Why had Lenin's loyalty to Larraz remained so steadfast?

"I could have ended up in jail. God knows my habit was bad enough. I was down to stealing the patients' morphine. You have any idea how hard it was to find a recovery program for a nurse? They prefer to kill their wounded. Juan helped find a rehab program that would take me. He saved my life in more ways than one."

As she spoke, Jeanne massaged her forearms, and Mesa could see the faint scars on her wrists that suggested she'd once tried to harm herself. Larraz could truly have saved her life.

"When was the last time you saw Dr. Larraz?" Mesa asked. It would have been difficult for Lenin to say no to him. Maybe he had coerced Jeanne into being his accomplice again.

"He came to see me after I sent him an announcement about starting the Bread and Roses project back when it was on Second Street. It's been more than ten years. I didn't expect to see him, but I wanted him to know his faith in me had amounted to something."

Mesa could tell by the look in her eyes that Jeanne was scared of losing everything she'd built. It was not pleasant seeing the other woman squirm. Still, questions needed to be asked. "Why did he come to see you?"

"He had this letter from a nun who had worked at the girls' boarding school where Mariposa had stayed when she first came to the States. The Sister talked about how she'd taken a liking to the little Cuban girl, and how much she worried and prayed for her. I could understand that."

"How do you mean?" Mesa asked.

"This woman had left her order and wanted to let Juan know what had really happened at that school. She wrote that two priests had been defrocked because of the molestations that had gone on there. The Sister was sure Mariposa had been one of the victims. Her behavior had become increasingly distressing. She wouldn't let anyone help her bathe, or tend to her bumps and bruises. That was why the Sisters had found a place for her at the Paul Clark Home, to get her away from her abuser."

"Did you actually see this letter?" Mesa asked.

"He stopped here one day to show it to me. Read it with my own eyes. He wanted me to understand why Mariposa is the way she is."

"And how is she?" asked Mesa, who had her own idea.

"Withdrawn. No kind of relationships outside the family. She couldn't even tolerate anyone touching her. She was in her forties by then and still living with him.

"Then he all but broke down, remembering the day that boy died. Told me that afternoon I had tended Mariposa, she'd had to fend off this boy Snake somehow, but I didn't realize he was dead. Juan said he never had been able to get Mariposa to tell him exactly what had happened.

"I can't imagine her torment," Jeanne continued. "She had spent three years at that school. Imagine, a nine-year-old abandoned like that, then abused by the very ones supposed to take care of her. Who could come back from that trauma so young? Still, she's finally managed to make something of her life. She uses that gallery of hers to help other refugees by selling their art. I read about it in the paper."

"You're sure you haven't seen him since?" Mesa said, nodding as if to convince her she couldn't lie.

Lenin shook her head and said, "I'm not making excuses for him, but Juan helped a lot of people. He helped me when I didn't think anybody could. If it hadn't been for him, who knows where Mariposa might have ended up. It would break his heart to see anything else happen to her, and it wouldn't do any good to punish her now, whatever she did."

Mesa took a bite of her donut and sighed. Lenin's story was depressing. She'd told Mesa a whole lot more than she'd expected to find out. And the picture Jeanne drew of Xavier-Larraz was even more confusing. He'd done everything to help his half-sister. Would he have killed for her? She needed to talk to Larraz again.

"I'm truly sorry Jessup is dead," Lenin said, "but you have to believe me. I never knew anything about what happened to him, let alone where he was, or that he'd be in any kind of danger. It's been thirty-some years since all this happened. I know what I did was to save myself. I've tried to make peace with God about that, and to make good since then. I do everything I can to help people like Jessup. I'm not to blame."

"Maybe so, but questions need to be asked until we get to the bottom of this. If nothing else, the *Messenger* will run a feature about Jessup so be prepared, because whatever happened will see the light of day one way or the other."

Chapter 18

Chance had returned to the DGH, and just spread Vicks VapoRub on his upper lip again when his cell phone rang.

"Chance, I need a big favor." It was Shane.

"I thought you were going to Dillon with the Senator."

"So did I. Change of plan. His mother's had a heart attack and he's had to fly back to Helena. They want me to go ahead to Dillon and accept the award on his behalf. It's one of those favors you'd like to be able to do, if you get my drift, but the luncheon starts in forty-five minutes, and I'm here at the airport with no plane. I'll be really late if I drive."

Chance understood Shane's predicament. Doing a favor for a D.C. politician never hurt a state legislator. But Chance did have other things to do, even if Shane was Mesa's latest squeeze. "Why don't you talk to Fitz or Tyler? One of them can fly you down. They'd be happy to have the Senator in their debt."

"Tyler gave a lesson this morning and then promptly left for Georgetown Lake. Can't even raise him on his cell. Mr. Fitzgerald is here but he's got those cracked bones in his ankle."

Chance cursed under his breath. "Oh yeah, I forgot." At the tender age of sixty-six, Sumner Fitzgerald, retired surgeon and owner of the local flying service, was still an avid downhiller, at least, until he'd taken a recent spill at Discovery. He couldn't operate the plane's foot controls with a medical boot supporting his injury.

"He did say we were welcome to use the trainer," Shane said. "It's already warmed-up and refueled."

Chance looked at his watch. It was only about sixty miles to Dillon. If he left for the airport now, they'd make it with time to spare. "All right, but you're gonna owe me big time."

Mesa drove to Alexis' place in Glen in record time. Fueled by what she had learned from Jeanne Lenin, her head was spinning. Suddenly the suave and debonair Dr. Larraz had been cast in a completely different light. Instead of being a savior, he was the great manipulator. He had concealed Snake's death all this time. Yet she found it hard to believe he had it in him to kill Jessup all these years later.

If Jeanne Lenin was to be believed, the psychiatrist had spent a lifetime taking care of Mariposa. She was the offspring of a father he hated and an exotic dancer, a child whose existence had probably tormented his own mother until the day she died, according to what Domenica Arroyo had told Alexis. How could a man capable of that kind of devotion and compassion kill someone?

Had he been afraid for himself, for Mariposa? Had Jessup turned into a psycho after all? If he had, J.D.

Firestone and Gladdie Pylypew hadn't noticed. To hear
Henry Gillis tell it, Jessup had been a good friend. Then
again, they didn't have Xavier-Larraz's expertise. Maybe
the doctor had legitimate reason to fear Jessup's neurosis,
and no way to help his former patient without risking
Mariposa's exposure.

As she sped south on the Interstate, Mesa reflected
on the mind's ability to justify its actions. They might
never know what got Jessup killed, but no one should be
able take justice into their own hands, no matter what the
reason. And no matter how many people would attest to
his good deeds, Larraz had to be held accountable.

Even if the cigarette lighter could be explained away,
confronting him about his connection to Grainger's
death would be a step in the right direction. The
knowledge of these new facts might prompt Larraz to
explain what else he knew, but wasn't telling. One thing
for sure, Mesa wanted answers and there was only one
way to get them.

She knew it would be Chance's instinct, especially
with his concern about the torched pickup, to take the
new information to Sheriff Solheim, and let them handle
Xavier-Larraz. Unfortunately, the authorities were big on
evidence, and she and Chance had none to back up their
suspicions about Jessup's death.

For all appearances, Xavier-Larraz was a respectable,
semi-retired member of the Montana medical
community. They had nothing to connect him to the
death of Dowling Jessup, and only the mention of the
lighter and Jeanne Lenin's circumstantial evidence to tie
the good doctor to a death that had occurred more than
thirty years ago.

Even Jeanne's statements couldn't put him at the scene of Snake's death. At best he'd be looking at an accessory charge if, and that was a big if, the authorities could prove the case against Mariposa. Mesa wondered if that could even happen. The gallery owner didn't look like she could survive an investigation, let alone prosecution or conviction.

Chance's suggestion that they check on Xavier-Larraz's alibi for the previous Saturday night was reasonable, but difficult to accomplish. Even without questioning him directly, he would find out about their inquiries, giving him the chance to create an alibi before police questioned him.

And without any clue as to motive, what case could they make? Had Xavier-Larraz killed Jessup because he knew who killed Snake? Then why hadn't Jessup gone to the police with that information long ago?

No, Mesa wanted to talk to Larraz first. She sensed that he might be ready for the story to come out. Maybe he had kept his secrets long enough. Why not give him the chance to tell the truth without being forced to do so by the authorities.

She had tried to call Chance three times to no avail and then decided she had tried hard enough. He would be adamant about going to the sheriff and she didn't want to waste the time.

Finally, she had decided to take Alexis with her. She might be unmoved by the pursuit of justice, but she was a damn good wing woman, even if she could be rash at times.

On the drive to Rancho Esmeralda, Mesa explained to Alexis why she wanted to talk with Larraz again. If he admitted that he had covered up Grainger's death, she would encourage him to come forward. She would take him to Solheim herself. She couldn't be entirely sure of the level of Mariposa's emotional trauma, but Mesa had no illusions about one of the oldest stories in the book, and that it somehow had led to Snake's death.

If Larraz denied responsibility, she would tell him she would go to the sheriff alone and tell them what she had learned. She couldn't be sure what would come of her efforts, but Larraz didn't know that. He could deny everything and take his chances. But hopefully the truth would come out.

"So what if he does admit he let Jessup take the blame? How does that get you any closer to knowing who killed Jessup?" Alexis had decided to play devil's advocate.

"I'm not sure it will, but it's worth confronting him."

"You get off on this, don't you?" Alexis said. "The whole investigative reporter gig."

"What do you mean? Vivian came to me with this story. I didn't go looking for it."

"I get that, but let's face it, Larraz, Mariposa, Domenica—they haven't really done anything but try to protect their own family. I didn't know this Jessup guy but his life was in the crapper from day one. Why make the Larraz family miserable now? If what you say about Mariposa is true, she's a victim in all this too."

"You'd actually take Larraz's side on this?"

"I'm not saying it's right. I'm just saying I think Larraz's intentions were not all bad."

"Maybe so. But the impact of his decisions led to Jessup's long-term institutionalization, the forensics ward, and then prison, when he could have had a chance at life. Larraz abused his position, his authority too. And it's not just about Jessup, but Vivian, even Mariposa. All their lives might have been different if all this had been handled openly. You don't get a pass on telling the truth because you have good intentions."

"After what he'd been through, first Castro, then Mariposa at the mercy of pedophile priests. You think he would expect that Mariposa would get a fair shake in the hands of some Montana prosecutor? The trial alone would probably have put her over the edge."

Mesa squirmed in her seat. "Okay, I'm not saying it would have been easy. But it was his job to see to the welfare of the patients in his care, all of them. He said that himself."

Alexis shrugged, "Well, maybe you can guilt the truth out of him."

"Or maybe he can set the record straight, and help us figure out what happened to Jessup."

≈৩৯

Once they were up in the air, Chance felt more relaxed than he had in a week. He was behind on the work on the DGH, and Henry was still unconscious. At least he'd had moments of talking in his sleep that Adrienne said were good signs that his brain was functioning normally.

Nevertheless, the stress weighed on Chance more than he cared to admit. Now, behind the controls of the Cessna with the wide open skies ahead, he felt the weight lifted. Everything would be fine, he told himself. And sitting next to Shane, suddenly they seemed like lifelong pals.

Not that they weren't friends. He had to admit he was surprised that Shane, straight shooter that he was, and his sister had hit it off as well as they did. Sure made Nana happy.

Though you could never tell about Mesa's relationships. She was a hard one to read. After their mother died, Mesa had grown up quick, or at least that was the image she created. Miss Independent, she had gone several thousand miles away to school. Everything became prescribed. Maybe that was what she liked about Shane. He was Mr. Cool, nothing out of control.

"Thanks for doing this, man," Shane said. "Short notice like."

"No problem. Any excuse to go flying and help a budding politician."

"I don't know about that. Mesa says you hate politics," Shane said, looking out over Mount Fleecer as the plane followed the Interstate south toward Dillon. "Think you could stand Mesa as a politician's wife?"

Holy shit, Chance thought. That came out of the blue. Maybe their relationship was way more serious than Chance realized. He laughed and said, "I don't know. She might still have some wild oats to sow."

"Tell me about it," Shane said. "Course if you could keep her away from Alexis Vandemere that might help. What's up with that chick, anyway? She's a looker but she's flat out crazy when she drinks. She nearly got us all arrested on St. Paddy's Day, throwing a drink on some guy at the Irish Times."

Mesa hadn't mentioned any details about this particular chain of events on Sunday night. But Shane's point of view was one Chance could agree with, except that it made him feel uncomfortable to trash Mesa's best friend, so he said nothing.

"Then there's this deal about the guy who died in the trailer. She really has a burr under her saddle about that one."

"That's Mesa," Chance said. "She never does anything halfway. The newspaper may be small but there's a bona fide journalist running it."

"Crusader, more like it," Shane said. "She always been that way?"

Chance smiled as he looked out at the Humbug Mountains, and thought about Shane's question. "I guess so. She's not big on expressing her personal views in public, but in the newspaper, nothing is sacred. She figures out who killed that Jessup guy, she'll come after them with both barrels."

Chapter 19

Alexis pulled her pickup in front of Domenica Arroyo's house at Rancho Esmeralda. "The ranch hands still call this place the Lorimar. They say it's been good enough for fifty years. Why'd anybody want to change it to some foo-foo name like The Emerald Ranch, I don't know."

Mesa nodded, and then said, "Maybe because the grass is really green in June?" to which, her friend rolled her eyes. Ranching communities were set in their ways. It could not have been easy for the Cuban family to fit in. Perhaps Larraz thought marrying into an established ranching family might make a difference.

"I hope you're right about this," Mesa said when they knocked on the señora's door.

"I just think you should at least talk to Mariposa before you go off on the señor. Everybody treats her with kid gloves, but she's a grown woman. We can still walk over to the main house and talk with the señor afterward."

Mesa knew Alexis had strong feelings about a family's right to protect its own. She'd seen her Grandmother Vandemere do it time and again with Alexis' father and mother and eventually Alexis herself.

"That's what money is for," Alexis had told Mesa more than once. "You can be so naïve about the truth, and what good it actually does. Just be glad I'm here to protect you from yourself," her friend had said.

Mariposa opened the door. She wore a pink cashmere sweater and a silk scarf, expensive clothes that certainly hadn't been purchased anywhere in the immediate hundred miles. Mariposa must travel to the big city, if for no other reason than to shop. "Hello again," Mesa said, curious to see if this second meeting would evoke a negative reaction. When the two had parted at the gallery, Mesa had the distinct impression Mariposa was glad to have an excuse to end their conversation.

Mariposa nodded curtly and invited them in, motioning them toward a crackling fire. The señora was sitting next to the fireplace in a large comfortable room where the kitchen melded into a family room, much cozier than the big house.

"Buenos dias, Alexis," Domenica said, "and you've brought your friend. Come in and warm yourself by the fire. You are hoping for a morning chat?"

Alexis smiled broadly just as she and Mesa had planned. Keep the mood light and let Mesa bring up the hard stuff. "We do have some good chats, don't we?" Alexis said.

Mesa had been surprised to hear that Alexis frequently dropped in on the señora. "She kinda reminds me of my grandmother," Alexis had said. "You know, feisty broads who haven't let their age get in the way of what they want.

"Mesa had hoped to spend more time with you at the Hacienda Club," Alexis said. "She didn't realize how busy you would be running the place."

Mesa chimed in. "As a matter of fact, I wanted to talk to Mariposa as well."

"Let us have coffee then," Domenica said and began to get up.

"Here, let me," Alexis said. "I think I know where everything is." She walked into the kitchen, apparently glad to have something to do.

Mesa could see Mariposa's eyes burning a hole in Alexis' back as she made her way past the counter that divided the large room.

"Mama," Mariposa said, "I have an appointment at the Galleria at one-thirty." She sat poised in an armchair across from her mother and looked at the gold watch that hung loosely at her wrist.

"This shouldn't take long," Mesa chimed in. She opened a file she'd brought with her and held out the first of the two sketches Adrienne had drawn. "I'm still working on this story about the death of a man named Dowling Jessup. This is a sketch of him. I stopped by the gallery Tuesday and showed it to Mariposa, who said Jessup had stopped by to see her the week before. I was hoping to find out if he had been here at the ranch as well."

Domenica looked at her daughter and then the sketch. "I don't recognize this man. What is this story about? Does his death have something to do with the ranch?" Domenica asked. Her manner was less welcoming now.

Mariposa's expression remained unchanged. Mesa tried to imagine this woman so enraged as to kill another human being. It didn't seem remotely possible. Even as she recalled Jeanne Lenin's description of Mariposa's hysteria, it had been hard to imagine.

"Que pasa?" Domenica said to her daughter.

Mariposa hesitated and then said, "A man by that name did come to my gallery last week, and introduced himself. I said I didn't remember ever meeting him before. That was all."

Mesa was surprised by Mariposa's directness. Her formal demeanor had faded, and she seemed anxious to please.

"He didn't mention anything about someone named Ethan Grainger? You both knew him when you lived at Warm Springs. He was also called Snake," Mesa said.

With the mention of this name, Mariposa diverted her attention to straightening a stack of magazines on a side table next to her chair. "No," she said.

"That name's not familiar to you ...?" Mesa said in a soft voice, not wanting the woman to withdraw.

"No, I'm sorry. I can't help you," she said and looked thankfully at Alexis who had appeared with coffee in a china cup and saucer.

"Dowling had a friend named Vivian Jobe," Mesa said, her tone as nonthreatening as if she were talking to a child. "The four of you—Dowling, Vivian, Snake, and you—used to be friends at Warm Springs. You remember that?"

Mariposa was stirring her coffee, and then took several quick sips.

"That would have been a long time ago. I don't remember. Now you'll forgive me, I must find Frisco."

"No need to rush, Mariposa," came a voice from the kitchen.

Mesa looked up to see that Xavier-Larraz had entered from the house's side door.

လပ္သ

When Mesa saw Larraz standing by the open door, motioning for her to leave with him, her first thought was that Jeanne Lenin had warned him about Mesa's threat to expose him. But even if that was the case, she was not worried.

True enough, he oozed control when he motioned Alexis and her through the side door of Domenica's kitchen and outside toward the big house, allowing them to go first. Clearly, he had been paying attention enough to know that she and Alexis had come calling.

He still came across as the charming host, though that opinion was fading now that Mesa considered what he had done. Now she also saw a man who may well have crossed the line. Nonetheless, Xavier-Larraz did not frighten her. She sensed that as long as his family was nearby, he would not harm anyone. He was there to protect Mariposa and her mother. Perhaps that was why he had appeared.

Rosita brought coffee into the den where the three of them sat. "Do you need anything else, Señor Larraz? I'm helping the señora this afternoon."

Larraz shook his head and Rosita disappeared. "So I gather you are here again about this man Jessup. What else can I tell you?" Xavier-Larraz said in a calm voice.

Mesa took a deep breath and thought about what she wanted to say. As much as she might be sympathetic to what had happened to Mariposa, Mesa had to be resolute. She needed to remind herself to think of what had happened to Jessup, and the pain his death had caused for Vivian and for Henry.

"I want you to know, Señor Larraz that I appreciate what a difficult situation you're in. I don't want to cause anyone any more grief," Mesa said in a quiet voice. "But I have done my homework, and I do mean to find out the truth. When we spoke on Thursday afternoon," she continued, "you said you didn't know anything about the evidence in the Grainger case, which was not true."

"Mesa," the señor said. "I don't expect you to understand the difficulties of dealing with these problems in a mental institution. Sometimes the spirit of the law is better served than the letter. In any event, there is nothing we can do now to change what happened."

"That may well be true," Mesa said, but we can revisit Snake's death long enough to consider some new evidence that's come to light. Another former patient has come forward. He saw you take a cigarette lighter from Jessup, the same lighter that ended up in Snake's pocket."

Xavier-Larraz's spine had stiffened and Mesa could feel him reverting to the arrogant doctor, as if he had the corner on the truth and knew his version would be the one accepted.

"Such details are meaningless," Xavier-Larraz said with confidence. "That unfortunate incident was laid to rest many years ago."

Mesa was having none of it. "It might have been for you and the authorities," she said, "but some of your patients were not as easy to fool as you think. Maybe you remember Tommy Little Boy, for example. He was diagnosed as a schizophrenic who didn't speak. Turns out, he was only deaf, and definitely not dumb. He's prepared to tell the police that he saw you take that lighter from Jessup that same day. You see, Tommy's been out of the system a long time. He's not strung out on medications or homeless, if that's what you're counting on. He can convince the county attorney to believe what he saw."

Xavier-Larraz's demeanor had begun to change as she continued to talk. The expression on his face suggested that his self-assuredness was giving way to concern.

"Want to tell me how that lighter ended up in Snake's pocket?" Mesa asked.

"Mesa, not everything in life fits into one of your absolutes of right and wrong," he said. He sounded almost penitent.

"Is that how you justify what happened to Snake?"

"He was mean and manipulative, a predator. I spent hours listening to him talk about his sick fantasies in the name of therapy."

"Mariposa seemed to like him."

"That was my mistake. She was ill. I brought her to the hospital with me because I thought the contact with the younger patients would eventually help her. She was never supposed to be alone with him."

"Was that what made you go looking for them when you realized that Dowl and Vivian hadn't gone to the gazebo? That's what happened, isn't it? You found Snake dead, and Mariposa in some sort of panic."

Larraz was clearly agitated. He stood up and walked over to the mantel and stood next to Alexis. "I really don't think any further discussion can change the past. What's done is done."

"You may be right, but Jessup's death is very much in the present, and I intend to write about it and the circumstances surrounding it. I will print the new information we have uncovered. This story will come out and it will include what Jeanne Lenin told me about that day in your cottage on the Hospital grounds when she saw Mariposa, where you lived less than three hundred yards from the Mound."

Mesa paused to let the weight of what she was saying sink in. "Dr. Larraz, I don't think you're a bad person. You've helped a great many people. Please, tell us what happened."

"If only I did know," he said and slammed the heel of his hand on the mantel. "When I got to the Mound, Mariposa was sitting on the top step of the Gazebo, hysterical, her clothes bloodied and torn. Grainger must have fallen over the gazebo railing, because he lay face down at the edge of the active part of the spring, the hot water bubbling around him."

Larraz's voiced had calmed and he turned and sat back in his chair. "He had torn the collar of her sun dress, and he still held the pink material in his hand."

"What did you do then?" Mesa asked. Her voice had softened as she sensed the resistance leaving him.

"I tried to help him. But it was too late. He had wounds on his head and face. They were covered in abrasions and burns. Perhaps his head had pierced the thermal crust when he fell, but I could do nothing for him. I removed the cloth from his hand and left him as he lay. I took Mariposa back to our cottage, expecting no one would see us. It was the dinner hour; most of the patients and the staff were in the cafeteria or the wards. I summoned Nurse Lenin to help with Mariposa. I couldn't leave her alone. Then I returned to my office in the main building so no one would wonder where I was. One of the orderlies found Grainger's body some hours later."

Mesa looked at Alexis who seemed genuinely distressed for the señor. Mesa, too, felt sympathy for him. She had pressured him to reveal a shameful secret he had kept hidden for three decades. She wondered if he had ever told anyone what he had done.

"I spent the rest of my career trying to unlock her mind, to free her of her anxieties. I could see into everyone's psyche, everyone's but hers."

He seemed close to tears, no doubt, years of frustration and fear coming to the surface. Then the fire crackled, and a spark popped out onto the rug. Larraz looked up, and quickly recouped. "But you can be sure, whatever happened, Snake brought it on himself."

"And Jessup?" Mesa said. "Did he deserve the blame for Snake's death?"

"I had to save Mariposa. Don't you see? I didn't have a choice," he argued. "She could not endure any scrutiny. Any further separation from her family would have killed her, or worse. What would you have done?"

The question was not lost on Mesa. She tried to imagine what Chance might have done to save her. "I wouldn't have put the blame on an innocent man. I know that much. You could have gone to the authorities."

"Justice for a mentally ill refugee? That's laughable. Even today, most people still think of us as foreigners. We wouldn't have stood a chance. Look at what the system did to Jessup."

"You did have a choice. He didn't. You could have helped him but instead you betrayed him and used your authority to condemn him."

"What could you possibly know of betrayal?" Larraz said, "My own father, my country—they betrayed me. And Mariposa, she was a child betrayed by the Church. I was the only one left to protect her. I did what I had to do."

"What you did to Jessup was as bad as what happened to Mariposa. You abandoned Jessup, left him to languish for years with no one to protect him," Mesa said with a fury she suddenly felt for the sad lives she had come to know in the past week—the Frito Lady, Henry Gillis, and Dowling Jessup—and what she knew Vivian had lost.

"You and your self-righteousness, don't think he was so innocent," Xavier-Larraz said, his words coming rapidly. "What I did was give him a place to think about how to get even. He was blackmailing me. See for yourself." Xavier-Larraz went over to a desk by the window and pulled a folded piece of stationery from a drawer and tossed it at her.

Carefully, she unfolded the paper. The note had been printed from a computer. "You have everything. I have nothing. It's only fair. We both know you owe me," it read. "One hundred thousand dollars. Meet me on Friday at the Galleria at closing time." No signature, but apparently Larraz knew who its author was. Jessup had contacted Larraz and the reason was all too familiar—money.

"He had found our ranch through an ad in the local paper, and he had been to the Galleria to see Mariposa. She is so fragile. Every time a news broadcast shows a

group of new refugees, wherever they are from—
Mexico, Haiti—her anxieties erupt again," he said with
resignation. "I couldn't risk the pressure his presence
might put on her."

Mesa thought about the newspaper cuttings in
Jessup's cabin. He had had a plan all along, and not
exactly a noble one. Edward Dantes would have
approved. "You expected mercy from someone you
showed none to?" Mesa asked. "What did you do?"

"I gave him what cash I had but he said it was not
enough," Xavier-Larraz said, talking now to himself. "He
said he'd be back for more. If I didn't raise it, then he
would hound Mariposa until she gave it to him. I tried to
make him understand. He said he wasn't afraid anymore.
God, how could I know it would come to this? He said
he would give me a day to raise the rest of the cash. I was
supposed to meet him in Butte last Saturday. I realize
now that I should have gone, but I sent someone to deal
with him instead."

Chapter 20

They sat in the Pilot's Center at the Dillon Flying Service, waiting for the courtesy car to get gassed up. Chance figured he might as well stay and attend the luncheon since the food was free.

He tried to picture his calendar and what days he might reschedule the pre-releasers for the Dead Guy House job, to compensate for the spur-of-the-moment decision. Truth was, a chance to go flying had made it an easy one—that and the fact that his client, the divorced professor, seemed to like him, and would understand.

They only thing that irritated him was that Mesa hadn't answered his text—a complaint she regularly made about him, he duly noted. He had this uneasy feeling that she might have headed to the Esmeralda Ranch without him. At least she would know he had flown to Dillon with Shane. He told himself not to worry, but he had yet to meet Señor Larraz and the other members of his family. Somehow, he would feel better if he at least had a feel for what kind of people they were.

"The señora is first class," Shane had said when Chance had voiced his concern. "I wouldn't worry."

Chance's call to Adrienne gave him more confidence, even if in a left-handed way. "She's a grown woman and a professional journalist, who just so happens to be your sister. Give her some credit and trust her instincts."

He knew in his head that Adrienne was right but, in his gut, he still had misgivings. He was the one who had grown up with Mesa. No one knew her blind spots better than he did. True, she didn't usually go off half-cocked, but she had been known to get her butt in a sling. Only six months ago, she'd ended up in a hostage situation and barely survived a crash landing in the same plane he was flying today.

The car pulled up, a beater Pontiac. "Sorry, about this," said Phil Damian, the Flight Service co-owner. "If I'd known you were coming, I'd have made sure the limo was ready."

Chance smiled and said, "Get what you pay for, right?"

His stomach growled. The luncheon was a steak feed at the Jaycee's Building in the Beaverhead Fairgrounds at the south end of town. Food, he thought, that'll make me feel better.

"Deal with him how?" Mesa said. What had Larraz decided to do? He certainly didn't look anything like the man Henry said he'd seen with Jessup.

Larraz's shoulders sank. He no longer held her gaze. For a split second, Mesa imagined a younger Juan Xavier-Larraz as Charlotte Haggis, Jeanne Lenin, and Ken Sandifer had described him—handsome, hard working, and compassionate. She found herself feeling sorry for him, for Mariposa, for everyone involved.

"My past will never let me rest," Xavier-Larraz was saying. "But it is not Mariposa's fault. I came to love her like my own child. I had to protect her, but I never meant for it to go this far."

"You've said enough." A voice came from the back of the room.

Mesa saw Alexis look toward the door. Her surprised expression morphed immediately into concern. Mesa looked over her shoulder to see Frisco standing in the doorway to the den holding what looked like a Colt .38.

Frisco motioned to Mesa with the barrel of the pistol. "Stand over there." He nodded toward Alexis.

Mesa was speechless. The sketch. She'd had the sketch with her this whole time and Frisco never even crossed her mind. How could she have been so thick?

Larraz, his voice taut, stepped toward Frisco. "You mustn't do this. You'll only make things worse."

"Juan, you know I won't go to prison," Frisco said. "I'll never forget what you did for me. God knows, I am truly sorry. I wish things could be different. But Jessup was never going to listen to reason. He was going to bleed you dry. Mariposa would be the one to suffer. You knew that. I did what needed to be done."

"Put the gun down," the señor said, "I won't have anyone else hurt. This is madness." He took another step toward Frisco. "We can still save Mariposa. She had nothing to do with this."

"I'll take care of Mariposa. Everything's going to be just fine, but you need to stop talking."

Mesa's hands had become clammy. A cold dread had come over her. She couldn't read Frisco at all. He seemed sober and deadly serious, not like some knucklehead who had pulled a pistol for shock value on a

Saturday night. That, she'd seen more than once in Butte. She took a quick look at Alexis, expecting some sort of miracle solution to the mess they were in. That's when Larraz made his move.

"It's too late for that," the señor said and charged Frisco.

Larraz was the taller of the two men and, though older, he seemed to carry his weight well. He grabbed Frisco's gun hand and slapped it against a sideboard.

For a split second, she thought he might overpower the younger man. But he fought back, his face a ferocious grimace, and then the gun went off. Larraz took one step back, and then collapsed.

Mesa's heart pounded so loud, she reached for her ears. She had seen deer and elk shot, but never a man.

Alexis went for a table lamp a few feet away, but before she could use it, Frisco had righted himself and had the pistol aimed at her.

Wiping blood from his cheek, he looked for a moment at Larraz, shook his head, and then said to Alexis, "Don't think for a second I won't use this on you."

"You pig. I always knew you were shit," Alexis said and dropped the lamp.

Frisco pushed her toward the door, motioning Mesa to follow. She took a last look at Larraz on the floor, a pool of blood forming under him as he clutched at the wound in his chest. She felt like she was moving in slow motion while the events around her were speeding by.

"Move," Frisco barked, and herded them across the hall and down a narrow set of stairs. He shoved them through a hallway to a door with a latch, and an open padlock with a key still in it. "Open the door," he said to Alexis.

Mesa's head was spinning; her stomach queasy. The cool air in the hall had startled her out of her daze, but now they were in such a confined space. She did not like their odds, even at two to one. She sensed that Alexis was mad enough to do something crazy.

"Make me," Alexis answered.

Jesus, Mesa thought, Alexis had picked *this* time to channel a ten year old? "I'll do it," Mesa said. She quickly removed the padlock and opened the door into what looked like a walk-in liquor cabinet. Thoughts were racing through her head. She didn't want to be in that tiny room. She had to do something right now.

Putting the key between her fingers, she gripped the padlock as tightly as she could. When she whipped back toward Frisco, she went for his eyes, but his reflexes were quick. He grabbed her wrist, and at the same time managed to point the long barrel of the Colt up under Alexis' chin.

"Drop it," he said to Mesa, "or, so help me God, I'll put her brain through the roof."

She could feel the heat of his breath, the acrid smell of anger. She did as he said, and then he shoved both women inside and slammed the door, but not before Alexis spit in his face.

Chance sat in the back of the banquet room, doing his best to doze with his eyes open. The combination of political speeches and an eight-ounce rib eye had gotten the best of him, not to mention the Blarney Stones for dessert. It was, after all, only a week after St. Paddy's Day.

Shane had just thanked the Jaycees for their understanding about the Senator's mother and segued his concern to the larger dedication that Krueger had to all Montanans. That was a good point and the time at which Chance's focus had begun to drift.

His mind wandered to the revelation that Larraz had likely planted the lighter on Jessup all those years ago. That was a long time to live with framing someone for a serious crime. While he hadn't met Larraz, from all reports everyone thought he was a stand-up guy. Ken Sandifer, Jeanne Lenin, Mitsy's aunt had all talked about Larraz as if he was a saint.

The only conclusion that made sense was that he was covering for someone else. And that someone had to be Mariposa. She was the only one left. If Tommy Little Boy remembered correctly, neither Vivian nor Jessup had been near the Mound, separate or together. Mariposa and Snake had been alone.

A burst of applause interrupted Chance's musing, and he brought the front two legs of his chair to the floor with a bang. He could see Shane at the head of the room, shaking hands and holding a big wooden and metal plaque. Hopefully, they wouldn't have to fly to Helena to deliver it to the Senator. Chance was much more concerned about finding Mesa.

He was willing to bet that she had come to the same conclusions he had. That meant she had probably gone to talk to Larraz alone. Damn her, he thought. Why hadn't she called him back? He decided to try her again, and realized he had left his phone in the plane.

❧❦❧

They were in absolute darkness.

"Alexis?" Mesa called. She forced herself to concentrate on her own voice, childlike as it sounded.

"Not to worry, sweetie," she said. "Just let me find the light switch and we'll be out of here in a jiff."

Mesa's heart was pounding, her breathing shallow. She didn't want to let out a scream, but one was building inside her.

"Damn," Alexis said. "There has to be a switch somewhere. There has to be."

Mesa felt her lungs tightening. The confined space presented panic enough to deal with, but in complete darkness, she was near hysteria. She tried to focus on the sound of Alexis's body moving in the dark.

"Ouch," her friend said and then the room was filled with light. "Damn thing smacked me in the head," Alexis said. A long string with a wooden ball hung from a shaded light above.

"Get me out of here," was all Mesa could say, her claustrophobia stifling her words. The only thing between her and outright panic was that Alexis was all too aware of Mesa's fear. They had once been stuck in a closet together at a party in college. One of Alexis' spurned boyfriends had propped a chair under the doorknob, saying that if that was the way they were going to act, that's where they belonged. Mesa had lost it, screaming hysterically. Alexis had all but kicked the door down before someone moved the chair, and then she went after the guy.

"Try to hurry," Mesa said, clammy sweat forming all over her. She was turning small circles in the tiny space while Alexis was inspecting the door.

"See if you can find anything we can use to pop these hinges."

The walls contained floor to ceiling shelves, stacked with wine bottles along the short side wall and along one long side wall. The other side contained hard liquor, rum, whisky, vodka, and even aged vinegars. Mesa started to focus on reading the labels on the bottles, and the first wave of panic began to subside.

"Shit," Alexis said, and then began pounding on the door. After about thirty seconds, she stopped and rubbed her hands. Then she pulled out her phone. She dialed a number and then said, "No service. These walls must be two feet thick. Try yours."

Mesa felt her eyes, filling with tears. "It's upstairs in my purse."

"It's okay. It's okay. A text might work," Alexis said. Then she looked at Mesa. "Jesse doesn't text."

"What time is it?" Mesa said, doubting that Alexis' foreman even carried his cell phone.

Alexis looked at the phone. "Almost one-thirty."

"Try Chance," Mesa said, wiping a tear from her cheek. She sank to the floor, willing herself to take deep breaths. The ebbing panic allowed her thoughts to shift to what had just happened, to Larraz upstairs bleeding to death if he wasn't dead already. "And Shane," she said. "They're both in Dillon."

"What should I say?" Alexis said. 'Knowing them, they probably have my number blocked. They both hate me."

"That's so not true," Mesa said and took a deeper breath. "Give me the damn phone."

Alexis slid down the shelves to sit next to Mesa. After a minute, Alexis said, "What's this? She reached across the floor under the next to last shelf. She pulled out a plastic toolbox.

❧

Headed back to the airport, Chance and Shane had just passed a field of grazing sheep on Airport Road guarded by a couple of llamas. They were talking about a proposed bill in the legislature to consider the odd-looking animals as livestock for wolf predation purposes.

"Well, what are they, if they're not livestock?" Chance was asking when he thought he heard the ping of Shane's cell phone.

"Pets? I don't know," Shane said with a chuckle.

"Can you check that?" Chance said when he heard the phone. "It might be Mesa."

Shane rooted around his brief case and then pulled out the phone. "Nah, it's just a 'no service' notification."

Chance heard a muted pop simultaneous with the car tugging to the right, then the sound of a persistent flop-flop made it official. "Shit," he said. "We just blew a tire."

"Courtesy cars," Shane muttered. "At least it didn't happen while we were on our way to the luncheon. How far are we from the airport?"

"Maybe a mile. You got your phone and we're headed uphill. Why don't you start walking and try phoning Phil at the Flying Service when you get over that rise. You should have service up there. The number's in the glove box. I'll start on the tire. Hopefully, you'll reach somebody, they'll come pick us up, and we can leave them to deal with this beater."

❧

"I've almost got the pin out," Alexis said. "You keep banging anyway."

Mesa hit the solid wood door for easily the hundredth time with a pipe wrench they'd found in the toolbox. The impact reverberated in her hand, but the sound seemed to fade in the small hallway outside the door. Alexis was pounding on a screwdriver with a hammer, trying to free the pin in the second hinge. Between them, they were making enough noise that someone would eventually find them.

Mesa couldn't help but wonder what condition Larraz would be in by then. Everything had happened so fast. What could they have done? What would they do if he died? If they didn't get out of this god-forsaken closet soon, she would go mad.

Neither Shane nor Chance had answered Alexis' text. Maybe they were already back in the air. The roar inside the cockpit would make it difficult for them to hear a text notification. Or maybe Alexis was right, and her message had been ignored.

"I got it! I got it!" Alexis said and the bottom hinge pin plopped out of the knuckle and onto the concrete floor next to the one from the middle hinge. She stood and looked at Mesa with a grin.

Mesa could not share her enthusiasm. Larraz was likely dead and Frisco on the run. She was the one who had pressed Larraz for answers. But he had decided on his own to attack Frisco. Still, she couldn't help feeling guilty, and sick.

Alexis sat back down on the floor and began kicking at the bottom of the door. "Help me," she said. "Maybe we can jar the latch loose."

Mesa joined her, anything to fight back the cloying dread. At least they were making more noise.

Bit by bit Chance unloaded the courtesy car trunk that appeared to contain the remnants of some barn sale, complete with handwritten signs that said *Vintage*, *Handmade*, *Repurposed*, and *Pay Here*. He stacked boxes of old tools, and horseshoes made into wall hooks and door knockers by the side of the road, along with several kerosene lanterns and a basketful of old china. Muttering to himself that there had better be a spare, he had kept one eye on Shane's distancing figure until he disappeared over the hill.

Then he found the spare and had begun to put together the bumper jack when he heard an approaching vehicle. Thank God, he thought, thankful not to have to bust his knuckles on any lug nuts. Chance took a step out in the road and made an up and down motion with his arm, expecting the driver would stop and give him a quick ride up to the Flying Service.

Instead, the white pickup swerved to the other lane of the road and flew by at such a high speed that Chance ended up with a face full of dust and gravel when he let out a curse. Ten minutes later, as he wrestled with the lug nuts that must have been tightened by the Marlboro man, and the nagging notion that the passenger in the pickup seemed vaguely familiar, he caught sight of Shane running back down the road.

Out of breath, he stammered as he spoke. "Phil's on his way from the other side of town. But you better see this." He handed Chance the cell phone and then rested his hands on his knees. "I saw the text when I finally got service."

It was from Alexis and read, "The sketch is Frisco. He shot Larraz and is on the run. M & me at Esmeralda. Send cavalry."

"Jesus," Chance said to Shane, "did you call 9-1-1?"

Shane stuttered again, "Well, no ... I wasn't sure."

"Gimme the phone. You grab the spare and help me get us on the road. You notice that white pickup pass by in a big hurry?"

"Damn near blew me off the road."

"That's the guy Henry saw with Jessup, and he has Mariposa Arroyo with him."

⟨≈⟩⟨≈⟩

"Just have one swig?" Alexis said. "It might help you to relax."

They'd been banging on the door for more than an hour. Sitting on the floor, sweaty and covered in the fine dust loosened by their constant banging on the door, they were exhausted.

In the last few minutes, Mesa had begun to think the walls of the closet were closing in. All she could think about was wanting to see the sky and taking a deep breath of fresh air.

"Here, take a whiff," Alexis said and held the bottle of brandy up to her friend's face. "This is expensive cognac."

She was beginning to think Alexis really didn't care. "I know you think this is funny," Mesa said, and she began to shriek, "but it's not. Don't you think I'd chug that whole bottle if I thought it would help?"

Alexis' slap caught her totally off guard.

"Damn it," Alexis yelled back. "I don't think it's funny. I hate seeing you like this. Down deep, you're the bravest person I know. You're the one who taught me not to give in, to stand up, and fight back, right?"

Mesa rubbed her cheek and wiped her nose on her sleeve. "Oh, Alexis, what would we do without each other?" she blubbered, and laid her head on her friend's shoulder.

It had been one of those nights when they should have gone home a lot earlier Mesa remembered. Alexis still had manic stages then. She liked to crash some trendy hotel bar, down a triple tequila, and dare anyone to try to keep up. This night a decent looking guy, dressed in a gray suit, tie undone, took the dare.

Despite her sense of loyalty to her BFF, Mesa wanted to go home. She was tired. Alexis had tossed her the Lexus keys, calling "Keep the porch light on, honey."

When Alexis stumbled back to the dorm at three a.m. with a split lip and a bruise swelling over her eye, Mesa was not prepared for the degree of anger that welled up in her. She thought about what Avalanche Annie would have done in such a situation.

"Where does he live?" Mesa wanted to know.

"I can't remember," Alexis said. "What difference does it make? What would we even do? I was stupid to go with him. It's my own fault."

"You went to his house. He got kinky. You decided to leave, so he slapped you around and pushed you down a flight of stairs, and that's your fault? Not in my world."

Alexis had two stitches by 7 a.m. Then Mesa drove around town, refusing to fill Alexis' pain medication until they found the prick's house, a duplex near the Dayton museum.

In the pre-dawn hours of the next morning, Mesa made use of her anger. Armed with a can of neon pink spray paint previously purchased at a crowded Walmart, Mesa had quietly walked through the neighborhood in her ninja outfit of black hoodie and jeans.

In no more than thirty seconds, she had sprayed A-S-S-H-O-L-E P-E-R-V-E-R-T in two-foot-high letters across the tasteful beige-sided duplex. They drove home across the Miami River Bridge, tossing the paint spray over the side.

Several times that semester they drove past the duplex, clearly visible from the bridge. Attempts to remove the paint, probably with sandpaper, were effective but slow, though the sight of the effort gave both Mesa and Alexis a profound sense of satisfaction.

Mesa took a deep breath. She conjured up her mother's voice saying, "Okay, let's get back to it."

She exhaled deep, looked at Alexis, and they resumed kicking the door.

≈⊱⊰≈

Chance turned past the last set of private hangars to park the courtesy car at the edge of the road. Now that he knew Mesa was with Alexis, and the sheriff was on his way, he wanted to find that pickup. Once they were in cell phone range on top of the hill, they had called to report Frisco's vehicle. Chance was sure they had to be headed for a plane.

In a state as large as Montana, most big ranches had access to a small plane and had at least one employee with a pilot's license. His intuition was rewarded when he saw the white pickup parked on the far side of the second row of hangars fifty yards away.

"They could be inside that hangar, getting ready to take off, if they haven't already," Chance said and looked at his watch. It had been a good fifteen minutes since the pickup had blown past. "I'm going inside."

"I'm going with you," Shane said. "You're not having all the fun."

Chance's heart was racing. "We don't know for sure if they're in there. You go over to the office and find out if anybody has taken off in the last fifteen minutes. If they have, call the sheriff and let him know. If not, then grab whoever is in there and find me."

Chance wasn't sure what he would do if he did find the fugitives, but he was ready to inflict some payback on Henry's behalf. At the very least, he could distract Frisco somehow, play dumb, and stall, if nothing else. The airport was four miles from town. The sheriff's office would send someone soon. The Esmeralda was more like nine or ten miles, he wasn't sure. Hopefully, Mesa and Alexis would have help soon as well. He knew the sheriff's department could make it faster than he could.

Shane took off at a run toward the next building, and Chance walked over to the door into the hangar. He put his ear to it and heard the hydraulic motor to the hangar's front door whirring. Frisco was on the move. Chance opened the side door and called, "Hey there, anybody here?"

He walked inside the double hangar, which had only the one plane inside, a Cessna 182. In the other space sat an aircraft tug, about the size of an ATV, used to tow parked planes off the tarmac. He saw Frisco and the woman he recognized from the news clipping as Mariposa. She was standing on the far side of the plane next to the open hangar door, Frisco next to her.

"This is a private hangar," Frisco said, his voice coarse and impatient. "You're in the wrong place."

"Well, I'll be," Chance said. "The guys in the Flying Service said you were thinking about selling this little beauty, and I thought maybe you could show me around." Chance walked as he spoke and came around to the same side of the Cessna as Frisco and Mariposa, hoping his wide-eyed rancher act would buy some time.

Mariposa lingered by the front door next to some folded lawn chairs while Frisco took a step toward Chance, who could now see the scar above the man's eye that had confused Henry. The dark eyebrow, thick and misshapen by a scar, had prompted Henry to say the man had mean eyes. Henry was right.

"The fuselage's in great shape," Chance said, meandering along the body of the plane, patting it mindlessly with his hand. "You getting ready to take her up? Maybe I could just take a quick peek inside the cabin." If he could get into the cockpit, Frisco might abandon the plane all together. At least Mariposa would be safe.

"I'll come around the other side." Chance took a few quick steps back around the tail, headed for the left side door. Frisco met him coming from the front of the plane. Only now, he was pointing a .38 Chance's way.

"Whoa, there," Chance said. "No need to get touchy."

Frisco grabbed Chance by the collar of his shirt and tossed him like an old rag toward the front corner of the hangar into a tangle of paint cans and miscellaneous hardware from a recent paint job.

"I know who you are, Frisco," Chance said, deciding to play his only card. He could see Mariposa frozen by the door and yelled to her. "He shot Larraz and he's going to get away with it unless we stop him."

Mariposa looked confused, and then said, "Someone shot Juan? No, it cannot be," she cried.

"I don't know where you think you're headed, but the sheriff is on his way," Chance said to Frisco. "Why don't you give it up now before somebody else gets hurt?"

"Everybody talks too much," Frisco said, and turned to Mariposa. "Get in the plane."

"No," she said defiantly, "we must go back and help Juan."

Frisco kept the gun on Chance and took a step toward Mariposa, reaching to grab her arm. Chance went for the pistol. Suddenly Mariposa was on Frisco hitting him with a folded aluminum chair—over and over and over.

Frisco tried to push her away and threw Chance down again. Finally, Mariposa fell to the ground. Frisco turned back toward Chance who tried to dodge the backhanded whip of the .38, to no avail. The pistol caught him on his glass jaw and down he went. The last thing he saw was Shane, crouched down and sneaking into the hangar through the back door.

Chance knew he must have been out a minute or two because, when he awoke, Frisco was in the cockpit. The roar of the Cessna's engine was ear-shattering. He tried to right himself, looking around to see if there was any way to stop the plane without getting himself killed. He sat halfway upright just as the plane's engine speed increased, and the propeller's thrust pressed him back to the ground. Frisco began to taxi out of the hangar.

The Cessna had hardly moved before it stopped again, the engine speed slowing. Chance could see Frisco motioning with his hand for someone to get out of the way. Crouching down to look below the fuselage, Chance saw that Mariposa had stepped to the middle of the hangar doorway, right in front of the propeller, blocking the plane's path.

At that moment, Chance heard a deafening crash as the rear of the plane careened into the hangar wall. He fell back to the ground, not sure what was happening. Then he saw the tires of the compact, but dense, little tug crushing the back of the aluminum fuselage, sufficiently lodging it against the wall. Frisco had no hope of taxiing, let alone flying, anywhere. The engine subsiding, he jumped from the cockpit, looked back to see the back door blocked by the plane, and then ran out the front of the hangar.

Shane came limping around the front of the plane with a grin on his face. "Quick," Chance said, not sure he could stand on his own. "He's probably headed for his truck. Help me up."

"No worries," Shane said, and held up the truck's car keys. "He won't get far."

❧

When the Beaverhead County sheriff's deputy finally unlocked the liquor closet door, Mesa was thankful that she could subdue her sense of relief enough to address the unfolding emergency upstairs.

Domenica Arroyo hovered over a stretcher as EMS squad members were preparing to load Larraz into an ambulance. She told them that although he was barely conscious, the señor had managed to tell the deputies to look for the women Frisco had taken away at gunpoint. He wanted to be sure they were not injured.

"I'm so sorry, Dr. Larraz," Mesa said as the stretcher approached. She felt deflated but she knew she had to say something.

"Frisco's devotion to Mariposa has always been extreme. I should have put a stop to it," Larraz said and began to cough. "It was his way of making amends."

"Don't try to talk," Mesa said, much as she wanted to know what he meant. The EMS guys rolled the stretcher away.

Mesa began to gather her things when her phone rang, and she jumped a foot. It was Shane.

"Hey," she said. "Where's Chance? Did you get our message? Are you still in Dillon?"

Strangely, Shane laughed. "Yep, everything's all taken care of. Here's your brother."

Chance sounded slightly groggy. He explained that they had arrived back at the airport in time to intercept Frisco with Mariposa.

"Is she okay? You don't sound so good either," Mesa said, holding back tears.

"She's fine, at least physically, but she's terrified for Larraz. I got a bump on the chin, but no worries. Shane hopped on the tug, fired it up, and saved the day."

"Hopped on the what?" Mesa said. No one was making any sense, or maybe it was that she was drained from all that had happened.

"Tell you later," Chance said. "The EMS is here to take us all over to the hospital to get checked out. Shane wrenched his knee and, apparently, one of the sheriff's part-time deputies roughed up Frisco when they caught up with him making a break for it across the airfield."

"Sounds like you and Shane are in no shape to fly home," she said, feeling too tired to think. "We'll meet you there."

Chapter 21

Chance had called Adrienne from the ER to fill her in on the showdown. When they dragged into her loft, Shane limping up the long stairwell, she had greeted the returning heroes, as she called them, with Moose Drool and Big Macs all around, a clear concession to Chance's belief that in times of crisis, McDonald's was the ideal comfort food.

"I'm fine," Shane kept saying to Mesa with a grin. Clearly, the adrenaline rush from the day's events and his painkillers had had their effect. They propped his leg up in front of the hearth with its roaring fire, and Mesa ordered him not to move for the rest of the evening. She took a glass of red wine from Adrienne and collapsed on the sofa next to Shane. Refilling their glasses throughout the night, they reflected on how the end of the day had transpired.

It had taken them the rest of the afternoon to finish up in Dillon. Barrett Hospital had all hands on deck in their ER when the sheriff showed up with one ambulance from the airfield, and a second from Rancho Esmeralda only minutes behind. Larraz had gone directly into surgery while Shane had to have an x-ray of his swollen knee.

Domenica was thankfully re-united with Mariposa; the two women sat together in one of the treatment bays to make a statement to the sheriff. Alexis did her best to help them along after she'd made a statement of her own.

Chance declined any medical treatment beyond an ice pack, which he applied to the welt on the side of his face. Mesa, fueled by a large cup of coffee, sat in the ER's waiting room with her brother while they filled in the gaps of each other's stories. Shane's x-ray seemed to take forever. So Chance and Mesa, despite growing exhaustion, obliged the sheriff with the details of the big picture.

After filling out statements of their own, the Beaverhead County sheriff promised his first call on Monday morning would be to his old pal, Rollie Solheim. Turned out they were fishing buddies. "You all doubled the felony crime report for the month," the sheriff said on his way out the door. "You head on back to Butte now 'fore anything else happens."

Domenica and Mariposa were finally allowed to go up to the surgery floor to await news of Larraz. As they headed down the hallway, two deputies appeared with a handcuffed Frisco, limping out of one of the treatment bays of the ER. He had a bandaged head and a boot on one ankle. He caught sight of the women and struggled with the deputy to cast a lingering look their way before they hauled him off to the county jail.

Watching Frisco struggle to see Mariposa, Mesa hoped she would be able to talk with Larraz about the pair. Exactly what there had been between them, she could not fathom. But she suspected some kind of love/hate madness had driven Frisco to kill to protect her.

Alexis plopped down in the chair next to Mesa and let out a long sigh. "Jesus, what a day."

"What do you think Larraz meant when he said Frisco was trying to make amends?"

"Give it a rest, will ya?" Alexis said with a yawn. "I told you from the beginning Frisco was weird. Montana is littered with ranch hands hiding from something or somebody. Isn't that enough to know?"

Finally, Shane was released with instructions to take the painkillers they'd given him and not to do any driving for a couple of days. They left the plane under the careful eye of the Dillon Flying Service and Alexis drove them all back to her place, where she offered to put them up for the night.

Mesa went inside to wash her face but declined the offer. Somehow, she had gotten a second wind, and she wanted to get Shane home. She would drive them back in her car. The two friends hugged in relieved affection, promising to check up on one another the next day. Alexis gave her a bottle of brandy for the drive back. "You all look like you could use a pick-me-up."

"What do you think Larraz's chances are?" Mesa asked Adrienne after finishing off one bottle of wine while Shane and Chance devoured all the food in sight.

"Hard to tell," she said. "Sounds like his heart wasn't involved or any major arteries, since he didn't bleed to death. If his general health is good and if they were able to repair whatever other organs might have been damaged …." Her voice trailed off. Those were a lot of ifs.

"I still don't understand what exactly went on between Mariposa and Frisco," Chance said. "Did she go with Frisco willingly? Were they running away together?"

"I don't think she had any idea what Frisco had done," Mesa said. Rosita had explained that Frisco had come into Domenica's house to say that he wanted to make a quick flight down to Idaho Falls to see about an Andalusian that was for sale. Mariposa had decided to go with him. The women hadn't heard the shot or had any idea what had transpired at the main house. Rosita had discovered the señor when she had returned for a vacuum cleaner. The county sheriff and an ambulance had arrived moments later.

"Saved by domestic science," Shane chimed in.

Mesa slapped him on the arm, and then kissed him on the cheek. "I'm damned glad too. I thought I was going to lose my mind in that liquor closet."

"You should have just started drinking the señor's booze," Shane said with a laugh. "Can't believe Alexis didn't think of that."

Mesa smiled and said nothing.

❧

Sunday morning, Mesa tried unsuccessfully to convince Shane to take a few days off. Nope. Nearing the end of the legislative session, second readings of bills were coming to the floor in droves. He needed to be there. In fact, he wanted to leave early so that he could figure out what accommodations his "bum knee" would require.

So, she had driven him to his apartment to help him pack for the week in Helena. At least she had convinced him to follow the doctor's orders and not drive. His buddy, the outreach director, a.k.a. a lobbyist, for the Montana Wilderness Federation, gave him a ride. Waving as the car pulled away, she reminded herself they really needed to talk. Next weekend, she told herself.

The sun was high but the air crisp. She knew spring was a ways off when she scurried down to the *Mess* to meet Chance with a stocking cap pulled over her ears. He had gone to see Henry, who had finally awakened from his semi-coma, to explain that he didn't have to be afraid to walk the streets anymore. The man in the sketch had been arrested, and Henry would achieve a notoriety that he could talk about for years. After all, if he hadn't come forward, Frisco would never have been brought to justice.

Before leaving her duplex, Mesa had called Vivian, wanting to give her the details of what had happened in person, but there was no answer. So, she sat at her office computer outlining the article she would write.

She received a call back from Vivian, who had been at church with Nana, but welcomed the invitation to stop by the office. She'd seen the Sunday Standard's late-breaking front-page story about Frisco's arrest and capture, and a local legislator's involvement in preventing the suspect's attempted escape. Mesa made a quick trip to the corner paper machine to buy a copy for Shane. She had to smile.

When Vivian arrived at the office, she definitely looked brighter and even more relaxed than after their trip to Warm Springs on Friday. She still had the boot on her left leg, but she was wide-eyed and curious for details.

She was glad to know that someone would be charged with Jessup's death, but she was reeling about the revelation of Larraz's involvement. "After all these years," she said in frank disbelief. "It was him? He was the one who lied? That is shameful." She took a deep breath and sat down on the sofa. She gave a quick hug to Buddha who nuzzled next to her. "All of this for Mariposa, poor woman."

The revelation about Dowl's attempt at blackmail had been disappointing too, even if they could both see why Dowl might have gone to those lengths. "It's so hard for me to imagine Dowl being angry," Vivian said in a quiet voice. "I could imagine it more of a slow burn where he had finally convinced himself that he had deserved better treatment and that the money was the fantasy, happy ending. I mean, I agree it still wasn't right."

She sighed and then, after a pause, said, "This all seems like a dream, a bad dream." She stopped talking and pulled a tissue from her coat pocket. Mesa moved to the sofa and put her arm around Vivian's shoulders.

"Look at me," Vivian said with a hesitant smile and tears running down her cheeks. "I suppose I had Dowl on a pedestal. Truth is nobody's all good or all bad, all strong or all weak. So much depends on what life throws at you. Your mother used to tell me that when I'd get down on myself."

Mesa nodded, remembering her mother expressing the same sentiment on more than one occasion. Then Mesa said, "But he didn't deserve to die."

"The thing Dowl never had was family," Vivian said. "No one to help and guide him. Even when I was at my worst, I had people around me who cared what happened to me, even my mother."

"At least we did accomplish what we set out to do," Mesa said. "You did clear his name."

Vivian wiped her nose and sighed. "For what good it did."

Mesa gave her a quick squeeze of encouragement, "You had the best intentions, Vivian."

"Don't worry," Vivian said and straightened up. "I'm all right. I know that what I did was as much for me as for Dowl, or at least the memory of us. He would have understood."

Mesa thought about Table Mountain and Abby and Walt Germane, glad to know that Vivian would be someone she could keep in contact with. She was looking forward to afternoon tea with her and Nana, reminiscing about her own mother.

The connection between Mariposa and Frisco was as confounding to Vivian as it was to everyone else. Their discussion about it was interrupted by Chance, who strolled into the office, fresh off the phone from Sheriff Solheim, whose detectives had taken a statement from Frisco that morning.

"Frisco confessed to dosing the coffee he'd bought Jessup at the Copper Pot," Chance said and explained how that was where Larraz had agreed to meet Jessup, only he had sent Frisco instead. Frisco had taken some of Mariposa's medications, but he claimed Larraz didn't know that. Once Dowl was woozy enough, Frisco led him up the hill to the trailer, doused him with whiskey and attached a lit cigarette to a book of matches that was taped to some paper and bedding, and then walked away.

"At least Rollie was able to pry the confession out of him."

"What do you mean, at least? Is there something Rollie missed?" Mesa said.

"Only capturing one of America's Most Wanted," Chance said with a grin. "The Beaverhead County sheriff ran the prints on Frisco, and the result was a big bingo. Warner John 'Frisco' Francisco had an outstanding warrant for negligent homicide that dated back to 1988."

"The story has already hit the wires," Chance said. He pulled up an article on the Seattle Times webpage on Mesa's computer. "Canadian man arrested in Montana after twenty-six years as a fugitive: Chelan County, Washington authorities have located a man sought after crashing a rented airplane into a lake and swimming away as it sank with his pregnant girlfriend inside."

The story explained that in an attempt to elope with his girlfriend, Frisco had flown across the border from British Columbia to Washington and crashed the plane. Apparently unable to free the girl, whose body was found with the plane in the lake at a depth of 220 feet, Francisco had swum to shore and then vanished—even after charges of negligent homicide were filed against him, even after being featured on "America's Most Wanted."

"You think Larraz knew about this and let him hide out at his ranch?" Vivian said.

Mesa thought about her last few words with Larraz and what he said about Frisco trying to make amends. "I think Frisco was one of a stable of people Larraz tried to save from one demon or another. According to Alexis' foreman, Larraz met Frisco when they still had a chemical dependency program at Warm Springs. Frisco had his own demons and Larraz hired him to help him out. I think Larraz was always trying to make up for what he'd done to Jessup by helping others. He knew what he'd done was wrong."

"Adrienne says Freud would have had a field day," Chance added. "Guilt, over-compensation, etc.—Larraz for Mariposa and Frisco for the girlfriend he couldn't save. Mariposa, suspended in another world, was the object of all their twisted efforts."

When Vivian got ready to leave, she said, "I see now why Sam has such faith in you." Then she looked at each of them for a long moment and said, "Your mother would be so proud. I can see her in both of you—smart, gentle, and funny. Mesa, thank you for listening to me that first day, really listening, and caring about me and Dowl."

She hugged them both and thanked them again for all they had risked to help her, not just to clear Jessup's name, but to give her some peace of mind. "There is one more thing."

They all chuckled, but Mesa said it. "There's always one more thing."

"I want to make sure that Dowl gets the proverbial decent burial. Who do I talk to?"

Chance promised to call Vivian after talking to Nick Philippoussis who could help make arrangements since he also worked at the funeral home. "Let's talk about what you want to do because I think Henry might want to be involved too."

They said their goodbyes, and Chance and Mesa went to the window, and watched Vivian cross the street to her truck. "What a difference a week makes," Chance muttered.

✑✑

The fading light of evening meant Mesa ought to turn on a lamp. But she couldn't move from the sofa. She had sat there all afternoon wrapped in an eiderdown quilt, waiting for the sunset. She kept repeating, "It's Shane. It's Shane."

A snow squall had moved across the valley from the south, meandering over the East Ridge amidst the pink and orange sunset. Clinging to the simple act of watching the weather unfold, the pins and needles in her foot went unnoticed until she heard the insistent pounding on the door. She realized the voice behind it belonged to her brother.

When she opened the door, Chance rushed in and hugged her, and then gave her a good shake. "My god, Mesa, you scared the hell out of me. Why didn't you answer the door when I first started knocking?"

Mesa stared at him, working to form the words. She felt like she was in slow motion, had been since Nick Philippoussis had showed up. His knock on the door that afternoon had a life of its own, a hollow reverberation she would hear in her sleep for months.

She had been standing at the counter in her tiny kitchen sampling Padang Thai peanut sauce from the bottle, thinking about the opening of a piece that would run in the upcoming week's edition. Irita would squawk but they would squeeze it in. She had made a good start.

Folks back East often think that mental health issues don't amount to much in places like Montana. That's because with so much wide-open space, everybody can go out into the middle of nowhere and scream to their heart's content. This week, in at least one case, the challenges of emotional trauma pointed to the harsh reality that many Montanans with mental illness are afraid to come out into the light.

The room to "act crazy," while it may benefit those who are uncomfortable witnesses, doesn't necessarily make the actor feel any better. Until we can accept that mental illness is no more shameful than cancer or heart disease, those among us who live with these hidden problems will continue to suffer in the shadows.

She wore her favorite writing outfit, a pair of plaid flannel boxer shorts over long johns and a faded Damascus College sweatshirt. She had left the *Mess* office at noon, energized by the possibility of a rare, uninterrupted Sunday afternoon to write, and she was on a roll.

Until recently, Dowling Jessup, who died last week in the Centerville trailer arson, had lived in the shadows. He had lived through traumatic events, been shuffled back and forth between Warm Springs, Deer Lodge prison, Pre-release, and a now defunct transitional housing program, suffered through medications with mind-numbing side effects, and a lack of therapists and adequate facilities.

She had prayed that the knock at her door was not someone she wanted to know intimately. "This better be a social call," she had teased Nick when she opened the door.

Nick had not smiled at her greeting. "Can I come in for a sec?" he had asked, his voice calm but serious.

She had dropped her arms to her sides, and stepped back from him, her heart racing. Nick had promptly provided the response she was desperate to hear.

"It's not Chance or your Nan. We got a call from the coroner's office in Helena. It's ...." and his voice had trailed off. "It's Shane."

≪∽

"I couldn't get here sooner," Chance was saying. "Adrienne and I took a couple of runs on the new snow up at Moulton after I left you and Vivian. I got Nick's text when we came back down to the cabin. Shane was such a strapping guy. A blood clot, man, what are the odds."

Mesa left him standing at the door, muttering, and returned to the sofa and the sky, watching it fill with stars, one by one. Chance sat next to her quietly, but she knew he wouldn't leave until he was absolutely sure she was okay, which she was on some level.

Mostly okay, though the sinkhole where her heart used to be suggested that she had deeper feelings for Shane Northey than she had been prepared to admit, or maybe it was the shock, the suddenness of it all.

"You know, when you're thirty-four years old and you die from a blood clot when your knee gets banged up ...." Chance was rambling. "Man, that's ... karmic, I guess. Adrienne says the odds against that happening, especially to someone in their thirties, are astronomical. She called it almost like a freak accident."

Astronomical, Mesa thought, and turned back to look at the stars. "Don't try to figure it out, Chance," she said, wondering if her voice sounded as odd aloud as it did in her head, like she was talking from one mountain peak to another, her voice echoing across a wide chasm. "He's gone. He's gone."

She felt her brother's arm around her shoulders. "I'm so sorry," he seemed to be saying but she couldn't really hear him.

The whole town was in shock. On Friday, the legislature canceled the day's sessions so members could drive down to Butte to attend the funeral, which was massive, at Holy Spirit Church. All the legislators came, at least the Democrats, some Republicans too. The governor gave a touching eulogy. He even brought his border collie, which Shane would have liked.

Mesa sat between Chance and Nana in the pew behind Shane's parents. When her mother had died, Mesa's sense of loss had been profound, but her death came as the end result of an unrelenting disease, and therefore made some sense. Shane's death was a mistake, and it was because of her.

Shane's grandfather had asked that Mesa write the obituary. She had done her best, professional but heartfelt—victim of a tragic accident, devoted and loyal, well-loved and sorely missed, trying to give some meaning to the short life he'd lived. She felt like a fraud.

The outpouring of love, after the fact—her own included, only made her feel worse. Why do we wait? Mesa had wondered. Death received all the attention while life got neglected, and she was the worst offender.

Ironically, Adrienne was the one who seemed to understand what was going on in Mesa's head. They were sitting on the front porch of Nana's house the Sunday following the funeral. It wasn't your fault, she had said. It was an accident.

"But he was there because of me," Mesa had countered. "He was good and kind and he should still be alive." And then the painful truth: "I didn't love him, you know. I cared about him, I did. But I didn't love him, not in the way everybody seems to think."

"I know."

Two simple words had broken through. Mesa looked up.

"When I found out that my husband was cheating on me with every nurse he could get his hands on," Adrienne said, "I wanted to kill him. Once we got divorced, he just went right on doing the same thing. I was the one who went into a shell for a year. And then when he died, I sobbed for weeks for the loss of him and the loss of the dream."

"How did you get over it?" Mesa asked, hardly expecting an answer.

"Time. One weekend, I got in my car and drove to Montana. I stared at Seeley Lake for a month and finally, one morning, I woke up and I had an epiphany. I realized that shared intimacy is worthwhile even if it only lasts a moment, a day, a week. It all counts. The illusion is that you can expect more."

"All that last week Shane was alive," Mesa said. "I kept thinking about how he wasn't the right guy. What if he was? What if he was my fairy tale ending? Did I blow it?"

Adrienne sat up straight and grabbed Mesa's hand. "Don't fall for that hype, Mesa, not now. Don't shortchange yourself by thinking that there's only one person for each of us, and somehow when we find them, we'll live happily ever after, or if we lose them, then it's all over."

"You don't think the fairy tale is attainable?"

Adrienne shrugged. "Maybe for a few, but you can count them on one hand. Besides, one woman's fairy tale is another one's nightmare. That, I know for sure."

Maybe Adrienne was right. At least she was honest, Mesa thought, and hugged herself as the wind came up.

"The point is, Mesa, punishing yourself won't change what's happened, and it won't help—not you or anyone around you."

"Why should I care?" Her voice was so flat; Mesa almost apologized for being rude.

"Because people depend on you—your grandmother, your crew at the *Mess*. They need you."

Then out of nowhere, or maybe out of a need for a little security, Mesa asked, "Do you love Chance?"

Adrienne hesitated, and then said. "At my age, it's different. I've been in love and out, been married, and then divorced. Chance too. We both know love is a roller coaster—it can be a tremendous thrill, but it can also make you sick." She paused and then said, "Your brother and I can talk about anything. There are no charades, but no promises either. That works for me."

Mesa read lots of poetry in the following month, usually when she awoke in the middle of the night, struggling to find meaning in Shane's death. It was a complete bust. At least she began to understand why most people didn't know what to say when someone dies, because no one did. Not even Emily Dickinson or John Donne or Dylan Thomas. Good effort, mind you, but not enough.

She discovered that pretending didn't help—pretending that she didn't feel anything, at least anything she wanted to share when people asked how she was doing. It only made the misery worse later. Grief, anger, guilt - they were all the same. Late at night, all alone, her tears probably came even harder than if she had shed them in the light of day in front of the crowd.

Focus was difficult. For weeks she struggled to remember exactly what she had said to Shane their last night together and that Sunday morning. The relief was palpable when she convinced herself that she had simply hugged him and said they would talk soon, that she had not been sarcastic or unkind. She doubted that he was concerned about their relationship when he had reached out to his friend, Skip, while getting out of the car, and said, "I got a hell of a headache …."

Sheriff Solheim was reported to be profoundly grateful when the arsonist was finally caught in mid-April, or rather arsonists. Three twenty-somethings were apprehended, thanks to the King's Lanes bowling alley surveillance camera. Drunk and stupid at four a.m., they had set fire to the trailer that served as a firework stand at the edge of the parking lot. How they had avoided arrest sooner, not to mention blowing themselves to

Kingdom Come, was the real question. Mesa gave the story to the new reporter to cover.

After confessing to his role in Dowl's death, Frisco's preliminary sentencing date was set for early June. Meanwhile, Sheriff Solheim, the state of Washington, and the province of British Columbia were in lengthy negotiations to determine which of numerous other charges Frisco would have to answer to first.

After Xavier-Larraz left the hospital, he had come back to the ranch and stayed in the señora's house. Alexis told Mesa about her visits there, her conversations with the señor. He had talked mostly about what would happen to Mariposa, which weighed on him. When his condition deteriorated, hospice had been called in during the day, and Mariposa sat with him all through the night. Vivian had even been to visit, and had talked with the señora about having Mariposa see Dr. Kaiser.

There being no statute of limitations on negligent homicide in Montana, the Powell County attorney reviewed possible charges in the death of Ethan Grainger. After various psychiatrists' evaluations, as well as an investigation of the evidence presented in the letter from the ex-nun, which Larraz had never thrown away, and supporting statements from Jeanne Lenin and a host of Larraz's professional colleagues, the Powell County Attorney decided not to charge Mariposa or Larraz.

Alexis had accompanied Mariposa and Domenica to the meeting with the county prosecutor, ostensibly as a translator, but mostly for moral support. Xavier-Larraz had been too frail to attend. She stopped by the *Mess* office one afternoon, and provided details.

"I think the prosecutor was totally bowled over," Alexis said. She couldn't be sure what he expected but

Mariposa had been straightforward, no nonsense. Since Frisco had shot Larraz, her shell seemed to have cracked and she had begun to talk. She had taken full responsibility for her part in Snake's death.

"I am deeply sorry for the violence that occurred on that day and since, particularly the death of Dowling Jessup, who played no part in the events at Warm Springs. After my arrival in the United States, I was placed in a girls' school. You have a letter that outlines my experiences there. I developed a phobia of being touched. Grainger tried to get me to undo the buttons of my dress. We fought and, so severe was my panic, that I hit him repeatedly until he lost his balance and fell over the railing of the gazebo on the Mound. I was so terrified and ashamed that I would not say what had happened. For years, my brother, Juan, has tried to help me understand the origins of my fears despite the deep shame it brought on our family. I realize his efforts to shelter me may not have always helped but whatever he may have done, he did to protect me."

Alexis said she had done her best to comfort Domenica who wept quietly throughout Mariposa's statement. On the drive back to the ranch, Domenica had confided that she and the señor had argued about encouraging Mariposa to become more independent, perhaps to take an apartment in town.

"She showed signs of being stronger than he realized," Domenica had said. "He maintained a traditional view of women. In Mariposa's case in particular, he barely saw her as more than a child."

A week later, after lingering for nearly two months, Juan Xavier-Larraz died from heart failure in his sleep.

Once the prosecutor had said no charges would be filed against Mariposa, the señor had been at peace.

Alexis called the next day to say that she would go to the funeral and could use a wing woman. Mesa declined, saying she sincerely doubted the señora and Mariposa would appreciate her presence. Alexis disagreed, but she understood and didn't question Mesa's excuse.

"Mariposa has asked me to find them a replacement for Frisco," Alexis said. "Those Andalusians are Mariposa's best therapy, and she knows it. Now all we have to figure out is what to do for you."

Chapter 22

Lunch at the Metals Bank Building with Tara McTeague, Mesa's childhood bestie turned real estate agent, was short and sweet, just as Mesa had hoped. Nearly two months since Shane's death, she still found it difficult to go anywhere in public. Somebody always wanted to express their condolences. Tara could be made to change the subject.

At work, Mesa had taken to coming in late and leaving early for much the same reason. She spent most of her time mentoring the newbie, JB. His actual name was Evan Llewellyn, and his great-grandfather had come from Wales to work in the mines. He was a Butte rat through and through, but Mesa could not let go of the John Belushi resemblance.

Everyone except JB and Irita seemed to tiptoe around her. Phade had ceased all rumblings about leaving and even brought her a daisy one morning. Irita would simply say, "Take all the time you need. I'll keep the ship afloat until you're ready to take the helm again." Mesa knew how lucky she was to have so much support around her, how hard they were all trying, but that seemed to do little to get her out of her funk. She had written nothing for weeks.

On the weekends, she would hole up in her duplex and not answer her phone. One weekend, at Nana's insistence, Mesa had gone up to Table Mountain where Vivian had put her up in the Leaning Tree cottage. After that first visit, she had returned several times. She enjoyed the long hikes they had taken where Vivian didn't press her to talk. One aftertoon they even made ojo de dios, which at first made Mesa laugh, and then cry. She was considering an appointment to see Dr. Kaiser again.

On the walk back to the *Messenger* office, Tara tried to convince Mesa to come to the Vu that night for a drink after work. "Jerry is taking the kids to his mom's. I almost never go out without all of them," she pleaded.

"Chance put you up to this, didn't he?" was her reply.

"I think I might be pregnant again, so this could be my last chance for nine months."

They walked to Tara's MINI Cooper, parked on Main Street, where they parted with Mesa's promise to think about the Vu. A cyclist weighed down with gear for an extended roadtrip had stopped just behind Tara's car as she pulled away.

He leaned a foot on the curb to rest, the ride up Main Street's steady incline being no easy haul. "Excuse me," he said to Mesa in heavily accented English. "Can you help me find some water. Hot water?"

Mesa thought about walking away. So many people on the road stopped in Butte that Mesa had begun to believe the rumor that there was an underground directory that listed the locals as easy marks, which they were.

"Just a little bit of water?" the young cyclist said. "For tea."

His accent sounded Spanish and with his thick wavy hair he looked like a model for an ad in Rolling Stone, not at all like a tea drinker—and fit too. Mesa was surprised that he wasn't more out of breath given the altitude.

"Follow me," she said and continued down the sidewalk. As she walked, the guy made a slow wide U-turn, his limbs lean and supple as he coasted down Main Street and onto Galena. She motioned him to lean his bike against the Cleveland building and waited while he pulled out a short metal thermos and a cup with a metal spoon from one of his many packs. Inside the *Messenger's* office, she led him to the water cooler with its two taps—a light blue one for cold water and a red tap for hot.

"Where I am coming from, I never see anything like this," he smiled and began to fill his thermos. "I make tea," he said and then he put hot water into the cup that was already filled with some green herb in a fitted sieve.

"And where would that be," she asked, her curiosity overcoming her ennui, "that you are coming from?"

"Argentina," he said. "I drink yerba maté. Very good drink from my country. You like some?" he said after taking a sip through what turned out be a metal straw, not a spoon. He offered her the cup with the straw.

"No, no," she said and held her hand up as if to keep him at bay. "I have to get back to work," and motioned toward the hallway to her office.

"Oh, I am so sorry, I didn't realize. You work here?" he said and gave a quick look around the small lobby, his glance coming to rest on the stack of newspapers on the coffee table in the middle of the room. "You write the newspaper?" he said with another charming smile.

Mesa sighed. "More or less," she said. "Here, have one," and she handed him a copy with a dismissive gesture toward the door.

"Gracias," he said, his slightly lisped accent, a genteel touch to his rugged masculinity.

Once again, Mesa felt a twinge of guilt. Like most of Butte, an unspoken tradition in her family was always to offer hospitality to travelers, especially international ones. She knew what it felt like to be in a foreign country and wish you could find a friendly local, yet she felt so impatient with him.

He stopped for a moment on the way out the door, and lifted his flat straw hat with one more smile, "Thank you again, beautiful lady, for the water and the newspaper," and then he was gone.

Mesa sat at her desk, her chair turned toward the window, the shades open. The Argentine was sitting on the curb drinking his maté and reading the paper, not seeming to care that he was thousands of miles from home relying on strangers for one of life's essential elements. Sometime later when he had moved on, she had not noticed. She was lost in her weariness again.

Hours later, prompted by yet another phone call, this time from Alexis, Mesa found herself headed to the Vu. As she entered, Tara waved and motioned to a beer at the ready next to her. The bar, which relied heavily on college students for business, was relatively empty now that the semester had ended. Mesa settled in and tried to rise to Tara's attempt to "enjoy herself for old time's sake."

Granted, the Vu had been the scene of many a celebration when the Copper Kings were playing baseball in Butte, and responsibilities went no further than to have a good time and make it home in one piece. Throughout the evening, they greeted a slow trickle of locals who were keen to say how good it was to see them, that they had not seen the pair out in forever. Tara had children for an excuse, which everyone understood, while Mesa tried to change the subject.

Alexis showed up in due time. She'd taken to wearing her ranch clothes into town, including a gray felt Stetson with a rawhide string. When she let the hat drop onto her back and her long blonde hair fell to her shoulders, every pair of eyes in the place turned toward her. Prudently, she had also taken to bringing along Jesse as a designated driver.

After a couple of beers, Mesa at least felt relaxed enough to look around the bar to see who she knew, not that she really cared. She did see that the cycling Argentine had found the student hangout. What a surprise. Standing at a tall table surrounded by a quartet of girls, his charms were creating lots of laughter. She found herself almost angry at the effortless way he seemed to be insinuating himself into her hometown bar.

Halfway through her third Heineken, Mesa began to formulate her leaving speech. Neither Tara nor Alexis would take her departure well as it was barely nine p.m. on a Friday night. But the truth was, Mesa's capacity for a good time was a long way from expanding.

"At least I made it through three beers," Mesa argued when Tara lamented, "I just don't know what to do with you, girl. Life has to go on."

"If I had a nickel for every platitude I've heard," she said then stopped as she saw her friend's expression droop. "Look, Tara. I appreciate what you're doing. I'm sure I couldn't be as patient as you, but you just have to let me do this at my own pace."

"I'm always here," Alexis said between shots of tequila. She knew better than to say anything else. They hugged and then Mesa was thankful to find herself outside taking a deep breath of the cool mountain air. She noticed Mr. Yerba Maté with his cup and straw untethering his bike from a parking sign in front.

"I am enjoying the beautiful night sky in your city," he said.

Mesa began walking along Park Street toward her duplex, and the Argentine with his bike fell into step with her. "You looked like you were enjoying our female population inside. What brought you out here?"

"They invite me to come home with them, but I don't want to go. They are very loud. But I don't want to offend them so I am making what you call the quick exit."

Mesa laughed. The quick exit was the term she would use to describe her own departure. "Where are you headed next?"

"I want to get an early start in the morning. I will ride to Three Forks."

Mesa had to chuckle. "That's a long way. How far did you travel today?"

"From Deer Log," he said with a puzzled face as if he knew he might not have the pronunciation down. "I have been working there for a few days, helping a man with his horses. Before that I was in Ronan working on another ranch."

Mesa had to give the guy credit. That yerbe maté must make him one able-bodied individual. "Deer Lodge," she said, letting him hear the correct pronunciation. "Must keep you in great shape," she added and wondered if exercise might be something she needed to start up again.

"I feel very strong," he said. "But I could use a good night's sleep. You have one of these travel hostels, maybe?"

"You mean a cheap place to stay?" Mesa said.

He nodded.

"Fraid not, unless you want to try the KOA. You got a tent in your gear?"

"No. But this KOA, I know it. Which way?"

They had reached Crystal Street and the temperature was dropping. She wanted to pick up her pace and turn the corner. "Look," she said. "I have a futon, and you'll be a good deal warmer there than sleeping on the ground. "I only live five minutes away."

"No, no," the Argentine said. "I do not wish to intrude. I know you are sad, and I would make the burden for you."

She dismissed what he said with a wave of her hand. "That's nothing to do with you. Come on. You can have your good night's rest and be gone in the morning."

They walked up Crystal to Granite Street with her guest walking his bike, accompanied by the intermittent clang of the metal sauce pans that hung from the cross bar. All the while, she was teed off. She hated the possibility that wherever she went, people like the young women in the Vu gossiped about her.

She unlocked the door to the duplex and invited the guileless Argentine to bring his bicycle inside for the night. "What's your name?" she asked as they walked up the stairs to the second floor.

"Francesco Leone," he said and took off his hat. "But my friends call me Frankie."

"Mesa Dawson," she said and he reached out and shook her hand, his touch warm and gentle. Then he walked over to the windows to look at the view of the red-lit mineframe. "This is beautiful." He sat down on the Moroccan cassock as if he had done it a thousand times. Her angered softened.

Mesa shook her head at his forthrightness and then went to the closet to pull down a pillow, a sheet, and a blanket. She patted the pillow and said, "I'm not just sad, I'm mad too, so watch it. Good night, 'my friends call me Frankie.'" Then she walked to her bedroom and closed the door.

Around two a.m., Mesa got up to find some water. She made sure to tiptoe but, when she opened the door, Frankie was still mesmerized by the view from the window, but this time he was standing in his Calvin Klein's. She grabbed a bottle of water from the fridge and tiptoed back to bed. She fell asleep thinking about his broad shoulders and narrow waist and how talking to a stranger seemed so comforting.

As the sun was coming up, she heard her door open. Frankie was placing a note on her dresser. "I'm sorry. I didn't mean to wake you. You are a special lady to be so kind. Please forgive me."

She sat up and motioned for him to bring her the note. It was in Spanish.

"It's the poet, Neruda, from Chile. You know him?"

She nodded. "Read it to me," she said and pulled the sheet closer. Again, his Spanish was so elegant and gentle and his eyes very blue.

"I don't translate well," Frankie said when he had finished. "But it means I love your darkness like a thing between the shadows and the soul." He smiled at her and looked down, and then he smoothed the sheet around her feet. "I wanted to give you something beautiful to comfort you," and then he touched her cheek.

Frankie did not get his early start, at least not on the road to Three Forks. Mesa had lost herself in the warmth of his kiss. They lay in bed exchanging stories for much of the day. Mostly she let him talk, holding her in his strong arms. He was twenty-three and from Buenos Aires, loved horses, rich soil, the tango, and homemade knives. He would travel through Europe, particularly Paris, where he intended to find a wife before he settled down to farm on the pampas.

Some time in the middle of the afternoon, he ran to Hennessy's Market and bought a bottle of wine from Mendoza and a steak that he cooked for her in what he called his special Argentinian way. When he left on Sunday morning, she was still asleep. She awoke to yet another note, this one next to her pillow. "Thank you for having a beautiful moment with me. May you have many more. Always, Frankie."

When she turned up at work on Monday at eight a.m., she had finally finished the feature about Vivian and Jessup which she had decided to call "Far from Home." Frankie's note was in her pocket.

Acknowledgements

Novel writing can seem like a joyride, even a flight of fancy, where the journey is often as important as the destination, but the road is by no means smooth. The drive requires the help of many. They deserve recognition and gratitude: Amy Kuenzi—super reader, who read this manuscript more times than I did; Louise Franklin—warrior writer whose efforts challenge me to keep going; Lynn Robbins—poet and BFF; and particularly Margaret Diehl—my editor whose gentle but incisive critique caused this book to blossom.

I relied on many content experts who helped me find my way—Louise Bruce and Jim Roscoe, my favorite ranch hands; Mike McNamee, friendly arson investigator; attorneys Tony DeNino and Craig Fitch, the Patient Advocate at the Montana State Hospital; Gloria Carter, social services for the mentally ill; Dave Daugherty, aviator extraordinaire; C.D. Holter, Butte-Silver Bow police officer; Butte-Silver Bow librarian, Stephanie Johnson; and the Butte-Silver Bow Archives staff.

Finally, thanks to my family who allow me the time to write, especially my daughter Lea whose adventures keep me informed about the lives of thirty-somethings.

About the Author

Marian Jensen has lived in Kentucky, West Virginia, and Ohio and, more recently, in Butte, Montana since 1999. *Grave Madness* is the second novel in her series, Mining City Mysteries. Trout fishing on the Big Hole River is still her favorite place to be.

HELP! Pass the word if you think this book is worth a read. While full-page ads in the NY Times may be ideal, that's out of reach for us. Surprisingly, perhaps, word of mouth is the next best thing! So, even if it's only a few lines, consider leaving a review where you purchased your book. The Mining City Mysteries thank you!

Not feeling so literate? Visit us on Facebook at Mining City Mysteries and like our page. Or read our blog at www.miningcitymysteries.com.